Abe Lincoln at Last!

More Magic Tree House®

Games and Puzzles from the Tree House

MAGIC TREE HOUSE® #47
A MERLIN MISSION

Abe Lincoln at Last!

by Mary Pope Osborne

illustrated by Sal Murdocca

SCHOLASTIC INC.

ISBN 978-0-545-68949-6

12 11 10   15 16 17 18 19/0

Printed in the U.S.A.   40

First Scholastic printing, January 2014

For Mary Sams

CONTENTS

Not often in the story of mankind does a man arrive on earth who is both steel and velvet, who is hard as rock and soft as drifting fog. . . .
—Carl Sandburg

Prologue

One summer day in Frog Creek, Pennsylvania, a mysterious tree house appeared in the woods. A brother and sister named Jack and Annie soon learned that the tree house was magic—it could take them to any time and any place in history.

Jack and Annie have since gone on many adventures in the magic tree house and have completed many missions for both Morgan le Fay and Merlin the magician of Camelot. On some of their journeys, Jack and Annie have received help from two young enchanters, Teddy and Kathleen, who are learning magic from Merlin and Morgan.

Now Teddy is in big trouble. While Merlin and Morgan were away, Teddy accidentally put a spell on Penny, Merlin's beloved penguin. The spell turned her into a stone statue. Teddy thinks that he could be banished from the kingdom—unless Jack and Annie can help!

Teddy and Kathleen have found an ancient spell that can undo Teddy's accidental magic. To make the ancient spell work, Jack and Annie must find four special things—each from a different time and place. They have already found two of these things: an emerald in the shape of a rose and a white and yellow flower.

Now Jack and Annie are waiting to find out what they must search for next. . . .

CHAPTER ONE

The Third Thing

Annie peeked into Jack's room.

"Ready?" she whispered.

"Yep," said Jack.

Even though it was two hours before school started, Jack and Annie were already dressed. Jack put his notebook and pencil into his backpack. Then he picked up the pack and his sneakers and followed Annie into the hall. In their sock feet, Jack and Annie tiptoed past their parents' bedroom. Then they slipped down the stairs.

When they reached the front hall, Jack and

Annie put on their jackets and shoes and stepped outside. The early-morning sky was gray. Everything was quiet, except for the sound of a gentle spring rain.

"Should we get our raincoats?" Jack asked.

"It's clearing up," said Annie. She pointed to blue sky in the distance.

"Oh, good," said Jack. "Let's hurry."

Jack and Annie stepped off their porch. Then they ran up the sidewalk and crossed the street. By the time they started into the Frog Creek woods, the rain had stopped. Misty rays of sunlight slanted down through the wet trees.

Jack and Annie kept going until they came to the tallest oak. The leaves at the top of the tree sparkled with raindrops, and the magic tree house was lit by the morning sun.

"It's waiting for us," said Jack.

"I knew it would be," said Annie. She grabbed the rope ladder and started up.

Jack climbed after her. Inside the tree house,

they looked around for the two special things they had found on their last missions.

"Great, they're still here," said Jack, pointing to a green jewel and a white and yellow flower in the corner.

"And it looks like Teddy and Kathleen sent some stuff for us," said Annie.

Lying in the shadows was a book. Next to it were a small folded note and a tiny blue bottle. Jack picked up the book. Its cover showed an old black-and-white photograph of a building. It looked like the White House in Washington, D.C.

Jack gasped. "Oh, man! Abraham Lincoln!"

THE LIFE OF ABRAHAM LINCOLN

"Wow," said Annie, looking at the book's cover. "He was a great president."

"No kidding," said Jack. "Do you think we're actually going to meet him?" He opened the book to the first page and read aloud:

Abraham Lincoln served as president of the United States from March 1861 until his assassination in April 1865. He led the country through the terrible crisis of the American Civil War. He preserved the union of states and outlawed slavery.

"I can't believe it," Jack said, closing the book. "Abraham Lincoln! Do you think *he's* supposed to help us find the third thing to break the spell that turned Penny into a statue?"

"Maybe," said Annie. "Let's see what else Teddy and Kathleen left for us. . . ." She picked up the tiny bottle and the note. She unfolded the note and read aloud:

The third thing to break the spell
is a single feather from a hero's hand.
Use it wisely to give him hope—
the hope he needs to heal his land.

"That sounds like a riddle," said Jack.

"I'll bet Abraham Lincoln is the hero," said Annie. "And"—she looked at the note again—"we have to get a feather from him. Then we'll use the feather to give him hope."

"Confusing," said Jack.

"A lot of our missions sound confusing at first, don't you think?" said Annie. "But in the end, they all make sense."

"Yeah, I guess," said Jack. "But that doesn't help us right now. There must be a magic potion in the bottle. What does the label say?"

Annie held up the small blue bottle and read the tiny writing on its label aloud:

Take a sip. Make a wish for <u>one thing</u> to help you on your mission. Remember: Trust the magic.

"That sounds kind of general," said Jack. "Wish for one thing to help us on our mission? That could be *anything.*"

"And remember to trust the magic," said Annie. She shrugged.

"Okay . . . we'll try to do that," said Jack. He took the bottle and the note from Annie and put them into his backpack.

"We've got everything we need," said Annie. "A mission, a research book, and a little bit of magic. Ready to go?"

"Yep," said Jack. He pointed to the picture of the White House on the cover of their book and said, "I wish we could go there!"

The wind started to blow.

The tree house started to spin.

It spun faster and faster.

Then everything was still.

Absolutely still.

CHAPTER TWO

Pirate Captain

Jack shivered. The air was chilly, but the sun was bright. Bare branches outside the tree house swayed in the wind. Annie was wearing a long dress with an apron. Jack wore a cotton shirt over a red undershirt and a pair of trousers with suspenders. His backpack had turned into a leather bag.

Jack looked into the bag. Inside were his notebook and pencil, the message from Teddy and Kathleen, and the bottle with the magic potion. "Good," he said, "it's all here."

"We've worn clothes like these before," said Annie.

"Yeah, when we ran from that twister on the prairie," said Jack.

"And when we helped Clara Barton in the Civil War," said Annie.

"Right," said Jack. "So, did we land at the White House?"

They looked out the window. The tree house had landed in a grove of bare, sunlit trees. Beyond the trees, horse-drawn carriages rumbled over a circular carriageway toward a stately white mansion with tall columns.

"Oh, man," whispered Jack.

The White House was breathtaking in the morning air, bathed in sunlight. A crowd was gathered outside the front entrance: men in long black coats and tall hats, and women in hoopskirts and bonnets with big bows.

"Looks like lots of people are visiting Abraham Lincoln today," said Annie.

Jack thumbed through their research book until he found another black-and-white photograph of the White House. He read aloud:

When Abraham Lincoln became president in 1861, the White House was considered to belong to all the citizens of the country, as well as to the president and his family. Anyone could walk right

in. President Lincoln sometimes found it hard to work in his White House office because of the number of people swarming through the building.

"So *anyone* can just walk right into the White House and look for the president?" said Annie.

"That's crazy," said Jack.

"But it's good for us!" said Annie.

"I guess," said Jack, "but I don't want to be one of those people who make it hard for the president to work."

"Don't forget," said Annie, "we're supposed to give him hope."

"With a feather that *he's* supposed to give *us*," said Jack. He shook his head, then took out their note from Teddy and Kathleen.

The third thing to break the spell
is a single feather from a hero's hand.
Use it wisely to give him hope—
the hope he needs to heal his land.

"How can we get a feather from him?" said Jack. "And how can it give him hope?"

"It's better to do just one thing at a time," said Annie. "First we have to find the president."

"Hey, Willie! Look!" someone shouted from below. "It's a tree house! See? See?"

"Oh, no!" whispered Jack.

Jack and Annie peeked out the window. A boy about seven or eight years old was looking up at the tree house. The boy wore baggy gray trousers with suspenders and a white shirt. He had dark, piercing eyes.

"Hello!" the boy shouted when he saw Jack and Annie. "Who are you? Why are you in our tree house?"

"*Your* tree house?" said Jack. "It's not your tree house!"

"Yes, it is!" the boy said confidently.

"Tad, hush!" An older boy ran to join the younger one. He had a friendly, open smile and looked to be around Jack's age. "Don't mind my brother Tad!" he shouted.

"But it's *ours*, Willie!" said Tad. "The White House is our house! And the tree house is in *our* yard!"

Oh, man, thought Jack. That was what the book said, too: the White House was considered to belong to all the citizens of the country, as well as to the president.

"I'm sorry, but this tree house is not like the White House," Jack called. "It doesn't belong to the citizens of the country. It's ours!"

"No, it's not!" yelled Tad. "I'm coming up!"

"No, you're not!" Jack yelled back. He reached for the rope ladder to pull it up. But Tad had already started climbing.

"Hide our stuff!" Jack said to Annie.

Jack quickly pushed the Lincoln book into his leather bag. Annie stuck their note and the tiny bottle into her apron pocket.

"Tad, come back!" called Willie. "Leave them alone!"

Tad scrambled into the tree house. He grinned at Jack and Annie, his dark eyes gleaming. "I'm a

pirate captain, and I'm taking over your ship!"
Tad shook his small fists in Jack's face. "Fight
me!" he shouted.

"Cut it out," said Jack, waving him away.

"Tad!" Willie shouted from below.

The boy just laughed like a maniac and danced around the tree house, trying to box with Jack. "This is my ship now, matey!"

"Quit it!" said Jack.

"Tad!" his brother yelled again.

"Your brother's calling you," Annie said firmly to Tad. "Go! Now!"

"Who are you to boss me, missy?" Tad said, jutting out his chin.

Annie laughed. "I'm not a *missy*, shrimp," she said. "I'm Annie. And this is my brother, Jack."

Tad lowered his fists. "Oh! Hello, Annie, I'm Tad." He put out his hand, and Annie shook it. "Pleased to meet you," said Tad, completely dropping his role as pirate captain. "What are you and Jack doing today?"

"Actually, we're hoping to meet with President Lincoln," Annie said.

"Really?" said Tad. "Me and Willie know a

secret. . . ." He gave them a sly grin. "If you come with us, we'll take you straight to the president. I give you my word."

"Thanks, but we can handle it ourselves," said Jack. The last thing he wanted was for this kid to get in their way.

"But I *want* to help you. Come with me," said Tad. He started down the ladder.

"Should we go with him?" Annie whispered.

"No, he's just making stuff up," said Jack.

"Are you coming down?" called Tad. "Or should I come back up so we can play?"

"Darn," said Jack under his breath. "Let's go, just to get him away from the tree house." Jack grabbed his bag.

Suddenly Tad poked his head back into the tree house. "Are you coming or not?" he said.

"Yes! Go!" said Annie.

"What's in your bag?" asked Tad.

"Nothing," said Jack. "Go back down!" He didn't want Tad to see their Lincoln book.

"Let me see," said Tad, climbing into the tree house again. "What's inside?"

"Nothing, he told you nothing," said Annie.

"Then why is he bringing it with him?" Tad asked her.

"Fine, I'll leave it!" Jack said crossly. He dropped the leather bag to the floor. "Happy? Let's go!"

"Yes! Let's go!" said Tad, and he disappeared down the ladder again.

Jack reached into his bag, grabbed his small notebook and pencil, and stuck them into the back pocket of his pants. "I'll come back later and get the book," Jack whispered, "after we get rid of this kid."

Annie smiled. "If we can," she said. Then she and Jack started down the rope ladder.

CHAPTER THREE

Hide! Hide!

Willie was waiting at the bottom of the ladder. "Hello," he said.

"Willie, this is Jack and Annie," said Tad. "I told them that you and I have a secret." He gave Willie a meaningful look. "I told them we'd take them to meet the president. I gave them my word."

"Oh, you did, did you?" said Willie. "Hello, Jack and Annie." He shook hands with them. "I apologize for Tad," he added. "My brother is very high-spirited."

"And Willie's sweet as pie," said Tad, making a face. "Come on, you all! To the White House!" He saluted, then took huge marching steps across the lawn.

"So does Tad really know the president?" Annie asked as she and Jack walked with Willie.

"He does," said Willie with a smile, "and so do I."

"Oh. Cool," said Jack. He liked Willie's kind, mature manner. He wouldn't mind if *Willie* introduced them to the president. "Do you think you could introduce us?"

"If Tad doesn't introduce you first," said Willie, "then I'd be happy to."

"That would be great," said Jack.

As Tad marched ahead of them, Jack, Annie, and Willie walked through the sun-dappled grove of trees. The air was chilly, but it smelled like spring. It looked like spring, too. Tiny buds sprouted from bare branches. Birds flitted from tree to tree, and robins hunted for worms in the green grass.

"Are your parents visiting the White House today?" Annie asked Willie.

"You could say that," said Willie.

"Look at me!" Tad called. He was running backward up the carriageway.

"Watch out, Tad!" shouted Willie.

Tad jumped out of the path of a horse-drawn carriage just in time. The carriage stopped in front of the president's house. The crowd was huge now. As people tried to squeeze through the front doors, some waved pieces of paper at the guard.

"Everyone wants to meet the new president!" said Tad. "They all want something from him."

"Don't talk that way, Tad," said Willie. He turned to Jack and Annie. "They're mostly looking for jobs in the government. They have to take care of their families."

Tad led the way past the carriages and between the columns to the crowd at the door. "Allow us to enter!" he shouted to the guard at the door. "Jack and Annie are here! Important friends of the president!"

To Jack's amazement, the guard did as Tad

commanded. The man moved people aside and let Tad, Willie, Annie, and Jack walk right into the White House!

Jack trailed behind as they all passed through the entranceway. From there, they went around a bronze screen and into a wide hall filled with grown-ups.

"Make way!" shouted Tad as he squeezed through the crowd. A few women squealed. Their hoopskirts rocked and swirled.

"Stop, Tad!" said Willie, grabbing his brother. "Calm yourself!"

No kidding! thought Jack. He liked Willie a lot, but Tad was too wild and unpredictable.

Tad laughed and broke loose from his big brother. He ran into a room off the hallway. Willie and Annie hurried after him. A moment later, Jack heard someone banging on a piano.

Jack followed cautiously. He went through a door into a huge parlor filled with women and girls sipping tea from china cups.

The room had furniture covered in red satin. There was a large portrait of George Washington on the wall by the tall windows. No one was paying any attention to Tad as he pounded away on the piano keys. Even Willie was ignoring him. He was busy introducing Annie to a plump, dark-haired woman sitting on a sofa.

Why don't the grown-ups stop this bratty kid?
Jack wondered. *Where are his parents? The White
House guards? The Secret Service?*

Tad turned his head and caught Jack frowning
at him. He jumped up from the piano bench,
rushed over, and grabbed Jack's hand. "Sorry,
mate! I almost forgot! I gave you my word!" he
said. "Come along!"

Jack tried to free himself from Tad as the boy pulled him out of the parlor.

"Stop! Let me go! I have to wait for my sister," said Jack. He looked back and saw Willie and Annie still talking with the woman on the sofa.

"They'll catch up to us," said Tad. "Come along! I have a secret that you won't believe!"

"Please! Leave me alone!" said Jack.

"No! Come with me, or I'll start screaming," said Tad. "And I can scream very, very loud." He had a wild look in his eye.

Oh, no! Jack thought. This kid was totally insane. "Don't scream, don't scream, just hold on a second." He called out, "Annie! Willie!" But neither of them looked up.

"C'mon! It's now or never!" said Tad. He pulled Jack down the carpeted hallway, toward a wide staircase.

"Let go! Let go of me! I'm serious!" Jack said.

Tad let go of him. "Please, please, come up the stairs with me," he begged. "If you don't, I'll . . ." He opened his mouth wide.

"Fine! I'll come!" Jack said through his teeth. He let Tad pull him through a group of grown-ups climbing the stairs. *When we get to the top, I'll run back down,* Jack thought. *Then he can scream as loud as he wants.*

As soon as they reached the hallway on the second floor, Jack turned around to run. But the stairway was packed with too many people to escape!

Tad grabbed Jack by the arm and pulled him to a door off the hall. "The president is right in there, I promise," he whispered. "Do you want to meet him? Or not?"

"Not," said Jack. *At least not with you,* he thought.

"But you said you did!" said Tad. He threw open the door and pulled Jack inside, then closed the door behind them.

Jack looked around. The room was empty of people. It had a huge wooden bed with purple drapes. Flying birds were carved into the black wood.

This must be the president's bedroom! Jack thought with awe and horror. He whirled around, but Tad gripped the door handle.

"We can't stay here, Tad," Jack whispered furiously. "We'll get in terrible trouble!"

"But President Lincoln is there, in his dressing room!" said Tad. He grinned, pointing to a closed door off the bedroom. "I told you I'd take you to him!"

"You are crazy," Jack whispered. "Move! I'm leaving! Before we get caught!"

Suddenly Tad groaned and fell to the floor.

"Tad?" said Jack. He bent down to check on him. "Tad, are you—"

Tad grabbed Jack's arm and pulled him to the floor, just as the dressing room door opened!

"Hide! Hide!" Tad whispered. He scrambled under the big wooden bed. Jack frantically crawled after him.

Jack held his breath as they lay on their stomachs under the bed. His heart was beating so hard that he thought he was going to have a heart attack! Tad covered his mouth and shook with silent laughter.

Two large feet in black socks stopped beside the bed. Jack felt the bed sink down. A pair of hands put a pair of large leather shoes down on the floor. The feet slipped into the shoes. Then the weight lifted off the bed, and the shoes stepped forward.

Tad crawled silently out from under the bed. Then he tackled the person wearing the shoes! The man yelled and fell to the floor. Tad sat on top of him and beat him with his small fists.

From his hiding place, Jack could see a dark-haired man lying on his side, groaning and moaning. Tad was attacking the president of the United States!

CHAPTER FOUR

Willie!

Jack was horrified. Would the Secret Service arrest him along with Tad? Jack had to stop him!

Suddenly the president burst out laughing. He wrapped his hands around Tad's fists. "You little tadpole," he said. "You didn't scare me one bit!" Then he started to tickle Tad.

"Pa, don't! Don't, Pa, don't!" Tad screamed and giggled and kicked.

Pa? Pa? Jack thought. *Abraham Lincoln is Tad's "pa"!*

The president laughed. He stopped tickling Tad and kissed the top of his head. "What are you doing in here, my boy?" he said.

"Pa, me and Willie found a tree house," said Tad. "Did you know there was a tree house here? Two kids were in it. Jack and Annie. Jack said it belonged to them. I told him it was mine because it's in our yard. Isn't it mine, Pa?"

Jack wanted to shout, *No, it's ours!* But he was afraid to be caught under the bed.

"Wait—what did you say their names were?" the president asked, sounding serious. "Jack and Annie?"

"Yes," said Tad. "They came out of nowhere. Don't you think the tree house is mine, Pa? Mine and Willie's?"

"They came out of nowhere?" said the president. "And their names are Jack and Annie? Are you sure?"

Why doesn't Tad tell him I'm right here—under the bed? Jack wondered. *Should I just crawl out?*

"Yes, Pa, Jack and Annie," said Tad. "But I want to know about the tree house. Do—"

The door opened. "Mr. President, you must come at once," a man said briskly. "You are late for your first meeting."

"Sorry, Mr. Nicolay," President Lincoln said. "I'll be right there." He stood up.

"The crowd is growing restless, sir," Mr. Nicolay said. "Before you know it, they'll storm your bedroom."

"Oh, they wouldn't dare," said the president, chuckling. "Not with my bodyguard here." He ruffled Tad's hair. "Come along, tadpole. Escort me to my new office down the hall."

"But when will you come and see the tree house, Pa?" Tad said as they started out of the door.

"Perhaps when I take my horseback ride later," the president said. "I'd like to meet this Jack and Annie." The door closed. And the room was quiet.

Tad forgot about me! Jack thought. He couldn't

believe it! Then he realized he'd better get out of the president's bedroom. He started to crawl out from under the bed, but the door opened again, so he quickly crawled back.

"Dust first?" Jack heard a girl say.

"Aye, then shake out the pillows and change the linens," said another.

Jack could only see the black stockings and shoes of the two maids as they bustled around the room. *Now,* he thought, *before they make the bed!* He scrambled out and ran to the door.

One of the girls screamed. Jack didn't look back. He threw open the door and headed for the stairs. As he bounded down the steps, one of the maids shrieked, "There was a boy under the bed!"

Jack reached the bottom of the stairs and squeezed through the crowd until he found a nook off the hallway. He scrunched against the wall, then peeked around the corner to see if anyone was coming after him.

Someone grabbed his arm.

"Ahh!" Jack yelled.

"It's me!" said Annie. "Where have you been? I've been looking all over for you!"

"I was upstairs! In President Lincoln's bedroom!" Jack said. "Tad made me go in there! Did you know that President Lincoln is Tad and Willie's dad?"

"That's what I was going to tell you. Willie introduced me to their mom!" said Annie. "She was really nice. Those were all her relatives in the parlor."

"Well, Tad tricked me into hiding under the bed, and I almost got caught!" Jack said. "And Tad didn't even remember I was there. He kept talking about the tree house, saying it was *his.*"

"Willie says Tad gets overly excited," said Annie. "He can't help it. Plus, it's their very first week in the White House."

"Well, it was awful," said Jack. "I was trapped under the president's bed!"

Annie giggled. "You know, that's actually pretty funny," she said.

"Not really," said Jack.

"Don't worry," said Annie. "Willie would have saved you. He told me to find you and then come upstairs to his dad's office and he'll introduce us. It's on the second floor at the end of the hall."

"Okay," said Jack, sighing. "I heard the president say he'd like to meet us."

"Really?" said Annie.

"Yep, when Tad told him about the tree house and you and me, the president kept saying, 'Jack and Annie? Jack and Annie? Are you sure their names are Jack and Annie?'"

"That's weird," said Annie. "But I'm glad he wants to meet us. Come on."

Jack and Annie headed down the hallway and up the stairs. On the second floor, Jack kept his head down, just in case the maids were looking for him. Jack followed Annie down the hall toward a group of people standing outside a door.

A skinny man with a small pointed beard was speaking to them. "Ladies and gentlemen, please! I'm sorry, but only the names on my list can meet with the president today!"

Jack recognized the man's voice. "That's Mr. Nicolay," he told Annie.

"Who are you to tell us we can't see the president?" a woman in a pink bonnet asked Mr. Nicolay.

"I am President Lincoln's secretary, ma'am," Mr. Nicolay said sourly, "and if you do not have an appointment, you must leave."

"Excuse me, Mr. Nicolay, but I believe that I am on your list," said a dignified man. He showed the secretary a piece of paper. The secretary checked the paper against his list.

"Of course. This way, Mr. Bennet," Mr. Nicolay said. He opened the door and nodded for Mr. Bennet to enter, then followed him inside. While the door was open, Jack and Annie peeked into the room.

Abraham Lincoln was sitting at a long table. Tad was perched on his lap, fiddling with his dad's tie. Willie was studying a map on the wall, while

the president was listening to one of the men at the table.

"Willie!" Annie whispered loudly.

Willie didn't hear, but Mr. Nicolay did—he rushed back out of the president's office.

"Willie!" Annie shouted.

Willie turned around just as Mr. Nicolay closed the door.

CHAPTER FIVE

Leave Now!

"Excuse me, young lady!" Mr. Nicolay said. "This is not a time for play."

"I'm not playing, sir," said Annie as she and Jack stood at the front of the crowd. "We're friends of Tad and Willie's, and Willie just told us to come here to the president's office. He wants to introduce us to his dad."

Mr. Nicolay scowled. "I'm afraid Mr. Willie misspoke. The president does not have time to meet you now," he said. "He is in a private

meeting with delegates from California, Indiana, and Maine."

"Maybe later, then?" said Annie.

"Not maybe later," said Mr. Nicolay. "After this meeting he is scheduled to have a meeting with his generals, and then a meeting with the Department of the Navy."

"Excuse me—" a man in the crowd called out.

"But I heard the president say he'd like to meet us!" Jack broke in.

"I can't imagine why he said that," said Mr. Nicolay, shaking his head. "Following all the meetings I just listed, President Lincoln will meet with foreign diplomats, then with a group of senators, and then with reporters from the *New York Times*."

"Mr. Nicolay! Listen to me!" someone shouted.

"So, sir," Annie interrupted, "you're saying he'll have no free time at all today?"

"Oh, he might have a free moment," said Mr. Nicolay. "But should that miracle occur, the president will go for a horseback ride in the country—and have a private meeting with himself!"

"Got it," said Annie. She took a deep breath. "Well, maybe you can just answer one question for us. Do you know if the president collects feathers?"

Mr. Nicolay threw up his hands. "This is no time for silly questions," he said. "Our country is divided, young lady. We are on the brink of war."

"What do you mean, sir?" one of the men in the crowd shouted. "What's the news from Fort Sumter?"

"Yes! What do you know that we don't know?" a lady called.

Everyone started shouting at once.

"That's it! Leave now, everyone!" Mr. Nicolay said. "The president is busy! He works night and day for you and for the unity of this nation!"

As the crowd shouted back at the secretary, Jack tugged on Annie's sleeve. "Let's get out of here," he said.

"We should wait for Willie," said Annie.

"I don't think Willie can help us," said Jack. "Come on. Let's go back to the tree house and look at our research book. Maybe we can think of something else."

"Okay," said Annie, sighing.

She and Jack hurried along the hallway, then down the stairs to the first floor. They wove through the crowd, then escaped out the main door.

"Phew! That place is nuts!" said Jack as they walked between the tall white columns of the White House.

"Are you sure we shouldn't wait for Willie?" said Annie.

"I'm sure," said Jack. He hurried down the carriageway. "Even if Willie took us back to the office to meet his dad, we wouldn't be alone with the president. Lots of other people would be there, too. We couldn't ask him for a feather. And we sure couldn't give him any hope. Everyone would laugh."

"You're right," said Annie.

Jack shook his head. "How can the president

even think in that place, with Tad jumping on him, his relatives visiting, his secretary yelling—"

"And a thousand people scheduled to meet with him," said Annie.

"And another thousand who are *trying* to meet with him!" said Jack.

They had arrived back at the tree house. "Whew. No wonder the president needs to take a ride in the countryside by himself," Jack said. He grabbed the sides of the ladder. "Let's go up and look at the book."

"Wait," said Annie. "I have a good idea."

"What?" asked Jack.

"Right now we really need to have our own meeting with Abraham Lincoln, alone," said Annie. "Right?"

"Yes . . . so?" said Jack.

"So if that's the one thing we need, our book can't really help," said Annie. "But I know something that *can*."

"What?" said Jack.

Annie reached into her apron pocket. She pulled

out the bottle and read the label aloud: "'Take a sip. Make a wish for *one thing* to help you on your mission. Remember: Trust the magic.'"

Annie looked up at Jack. "So why don't we make a wish to have a private meeting with Abraham Lincoln?"

"Isn't it too soon to use our only magic?" said Jack.

"Maybe. But maybe it's the perfect time," said Annie.

"So we wish to have a meeting with the president all by ourselves?" said Jack.

"Yep," said Annie.

Jack couldn't think of another plan. "Well . . . okay," he said. "Let's do it."

"Just remember, we have to trust the magic," said Annie.

Jack nodded.

Annie took the top off the bottle. She raised the bottle to her lips, then swallowed a quick sip of the potion. She handed the bottle to Jack, and he did the same.

"You can make our wish," said Annie.

Jack squeezed his eyes shut. "We wish to have a meeting with Abraham Lincoln!" he said. "Alone!"

There was a deafening *WHOOSH* and a *ROAR*. The earth shook, like a speeding train passing by. The ground opened, and Jack felt as if he were falling through space,

through a tunnel,

down through blackness,

into a world of daylight.

CHAPTER SIX

Trust the Magic

Clouds hid the sun. Jack and Annie sat in a clump of dead weeds beside a dirt road in the countryside. A chilly wind blew the creaky limbs of bare trees.

"You okay?" asked Annie.

"I think so," said Jack. "Where are we?"

"Looks like we're somewhere in the country," said Annie.

"No kidding, but where? Why?" said Jack.

"Wait, wait," said Annie. "Mr. Nicolay said if the president had a free moment, he'd take a ride in the country. I'll bet we've come to a spot where we can catch Abraham Lincoln on his ride! Alone!"

"Oh, wow . . . cool," said Jack.

"Look!" said Annie. "Someone's coming this way now! On a horse!"

A slim figure on a horse was coming down the dirt road. Jack and Annie jumped to their feet. When the rider on the bony white horse got closer, Jack sighed. "It's not the president," he said. "It's just some kid on an old horse."

"Maybe this kid is supposed to help us somehow," said Annie. "Remember, *trust the magic*."

Jack nodded, but he couldn't imagine the boy would be much help. He looked to be ten or maybe eleven years old. His matted black hair stuck out from under a coonskin cap. His thin face was dirty, and his buckskin pants and moccasins were stained and torn. A frayed burlap sack hung from his shoulder.

Annie stepped into the road and waved. "Hello!" she called.

The boy pulled the old horse to a halt. He took off his cap and bowed his head. Then he put his cap back on and looked at them with tired gray eyes. "How do?" he said without a smile.

"We do good," said Annie. "We're wondering if you can help us. We're looking for Abraham Lincoln. Does he ride his horse around here? Have you ever seen him?"

The boy's eyes brightened. "You're looking for Abraham Lincoln?" he asked.

"Yes, we are," said Jack.

"Why?" the boy asked.

"Um . . . well, we just want to say hi to him," said Jack. "Do you know if he goes riding in this area?"

The boy nodded. "He does," he said. "In fact, he is in this area as we speak."

"Really?" said Annie. She smiled at Jack, as if to say, *See! The magic's working!*

Jack couldn't help smiling back. "So, can you tell us where we can find him?" he asked the boy.

"Yes," said the boy, nodding. "But I think it's better if I take you to him myself. I just have to grind some corn at the mill first."

How long will that take? Jack wondered. *How*

long will the president be riding in the country-side?

"Maybe you could just tell us where we could find him," said Jack. "We don't have much time."

"Wait," said Annie. She whispered to Jack, "We have to trust the magic."

Jack sighed. He looked back at the boy. "Okay, we'll go to the mill with you," he said, "but it would be good if we could hurry, so we don't miss finding Abraham Lincoln."

"You won't miss him. I give you my word," said the boy. "Come along. The grinder's around the bend. Giddyup, girl." He shook his reins, and the old horse started plodding down the road again.

Jack and Annie walked after the slow-moving horse. "Our names are Jack and Annie," Annie called. "What's yours?"

"You can call me Sam," the boy said over his shoulder.

"Okay, Sam," said Annie. "Thanks for helping us."

A gust of wind stirred the branches of the trees. The old horse neighed and stopped. "Keep going, girl," said Sam.

But the horse wouldn't budge.

"She doesn't hear well. She gets spooked by the wind," Sam explained to Jack and Annie.

The lonely sound of the wind spooked Jack, too. Something felt wrong. This weather was different from the weather at the White House.

"Giddyup, girl!" said Sam.

The horse started plodding down the road again. When they rounded the bend, Jack saw a strange-looking machine in a clearing. It had a barrel-like container with a wooden beam attached to it. Metal rods hung from the end of the beam.

"What's that?" said Jack.

"The grinder," said Sam. "You ain't never seen one before?"

"Sure, we have," said Annie.

No one was tending the grinder or waiting to use it. Sam dropped his sack to the ground and dismounted. He was tall and skinny. His buckskin pants were too short for him.

"What's in your bag?" asked Annie.

"Twenty pounds of corn," Sam said. "Shelled it all by hand."

"Wow," said Annie.

Sam poured the corn kernels into a funnel over the barrel. Then he hitched his old horse to leather straps attached to the metal rods.

Jack and Annie stood to the side and watched Sam walk his horse around in a circle. After a while, Jack grew impatient. The corn grinding seemed to be taking forever. Before he could say anything, though, a gust of wind came up and the horse reared.

"Keep moving, girl!" said Sam.

The horse neighed and tossed her head.

"Go on, girl! Giddyup!" said Sam. He slapped her backside. "Giddyup, I said!"

The horse didn't budge.

"These nice folks are waitin' on us!" said Sam. He pushed the horse from behind.

The wind picked up, tossing dead leaves into

the air. The horse neighed again, then kicked out with her hind foot. Her hoof hit Sam in the head! His coonskin cap flew off as he fell backward and sprawled across the ground.

"Sam!" cried Annie.

Annie and Jack knelt in the dirt beside the boy.

A trickle of blood ran down the side of his head. His eyes were closed.

"Sam?" said Annie. "Can you hear me?" She wiped the blood with her apron.

Sam didn't answer or open his eyes.

"Hey, Sam!" Jack said loudly. "Wake up!"

But Sam didn't move. He didn't even seem to be breathing.

Jack and Annie looked at each other.

"Is he dead?" whispered Annie.

CHAPTER SEVEN

Sam's Farm

"I don't know," said Jack. This was one of the worst things that had ever happened. He pressed his finger against Sam's wrist to feel for his pulse, like he'd seen on TV and in movies.

Sam's eyes opened. "Giddyup," he said weakly.

Jack laughed with relief. "Whew, we were afraid you were dead!" he said.

"Ain't dead yet," Sam whispered, blinking, "but I am seeing stars and my ears are ringing."

"Does your head hurt?" asked Annie.

"Yes, bad," Sam said quietly, his eyes squinting with pain.

"You might have a concussion," Jack said. "Is there a doctor nearby?"

"Thirty-five . . . ," said Sam.

"Minutes?" asked Jack.

"Miles," Sam whispered.

"Whoa, that's really far," said Annie.

"I have to go home . . . to our farm," said Sam. He struggled to sit up.

"Careful," said Jack. He couldn't remember what to do if someone had a concussion.

With Jack and Annie's help, Sam managed to get on his feet. "Thanks," the boy said. He staggered toward his horse, then swayed and collapsed onto the ground again.

"Sam!" said Annie. She and Jack gently helped him back up to a standing position.

"Dizzy . . . just dizzy," whispered Sam.

"We'll help you get home," said Annie. "You can't do it by yourself. Right, Jack?"

"Right," said Jack. He knew it was the right thing to do. *But as soon as we get him home to his parents, we have to find Abraham Lincoln,* he thought.

"Sam can sit in front of me and I'll hold on to him," Annie said to Jack. "You can take the reins and walk alongside us."

"Okay." Jack kept holding Sam, while Annie unhitched the straps, freeing the horse.

The wind had died down. The horse was calm as Annie coaxed her to a tree stump. She climbed onto the stump and then onto the horse's back.

"Your turn, Sam," said Jack.

Jack held Sam's elbow as the gangly boy climbed onto the stump. Then Sam hauled himself onto the horse in front of Annie. He started to slump forward. Before he could slide off, Annie grabbed him and held him up.

"Got him?" said Jack.

"My cornmeal," Sam whispered.

"I'll get it," said Jack. He found a panel in the

bottom of the grinder and opened it. Then he grabbed the empty sack and scooped the ground corn inside.

Jack slung the sack over his shoulder. Then he picked up the reins and turned the horse around. Annie held Sam as Jack led the horse along the lonely road back the way they had come.

This isn't the way things are supposed to happen, Jack thought. He knew they were supposed to trust the magic. But now they were helping the person who was supposed to help *them.*

"Where is your farm, Sam?" Jack asked after a while.

The boy didn't answer.

"Sam!" said Annie, giving him a little shake. "Your farm? Where is it?"

Sam opened his eyes. "Here," he said.

Jack didn't see any sign of a farm. The only things up ahead were a small, windowless log cabin and a shed. A curl of smoke rose into the white sky.

"Here *where*?" asked Jack.

Sam pointed to the cabin and shed.

That's it? Jack thought. *Sam's family must be really poor.*

The cabin and shed were in a scrubby clearing. The clearing was dotted with piles of stones and stumps where trees had been chopped down.

Not much of a farm, Jack thought. But at least they hadn't wasted a lot of time getting Sam home.

Jack led the horse toward Sam's farm. The cabin not only had no windows—it didn't even have a door! A black bearskin hung over the entrance. The horse stopped near the lean-to shed. The sound of a cow mooing came from inside.

"I'll help you, Sam," Jack said, dropping the sack of cornmeal to the ground. "Careful, careful."

Sam lowered himself down from the horse. When his feet touched the ground, Jack grabbed him. "Lean on me," he said. He put Sam's arm around his shoulders.

"Got him?" said Annie.

"Yep," said Jack.

As Jack and Sam stumbled toward the cabin, Annie slid off the horse and tied her to a fence post beside the shed. Then Annie grabbed the sack of cornmeal. She ran to the cabin and pushed aside the bearskin, so Jack could help Sam inside.

No one was home. The only light in the one-room cabin came from daylight streaming through big cracks between the logs of the walls. A low fire burned in a fireplace, but the air was cold and damp. The floor was made of dirt, and the crude furniture was made of planks of wood and tree stumps.

"Thank—thank you, Jack," Sam said, breathing heavily. "You can just leave me right here." He took his arm from Jack's shoulders and crumpled onto the dirt floor. He curled up and lay shivering on his side.

This is not good, thought Jack.

"You can't lie on the dirt, Sam," said Annie. "Don't you have a bed?"

Sam pointed to a loft.

"We'll help you," said Jack.

Jack and Annie pulled Sam up from the floor. He put his arms around their shoulders, and they brought him to a row of wooden pegs that led to the loft. Sam managed to pull himself up the row of pegs. When he reached the top, he disappeared.

"Now what?" Jack whispered to Annie.

Sam moaned from the loft above.

"Poor kid," Annie murmured to Jack. "There's no one here to take care of him."

Jack didn't know what to do. He wanted to help Sam, but they still had to find Abraham Lincoln in the countryside before he returned to the White House. And he wasn't sure how long the magic would work.

Another moan came from the loft.

"We have to help Sam," Annie said decisively. She climbed up the wooden pegs. Jack followed. As he crawled into the loft, he had to be careful not to bump his head on the ceiling.

Light and cold air came through the cracks between the logs. Sam was lying on a bed of corn husks and dried leaves. His fingers were pressed against his head.

"Does your head still hurt?" asked Annie.

"Bad," said Sam. He kept pressing his fore-head, as if trying to push away the pain.

"Where are your parents, Sam?" asked Jack.

"Pa's gone," Sam said hoarsely. His eyes were squeezed shut. "Went to Kentucky last month."

"Where's your mother?" asked Annie.

Sam just shook his head.

"Can you tell us where your mother is?" Annie asked.

"Dead. She's dead. She died last year," said Sam. He covered his eyes with his arm.

"Oh, no," said Annie.

"Is there anyone who can take care of you?" Jack asked. He couldn't imagine being so alone.

"My sister, Sarah," Sam said in a muffled voice.

"Where's Sarah now?" asked Jack.

"School," said Sam.

"When does she get home?" asked Jack.

"After dark," said Sam.

"After dark?" said Annie.

"Short days in December," said Sam.

December? thought Jack. When they'd landed at the White House, it had been March. Maybe Sam's head injury had confused him.

"We're not leaving you, Sam," said Annie, "not until Sarah comes home."

"Don't . . . have to stay," said Sam, wincing with pain.

"We know we don't have to," said Jack. "But we want to."

And he meant it.

CHAPTER EIGHT

Into the Rough

Jack and Annie huddled in the loft near Sam. As the wind whistled between the logs, Jack could feel the boy's sadness.

"Thank you," Sam said. "But I have to get up now—have to do chores—help Sarah."

"No, not now," said Annie. "Maybe Sarah can take care of your chores when she gets home."

"She'll be too tired," said Sam. "She has to walk a long way home. With Pa gone, she can't sleep—hears wolves and wildcats all night."

"Really? Are there wolves and wildcats around here?" said Jack.

"Plenty," Sam said. "I have to do my chores—" He tried to sit up.

"Not until you feel better," Annie said firmly. "You lie here and rest. *We'll* do your chores. Just tell us what to do. We'll be happy to do it. Won't we, Jack?"

"Uh, sure . . . ," said Jack. "What are your chores, Sam?"

Sam lay back and took a deep breath. "Split wood," he said, closing his eyes, "milk cow, get water from spring . . ."

Jack slipped the pencil and notebook out of his back pocket and wrote:

> split wood
> milk cow
> get water from spring

"Where's the spring?" asked Jack.

"Just a mile away, through the rough," said Sam.

"The rough?" said Jack.

"No problem," said Annie. "Anything else to do?"

"Make corn bread, then do homework in speller book . . . ," said Sam.

Jack added to his list:

make corn bread
homework in speller book

"That's it?" said Jack.

"Yes," said Sam.

"Good. We can do that!" said Annie.

We can? thought Jack. *Milk cow? Make corn bread? And what's "the rough"?*

"Sam, where's the rough?" asked Jack.

But Sam had fallen asleep.

"Sam?" said Jack.

"Shhh, let him sleep," Annie whispered.

Jack nodded. He followed Annie down from

the loft and across the dirt floor. She pushed aside the bearskin, and they stepped out of the cabin.

"Why did you promise to do Sam's chores?" said Jack. "We don't know how to do all that stuff."

"It was the only way to keep him from trying to work," said Annie. "He really needs to rest. Don't worry. We can figure them out. What's first?"

Jack looked at their list.

"Split wood," he said.

"How hard could that be?" said Annie. "There's the woodpile. There's the ax." She strode over to a stack of wood in the front yard. An ax was sunk into a fat log.

Annie rubbed her hands together, then wrapped them around the ax's long handle. She pulled and pulled, but the ax didn't budge.

"Let me try," said Jack. Annie stepped aside. Jack gripped the handle and pulled as hard as he could. But the ax stayed in the log.

"Forget it," said Jack. "It's like trying to pull the sword from the stone."

Annie laughed. "I guess we're not meant to be king," she said. "So, what's next?"

"Milk cow," Jack read from his list.

"All righty," Annie said cheerfully. She led the way to the shed next to the cabin.

Inside the shed, a cow was eating hay and swishing her tail. A three-legged stool and a tin pail stood in the corner.

"You try first," said Annie.

"Me?" said Jack.

"I tried the ax first," said Annie.

Jack put the pail under the cow and moved the stool close to her. Then he sat down.

The cow gave Jack a look. Then she whipped him in the face with her tail.

"Oww!" said Jack. He leaned forward and stared at the cow's udder.

Jack looked up at Annie. "I have no idea what to do," he said.

Annie laughed again. "Me neither," she said. "We'll come back to this, too. What's next?"

Jack jumped up from the stool and looked at

their list. "Get water from the spring," he said.

"I saw two jugs by the door," said Annie. "I'll get them." She ran to the cabin and came back a moment later with two brown jugs.

"Heavy," Annie warned. She gave one to Jack.

The jug *was* surprisingly heavy. "They'll be heavier with water," said Jack. "This isn't going to be easy, since the spring is a mile away, 'through the rough.' Whatever that means."

"I'll bet that's the rough over there," said Annie. She pointed to the woods on the other side of the clearing.

Jack and Annie wound their way through the stumps and stone piles until they came to the woodsy area, thick with underbrush. Wild grapevines twisted through bushes and around bare branches of small trees, binding it all together.

"It looks rough all right," said Jack.

Annie pointed to a narrow path. "I'll bet that's how to get to the spring," she said. "Want to give it a try?"

"Sure," said Jack. "Let's go."

Carrying the jugs, Jack and Annie started down the path. They pushed aside tangled vines and branches. Crows, sparrows, and woodpeckers swooped overhead. Squirrels ran up and down the small, bare trees.

Down the path, the rough got rougher. The path nearly disappeared. The tangle of undergrowth was so thick that Jack began to lose what little hope he had.

"I can't see pushing our way through this stuff for a whole mile," he said.

"Me neither," said Annie. "Let's go just a little further and see if it opens up again."

Jack and Annie pushed past more brambles and vines. "This whole journey is leading nowhere," Jack grumbled. "No spring water, no split wood, no cow's milk. Worst of all, no Abraham Lincoln. We've missed our only chance to use the magic to have a private meeting with him."

"I know," said Annie. "But we couldn't just leave Sam to try to do his chores. Offering to help him was the right thing to do."

"I know," said Jack.

"It's weird," said Annie. "Even though helping Sam isn't part of our mission, I feel like doing one good thing is somehow connected to doing another good thing. If we're helping Sam, we're also helping Penny."

"Yeah . . . ," said Jack. Despite his worries, he agreed with what Annie said. "There's only one problem: we have to get this feather from—"

"Yikes!" said Annie.

Jack looked back at her. "Yikes, what? You forgot we had to get a feather?"

"No. Yikes, did you hear that?" she whispered.

"Hear what?" whispered Jack. He held his breath and listened.

"A growl," whispered Annie.

Jack looked around, his heart pounding. "Like, uh—a wildcat growl? Or a wolf growl?" he asked.

"Like—*that* growl," said Annie.

Jack heard the long, low growl. He heard twigs breaking. The hair went up on the back of his neck.

CHAPTER NINE

Corn Bread and Molasses

"Turn around slowly," Jack said to Annie.

Clutching the water jugs, Jack and Annie turned around and started back the way they'd come. They tried not to make noise, but sticks and branches cracked and snapped.

The growl came again. *Louder.*

"Forget slow!" said Jack. "Run!"

Annie bolted ahead through the brush. Jack ran after her. His heart pounded. Brambles and vines blocked their way. Thorns snagged their clothes. They ran as fast as they could, not knowing if all the breathing and thrashing sounds were coming from them—or from the beast chasing them.

They burst into the clearing. Jack looked back. He didn't see a wolf or wildcat, but he wasn't ready to stop yet. "Keep going!" he cried.

Jack and Annie tore across the scrubby clearing. Finally they came to the cabin.

Sam was standing by the woodpile, swinging the ax! He gracefully split a log in two. He looked up at Jack and Annie and smiled. "How do?" he said.

Jack and Annie laughed as they tried to catch their breath. For some reason, Jack felt safe now, with Sam. "Fine!" he said. "Fine, fine, fine!"

"How do *you* do?" said Annie. "Why are you splitting wood?"

"I said to myself, I ain't going to lie in bed forever," said Sam. "My headache stopped as soon as I started my chores. I figured the two of you had left."

"Oh, no, we tried to do your chores," said Jack. "But—"

"We were headed to the spring to get water and we heard a growl," said Annie.

"Like a wolf," said Jack.

"Or a wildcat," Annie said.

"So we ran," said Jack.

Annie held up a jug. "No water. Sorry."

"No milk, either," said Jack.

"No split wood," said Annie.

"No corn bread," said Jack.

Sam gave them a big grin. "Don't worry. I took care of milking the cow, and I found water in the rain bucket. The corn bread's baking now."

"Wow," said Annie.

"That's amazing," said Jack. Now that Sam was better, he wondered if he could lead them to the president. "Do you still have time to help us find Abraham Lincoln?" he asked.

"Sure," said Sam. "I gave you my word."

"Great. Do you think he's still riding his horse in the country?" said Jack.

"Nope. He's not riding anymore," said Sam.

"But I guarantee you he's around here."

"Like where?" said Jack.

"Don't worry. I'll introduce you to him very soon," said Sam. "Let's go inside first."

Sam stuck his ax in a log. He picked up an armload of wood and headed into the cabin. As Jack and Annie followed, Jack glanced at the sky. The sun would be going down soon.

Inside, Sam put more wood on the fire. Then he lit two oil lamps. "Would you like to have some corn bread with butter and molasses?" he asked.

"Oh . . . wow . . ." Jack didn't know what to say. He was desperate to look for Abraham Lincoln, but he was also *very* hungry.

"I'd love it!" said Annie.

"Me too," said Jack, relieved. "We'll eat fast. And then we can look for Abraham Lincoln, okay?"

"Yes indeed. But first, you-all sit down," said Sam.

Jack and Annie sat on small tree stumps that served as stools. Sam lifted the lid on a pot

hanging over the fire. The delicious smell of corn bread filled the air.

Sam moved the pot to the wood table. Then he sliced pieces of steaming bread and put them on wooden plates. He smeared butter and dark molasses over the bread and ladled milk from the pail into wooden cups.

Jack sipped the sweet milk and ate the hot, buttery corn bread. "Yum," he said. He thought it might be the best meal he'd ever had.

"You really worked hard after we left," Annie said to Sam.

"I like to make things nice for Sarah for when she gets home from school," the boy said.

"Do *you* ever go to school?" asked Jack, his mouth full.

Sam nodded. "Since Pa left, I stay here to watch over things and do chores. But Sarah comes home and shares what she's learned. I do home-work and everything."

"Have you lived here a long time?" Jack asked, looking around at the crude cabin.

"A few years," said Sam. "We came from Kentucky. Pa and I cut our cabin out of the wilderness. We chopped down trees to make a road. We rolled fifty logs to this site and put up these walls. Did it all by hand and all without nails."

"Whoa," said Jack. It sounded like work for the strongest men, he thought, but Sam couldn't have been more than seven or eight at the time.

"We did as best we could with the furniture," Sam said with a laugh. "Someday we'll do better."

"It's not bad," said Jack. He looked at the cabin with new eyes. It seemed like a miracle now—everything made by hand, without the help of machines or even nails.

"You make all your own food, too, don't you?" asked Annie.

"'Course," said Sam. "We have our crops, and Pa hunts for our meat, or he did when he was here."

"I wouldn't be a good hunter," said Annie.

"Me neither," said Jack.

"Me neither," said Sam. "I shot a turkey once. Then I took a good hard look at the bird. I was so taken with its beauty, I ain't pulled a trigger on a wild creature since. That's why we haven't had any meat since Pa left."

"Well, you do a great job making corn bread," said Annie.

"You sure do," said Jack. He took his last bite, finished his milk, and wiped his mouth on his sleeve. Okay. Now they had to look for the president. Through the cracks in the cabin, he could see it was getting darker.

"Did you get all your chores done?" said Annie.

"Nope. I ain't worked in my Dilworth speller yet," said Sam. "But I don't really consider that a chore. It's my favorite thing. You could say I have a great thirst for learnin'."

"So do we," said Annie. "What's your homework for today?"

"Annie," said Jack, trying to catch her eye.

"Hold on, I'll get the speller that Sarah brought me from school and show you." Sam crossed the room and scrambled up to the loft. "The lesson I studied this morning is parts of speech," he called down.

"We have to go," Jack whispered to Annie.

"We can't hurt his feelings," whispered Annie. "Just let him show us the speller."

"But we have a mission—" Jack started.

"Here it is!" said Sam, climbing down from the loft. He grinned at them and held up a tattered book. "Would you mind giving me a little test?"

CHAPTER TEN

Readin' and Writin'

"We don't mind," said Annie.

"Annie," said Jack.

But Sam opened the speller and handed it to Annie. "Parts of speech," he said.

"Okay," Annie said. "What is a conjunction?"

Sam bit his lip. "Let's see . . . a conjunction is a part of speech that joins words and sentences together," he said. "Some conjunctions are *and, but,* and *because.*"

"Perfect!" said Annie.

"Yes, perfect," said Jack. "Here's an example: Jack wants to leave, *but* Annie is ignoring him."

"Good example," said Annie. "What is an interjection?" she asked Sam.

"That's a part of speech that expresses a sudden passion of the mind," said Sam, "such as 'Alack!' or 'Alas!' or 'Fie!' "

"Good," said Annie, laughing, "except Jack and I don't use interjections like those. We express a passion of the mind by saying things like 'Oh, man!' or 'Oh, wow!' or 'Whoa!'"

"Yes, that's right," said Jack, glaring at Annie. "Like 'Oh, man, time is running out!' Or 'Oh, wow, the sun is going down!' Or 'Whoa, we have a mission to complete!' "

Annie laughed again. "Right, that's how we use our interjections," she said to Sam. "What else is in your book?"

"Spelling and grammar rules," said Sam. "And quotes from the Bible and fables."

"Cool," said Annie.

Sam closed his speller. "I only wish I had more books," he said. "Anyone who'll give me a book is my best friend. I'll walk miles to borrow it."

"Jack would, too," said Annie. "And Jack and I both love to write, too. Don't we?" She looked at Jack.

"Yes, we do," said Jack, sighing.

"Oh, I do, too!" said Sam. "Neither my pa nor my ma ever learned to write. But I love it. I write words in the dust or the sand, even in the snow. I write them in the dirt floor with a stick." Sam laughed. Jack couldn't help smiling. "Why, I write on wooden shovels with charcoal!" Sam leaned forward and said in a hushed voice, "But the *best* thing in the world to write with is my quill pen and my blackberry ink!" Sam's face glowed in the firelight.

"Oh, wow, you do love to write," said Jack. "So do I." Jack forgot about Abraham Lincoln for the moment. "I love to make up my own stories."

Sam smiled. "Me too," he said. "And now I

want to tell you-all a good one. I meant to tell you this before, but I got kicked in the head before I could. I'm kind of famous for playing pranks on folks. But the two of you don't deserve—"

Suddenly noises came from outside: rumbling and neighing.

"What's that?" said Annie.

Sam froze. Then he turned to Jack and Annie, his eyes wide. "A wagon!" he said. He jumped up and rushed to the entrance of the cabin and pushed aside the bearskin.

"Pa!" Sam shouted, and he disappeared outside.

"His dad's back?" said Annie.

She and Jack hurried to the doorway and peeked out. Four horses were pulling a wagon through the cold dusk. The rickety wagon was filled with kids and furniture.

They watched as Sam ran toward the wagon and the driver pulled the horses to a halt. Sam's pa jumped down from his bench and threw his arms around Sam. They hugged for a long time.

Then a woman stepped down from the driver's bench. Three children scrambled down from the back. They stood smiling and giggling beside her.

"Son, I want you to meet my wife and your new ma from Kentucky," Sam's pa said. "And these are her children and your new sisters and brother, Elizabeth, Matilda, and John."

Each kid said "howdy" in turn.

"Howdy, son," Sam's new ma said. "I've so looked forward to meeting you. Thomas is awful proud of you and your sister. He says you're a good reader and a good writer."

"We hear you're a good woodchopper, too!" said the boy named John.

"And you like to tell stories!" said the girl named Elizabeth.

"And play pranks!" said the girl named Matilda.

"We brought you some books!" John piped up.

"And a feather mattress!" said Elizabeth.

"And a washstand and some soap!" said
Matilda. "Come look!"

The children grabbed Sam. He laughed as they
pulled him toward the wagon and started showing
him all the things they'd hauled from Kentucky.

Jack smiled. Sam wouldn't be sad or lonely anymore, he thought. It made him feel happy to see such a good thing happen to Sam.

"Let's slip outside and hide in the shed," Jack said to Annie. "So we don't have to explain where we came from."

Jack and Annie pushed past the bearskin into the shadows of twilight. They crept into the cowshed and peeked out.

"Pa?" someone shouted. "Paaaa!!!"

Across the clearing, a girl came running. She wore a black cape with a hood.

"Sarah! My girl!" Sam and Sarah's father rushed forward and threw his arms around his daughter.

Sarah started sobbing.

Her father hugged her. "Don't cry, girl," he said. "I brought you a whole new family. We'll all take good care of each other now. Come on, let's go in, and you can meet everyone. You'll love them all, Sarah, I promise. I give you my word."

As everyone headed into the cabin, Matilda exclaimed, "My goodness, you built this by hand?"

"What a wonderful job you did," said Sam's new ma.

"It's going to get better," said Sam's pa. "We're going to make a real door, aren't we, boys? And we'll make a real floor with wood, patch the roof, and put mud in the chinks between the logs."

"Yes, sir," said Sam and John together.

Thomas held the bearskin for his wife and all the children. Then he followed them inside.

Jack and Annie could hear the sounds of happy conversation coming from the cabin.

"Wow, what a day to be with Sam, huh?" Annie said to Jack.

"Really," said Jack. "But what should we do now?"

"I don't know," said Annie. "I think Sam forgot us in all the excitement."

"Like when Tad forgot me under the bed in the White House," said Jack.

"Jack! Annie!" Sam came running out of the cabin, calling to them in the fading light.

"He didn't forget us!" said Annie.

She and Jack stepped out of the cowshed.

"We're here!" Annie called.

"I want to give you something!" said Sam. He

held up a quill pen and a small bottle. "I told you about these. The pen's made from the feather of a goose, and the ink's from the roots of a blackberry bush. I want you to have them."

"Oh, no, Sam," said Jack. "You keep them. You need them more."

"Take 'em," said Sam. "I want to thank you for staying by me when I was feeling poorly, and for trying to do my chores. Your kindness truly helped me."

"But we didn't do any chores, not one!" said Annie.

"You tried, though," said Sam. "And most important, you both love what I love most: readin' and writin'. Please." Sam handed Jack the quill pen and the ink bottle. "Use them to write something special."

"We will," said Annie. "I can carry them, Jack." He handed her Sam's treasures, and she put them into her apron pocket. "Thank you."

"You're welcome," said Sam. "And what I was going to tell you is—"

"Yes—" Jack started.

But before Jack could finish, a *WHOOSH* and a *ROAR* shook the earth, like a speeding train passing by. The ground opened, and Jack felt as if he were falling through space,

through a tunnel,

down through blackness,

into a world of daylight.

CHAPTER ELEVEN

Abe Lincoln at Last!

Jack and Annie looked around in a daze. They were under the trees near the tree house, standing in the same spot where they'd sipped the potion. The air was chilly but bright. A fresh breeze rustled the branches.

"The magic ended," said Jack, stunned. "It ended before we could complete our mission."

"I know," Annie said. "And we didn't get to say good-bye to Sam."

"I didn't even thank him for the quill pen and the ink," said Jack.

"I know. These were his treasures," said Annie. She held up the goose feather and the ink jar that Sam had given them.

"Wait, that's so weird," said Jack. "We're looking for a feather, and Sam gives us a pen made out of a feather—"

Annie gasped. "Look, Jack!" She pointed toward the carriageway.

A tall man in a dark coat and a high black hat was striding toward the grove of trees. He turned his head, as if he were searching for something.

"At last!" said Jack.

"Mr. President!" Annie called. She thrust the quill pen and ink bottle back into her pocket and ran toward Abraham Lincoln.

"Wait!" said Jack, running after her. "What'll we say?"

"We'll figure it out!" said Annie. "Mr. President!"

Abraham Lincoln turned and looked in their direction. He froze and stared at them, as if he were both astonished and afraid.

What's wrong with him? thought Jack. As they got closer to the president, Jack and Annie slowed to a walk. Abraham Lincoln kept staring at them as if they were ghosts.

"Hello, sir," Annie said shyly.

Jack was speechless.

The creases in the president's face gave him a deeply worried look. His gray eyes stared at them

without blinking. "So it *is* you," he said in a hushed voice. "Tad told me your names, but I could not believe it might really be you."

"What do you mean?" Annie asked.

"You don't know who I am?" he said.

"You're Abraham Lincoln," said Annie. "President of the United States."

"Yes, but I spent the day with you once long ago," said the president. "And you vanished, right before my eyes."

"We did?" said Annie.

"Outside our log cabin in Indiana," said the president.

"Indiana?" said Jack.

"Yes, it was the day my father brought my stepmother home—and my new sisters and brother."

"Oh . . . *oh!*" said Annie.

"What?" said Jack.

"You were Sam!" said Annie.

"You were *Sam*?" said Jack. He couldn't believe it.

The president nodded.

Annie laughed. "So when we told you we were looking for Abraham Lincoln, you played a prank on us and told us your name was Sam!"

Abraham Lincoln smiled. "I haven't seen you since that day so long ago," he said. "And you haven't changed at all. I don't understand. Are you angels? Are you a dream?"

Jack was too stunned to answer. *It wasn't long ago, it was today,* he thought. *Or—maybe not.* Time and magic were confusing things.

"We're just regular kids, not angels," said Annie. "But maybe you should think of it all as a dream—a dream with a little magic thrown in."

Abraham Lincoln nodded slowly. Then he smiled. "I remember you tried to do my chores," he said, "and you thought some wild creature was chasing you. And you told me that your interjections were 'Oh, wow!' and 'Oh, man!'"

"Right," said Jack, smiling.

"You also said you loved learning and you loved

to read," said the president. "And you loved to write stories."

"And you said you loved to do that, too," said Annie. "So you gave us these." She pulled the ink bottle and the quill pen out of her apron pocket. "These were yours once, remember?"

Abraham Lincoln stared at the ink bottle and feather pen. "Yes," he said. "I made them from blackberry roots and a goose feather."

"Oh, man," whispered Jack. For the first time it fully dawned on him that Sam—who was really Abraham Lincoln—had given them a feather! The rhyme was starting to make perfect sense!

"Why have you come back?" asked the president.

Now Jack knew exactly what to say. "We have to give you a message of hope," he answered. He reached for the notebook in his pocket.

"Jack's right," said Annie. "Just a second." She opened the ink bottle and dipped the goose-feather pen into the ink. Then she handed the pen to Jack. "What should we say?" she whispered.

"Well, the Civil War is going to have a good ending," Jack whispered back. "All the country will come together."

"With freedom for everybody," whispered Annie.

"I'll write something about all that," said Jack. He thought for a second, and using the goose-feather pen, he scratched a message on a page in his notebook:

> Never lose hope. This land will live
> peacefully as one nation one day,
> with freedom for everyone.

"You told us to use your quill pen and your blackberry ink to write something special," Jack said. He tore out the page and handed it to the president of the United States. "This is it."

Abraham Lincoln read the words on the paper. When he looked at Jack and Annie, the creases in his face had softened. His eyes had grown bright. "Oh, wow," he said softly.

Jack and Annie laughed.

"Do you really think so?" the president asked. "Do you promise?"

"Yes. I need to add something," said Jack. He took the note back from the president and wrote:

We give you our word.
—Jack and Annie

A shout came from the distance: "Pa! Pa!"

It was Tad. He was running up the carriage-way, with Willie right behind him.

"Mr. President, we have to leave now," said Jack.

"Really?" said Abraham Lincoln. He looked sad for a moment. Then he looked at his boys running toward him. "Yes, of course, I understand," he said.

"We'll never forget our times with you, Sam," said Annie.

"Nor will I forget," said Abraham Lincoln.

The boys were getting closer.

"Here, sir," said Jack. He gave the note back to the president. Then he and Annie started moving away.

"Good-bye!" they called to Abraham Lincoln.

The president waved and put their note in his pocket.

Then Jack and Annie quickly climbed up the ladder. Inside the tree house, they looked out the window. They saw Abraham Lincoln hurrying to meet his boys. When he caught up to them, he wrapped his arms around them both. They were all laughing.

"Abraham Lincoln's a good dad," said Annie.

"Yeah," said Jack, smiling. "Well, we'd better go now. Before Tad tries to take the tree house away from us."

Annie laughed. "He'll be pretty surprised when he discovers it's disappeared," she said. She picked up the Pennsylvania book and pointed to a picture of the Frog Creek woods. "I wish we could go home!" she said.

The wind began to blow.

The tree house started to spin.

It spun faster and faster.

Then everything was still.

Absolutely still.

CHAPTER TWELVE

The Feather of Hope

A spring breeze was whispering through the trees. "We're home," said Jack. They were back in Frog Creek, wearing their own clothes again. Jack looked in his backpack and pulled out their book on Abraham Lincoln.

Annie reached into one of her jacket pockets. "Good, they're still here!" she said. She took out Abraham Lincoln's gifts: the bottle of blackberry ink and the goose-feather pen.

"Cool," said Jack.

"Before we go, I want to look in our book and

see if there's a picture of Willie and Tad," said Annie. She took the book from Jack and checked the index. "Yes!" Then she turned to a page on the Lincoln children.

Annie read for a moment, then she whispered a sad "Oh, no." She closed the book and put it down. She looked terribly sad.

"What's wrong? What did you read?" said Jack.

"I just read that Willie died of typhoid fever in 1862," said Annie.

"Oh, no," said Jack. "That was the year after we met him."

"Poor Abraham Lincoln," said Annie.

"Poor Tad," said Jack.

"Yeah, he really needed Willie," said Annie.

"And then Tad will lose his dad just four years later," said Jack. "President Lincoln will get assassinated."

"I know," said Annie softly.

Jack didn't know what to say. He felt like the wind had been knocked out of him. All his annoyance at Tad disappeared. He wished he'd been kinder to him.

"It doesn't make sense, does it?" said Annie.

"I guess that's why *hope* is such an important thing," Jack said.

"What do you mean?" said Annie.

"We can't explain why sad things happen," Jack said. "All we can do is hope they make sense someday."

"Like when?" said Annie. "When will they make sense?"

"I don't know when," said Jack. "Maybe not even in a person's lifetime. Maybe in a world beyond this world." He sighed. "Maybe we just have to accept that it's a mystery."

Annie nodded, blinking back tears. "Well, we brought back the feather of hope," she said.

"And we gave hope to Abraham Lincoln," said Jack.

"And he did really great things as president, didn't he?" Annie said.

"Yeah, and he was a great dad, too," said Jack.

Jack placed the feather of hope in the corner of the tree house next to the glacial buttercup and the emerald rose.

"There's one more thing to get to save Penny," said Annie.

"Tomorrow," said Jack.

"Definitely," said Annie. "Today I just want to live my normal life: have breakfast with Mom and Dad—"

"And go to school," added Jack.

"We're lucky we can go to school," said Annie.

"Yeah," said Jack. "And we're lucky to have a nice house with heat and running water."

"And comfortable beds," said Annie. She started down the rope ladder.

"And lots of books," said Jack. He grabbed his backpack and climbed down after her.

As Jack and Annie headed home between the trees, a breeze shook the wet branches. Sparkling raindrops filled the Frog Creek woods.

Author's Note

When researching Abraham Lincoln, I was inspired by what his friends and family said about him. The sampling below taught me a lot about what kind of person he was.

From Dennis Hanks, Abraham Lincoln's cousin:

"Abe was getting hungry for books, reading everything he could lay his hands on. . . . He would go to the cupboard, snatch a piece of corn bread, take down a book, sit down in a chair, cock his leg up as high as his head, and read."

"[Abe] would commence his pranks, tricks,

jokes, stories, and . . . all would stop—gather around Abe and listen."

From Sarah Lincoln, Abraham Lincoln's stepmother:

"Abe was a good boy . . . was diligent for knowledge . . . and if pains and labor would get it, he was sure to get it. He was the best boy I ever saw. He read all the books he could lay his hands on."

"When he came across a passage [in a book] that struck him, he would write it down on boards if he had no paper and keep it there till he did get paper—then he would rewrite it, look at it [and] repeat it."

"Abe never gave me a cross word or look, and never refused in fact, or even in appearance, to do anything I requested him."

From a family friend of the Lincolns':

"If there was any motto or slogan of the White House during the early years of the Lincolns' occupancy it was this: 'Let the children have a good time. . . .' When the president came into the family sitting room and sat down to read, the boys would rush at him and demand a story. Tad perched precariously on the back of the big chair, Willie on one knee...."

Now I hope that *you* will do your own fact-tracking—and enjoy learning more in the Magic Tree House Fact Tracker: *Abraham Lincoln*.

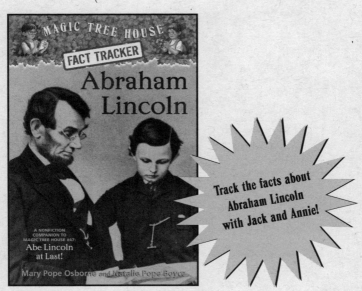

Track the facts about Abraham Lincoln with Jack and Annie!

Mary Pope Osborne

is the author of many novels, picture books, story collections, and nonfiction books. Her *New York Times* number one bestselling Magic Tree House series has been translated into numerous languages around the world. Highly recommended by parents and educators everywhere, the series introduces young readers to different cultures and times in history, as well as to the world's legacy of ancient myth and storytelling. She and her husband, writer Will Osborne (author of *Magic Tree House: The Musical*), live in northwestern Connecticut with their three dogs. Ms. Osborne is coauthor of the companion Magic Tree House Fact Trackers with Will and with her sister, Natalie Pope Boyce.

Praise for Jaine Fenn

"A fast-paced, passionate adventure with a scientist at the heart of it, whose courage stays with you long after the story is over. Jaine Fenn deserves to be at the top table of British SFF."
Paul Cornell, *Doctor Who* writer

"Brilliantly written; an excellent book that I struggled to put down. Hidden Sun draws you into a strange and evocative world, both alien and oddly familiar."
Gavin G Smith, author of *Age of Scorpio* and the *Bastard Legion series*

"A great talent. One of the most original voices in contemporary fantasy."
Gareth L. Powell, author of *Embers of War*

"Intriguing world building and complex cultures are a Jaine Fenn specialty, and Hidden Sun takes these elements to the next level. Fenn fans will enjoy this one!"
Patrice Sarath, author of *The Sisters Mederos* and *Fog Seaon*

"Exciting… complex and unusual."
Liz Williams, Philip K Dick Award Nominee of *Empire of Bones*

JAINE FENN

BROKEN SHADOW
SHADOWLANDS BOOK II

**ANGRY
ROBOT**

An imprint of Watkins Media Ltd

Unit 11, Shepperton House
89 Shepperton Road
London N1 3DF
UK

angryrobotbooks.com
twitter.com/angryrobotbooks

An Angry Robot paperback original,
2019

Copyright © Jaine Fenn 2019

Cover by Andreas Rocha
Set in Adobe Garamond Pro

Angry Robot and the Angry Robot
icon are registered trademarks of
Watkins Media Ltd.

ISBN 978 0 85766 803 5
Ebook ISBN 978 0 85766 804 2

Printed and bound in the United
Kingdom by TJ International Ltd.

9 8 7 6 5 4 3 2 1

For Dr Mark Thompson,
who does the maths.

CHAPTER 1

"The charge," intoned the cardinal, "is heresy."

Rhia Harlyn met Marsan's gaze. "Right." She had known this day might come. But not yet. It was too soon. "I see. Can you be more specific, Your Holiness?"

Cardinal Marsan looked down from his high-backed chair. Rhia had last been in this small private courtroom two years ago, for her brother's trial. She had hoped never to see it again. "Heresy is heresy," he said with a sniff.

If she sighed, the cardinal might hear. The two guards behind her and the young clerk sitting to one side certainly would. So she inclined her head as though accepting this idiocy as wisdom and said, "Of course. Yet I have a right to know the details of the charge against me, in order to prepare my defence."

The cardinal's left eyebrow twitched, as though expressing his outrage at the idea that there was a proper defence against heresy. "You have proposed, against all common sense and, more importantly against the teachings of the First, that the world is not at the centre of the universe."

Damnation! But what else could it be? The Church might not approve of the natural enquirers, but it tolerated them – if they

1

kept quiet. She had been betrayed.

"Well?"

The wretched man wanted an answer. Should she lie? Feign ignorance? No, her words were being recorded by the clerk. Lying now could make things worse later. She drew a deep breath and said, "Yes. I am indeed working on a theory that rather than the Sun and all the stars going around the world, our world and certain other celestial bodies go around the Sun."

"Preposterous."

Rhia clenched and unclenched her jaw. "It would be if the world was flat, yes."

"So you also propose that the world is not flat?"

Actually she had got that from the writings of Watcher of Valt. But she was not about to break the enquirers' code, even if someone else had. "I do, yes."

"Hmmm. That is indeed a heretical concept. And did you come up with this 'theory' by yourself?"

"I am not sure what you mean, Holiness."

"I know you are unmarried but perhaps a man of your acquaintance proposed the concept to you?"

Now Rhia did sigh. Then she made herself take a fresh breath, and force a smile, before replying, "Were you thinking of any man in particular, or merely commenting on the general inferiority of the female mind?"

"It is a reasonable question."

The cardinal's icy tone froze her ire.

"No. This theory is all my own."

"Really." Marsan sniffed again.

"Yes, really." She could feel her voice rising. "With respect, Cardinal, I do not believe that the relative locations and movements of the Sun and stars are explicitly stated in the Scriptures." Had she been given any notice, she might have researched this but the pair of militiamen sent with the summons had been instructed to bring her straight to the palace.

"And you are an expert on the Scriptures, are you?"

A tremor of tension danced down her spine, "Of course not, Your Holiness." She swallowed, "If there is such a passage, please tell me." *Just put me out of my misery, because if I really have contradicted the Scriptures, I may as well burn my papers now.* Despite the close heat of the small room, her blood ran chill.

The cardinal held up a finger. "The First, in his wisdom, felt no need to impart such a self-evident truth as the disposition of heavens."

Rhia let herself breathe. "Then I would humbly suggest that this interpretation of the skies might not go against the Church's teachings."

"It is not for you to interpret the will of the First!"

No, that's your job. A lightheaded and inappropriate sense of relief settled on her. She – and more importantly her work – was not doomed. But the Church still had a case. She kept her gaze low and took a deep breath before replying. "My apologies, Holiness. I spoke out of turn."

"So you did. Now that you have formally heard the charge, I will confer with my fellows and set a date for your trial."

"Trial?" Of course there would be a trial.

"Yes. Do not think your status will protect you, Countess."

"I never do. I put my faith in the truth."

The cardinal shook his head slowly, his eyes narrow. "We will inform you of the process in due course. You may go."

Her heart heavy in her chest, Rhia turned away. The two militia guards stood aside to let her pass.

As soon as she was back in the corridors of the palace proper she accosted a footman. "I must speak to the duke at once!" Despite her foolish words to the cardinal, she intended to use every advantage her position gave her.

The footman's alarm might have been comical in other circumstances. "I… I do not know where his Grace is at this moment, Countess." The servant knew who she was of course: everyone at court knew of the eccentric noblewoman with the quarter-mask.

"Then find him!" But even if she managed to locate Francin, he might not grant her an immediate audience. "Find him and tell him that I, and my work, are in danger, and I need to talk to him. I will be at my house. You understand the message?"

"Yes m'lady."

"Good. Thank you. Now off you go!"

Outside, evening was creeping across the city, cooling the hot, dry air. The streets were empty, though Rhia caught faint sounds of a commotion from the lower city. There was often some commotion in the lower city these days.

Back home, she had just put a foot on the stair when the kitchen door opened and Markave emerged. "Is all well, m'lady?"

"Not really." Sometimes she wanted to confide in her steward, however inappropriate that might be. "It's... it's nothing you need worry about though."

"If you are sure... Will you want supper in your study?"

"Please." She could not remember the last time she had eaten in the townhouse's grand dining room.

Halfway up the stairs a black-and-white streak darted out from the landing. Rhia leaned down and scooped up the cat. "Got you!" The furry bundle squirmed in her grasp, purring all the while. "You know what, Yithi?"

The cat favoured her with a blank golden stare.

"Some days I wish I was a cat."

Yithi's response was to kick her legs, claws extended. She had always been more Etyan's than hers. Insofar as any cat was anyone's. Rhia took the hint and put her down. "Go on then."

When Rhia reached the room at the top of the house, her gaze skittered over the usual comfortable mess – papers, books and instruments piled high on desks and workbenches – before settling for a moment on her unfinished celestial model. She had just been getting somewhere with it when the summons arrived, having wound the Maiden a quarter circuit around the Sun without the mechanism sticking. The model was still not even half-finished but right now she needed the comfort of the sky.

She strode across her study, grabbing the sightglass from its stand as she passed. She climbed the wooden ladder, slammed the trapdoor at the top open, then pulled herself onto the observation platform tucked into the high roof. She clicked the sightglass into its tripod with a sigh.

Whitemoon was up, though low. The Harbinger dominated the other side of the sky, a bright point trailed by a smeared arc of spangled light. The wandering star appeared larger than it had when it rode overhead a few weeks ago – an illusion; she had observed the same phenomenon with the Moons – yet also dimmer. The bright tail which streamed behind it like a shower of water droplets frozen in place was straighter than it had been when she first sketched it, though not as straight as the second, dimmer tail which the star had recently developed. No enquirer had mentioned this second tail. But her ironwood chest contained only a subset of the knowledge in the enquirers' network, and it had been several generations since the Harbinger's last appearance. So many glorious questions… Faced with matters of such cosmic importance, the opinion of one set of churchmen in one shadowland was nothing.

People saw this "bearded star" as a grim portent. Combined with yet another rain-year that brought little rain, its return had triggered unrest. But for all its dramatic appearance, the Harbinger was just a celestial body of irregular habits. Her observations showed its slow crawl across the sky to be an illusion borne of perspective. She was sure the Harbinger's true path was around the Sun and if she could prove this, she could also prove her wider theory of celestial mechanics.

But her interest lay in observing, and finding patterns. Numbers were a necessary evil. Yet for her theory to have weight, and be irrefutable by scholar, guildmaster or priest, it must be backed up by calculations; and she could not make her calculations fit her observations. Which was why she had asked someone more comfortable with mathematics to aid her. A mistake, it now turned out.

What if this was *all* a mistake? Perhaps the reason she could not prove the Sun was the centre of the universe was because it wasn't. She had staked her reputation on a near-death revelation. It had seemed so obvious at the time, but perhaps she was about to be tried for an unprovable fever-dream.

CHAPTER 2

Dej let Etyan lead the way through the umbral forest. Although his hunter's crouch wasn't necessary – they were only rabbits for First's sake! – she liked the way his breeches pulled tight over his backside when he bent over like that.

Etyan had found the warren a few days ago. He'd gone out looking for water and come back with a waterskin half full of brackish brown liquid and a head full of enthusiasm.

His excitement at finding the rabbits had coaxed a rare smile from her. He'd stood in the doorway of their shack and gestured with the slack waterskin, saying how hunting rabbits would be like hunting deer. Dej, rather than admit she didn't know what a deer was, had said, "So you used to hunt deer?"

He'd shrugged. "A couple of times. The duke kept a few dozen on his estate."

"Which you got invited to?" She pounced on the chance to get him talking about his old life.

"Of course. He had the servants block off some of their normal routes then we'd ride after the deer, forcing them into a dead end, where they couldn't get out."

This didn't sound very fair on the deer. "And then you killed and ate them?"

Etyan hung the waterskin on the hook by the door. "No, like

I said, the duke didn't have that many. But he'd give a noble the honour of killing one specially chosen deer. We'd have a feast, later."

Deer were, presumably, rather larger than rabbits. "Did he ever choose you?"

Etyan grimaced. "No. I was too young."

"But we can hunt rabbits the same way." Back at the crèche, they'd put up fences to discourage rabbits from eating delicate crops, but that was to keep them out, not hem them in. And they'd been too fast to consider chasing, before her bonding.

"I don't see why not."

The next day, they'd gathered planks left over from building their shack, and a couple of spare blankets, and carried them to the warren. They'd used these planks and strips of blanket to set up barriers between some of the trees, limiting the rabbits' access to their home. Etyan said not to block the actual holes; they needed the animals to stay there, and get used to the changes.

Now she and Etyan were back, armed with the netting bag they stored vegetables in and the empty stew pot from the hearth. The glow of the skyland, glimpsed through the tree-trunks to the west, was dimming. They had to time their arrival for the early evening, when the rabbits were returning from foraging in the shadowland to the east of the umbral.

The ironwoods here were huge, with smooth silver-grey trunks nearly as wide as their shack. The trees must be due for harvesting soon. Was this still Harlyn territory? She shook her head: it didn't matter; owning the land was shadowkin thinking.

Etyan stopped, and pointed at the ground ahead where the forest floor was peppered with burrows and small mounds of earth – along with their efforts from a few days earlier. A couple of bunnies were hopping around; as they watched, one of them went into a hole.

"You go round the far side while I stay here," whispered Etyan. "Stay downwind and make sure we can still see each other."

"Obviously." Moving with slow care, Dej circled right. She

found a place with a perfect view of the warren, but there was a tree bole between her and Etyan. She moved round until she could see him. He raised a hand to show he could see her too.

Only one rabbit was visible, hopping round on the far side of one of the barriers, a knee-high strip of fine woollen cloth woven in a complex red-and-orange checkerboard design. Dej felt smugly pleased at seeing the rich, showy blanket shredded and put to practical use.

The rattle of wind through treetops overhead picked up, and a chill eddy made the scales along her bare arms tighten against the cold; the ever-present umbral breeze sharpened at morning and evening. A shadowkin would be having trouble seeing by now, as twilight deepened the thick gloom beneath the ironwoods.

Two more rabbits loped into view. One headed for a hole, then paused and sat back on its haunches. It sniffed the air. Dej tensed, but the animal just dropped down onto all fours and continued into its burrow, unconcerned. The other one came over to the rabbit Dej had first seen. Noses met, and the two of them hopped a couple of paces nearer the cloth barrier. This looked like a good moment to make a move, maybe even bag the pair. She looked over at Etyan, then raised her hand. Though his skin wasn't scaly like hers its unique patterning still made him blend into the shadows; the shake of his head was no more than a slight change in the dark shape he made beside his tree.

Fine. It was his plan.

One of the bunnies was hopping round the other now. If that meant what she thought, they'd be well distracted. Movement near Etyan; he had at least one rabbit in range too. This was the perfect moment. She raised her hand again.

The second rabbit was sniffing at the other one's rear. Dej smiled. Etyan still hadn't moved. Well, she was the experienced hunter here. It was time to strike. She raised her hand: *Go.* Without waiting to see what Etyan did, she pushed off from the tree, cutting in to come at the amorous bunnies from the shadowland side, transferring the net into a two-handed grip as she moved.

She leapt over the low barrier. A furry head went up. The rabbits broke away in opposite directions. They were faster than she expected. The one heading for a plank barrier was closest. She waited for it to turn, trying to gauge whether it would go left or right. It did neither: it leapt straight over the plank.

The other rabbit jinked to one side. She adjusted her course, toes pushing off the compacted earth, arms outstretched.

Off to one side she heard a thud and an oath.

The rabbit came up against the red-and-orange cloth. This was a higher barrier than the plank, but flimsier; it put its head down and started to scrabble underneath. Dej threw herself forward and caught fur and warm flesh. The rabbit, pinned to the ground, kicked back hard. Dej pressed down on it, flinching when a claw scratched her arm. She eased the net over the panicking creature. To her relief, it froze.

She looked across to Etyan. He was picking himself up off the ground, empty-handed.

Holding her prize, Dej stepped over the cloth barrier. Although these rabbits didn't communicate head-to-head like some creatures in the skyland, the fuss might have alerted the others.

Etyan strode across and grabbed her arm. "Why'd you go off like that?"

"Because that was our best chance! Let's get clear of the warren and stay quiet. Maybe they'll come back."

"What about that?" He gestured at the netted rabbit.

"Well, we'll have to kill it if we don't want it scaring the others off." She looked at his expression. "Which I'm guessing you want me to do."

He looked away. "Please."

She stepped over the final plank, holding her prize high. She could see, hear and feel its terror. Just get it over with. Once she was clear of the warren she dropped to one knee and laid the bag on the ground. The rabbit burst back into life, twisting and kicking in the netting. "Etyan! Can you hold the bag steady?"

He nodded and crouched down to pull the other end of the net's drawstring. The rabbit was stretched out, wide-eyed and panting. She'd brought her paring knife but the short flint blade would more likely cut the net than the rabbit. Something less subtle then. As she brought her foot down Etyan looked away. The first blow crunched fur and bone. The rabbit spasmed and gasped; in agony, but still alive. As Dej stamped on its head again, a weird combination of revulsion and elation coursed through her. The rabbit went limp and silent. She felt the life leave it.

To hide the warm, dizzy rush the small death had triggered, she spoke brusquely. "Right. We'll need the net to carry it back, so if we want to catch another we should use..." Her voice trailed away. "Where's the stew pot?'

"I tripped on a rabbit-hole and fell. It broke."

"You broke it." She'd said using a clay pot was a dumb idea, but he'd talked her into it.

Etyan gestured airily. "It's all right, we'll get another one from Ree next time we visit the estate."

The twisted warmth flared into annoyance. "Of course. If all else fails, ask your big sister. Why don't we just get some rabbits and a few deer from her as well? Oh, and I'm sure she'll offer more lovely embroidered blankets. And while I think of it, how about a *proper wife*!" She spat the last two words.

For a moment they stared at each other over the body of the dead rabbit. Had she gone too far? Maybe, but right now she was full of fire.

Then Etyan said, "You know you're all I need, all I'll ever need." He smiled. She knew that smile: it destroyed her. Or rather, it destroyed her will, made her want just one thing. And he wanted it too... The ire was gone; the fire remained.

He put his hands on her shoulders and pulled her upright. She let him.

She stepped over the animal she'd just killed to stand toe-to-toe with him. She pushed him backwards, and he fell, pulling her with him onto the bare, scented earth.

CHAPTER 3

"You brought the treatise. Marvellous!" Duke Francin clapped his hands, startling the miniature dog dozing on his lap.

"I did." The latest delivery of writings from the enquirers' network had arrived this morning, a small consolation after a sleepless night worrying and waiting for Francin to get in contact. When a messenger arrived around noon to say the duke would see her, Rhia had decided to bring this new paper with her.

"I was beginning to wonder if you'd forgotten my request. Not that I'm complaining." He slid the tray of tisane and biscuits to one side, making space on the lacquered table between them. They were in one of the palace's smaller drawing rooms, alone save the ubiquitous footman by the door.

As Rhia put the parchment bundle down she said, "I did warn you this one might take a while. Durn is some distance from Shen."

"Of course, of course. Thank you again for asking your learned friend in Durn about this 'blue iron'. If we can master the technique it could make all the difference!"

"All the difference to what, *Francin*?" When he first mentioned having problems smelting the iron from the skyland he had been characteristically vague about uses for the metal. She would like some iron for her own projects but although the duke had been

13

processing the rocks from the red valley for over a year now she had yet to see so much as an iron nail.

"To… everything!" He favoured her with his infectious smile. The dog settled again.

She hadn't expected him to tell her. Despite their kinship, friendship and her use as a natural enquirer, he rarely shared his business with her unless forced by circumstance – such as when she had threatened to withhold the location of the red valley unless he arrested his traitorous wife.

Oh, Alharet. The betrayal by the one person she had thought of as her true friend still cut like a shard of flint.

"But these writings are not why you wanted to see me so urgently, are they?" Francin was staring at her with apparent sympathy, one hand on the papers. "It's this heresy business."

Of course he knew. He had probably known before she did. "Yes. That."

"I assume the Church has issues with your Sun-centred universe?"

Rhia had shared her theory with her royal cousin: once perfected she had planned to release the detailed theory publicly, disseminating it to the nobles and guildmasters of Shen all at once and with the duke's blessing, at which point the Church would not dare to speak against it. "They do. Not that it is much more than an idea as yet."

"Hmm. Do you know how the cardinals found out?" Not from him: Francin would never betray her. She was too useful.

"I believe I do."

"Ah. And do you need any assistance in that regard?"

"No. It's… my business. What I need help with is the situation I'm in now. Will there really have to be a trial?"

"Unless you recant, yes."

"That's 'recant' as in say I'm deluded, and that despite discovering how the universe really works I'm going to pretend I didn't, and cover it all up?"

"From your tone I surmise you will not be recanting."

"You surmise correctly, cousin." She experienced a stab of apprehension at the possible consequences of sticking to her principles. But this revelation was what she had been born for. "So, a trial then? How will that work?"

"As the Church rarely holds heresy trials – the last time was in my grandfather's day, and that was a forbidden artefact – they must use the processes of our civil judiciary, even though they are trying to prove you have committed an offence against the First."

"Meaning, the trial will be secular?" That was good news.

"Its form will be. However, the cardinals will want to sit in judgement."

"Ah." Not so good. "So how does that help me?"

"Well, I was mulling this over during my morning toilette. This is a trial about a dangerous idea. The less people get to hear about the idea the better, from the Church's point of view. So I'm pretty sure they'll want a closed hearing."

"Is that what happened with the enquiry about Etyan and the girl?" Derry: the dead girl's name had been Derry. She needed to name her, to remember that Derry had been someone's daughter, someone's sister, before the duchess's scheming had ended her life.

"Quite so."

"Then that's what we'll do!" Etyan's own hearing had turned out better than she'd hoped. Better, in fact, than her brother deserved.

"A closed hearing is the, ahem, quick and dirty solution. You will not be allowed to argue your case beyond incontrovertible facts, and your fate will be swiftly determined by a single judge – a judge that, in this case, the Church has appointed."

"In other words, a cardinal. Right. Well he's unlikely to find in my favour."

"I fear so." Francin ran a finger along the outstretched neck of his lapdog. The animal sighed in its sleep. "The preferred option would be an open session allowing the matter to be explored fully in the public eye. The Church would never accept that, given they want this idea buried, not publicly discussed."

"So I must dance to their tune?"

"Not necessarily. Your noble status gives you the right to a grand trial. This is still a closed session but with a proper chance for evidence, argument, appeals and suchlike. More importantly, there are three judges: one appointed by the party bringing the action – the Church – but the others a member of the nobility and a respected member of the populace, chosen by lot."

"The noble... could it be anyone?"

"The appointment is made by the judiciary administrators but I have final oversight."

"It couldn't actually be you though?"

"Alas no. I must maintain neutrality. The cardinals cannot thrive without my support but I cannot rule well without theirs. I must play my hand with care. Especially now, with that damn wandering star glaring down at us out of a cloudless sky." He frowned. "And you need to be aware of the consequences of a grand trial: there is no limit to the penalty that can be imposed."

"So I could... They could... If I'm found guilty I could be sentenced to death?" She was so busy worrying about the Church confiscating her papers she had not considered what might happen to her, personally.

"We must acknowledge the possibility."

"Ah. Right." So her choice came down to a foregone conclusion, or to risk everything. "Cardinal Marsan said he'd let me know what was happening, implying I didn't have any choice."

"He wanted you to think that. But you do, if you are willing to risk the penalty."

"I... I believe I am."

"Then you must write to Marsan at once. Oh, and make sure you ask for the full year to prepare for the trial."

"A year to prepare?" For the first time since the cardinal's summons, Rhia felt hope. Surely she could perfect her theory in a year.

"Up to a year. In practice they will not grant that long, but you must ask." Francin frowned. "Oh, and best not mention I advised you in this."

"I wouldn't dream of it." Now the tension within had unclenched a fraction, Rhia found herself considering a further matter, not entirely unrelated. "I think I need to ask you another favour."

"You *think* you do?"

"It's… something I've been considering for a while but, well, it's become unavoidable." She took a deep breath. "I need a husband."

"Ah. I must say you've changed your tune. When we last discussed matters matrimonial you made it clear you did not wish to be married off."

"I still don't. But I need to think about the future of my House." And of the enquirers' papers.

"Of course. I assume your little brother has shown no sign of facing up to his duties?"

"No." She must write to him too. "If he does see sense and return to the city then I will be asking you to find him a wife instead."

"Not really my area of expertise." The duke grimaced, no doubt thinking of the duchess's talents in that direction. "But I will make sure the other Houses' major are aware of your desire for a spouse. Or Etyan's should he decide to come home."

"One more thing, Francin. Whoever I marry must undertake not to interfere in my work. I will be subject to a husband in matters of the House but not in matters of enquiry."

"When you say 'undertake'…"

"In writing, before we are married."

Francin laughed. "Ah, my presumptuous cousin. It is fortunate I both like and value you."

CHAPTER 4

If only they never had to leave the bed. Or floor, or ground, or wherever they ended up. Not that they screwed as often these days. But when they did... when they did Dej could forget everything else for a while.

It wasn't just the sex. When she woke up before him, she would watch Etyan sleep and feel her chest and belly fill with warmth. In those moments, he was the centre of everything. It was the two of them against the world. In those moments, she would kill, would die, would do anything for him.

But those moments didn't last.

They'd only caught the one rabbit; by the time they were done with each other it'd been dark, and all the rabbits were back in their burrows. When they got home they'd tried to rig up a spit, but the rabbit had ended up falling into the fire. That, combined with the fact neither of them really knew how to deal with the fur and guts, meant they only got a couple of mouthfuls of edible meat each. They'd eaten in silence, neither wanting to be the one to start the next argument.

"I'll go dig for honey-grubs later," said Dej the next morning, when Etyan came back from taking a dump farther in the woods.

"Honey-grubs. Yum." He'd been gone a while; perhaps the rabbit meat had disagreed with him. She wasn't feeling too good herself. "Thought you said there weren't any."

"No, just that I've dug up all the nearby burrows so I'll have to go farther out to find them." She hazarded a smile. "You can come with me if you like, see what we can find together."

He shook his head. "No thanks. All we'll find out there is wastelands and weird critters and maybe some real skykin who'll chase us off."

She ignored the jibe about real skykin. "It's not that bad. And the skyland's huge." When they'd first got together they'd planned to explore the skyland together. But, other than the odd foraging foray, it hadn't happened. "There's loads of interesting stuff out there."

"Stuff that's interested in eating us, you mean. You go if you want." He shrugged and brushed past her into the shack.

She sighed. If she'd suggested going the other way, east into the shadowland, he'd probably have jumped at the chance.

She pulled her flute out of her belt. Perhaps she shouldn't be so against visiting the Harlyn family estate. After all, she'd picked up this old ironwood flute on their first visit – and been allowed to keep it – and they never went hungry there. But not being able to see the Sun properly made her feel nervy, trapped, incomplete. On the estate, or even worse, in the city, she felt the sky bearing down on her, the people all around suffocating her.

And she hated having to take charity from Etyan's sister. The Countess always stressed how welcome they were to visit, at any time. Whenever they were in Shen, Dej was on edge, scared that, despite saying he'd never live in the city and was only here to see Rhia, Etyan might decide he liked having servants and decent food more than he liked living in the umbral with her in their ramshackle home.

She leaned back against the wall and closed her eyes, enjoying what little dappled and diffuse sunlight made its way through the immature trees. Then she put her flute to her lips and began to play. Etyan wasn't all that musical, but she loved to play for him. She would've loved to sing for him too, if her animus hadn't taken that ability from her. Today, she didn't look back inside to check whether he was enjoying the music or not. She was soon too thirsty to play anyway. She opened her eyes and reached back for the waterskin.

When she twisted round to return the near-empty skin to its hook she saw Etyan sitting on their straw-stuffed pallet, looking at her. All he had to do was smile now, and she'd go over. But instead he said, "Let's go to the estate early."

Her heart sank. "We're not due for another week."

"Six days actually." Etyan insisted on keeping a tally of days by carving notches on sticks. "If we go early it would just be the two of us."

He was right; the Countess only visited her estate when they were due there. But that wasn't the point. "Etyan, it's not that I don't like your sister, I just find her hard to cope with. Especially last time, when she started going on about whoever-it-was's lovely daughter, and how their House was looking for a good marriage for her, and she had tits like melons and all her own teeth."

"I don't remember the bits about the tits and teeth. Perhaps I should have paid more attention... Ow!" He ducked the thrown waterskin. "Anyway she can hint all she likes; I'm not getting married."

She nearly said: *not even to me?* But that would break an unspoken rule. Getting married was what normal people did. "I still don't see why Rhia can't find a husband for herself, assuming anyone'll have her at her age." Given Etyan's sister was more than a decade older than him, Dej sometimes thought of her as more like his mother. She certainly acted like it.

"That's harsh."

"But true."

"You know why Ree won't marry."

"Because a husband would stop her doing her 'work'. I don't see what's so important about staring at the sky all night then spending all day scribbling."

"Neither do I. But that won't stop her. So, are we going?"

She was tempted. But she gave into him too much. She couldn't remember the last time he'd given in to her, outside of bed. She came over, waiting for the cue to forget reality for a while. But he wasn't smiling, and he didn't meet her eyes. She grabbed the waterskin and trowel. "We need more water. We'll talk about it when I get back."

"Fine." He gestured at the air without looking at her. "See you later."

She headed east; despite the drought, the best chance of finding standing water was in the shadowland – with or without Etyan. After a while the trees thinned, diffuse golden light visible between the wide, straight trunks. Beyond the ironwoods bleached brown crops wilted in the fields. The clouds that hovered on the skyland side of the umbral sometimes spilled over into Shen itself and dropped their rain on the farmland nearest the umbral, but that hadn't happened in months.

When she came out from the cover of the umbral she looked up at the Sun, reduced to a bright patch in the pale shadowland sky, then back down over the fields. She skirted the first field then crossed an irrigation ditch lined with hard, cracked earth to cut farther in towards where the land dipped. The buzzing whisper of the umbral breeze through the treetops fell away.

The next field had some sort of corn growing in it, stems bent and heads dried out. But there was a handbreadth of water in the irrigation ditch on the far side. She scooped up enough to drink – muddy, but she was used to that – then used her ironwood trowel to dig into the ditch, creating a pool deep enough to half fill the waterskin.

That was a lucky break; some days she visited a dozen fields before finding any water. She decided to carry on anyway; the waterskin needed filling completely if possible, and staying out postponed having to face Etyan.

In the next field paper-thin leaves wilted across dusty ground; beets of some sort, maybe already dead. The next field was covered in a blue-grey tangle of oilseed, one of the few plants that tolerated the drought.

The field upslope held rows of knee-high bean plants. She leapt the ditch, which had a trickle of liquid mud in the bottom, then crouched down and pulled a pod from the nearest plant. When she cracked it with a fingernail it tore like dry skin but revealed beans that looked plump and relatively moist. Tasted good too. There were several dozen pods within easy reach. Good job she'd brought the veg net.

Etyan was dozing outside the shack when she got back. She plumped the half-full waterskin and bulging net down next to him. "Tonight we dine on the finest beans!"

"Where from?"

"From a field." She pointed vaguely behind her. "Over there."

He stood to look her in the eye. "We talked about this. Those belong to a farmer."

"A farmer planted those beans, yes." She had been aware, as she picked the beans, that this was stealing; it had added pleasure to the experience, a pleasure she'd almost forgotten.

"But they need those beans. The drought is making it hard for people."

"The drought is making it hard for *us*, Etyan."

"Yes, but we can go out into the skyland and find stuff to eat. And there's always my sister."

"Isn't there just."

"Farmers don't have those options. This is all they've got."

"This," she kicked the bag, "is a tiny amount of what they've got. So tiny I doubt they'll miss it. Anyway, since when did you care about farmers?"

"Since I was taught to. It is a noble's duty to ensure the people who provide your food are well cared for."

The nobility card: she hated that. "Those lands don't even belong to your House. Why do you care if they're not your farmers?"

"That makes it worse!"

"What? Why?" Her voice was rising.

"Because if the farmer owed allegiance to House Harlyn I could ask Ree to compensate him."

"For a handful of beans? Really?"

"It's the principle, Dej."

"Oh right, and you're all about *principles*."

"What's that supposed to mean?"

"You know what. If principles matter *so much* to you then why did you run away when you were accused of murder, rather than face your accusers!"

"I did not kill that girl!"

He always called her "that girl". Not that Dej ever met the poor bitch. But "that girl" must've had a name, and a life. "No, but you acted like you had. And *something* happened that night–"

"Drop it, Dej! I was set up. The court exonerated me."

That was what he always said, or some variation on it. But she wasn't going to drop it today. "Why won't you trust me enough to tell me the truth?"

He looked hurt. "Because I want to let the past go! Don't you?"

"Yes. No. But I've told you how I got here, about the crèche and the clanless and everything. I know almost nothing about your old life. I don't even understand why you left Shen."

Etyan shook his head and whispered, "Because I'm an idiot." He looked past her into the trees.

"Are you an idiot for going off with me?" she whispered.

"Of course not! You're my future." The first time he'd said that she'd been filled with joy, but now it sounded like a well-worn phrase. His voice hardening further, he added, "It was nothing to do with you. Can't you just accept that?"

"I guess I'll have to." She threw her hands up and turned on her heel.

"Dej! Where are you going?"

"To get us a nice fat horrible grub to eat. Feel free to return those beans to the farmer while I'm gone!"

CHAPTER 5

Rhia wrote two letters immediately after her visit to the duke. One to Cardinal Marsan, requesting a grand trial with a full year to prepare. The other letter, to Etyan, explained her situation and asked, no *told*, him to come to the city at once. She softened the tone with an apology: he would be expecting her, not merely a letter, to be waiting at the estate for his next scheduled visit, but she dare not leave the city until she had the Church's answer.

She had also faced up to the growing pile of household correspondence. Markave ran the townhouse efficiently despite not having a housekeeper since the unfortunate business with his wife. Mereut, her estate manager, did an equally good job in their holdings beyond the city. But some items still needed her attention, as nominal head of House Harlyn while her brother was "indefinitely absent".

The two dozen other letters she wrote over the next few days took more thought. Assuming she was granted a grand trial, she could call up to five witnesses and read depositions from up to twenty more. The obvious witnesses would be her fellow enquirers, assuming any were willing to travel to Shen.

The right words were essential, and as words were not her strong point, it took a full day just to compose a draft. She then had to modify and tailor her request to each enquirer, depending on their area of knowledge and previous dealings with her.

The enquirers in the six shadowlands adjacent to Shen were close enough to consider appearing in person but those farther afield might offer written testimony, and she needed to allow time for them to receive her request and send their answers.

Her defence would rest on two pillars: the provability of her theory, and the fact that it did not directly contradict the Scriptures. For the former, she was on her own. For the latter, there was one obvious ally in the enquirers, a respected religious scholar from a nearby shadowland who nonetheless kept an admirably open mind. But she had reason to distrust Meddler of Zekt. She did not write to him.

When the effort of dealing with words got too much she returned to the more-vital-than-ever task of making the numbers fit the observations. The real problem was the Strays; none of her calculations explained their erratic movement across the sky – which was ironic, as her observations of these three most prominent stars had prompted the realisation that the Sun was at the centre of the universe.

When she could no longer hold a pen she either went up to her observation platform or, in daylight, tinkered with her celestial model. She had used her father's writings to design it, employing cogs and wheels to build a device that would – hopefully – emulate the movements of heavenly bodies. But she was not the engineer he had been; whenever she fixed one part, something else jammed or broke. Again, the Strays were the problem. The spheres on sticks representing the outer two, the Matriarch and the Crone, had not moved for weeks. Of course, had Francin provided iron cogs then perhaps the mechanism might run more smoothly.

The longer she waited for the Church's response, the harder it became to concentrate. She kept coming back to how little control she had over events, and how matters might play out.

There was one matter she had control over, however distasteful. And it needed to be resolved. She could not put off confronting her colleague any longer.

Rhia did not visit the middle city much, save occasional trips to the guilds to order items for her work, and it took a while to find Theorist of Shen's house. Then again she had only visited Shen's other natural enquirer once, long ago.

When his housekeeper answered the door Rhia said, "I wish to speak to Andar Olashin." She had considered sending a note ahead, but did not want to give him the chance to find some excuse not to see her.

The woman's gaze pulled away from the lacquered mask covering the area around Rhia's left eye – always the first thing a stranger's glance went to – to take in her fine clothes and lack of escort.

"Who shall I say is calling please?"

"Rhia Harlyn." Enquirers needed to know each other's real names in order to write to each other.

"Of course, m'lady. If you will wait in the parlour I will bring refreshments."

"Just some cordial please." It was too hot for tisane.

Andar Olashin was an architect by trade, and his minimal but pleasing decor and furnishings reflected this. He – or perhaps his wife – had a good eye for colour, matching pale golds with lavender and pastel blues.

The housekeeper returned with a cool beaker of cordial. After the servant curtseyed and left, Rhia suppressed the image of Sur Olashin creeping out the back door to avoid her.

The natural enquirers valued independent thought; meeting in person was frowned upon. Hence also, the two enquirers in a given shadowland focused on different areas. So she, like Father before her, was Observer of Shen, a position stressing the practical side of enquiry, in contrast to Theorist of Shen's more abstract concerns.

Father knew his son was not as suited to inherit his role as his daughter; by the age of fifteen Rhia had already compiled books of sketches and observations of the natural world and begun the study of optics that would culminate in her sightglass. Ever one to think the best of people, he had wanted Shen's other enquirer to get used to the idea of a woman in the network. Their reception by Theorist of Shen had been somewhat cool. She expected no better today.

The door opened.

"Good afternoon, Sur Olashin."

"M'lady." He had not been young when they first met, and was truly old now, his hair reduced to wisps and his movements ponderous. He lowered himself into the seat farthest from her with a grunt. "To what do I owe the pleasure of this visitation?"

"I find myself in trouble with the Church."

His face remained suspiciously bland. "How unfortunate."

"I am being called to task for some of my work for the enquirers."

"Are you now? That sounds quite serious."

"It is. And I am guessing by your reaction that you are not overly concerned for me, or my work."

"I fear you may be right, m'lady."

He was enjoying this, damn him. She may as well come out with it. "Did you inform the Church of my new theory?"

"I did, m'lady." To his credit, he held her gaze.

"And would you have done so were I a man?"

For a moment, Andar Olashin was silent. When he spoke his voice was pensive. "I find a feminine presence in the arena of knowledge... disconcerting. However I would have alerted the cardinals to your heretical theory regardless. I acted according to my conscience and my faith."

And there was, Rhia knew, no arguing with faith. "Well, at least you had the good grace to admit it to my face."

"We are enquirers. I owe you the truth."

"Indeed you do." Through her disappointment, cold anger flared. "Even though your actions broke our code. Our work is not to be shared with unsympathetic parties."

Sur Olashin made a *hmm* noise deep in this throat, then said, "It is not, no. But the enquirers' code is not a binding and enforceable law." He was right. And calling for his censure from their peers might not endear her to those very people she had just written to seek aid from. Sur Olashin continued, "And I had the interests of the network at heart."

"Really? I fail to see how bringing our work to the attention of the Church will benefit the enquirers. Quite the contrary, in fact."

"I am bringing *your* work to the attention of the Church. Not the network's as a whole. If we lived in a shadowland where enquirers are persecuted, I would have stayed silent rather than draw any attention. But in Shen we are lucky. We can work freely – provided our work does not offend Church or State. Your radical theory offends not only my own beliefs but the institution of our Church. Better to dissociate the enquirers from it now than have it become public knowledge, and bring our wider work into question."

"So betraying me was a matter of expedience as much as faith?"

"My decision to pass on your work served both causes. I do not regret it."

"Then I will not take any more of your time." She stood. "I can see myself out." She turned on her heel and strode over to the parlour door, yanking it open, only to stop on the threshold. Two young men stood immediately outside, one leaning forward as though to hear better the proceedings in the room, the other with a warning hand on his arm. They looked as shocked to see her as she was to see them.

"Oh," said the younger one, straightening.

The other, slightly older, managed a hasty bow, "M'lady!"

His companion shadowed the bow, clumsily.

From behind her Sur Olashin shouted, "Boys! What is this?" These must be Sur Olashin's apprentices.

Under other circumstances she might have enjoyed the absurdity of the situation. But right now she just wanted to get out of this man's house, so she swept past, and out the front door.

CHAPTER 6

Dej stalked through the thinning trees towards the light. She should return to the shack and get a bag for the grub but she'd rather spend a week locked in his sister's study than go back to Etyan right now.

Her route through the nearby skyland was so familiar she barely noticed the usual towers of cloud above and the patchy bushes, scrubland and occasional vegetation-furred rocky outcrop below. The landscape immediately beyond the umbral was quite healthy, thanks to the occasional downpour from the umbral storms. It smelled good too; she'd forgotten the richness of smells-with-added-sensation that filled the skyland: sweet-sharp like fresh orange, spicy like warm stew, clean like crushed mint. All at once. She breathed deep.

She needed a drink. The ground was damp from a recent cloudburst but there weren't any springs or standing water. So, honey-bug later, water-bug now. They were easier to find anyway. She cast around until she saw a tell-tale patch of mauve-grey lichen-stuff, by which time she was out of the umbral overcast and into the silvery skyland Sun. Half dried-out and not much bigger than her palm, the bug's surface parts were easy to miss by sight alone but it also smelt sweet, like drying hay, and dormant though the bug below was, she sensed its life.

She pulled the trowel from her belt and concentrated on pinpointing the bug. Sometimes they strayed to one side of the surface mat that absorbed water for them. Nope, directly below. Good. She stabbed the trowel-blade into the middle of the mat then dug down as fast as she could. Half a dozen hastily shovelled scoops of soil later she glimpsed a dark brown shape. She thrust her hand down and grabbed the bug. Small one, no longer than her hand, and its casing had already began to harden. Getting the trowel under it she lifted her prize, then slammed it down on the baked earth and stabbed it with her trowel-point. A smell/sound of rot/insolent fear hit Dej between the eyes, but she'd expected that. She lifted the brown lump in both hands, tipped her head back, and pulled the punctured beastie apart. Cool liquid rained into her open mouth. Not water, but thirst-quenching enough and better tasting than a lot of skyland life. The first time she'd brought Etyan out here and caught a bug for him he'd said the taste reminded him of wheat beer. She had no idea what wheat beer tasted like, but she'd enjoyed impressing him with her animus-given knowledge and competence. Shame it only worked in the skyland.

She teased out the bug's stringy flesh with her teeth, then threw the drained husk to one side and sat back on her heels. Her heart was pounding. She smiled to herself. Surprisingly exciting to hunt, water-bugs. They'd never fight back, but they'd harden their skin into an impermeable casing as you watched. She'd once tried carrying the encased bugs back to the shack but nothing short of dropping a huge rock on them cracked the shell, and that just left a useless spatter of bug bits. Find them, kill them, eat them. Nice and simple.

The evening Sun was lighting the undersides of the high, sculpted clouds clinging to the edge of the shadowland. Dark soon. But she could picture Etyan's expression if she returned empty-handed now.

The remains of last night's rabbit were a distant, queasy memory. Honey-bugs had to be cooked, so even if she found one she couldn't eat it. She cast about, looking for a bush whose leaves smelled safe to eat, or even better, one with proper fruits.

She located a stand of pale knee-high spikes that exuded a lemony scent: lemon-spikes, as she called them; no point making up fancy names. Only the central cream-coloured spine was edible and it didn't taste of lemon, or of anything she'd ever eaten before, but the spongy mass was good and filling.

By the time she'd eaten, the Sun was touching the horizon. She wouldn't be going back tonight. Whitemoon was already up, and Greymoon was rising. The Harbinger was up too, nearer the horizon than the last time she'd seen it. She lay down on the cooling earth and watched the night sky blaze into brilliance around her. She might not feel the need to write stuff down about the heavens, but that didn't mean she couldn't enjoy them when her view wasn't blocked by trees or clouds.

After a while just looking and not thinking, she felt better. Lighter, less worn down. But not tired.

She sat up, then stood, revelling in the feeling of shedding something invisible yet heavy. With both Moons up and the night-glow of the plants she could see well enough to avoid any nasty night-time critters on the ground, and it wasn't like you got nightwings round here. She may as well carry on. She kept just enough of her attention on her surroundings to distract herself.

She only spotted the road as she crossed it, and the whiff of rhinobeast shit hit her nostrils. She stopped and looked along the straight track of cleared earth. The road to Xuin. This was the farthest she'd ever come with Etyan, back when he'd foraged with her, unwilling to be parted even for a day. They'd been wary of the road, although the chances of meeting the caravan were low. Even if they had, so what? No doubt the skykin who ran it would look down on her, with her incompletely bonded animus and shadowkin habits. First alone knew what they'd make of Etyan, neither skykin nor shadowkin. But that was their problem. She didn't care what "real" skykin thought of her. She didn't care what anyone thought of her.

Except Etyan.

What was he doing now? He'd be worried, wondering where she was.

She shook her head and carried on, though her steps were beginning to drag. Perhaps they spent too much time together. The early days had been all about making their home – literally building it, because she insisted they did that, rather than getting the Countess' people to do it for them – and finding how to live as a couple. And the sex, of course. But when the sex became more routine with time, and the living became harder with the drought, they started to take things out on each other. When they weren't screwing or surviving, there wasn't much else to do. They'd talked about everything they were going to talk about – or at least, everything Etyan *would* talk about. She knew she shouldn't pick fights but when they rowed she saw the fire in him, the spark that made her love him. And eventually they'd make up, and remember what they were to each other.

Making up after this would recapture the fire. If he thought she was leaving him then when she didn't maybe Etyan would finally share everything with her, the way she shared everything with him.

Eventually, with Whitemoon setting, she stumbled. Exhaustion had crept up on her. She found a pus-bush by its smell; that would be enough to keep most creatures off her while she slept. Fighting the instinct to lie straight out along the axis of the world, she curled up, her back against the disconcertingly rubbery stems, and concentrated on ignoring the discomfort of the bare ground, the pull of the north, and the stink of her hiding place.

Light woke her: she'd slept through to dawn. Her limbs felt stiff and heavy; the cold had got into her overnight.

She rolled out from under the bush, crouched to pee, then stood and stretched.

If she turned around now she could be back at the umbral for dusk. That would be the obvious option. That would be what Etyan wanted, what he expected.

Which was why she wasn't going to do it. She was going to stay out longer. Make him wait.

But where should she go?

She looked around. The mountains of the Northern Divide broke up the horizon ahead. She'd come a fair way already but Shen still dominated the view to the east, a looming dark patch rimmed with clouds. She'd just been travelling around the shadowland, not away from it. She'd been raised in Shen, gone out to be bonded, fled, and come back. It was like the shadowland wouldn't release her: she could circle it but not escape its influence.

Oh yes I can! She knew just where to go now.

CHAPTER 7

"Holiness?"

He was in a dark place. Not a bad place, but dark. He had been here some time, though he was only just realising it. He knew this place. It had been his home once.

The cave.

Of course! His ghost was right—

I always am.

Ah, that familiar, infuriating reassurance. This place though, was from before, back when he was alone. No, not always alone. They came to him every few days, to tell him about the world beyond: the healers and hunters, the pathfinders and builders, the seer—

"Holiness? Can you hear me?"

The voice came from outside the cave. From outside the memory of the cave. The fast-receding memory of the cave…

That was *then*, this is *now*.

He blinked, and opened his eyes.

A calm-eyed man of middle years leant over him, his expression relieved. "Holiness! You have returned to us!"

The man's name would come in a moment. He felt weak, fuzzy-headed. But better all the time.

"Holiness, can you speak?"

A good question. He swallowed, and tried to clear his throat. A dry rasp emerged.

"Ah!" The man looked concerned. "You must be thirsty, of course." The face moved away, replaced by a view of a wooden ceiling, darkened by lamp-smoke.

The man returned. A beaker was pressed to his lips. He drank. Tephat. The man's name was Tephat. And Tephat is—

Your head hospitaller, his ghost supplied.

Of course he was.

"Holiness?" He focused on hospitaller Tephat. "You said I should I ask your name, when you awoke." He sounded perplexed at the request.

But it made sense. With every passing moment, everything made more sense. He cleared his throat, and gave a brief "Hah!" to check his voice was still working. It was. "I am Sadakh, Eparch of the Church of the First Light and—" he turned his head, which felt a little light on the pillow but moved without pain or discomfort, "—I am in the infirmary of my priory, in the city of Mirror-of-the-Sky in the shadowland of Zekt." A long, long way from the cave where he had spent the first third of his life.

Tephat smiled. "Yes, Holiness. That is so." He continued, "I did as you commanded, and watched you every moment I could. When I had to rest or attend my other duties, one of my trusted subordinates took over the vigil."

"Good. And how long was I unconscious?"

"Two days."

As predicted.

His ghost sounded smug. Yes, this fitted with the earlier trials. "How fare my flock?"

"Poliarchs Hekmat and Antreph stepped in to carry out your duties after you, ah, collapsed. There has been much concern."

"But nothing untoward happened while I was oblivious to the world."

"I am not sure what you mean, Holiness."

He was being too obtuse. This man was a healer, not a politician. "As far as you are aware, neither the priory nor any of my flock experienced any unwanted attention from the Eternal Isle these last two days."

"I do not believe so."

He would get a full report later from his various sources. What mattered was that the prince had not taken advantage of the eparch's temporary indisposition. "What did you tell your subordinates, when they kept watch over me?"

"Only that this malady appeared similar to one I had seen before, which the sufferer recovered from." Tephat leaned closer, though they were alone in this corner of the infirmary. "No one else knows that it was a trial you inflicted upon yourself, Holiness."

Tephat wanted him to know that his secret was safe, but the man was troubled at having to keep it. That might be a problem, down the line. If action had to be taken it would be a shame, as Tephat combined good medical skills with administrative acumen, making him an excellent choice to run the infirmary. He would be hard to replace. "And while I was unconscious, did I talk in my sleep?" Letting out secrets while unable to control his tongue had been another concern.

"You muttered to yourself when the fever burned high, but only odd phrases which made little sense. At one point you demanded someone tell you more, and on another occasion you appeared–" the hospitaller flushed, "–you were telling someone that you loved them."

Your first life relived, his ghost commented wryly. But not in a way that could be used against him. That was a relief. "Bring my robes please, Tephat."

"If you are sure, Holiness. You are still weak."

"I have left my flock leaderless for too long already." He smiled at his hospitaller. "Do not worry, I will be easy on myself. But at the very least I should be seen at the daily offices, even if my poliarchs still preside over them."

"Of course, Holiness." The hospitaller bustled off.

He took a deep breath, then sat up. Still a little dizzy yes, a little weak. That was to be expected. And, looking at the back of his hands, he saw the expected rash; going on the previous two tests, it should fade in a week or two. Otherwise, he felt well. But unchanged.

Has it worked?

Now that was the question.

CHAPTER 8

"M'lady, there's a letter!"

"What?" Rhia blinked at the maidservant standing at the foot of her bed. "A letter, you say…" It had better be important to warrant waking her, although from the sunlight edging the shutters she had slept late. She had stayed up beyond the twenty-fifth hour, watching the last vestiges of the Harbinger's tail sink below the horizon. "Who from, Nerilyn?" Perhaps Etyan had finally answered her letter, though his presence would have been more useful than a written excuse.

"I don't know, m'lady. But it was brought by a priest, and he said I was to give it to you at once."

A priest. Rhia's heart flipped. "Hand it over, please." She struggled to sit up.

Nerilyn did so. "Shall I open the shutters?"

"Yes. Thank you." Light and heat flood the room. The letter was a single sheet of milk-white parchment addressed to "Rhia Harlyn" – no title or honorific. The seal showed the world-encircled Pillar of Light; Rhia had always thought the Church of Shen's official sigil looked like the number one inside the number zero. She tore it open, unfolded the parchment and read:

From Cardinals Marsan, Vansel and Charain to Rhia Harlyn of House Harlyn, given on the 28th day of the 7th month of year of

Separation 5361:
We have duly and fully considered your request and are willing
to hold a grand trial to uncover the full truth.

The truth indeed! The cardinals wouldn't know the truth if it fell on them!

The trial will commence on the first day of the new year.

Less than four months away. So little time to prepare…

While you await trial you are requested not to leave the city save
in exceptional circumstances.

Meaning: don't think of running off to another shadowland. Again.

We also advise against further dissemination of any potentially
heretical material.

Of course they did. She should have expected that. But she had no intention of letting the Church stop her corresponding with other enquirers.

Finally, be aware that should your guilt as a heretic be
established, the Church of the First in Shen intends to impose the
maximum penalty, by the traditional means.

The paper quivered in her grasp. Rhia closed her eyes. They meant the death of the damned: to be bound, placed in a pit outside the city walls, and buried alive. They were calling her bluff. But they were also worried that she had the truth on her side: why else remind her not to spread her theory?

"M'lady? Are you all right?"

"Nerilyn!" She had forgotten her maidservant. "I…" The day's warmth had receded from the room. These last couple of weeks she had been wilfully lost in her work, telling herself that honing her theory would avert the trouble ahead. But this letter made it real, inescapable. This time next year she could be dead, her papers burned, her household… She blinked back stupid, weak tears and said, "Nerilyn, fetch Markave and Brynan."

"Brynan is at the market, m'lady."

"What?"

"He has been going in my stead. With all the fuss in the lower city Markave was concerned for my safety."

"Oh. Of course. Just fetch Markave then."

She pulled up the thin bedsheet to give some semblance of dignity. She did not trust herself to stand. She must ignore both the heat of emotion and the chill of fear. She must be strong, for herself, for the truth – and for those who relied on her.

Nerilyn returned with her steward.

Rhia took a deep breath and said, "The Church is calling me to account for my work."

Markave gave an odd look to Nerilyn, who stood next to him.

Rhia frowned. "What is it? I know I should have mentioned this earlier, but..."

"M'lady does not have to confide her business in us," said Markave. "However, there was a rumour. Nerilyn?"

"Begging your pardon, but I heard you spoke to one of the cardinals when you got summoned to the palace a few weeks back, then went to see the duke the next day. We did wonder."

"Please tell me when you have such concerns! You know I would not consider it improper."

"You were so busy, I didn't want to bother you..."

"Wait, how did you hear this?" said Rhia.

"Adern told me. He's an under-footman. We're... I'm seeing him, m'lady."

Rhia had noticed a new spring in Nerilyn's step. "Ah. That's... nice. But I would be very interested in any other snippets Adern might overhear." Servants were a useful source of information... although they could also be used against you. "Assuming he would be comfortable passing such information on." She did not say assuming you can trust him. With Alharet safely locked away there was no reason to suspect Nerilyn's young man was more than he seemed.

"I will report back, m'lady."

"M'lady, how serious is this?" Markave asked.

Rhia met her steward's pale gaze. "I am being tried for heresy in a grand trial. The penalty is death." It still felt unreal to say it.

Nerilyn's hand went to her mouth and Markave's high forehead crumpled.

Rhia tried for a light tone. "But only if I am found guilty! And… even if that happens, there is no reason my guilt should taint you. If I am… gone, then I would hope that my brother would, finally, take on his duties as head of House Harlyn." Assuming the Church did not try to have her House dissolved; no, they had no right. "Even if Etyan does not return, the duke will intervene to curb the Church's zeal. You will not suffer for my actions, I promise." She only hoped she could keep that promise if it came to it.

"Thank you, m'lady." Markave still looked concerned, though he had relaxed a fraction. "We should let you rest now. Did you want food sent up?"

"I… in a while. Nerilyn, I have disturbed your day enough. Please go to your duties. Markave, please stay."

The maidservant bobbed a curtsey and left.

Rhia did her best to find a reassuring smile for her steward. "There is a matter related to my current predicament which I need your help with." This morning's news prompted a decision she had been putting off.

"Whatever I may do to assist, m'lady."

"Your two boys, how are they doing?" After Markave lost his first wife to the same plague that had taken Father, his young sons had been brought up by his sister and her husband.

"Tador is working at one of the minor Houses, learning his trade."

Markave intended his older son to inherit his place as steward of House Harlyn; Rhia had agreed he could move in once he had been trained in household management.

"And Kerne?"

"Kerne lives with my sister still, though he is apprenticed to the plantsmen."

"The horticulturists guild?"

"Yes m'lady."

"You have told me of his interest in the natural world before. He is a sharp boy, yes?"

Markave gave a rare smile. "I think so. But I am biased."

"Then I would like to speak to him as soon as possible."

"To what end, if I may ask?" Markave sounded understandably puzzled.

"I wish to take on an apprentice." She had planned to train an apprentice before she grew old and infirm, but the Church might not give her the chance to grow old and infirm.

"An apprentice?" Now her steward sounded downright confused.

"Yes. To inherit my role as Observer of Shen, should I… no longer be in a position to carry it out." Markave knew of the enquirers, in broad terms. She did not keep secrets from him.

"I had assumed when your brother had a family, one of his children…"

"That is what I had hoped, but there is no immediate sign of that, is there?" She tried to keep the bitterness out of her tone. If she did not have a nominated successor then Theorist of Shen could put someone forward. After all, he had two apprentices.

"But Kerne is… He is not of noble birth, m'lady."

"I know that." She had considered asking Francin if any youths at court had the potential to become a natural enquirer but even if a boy – or girl – with promise could be found amongst those little fops and rakes, such an appointment would start tongues wagging. Although no one in the palace save Francin knew she was an enquirer, everyone at the top of the hill knew about her "unseemly" interests, and schooling a courtier's offspring or House scion in them would cause a scandal, and might be used against her in the Houses' interminable games of politics. "But I will take a sharp mind over blue blood any day."

CHAPTER 9

On the third day out from Shen, Dej spotted a pair of blocky shapes in the sparse landscape, between her and the now barely visible smudge that marked the shadowland. A tent and a covered wagon, resting out the day at one of the duke's way-stations: confirmation she was on track. Not that she needed it. She might be incompletely bonded but there was one skykin ability that never failed her. Plus, she'd been this way before.

That evening she stopped early, rather than brave the mountains in the dark. She got out her flute. She often played for Etyan in the evening. This was the longest they'd ever been apart. He'd be worried. And maybe annoyed. But she wasn't going to turn back now. She was making this journey not because anyone expected her to do it or to please someone else. She was doing it for herself. She'd go back when she was ready. The hollowness growing inside her wasn't the old familiar need, the drive that led to errors of judgment, to trusting too easily, caring too much. It was just a physical thing: she was hungry, that was all.

She played a few airs, ones Etyan didn't like so much. The thin notes disappeared into the wide, star-spangled night.

Once in the mountains she relied on a combination of memory and the constant sense of the direction of north. This land was wetter, with streams and pools to drink from, and more vines and fruits and crawling creatures to eat.

She felt the red valley before she saw it. Her first time here, with the clanless, she'd thought she imagined the odd pull of the land, but when she returned later with Etyan and his sister she'd been sure. Etyan said the valley's rocks were full of iron, which must interfere with her pathfinding abilities.

She was arriving from the south, as she had when she led the duke's rescue party to save Etyan and Rhia. The route had become a well-worn path now, wide enough for a small cart.

She spent the night in a huddle of rocks just off the path, and timed her arrival for the middle of the next day, when the shadowkin would be resting in the shade.

As she approached she slowed, then stopped, shocked at the changes since her last visit. Over a quarter of the bowl-shaped valley had been ravaged. Great swathes of reddish rocks were gathered into piles. In some places, scrapes and trenches had been dug. The activity centred on the row of caves set into the valley side. This made sense – the caves were ready-made shelters for the delicate shadowkin – but it also made Dej's heart sink. In one of those caves she'd had her first, inconsequential conversation with Etyan, while his sister lay sick and delirious. It had been an uncertain, fearful time but also a glorious one, full of possibility. She'd come here to recapture that first flush of wonder at finally finding the person who filled the emptiness inside. Once she'd gone back to Etyan in her mind and heart, she'd be ready to go back for real.

But the place had changed beyond recognition.

Now the cave mouths were hidden behind a dozen or so large tents. Beyond the tents, directly in front of the caves, Dej glimpsed two great brickwork cones, one with wisps of smoke rising from it.

She crept closer.

Some of the tents were fully enclosed; others had shaded gaps for ventilation. The nearest vented one contained half a dozen donkeys sitting down or dozing on their feet. The next tent along was closed. One of these sealed tents would hold stores of food for

the men working here. Etyan might not like her stealing farmers'
crops but he could hardly object to taking a few supplies from
the richest man in Shen. Plus, the duke owed her: she'd told him
where to find his missing kinsfolk, then later led his men back here
so they could take advantage of the iron.

Once she'd taken whatever supplies she could carry, what
was to stop her carrying on deeper into the skyland? One of the
reasons Etyan gave for them not venturing far from Shen was
her occasional need for shadowkin food, another legacy of her
incomplete bonding. With shadowkin supplies she – maybe they –
could go far.

She could just take what she wanted while the shadowkin slept
the day away. But she was curious about those odd brick cones, the
shape of elongated beehives, higher than a man. Each had a small
opening at the front and what looked like a giant set of bellows set
into the side. The bellows were attached via wooden frames to a
more familiar-looking structure between the two cones: a pair of
wooden wheels on their sides that looked like the pump over the
main well back at the crèche. She could even see donkey harnesses
on them. But there was no well here.

She looked around. No movement. No sound except the breeze
snapping the canvas and a duet of snores coming from one of the
vented tents. As far as her other senses could tell, everyone was
asleep. She edged out from cover. The area directly in front of the
beehives was covered by a huge awning, with all sorts of objects
strewn around: piles of red rocks and a large mound of something
black near the beehives; boxes, barrels and some odd rectangular
clay lumps, squared off roughly and held in ironwood frames. She
darted over to the awning. Unlit lamps hung from its underside
and in the centre a large flat stone was set into the ground; it
looked chipped and scorched in places. Nearby, something shiny
caught her eye. There, propped up against a tentpole, was a huge
hammer, the dark ironwood haft set with a head of pure iron.

The crèche kept a handful of precious iron implements for tasks
that neither ironwood, flint nor diamond were good for. The only

one Dej had ever handled was an iron-tipped awl for piercing tough leather hides. The iron awl was one of the few items of worth she'd never considered stealing, because it was so valuable that she risked more than a cane across the palm or a day in the hole if she got caught. Yet here was a lump of iron as big as two clenched fists. Mesmerised, she slinked over to the hammer and crouched next to it. The head wasn't perfectly smooth: one end looked battered; it was pitted along the side and sported rough reddish-brown patches. She touched it, expecting the iron to be cold, but the hammer-head was warm. Odd.

The lumpy clay thing next to it looked like a torso-sized mud-brick that came apart into two halves, currently held together by the wooden frame. A row of four small holes ran along the top, like someone had poked a finger into the clay.

She looked beyond the giant brick in its frame. Lying on the ground behind was another brick, or rather half a brick, as this one had been split open and laid on its side. Nestling in hollows in the upper surface were slivers of iron longer than her hand, shaped like elongated leaves. Dej reached out. This iron was even warmer, almost uncomfortably so. Despite this, she lifted a leaf from its hollow, smiling at the idea of holding so much iron in her hands. Even before she straightened she knew she'd be taking this with her.

"Hey you!"

Dej looked up to see a man standing in the cave mouth, holding something up to his chest. She began to turn, ready to run.

Movement too fast to follow out of the corner of her eye.

Something punched into her side, just below her upraised arm.

The iron leaf went flying. The blow whirled her around, drove the breath out of her. She caught herself, tried to carry on running.

But the strength had gone from her legs and what felt like a great hot stone had lodged in the side of her chest. She stumbled, batting an inept hand at the pain in her flank. Her fingers caught on a spike, sticking out of her. Touching it set off a web of agony across her ribs.

She gasped, and fell forward, head just missing one of the bricks. She couldn't draw breath. All the air had gone and been replaced by hurt.

Beyond where she lay shouts started up, shouts and movement, but it took all her concentration to not suffocate against the hot weight filling her chest.

She thought how stupid it was, to die like this.

She thought that she would give anything to hold Etyan, once more before the end.

Then she stopped thinking at all.

CHAPTER 10

The boy was late. Rhia looked out the parlour window, past shutters thrown wide to catch the minimal breeze. The view showed a slice of the townhouse across the street, the side of the next house down the hill, then a falling vista of hazy walls and tiled roofs. Beyond the city, the heat-washed fields of beige and tawny brown would have merged with the pale sky were it not for the thin bright line marking the edge of the skyland. Although the Harbinger was gone from the skies, they remained cloud-free, with no sign of the rains.

Yesterday, still stunned from the Church's letter, she had dressed in haste and gone to find Francin. He needed to know what the cardinals had said, and she needed his reassurance that he was doing all he could for her. But the Duke of Shen was nowhere to be found. She did see his two younger children, trotting down the corridor with a guard in tow, probably on the way to visit their mother.

Unwilling to be fobbed off by servants and courtiers she had eventually intercepted the aged but hale Lord Crethen, one of the duke's most trusted advisors. He apologised, with passable sincerity, for the duke's absence. But the only explanation he offered was that "His Grace was unavoidably called away."

"How long for?" she insisted.

"No more than a couple of days."

The duke only left Shen city to visit his estate, a formal event attended by pomp and spectacle. Where would he sneak off to by himself for "a couple of days"? It was not as though he needed to leave the palace to enjoy whichever mistress currently engaged his lower regions.

"Then I will write him a note," she snapped, her dismay heating to irritation. "Which I hope he will receive promptly." But her temper had cooled again by the time pen, paper and sealing wax arrived; being rude achieved nothing save causing offence.

When she returned to the townhouse she called for Nerilyn. "The next time you see your under-footman friend please ask him what he knows about the duke taking a secret trip from the palace for several days."

Now, waiting for Markave's son, the irritation she had felt at Francin's absence stirred again, born of frustration and fear. The duke's agenda was so often hidden from her: witness the actions of Captain Sorne, who had led the expedition to Zekt to retrieve Etyan, then unexpectedly stayed there "on the duke's orders".

Some of her ill temper came from her current pastime: she was trying to read the Book of Separation. But even when she managed to penetrate the pretentious style and unhelpful interjections – what did "Give Glory to the First in All Things" even mean? – the actual content was often unclear, illogical, or downright contradictory. How could the First turn people into stars, as He had supposedly done with the Strays? And taken at face value "put nothing made by the hand of man into the body the First gave you" would make it heresy to eat biscuits, or any prepared food. So far, she had not found anything to contradict her theory of the universe. However, hundreds of subsidiary commentaries, interpretations and addendums had accreted down the millennia and she could spend every waking hour between now and the new year reading and still not get through them all.

Someone rapped on the front door. She heard Nerilyn answer it, and a few moments later the maid showed Kerne in.

JAINE FENN

The boy who entered was a stranger to her; she had not seen
him since he went to his aunt's. She did recognise Markave's
blade-like nose and wide forehead. He stopped twisting his cap in
his hands long enough to give an unnecessarily deep bow. "I'm so
sorry I'm late, m'lady." From the sound of it, his voice had only
recently broken.

"No matter. You're here now. Sit down."

Kerne eyed the plush seat Rhia had indicated as though
expecting it to bite.

"Sit. Please. Did your father explain the situation?"

Kerne sat abruptly. "You wish to take me on as an apprentice."
He sounded incredulous.

"You are currently apprenticed to the horticulturists, I believe.
Tell me what you do there."

"Uh, these days the guild is mainly working on new food-crops
that can survive with as little water as possible."

"I imagine they are. This would be in their fields just outside
the city, yes?"

"Yes." He gulped.

"And is that where you work, in the fields?" She could not see any
dirt under the nails of the hands currently strangling his cap.

"Sometimes. Mainly I record the results, taking measurements
and counting yields."

Observational skills: good. "And what are you working on
now?"

"We have a new type of barley that, if watered well when it first
sprouts, requires little or no water to mature."

And he sounded excited about his work: excellent. "If you work
with me, it would not be with plants but with other observations
of the natural world. Have you any such experience?"

"I'm not sure what you mean, m'lady."

"Have you ever, say, recorded the comings and goings of bees
in a hive over a day, to note their direction of flight?" That had
been one of her earliest observation projects, out at the villa on the
family estate. She was not sure how old she had been, but Mother

had still been alive and in reasonable health, so it was before Etyan's birth.

"I… I have not had cause to watch a hive for that long, m'lady."

Rhia realised her mistake. Her early life had been filled with days of leisure when, encouraged by Father, she indulged her curiosity at length. Most people had work or other obligations to fill their time. "I see. Of course." He had stopped mangling his hat and she noticed now that his nails were bitten, just as hers had been when she was a girl, before Father had given her a bitter salve to stop such behaviour. Her frustration – at the boy and at herself – eased a little. Lack of opportunity did not mean lack of capacity. "The work I do is of a different nature anyway. Let me show you."

She ushered him up the great staircase running through the centre of the townhouse, their progress made more complicated by his unease at going ahead of her instead of walking behind as their respective statuses required.

When she opened the study door she watched his reaction. His face went from confusion (it was a little untidy in here) to surprise – he had probably never seen so many papers – to, she was relieved to see, genuine interest.

"Well?" she prompted.

"I am sorry m'lady, this place is…"

"It would be where you would work, with me. Does that appeal?"

"I.. it is… amazing." His eyes darted across the shelves and desks. His expression held wonderment but also what looked like suppressed panic. His gaze fell on her celestial model.

"Aha," Rhia tried to sound reassuring. "Now that is a model of the universe."

The boy looked at her. Definitely panic. But Rhia would not give up on him yet. "Come and see."

He followed her past the overflowing desks and workbenches, clutching his hat. "I understand your confusion," she conceded, "so allow me to explain." She pointed to the perforated pottery sphere in the centre of the contraption; she had lit the lamp within in anticipation of this conversation. "This represents the Sun, giving its light." She leaned over to not-quite-touch a slightly smaller sphere standing proud on its thin pole. "And this is the world." She pointed to the other three, yet smaller, spheres, one positioned between the world and Sun and two outside the world's run. "These are the Strays: the Maiden, Matriarch and Crone." Dare she try turning the mechanism? Best not. "You see how each sphere on its stick sits in a hoop of ironwood with cogs set into it."

"Cogs?"

"These toothed plates, here. See how they interlock? By turning a series of handles it should be possible to make each heavenly body move in its track."

"That is most interesting, m'lady."

"From your tone, I see this is not entirely clear to you. Which is fine! You must say what you think Kerne. Always say what you think."

"I think, begging m'lady's pardon, that this is beyond my wit to comprehend. I am sorry, m'lady."

"Where does your confusion lie? There is no shame in not understanding, only in not *trying* to understand." She went on to explain the essence of her theory, being careful to define new-to-him terms like "orbit" and "gravity". He nodded a lot, and asked questions, though these mainly revealed how little he understood as yet. And then, finally, he frowned and said, "I am unsure why the First would make the universe so complicated."

Her heart sank. But rather than challenge his beliefs she settled for saying, "I do not know. But I believe it is our duty to try and understand it. Would you be willing to join me in that quest?"

"As m'lady pleases." He did not sound certain.

"Do you want to do this, Kerne? I am ripping you from what you know and no matter how noble the cause, that will be a disruption."

His head dropped. "May I speak frankly?"

"Always."

"I'm not sure. I do not know if I am up to this great work.

Also…" he added in a rush, "I've got friends at the guild, and work I enjoy there."

She had considered this. "Then I suggest a compromise. You may split your time equally between your work for the horticulturists and your work for me. Would that suit?"

His head stayed down, looking at his cap. He gave it a last squeeze and looked up. "Yes m'lady."

"Then I will speak to your guildmaster."

After the boy had gone Rhia's spirits lifted. She had taken a positive step.

But the next day a letter arrived, addressed with Empiricist of Marn's elegant handwriting. The note inside was brief: *I am afraid that I cannot provide any assistance in your current dealings with the Church of Shen.*

Given the timing of the caravan to Marn, he could not even have given her request a full day's consideration before refusing it.

CHAPTER 11

Now who will we meet this time?

Sadakh suppressed a smile at his ghost's question. He invariably "just happened" to run into one or other faction whenever he visited the Eternal Isle.

As well as a pair of palace guards, he had the single permitted servitor who, as usual, was a disguised bodyguard. One day he expected to need their services.

But not today. The lone figure ambling along the wide-windowed corridor was all smiles. Sadakh searched his memory for a name as the eunuch halted before him. Each of the forty "immortal advisors" had a complicated, if largely ceremonial, job title, as indicated by their clothes and accoutrements. If he got the title he'd get the name. Short tunic, narrow pectoral with tablet-woven design of a stand of reeds in rich shades of green... ah yes: First Scribe of the shallows, servant of the knowledge of numbers. A senior administrator. Traditionalist by allegiance and cautious by nature.

As the eunuch straightened after giving a fulsome obeisance Sadakh returned his smile and said, "Advisor Eneph, how are you? Your joints are troubling you in this weather, perhaps."

"Ah yes, how this rain gets into my old bones! Will it never end?" Eneph gestured a knobble-knuckled hand at the nearest unshuttered window where, far below, the lesser islets of Mirror-of-the-Sky were visible only as vague, pale, mist-shrouded patches in the dark lake. At least the cloudy skies had hidden the Harbinger from sight; weak minds tended to treat such celestial phenomena as evil omens.

"The First only knows."

"And has not informed you. You have also been unwell, I believe. You still look a little... flushed."

Of course he knows. As so often, the ghost mirrored his thoughts. "Just the legacy of a recent fever."

"I am glad you are on the mend. But it is our dear caliarch's health that concerns me most." The advisor meant that: unlike Prince Mekteph, the eunuchs had little interest in personal power, only in the stability of the state.

"Is there particular cause for worry?" Sadakh kept his tone light. His sources on the Eternal Isle were limited, so any information the eunuchs chose to volunteer was welcome.

"His melancholy grows. He believes his death is near."

Not if you can help it... Ignoring his ghost Sadakh said, "I pray for him daily."

He thought that was it, but then the eunuch's high brow furrowed. "If...no, we must say *when*... the caliarch joins his blessed ancestors, given his childless state we fear for a return to troubled times."

"Should that sad day occur soon then no doubt the prince will step forward to act as regent until young Shirakeph comes of age." *And woe betide anyone who tries to stop him.* Mekteph's personal claim was weak, being through his mother, but his son had benefited from the Zekti royals' habit of interbreeding, cousin marrying cousin, giving the boy a solid double claim. Plus, he was an innocent child untainted by the suspicious deaths that had brought his father so close to the throne.

"So we all expect. And in that case the people will need spiritual certainty more than ever."

"They will indeed." Sadakh had wondered when this particular conversation would occur. The immortal advisors really must fear for the caliarch's end.

"We wonder if the time is right for overtures of peace to be made between yourself and the prince."

Sadakh let the eunuch hear his sigh. "I would welcome it, but Mekteph greatly dislikes me." He was unsure of the precise reasons but it appeared to be a combination of his outsider status and his choice to back the winning side, seasoned with a dose of the family irrationality.

"So we understand. However, if there were some way of restoring relations, I am sure you would seek it out now."

"I would. But I prefer to think that the First will favour Numak with more years yet." *And when that is a certainty, the prince will need dealing with...* His ghost sounded gleeful.

"As do we all. But we must consider all possibilities." Eneph's traditionalist tendencies might lead him to favour breeding over common sense, but like all the eunuchs who effectively ran the Zekti state, he was at heart a pragmatist. Sadakh could not blame him for trying to force a rapprochement between prince and eparch as the caliarch's end approached. "I will not keep you from his majesty any longer. Good day, Holiness."

If Sadakh's plans came to fruition he would need all the eunuchs on side, traditionalist or reformist. "And I will consider your advice, and wish you a good day also, Advisor."

He half expected a matching encounter with the prince or one of his courtly allies, but the rest of the climb to the summit of the Eternal Isle was uneventful. As he stepped outside, he found the final set of steps slick with rain, the calls of the sacred gyraptors circling overhead muted by the damp air.

At the entrance to the Hall of Eternal Guardians his aide stood silently aside, joining the pair of impassive guards stationed at the caliarch's sanctum. Sadakh would also lose a less tangible presence for the duration of the visit: for some unknown reason his ghost never spoke up in this house of the dead.

He was used to the caliarch reacting with mild surprise to his arrival for their weekly meetings; Numak's memory was not good these days. That normally meant he caught the caliarch reading, or dozing, or at one of the odd crafting hobbies he felt brought him closer to his people. But today, Zekt's supreme ruler was lying on the floor.

Numak had stretched out next to one of the two-hundred-and-thirty-six niches that lined the walls of the long, low hall. Each niche contained the reclining body of a previous caliarch: preserved, bejewelled and dressed in their full finery, laid out amongst models of those persons and objects important to them in life. The niche Numak lay beside contained the body of his father.

Amenteph the Fourteenth had been a good ruler, save for one fatal flaw. He had taken the symbolic act of marrying his sister literally, ignoring the courtesans in his harem in favour of bedding his own flesh and blood. The three sons and one daughter who had resulted had each shown disturbances of the mind, from melancholy to fratricide. Numak, the last survivor from that too-close union, was the youngest of Amenteph's offspring, and had never expected to become caliarch.

Sadakh stood a little way off and cleared his throat.

The caliarch started, then sat up. "Oh, it's you." His gaze sharpened. "Did it work?"

"I am, as you see, hale and hearty." Unlike most of his early test subjects; the knowledge gained since joining the natural enquirers two years ago had been invaluable in creating a proper, safe serum from the animus extract.

"Yes, but did it *work?*"

Sadakh had expected this question. "Majesty, we cannot know."

"Do you not feel more alive? Can you sense an extended life stretching ahead of you?" A wheedling desperation entered Numak's tone.

Sadakh had considered lying, but when – if – he administered the serum to Numak he had to be sure it worked. For the caliarch to be incapacitated for several days would put the court in turmoil. "I feel no different." Neither had the other two recent successful test subjects, although when it came to Ritek and Ereket he could not expect a detailed health report, given those two loyal servants had no tongues.

"Then how do you know it has granted you more life."

"As I say, I cannot but—"

"I was dreaming of poor Kenerit when you came in."

His long-dead wife. This was not good. "Dreams are merely the mind's rumblings, Majesty. They come from nowhere and to give them much credence is unwise. Here, let me help you up." Sadakh held out a hand.

Numak shook his head. "I am fine here. I dream of my dead family a lot recently. Even my honoured father..." He half raised a hand towards the niche. "And if he, who remains to watch over us, wishes to communicate his unease at what we are trying to do, perhaps I should listen."

Sadakh's heart sank. Numak supported his work because the caliarch believed that having a corporally eternal ruler would free the spirit of his father and the hundreds of other dead caliarchs. No longer bound by their mortal remains to watch over their descendants on the Eternal Isle, they could move on. If he had changed his mind, then Sadakh had lost his greatest ally. "You must do what your conscience dictates, Majesty. But if you were given the gift of immortality, then your ancestors would not have to abandon Zekt. It would be their choice whether to take their heavenly reward or remain in the world with their greatest, and last, scion." He hated resorting to flattery, but Numak's ego was as fragile as his sanity.

"But if it truly is the will of the First that I live forever and take on this burden, then surely you, as His representative in the world, would have succeeded by now."

"I can do this Majesty. I will do, for you and for Zekt." And, his ghost would no doubt remind him if she were not struck dumb here, for himself. He was not that much younger than Numak and, given his heritage, he could not expect to live as long as the Zekti monarch.

"If only you could show me some change, some sign…"

"I wish I could. Perhaps the change takes time. I took the serum little more than a week ago. Do you remember the Shenese boy who survived the first experiment? He experienced changes, but they took a while to manifest." Not that Sadakh had seen those changes for himself.

"Didn't he run away?"

"Not exactly, Majesty. But he is no longer in Zekt."

"Can't you get him back, and study him or whatever?"

"I have tried, believe me. But I placed more importance on securing the right raw ingredients." Since the accident that had killed most of his skyland agents, that had been hard enough; the animus that had provided the serum was only the second they had procured in as many years.

"Well, perhaps the full change will come to you soon." The caliarch frowned. "You will keep me informed."

"Always." Insofar as it was safe. Messages could be intercepted and unscheduled meetings drew unwanted attention. The caliarch was not threatening to withdraw support, but if he was losing faith then perhaps it was time to change strategy. Maybe he should take the eunuchs' hint, and try to make peace with Prince Mekteph.

CHAPTER 12

"Pleased to meet you, Sur Lectel." Rhia produced her best courtly smile for the lawyer. He could have passed for a courtier with that upright bearing and raised chin, though he was dressed in sombre robes, rather than the slashed-doublet-with-excessive-braid which appeared to be the current fashion at court.

"Likewise, Countess." He bowed low enough to be respectful without seeming obsequious. If only his eyes were not so close together she might take to this man, despite his profession. "His Grace has acquainted me with the particulars of your case," he added, his gaze sliding across to the duke, who sat next to her in the meeting room.

"Yes indeed." Francin did wear a slashed and braided doublet, of course. Rhia had squeezed herself into the required skirts and corsetry, though a mischievous streak had made her choose the mask poor Uncle Petren had painted, the one that made it look like her left eye was peeking between the fingers of someone reaching round from behind her. "Do sit down, Sur Lectel," the duke continued, "You're giving me a cricked neck."

"Thank you, Your Grace." After sitting and briefly fussing with his robes the lawyer turned to Rhia. "Countess, are you able to provide copies of the material the Church is in possession of, so we may see precisely what they are objecting to?"

"I think so, yes." She had copied out a selection of notes for Theorist of Shen. She could recopy them. Or perhaps she should just ask for them back, given he found them so offensive. She stifled a bitter smile.

"Excellent." The lawyer cleared his throat. "If there are any supporting papers the Church has not seen, they may be of use too."

"I have a lot of papers. And most of the calculations – the mathematics that support my theory – exist only as rough jottings."

"I was thinking more of any writings of a more philosophical nature, something which might present your startling theory in the context of a life lived within the Church's precepts, or show how it is congruent with aspects of the scriptures."

"I am not a philosopher or theologian, Sur Lectel. I deal in observations, and facts."

"And... calculations." He made the word sound unpalatable.

"Yes! Calculations produce proofs that cannot be argued with!"

Francin's response was gentle. "Or, sadly, understood. Not by most people anyway."

Her shoulders drooped. "I know that. The cardinals won't accept mathematical proofs alone as a reason to drop the charges. Even if – when – I produce complete calculations I imagine all it will prove to them is that women should not think too hard."

"I fear you may be correct. So, cousin, may I ask why these proofs matter so much?"

"Because if I find I am wrong I will recant."

"I see." Francin's tone was neutral, his face in the corner of her eye as inoffensively vacuous as that of the dog sitting at his feet.

"But if I am right, then the proofs will serve not only to vindicate my theory but be of use to others who come after me. Even if... the worst happens, my work will live on."

"An admirable sentiment, Countess." The lawyer sounded more puzzled than admiring. "But not, perhaps, of immediate use to our case."

"Wait a moment," Francin tapped his chin. "Weren't you working on a model of the heavens, Rhia? That might provide a more accessible demonstration for the court."

"It could, yes!" She had been keeping the two matters separate, even reading the scriptures downstairs, then going upstairs to do proper work in her study. But the celestial model might be of use in the trial. Assuming she could get it working. "But it isn't operating as it should yet. It might help if I had iron cogs."

"I will see what I can do."

The lawyer cleared his throat. "So, am I to understand that you may be able to demonstrate the truth of your theory in a way comprehensible to all, through this model?"

"Yes. I hope."

He nodded slowly. "That could help greatly. Regarding the other part of your defence, I have done some preliminary reading."

"As have I."

"Good. You will need to be well-versed in the Book of Separation, ready to answer any question."

"I will be." She had nothing to fear if she prepared properly, so why was her heart hammering?

"Do not worry yourself, Countess. I will guide you through this."

"Thank you, Sur Lectel."

"So, you will have the papers sent over?"

"Once I have copied them, yes."

"Then I have all I need for now. I will take my leave, if I may."

Once the lawyer had bowed his way out, Francin turned to her and said, "You are set on this course, are you not?"

"You know I am."

"Even the possibility of the Death of the Damned does not deter you?"

She flinched to hear him state it so baldly. "It does not." She forced a smile. "Having examined the surface of Whitemoon with my sightglass, I can assure you it is not covered in harmonious cities populated by the worthy dead anyway. Just craters." Itself an interesting find.

"Oh. Best not mention that at your trial, eh?" He gave a wry grin. "But if you cannot prove your theory, you will admit the Church is right?"

"I have no intention of risking myself, or my papers, for a lie."

"No," his voice was soft, "but you would risk death for the truth."

"You know I would." She narrowed her eyes at him. "But it won't come to that, will it? Will it, Francin?"

"I am doing all I can, up to and including procuring that excellent lawyer and making sure he has every incentive to get you acquitted." Rhia preferred not to imagine the kind of incentives her cousin might apply. "But I still want to give you a chance to change your mind before it is too late. You could lose both your life and your work."

"I know that. Although..." She had been looking for a way to broach this subject for some time, and this latest unpleasant development made it even more vital "...when it comes to my work, it would be less distressing if I knew there were copies."

"Copies?"

"Of the papers in my ironwood chest. The one you removed from my house to stop your wife getting her hands on it two years ago."

"I believe that chest had a sturdy lock on it."

"It did. Nevertheless... oh, let us stop this play! Francin, did you take copies of my papers when I was in Zekt?"

"I opened the chest and examined the contents, yes. But I saw no need to replicate them all as if, First forbid, you did not make it home then I would have plenty of time to do so before a new claimant to your position came forward. From what little I know of the natural enquirers, I do not believe they act in haste. But surely other enquirers have copies?"

She shook her head. "Some. I have a subset of a subset – so much has been lost down the ages! But there may well be items in my collection no one else has."

"I see."

She sighed, and found the sigh wanting to turn into a sob. "Why is the Church doing this, Francin?"

"Good question." He paused to fuss the dog at his feet. "Given my ongoing dance with the cardinals, I think what you really mean is 'Why are they doing this to *you* and why *now?*' I suspect someone, to use the lower city parlance, has it in for you. Possibly more than one person."

"Meaning?"

"Well, for a start someone provided information about your theory to the Church."

"Yes they did. And I have dealt with that." As best she could, anyway. "But why did the Church decide to invoke a trial?"

"I suspect their... robust response to the informant may come down to politics. Some of the other Houses may have, ah, put in a bad word. You have enemies, Rhia."

"I know." House Escar for a start.

"Another reason is one you spent some weeks observing for yourself."

"The Harbinger?"

"It made people scared and volatile. I am, incidentally, indebted to you for warning me of its imminent return, even if it arrived somewhat sooner than we had feared."

"I did say these celestial appearances are hard to predict. So the Church is taking advantage of the unrest?"

"As is their wont. Frightened people are easily led." Francin sounded almost pleased by the challenge of tussling over the loyalties of a fearful populace. "Returning to your predicament, I suspect the Church were expecting a quiet capitulation. Instead, you called their bluff."

"By requesting a grand trial."

"Precisely."

And it was done now, the wheels set in motion. But talk of the other Houses reminded her of another matter. "I am guessing you've had no luck finding me a husband."

"I have not had time to make much progress – I assumed a

good lawyer was more important than a compliant spouse right now – but you are correct. Your House's comparative wealth is not proving as attractive a lure as expected. Your proviso regarding retention of all your freedoms might be an issue. That and your current disfavour with the Church."

Politics, again. But he had reminded her of the final item on her mental checklist. "When you say you have not had time, might that be because of unexpected errands?"

"Unexpected errands? Really cousin, you are not one to insinuate when you can state. What do you mean?"

"I tried to see you earlier this week, but was told you were 'away'. Where were you, Francin? You never leave the palace."

"I do not make a habit of it, no."

"But you were gone for several days."

"There is more to Shen than the city, cousin. I had business elsewhere in my realm."

"Or beyond it, at the red valley?" She could not think where else he might go, although that would have taken him away for a week or more.

"Goodness no. Operations there run themselves. I need hardly–"

The door burst open. A breathless footman bowed then blurted, "Your Grace, you must come at once!"

Francin frowned. "What is it?"

"The duchess, Your Grace. She has tried to take her own life!"

CHAPTER 13

Someone was saying something about dice. Dej was aware of that, now. She hadn't been aware of anything for some time. She strained to make out the man's voice.

"…end up owing me your month's wages!"

"I let you win last night."

Two strangers, some way off, talking about a game. A game of dice. Where was she? What had she been doing before this? Why did her body feel so odd?

"Oh, and the night before too." The first man laughed, and his voice receded further. She listened, but heard only wind through canvas and a distant shout that sounded like a warning to "stand clear".

Everything came rushing back.

She'd been stupid. She scrunched up her face until the eyelids ungummed themselves, then opened her eyes to see lamp-lit rock overhead. She was in one of the caves, in the red valley. She'd been caught. She had to get away. But her chest ached like she'd been kicked by an ox, and the rest of her body wasn't up to moving much.

With some effort, she turned her head. She was on a pallet-bed in the largest cave; three more pallets lined the walls, all empty, with various personal possessions – eating utensils, clothes, boots, and some weapons – piled under, on or beside them. It was dark beyond the cave entrance but she made out the back of one of the brick beehives, with people moving around under the lamp-hung awning beyond.

A figure loomed out of the lamplight. She tried closing her eyes but she'd been seen.

"You're awake. Good."

She swallowed, and realised how thirsty she was. "Water. Please." It came out as a pathetic croak. She let it. The fact she wasn't dead meant they had some sympathy for her. She could use that.

The man who came over had a jowly face and heavy eyebrows. She knew him from somewhere. She let him help her drink. The water made her tongue feel odd, sort of itchy. He was gentle with her, not like a jailer. "I'm sorry," she said.

"For what?" His voice was soft.

"Taking the… leaf thing." She considered adding that she was going to put it back but decided against an outright lie, given how nice the man was being.

"I'm glad to hear it. Good job I realised it was you. The Captain was all for finishing you off."

She realised who this was. "You're the medic, the one who came with the soldiers to rescue Etyan."

"That's right. I'm Gerthen, official medic to the duke's outpost in the red valley. And you're Dej. Young Lanen saw a skykin poking round and decided to shoot rather than asking questions."

"Shoot?"

"You took a handbow bolt to the chest. Broke two ribs and made a mess of one of your lungs. We almost lost you. Fortunately it's true what they say about skykin being tough. You've been out of it a while though."

"How long?"

"Best part of a week."

"A week?" Etyan would be frantic!

"Even with your advantages a wound like that takes time to

72

heal. I'll let you rest up again now."

"Wait… I'm not a prisoner here, am I?"

"No." Gerthen pursed his lips, "Though the Captain would like a word with you later."

"Captain… " she searched her memory and came up with "Remeth?"

"No, Remeth's not on the current rotation. It's Captain Govand. Get some rest, Dej."

Given how weak she felt, she had little choice. They didn't mean her any harm; she could hardly blame the duke's men for shooting her and she was safe enough here, for now.

She dozed until near sunrise, when Gerthen returned with an older man with a limp. He introduced Captain Govand then went to sit on the pallet across from hers.

"Dej, isn't it?"

She nodded.

"You're not in trouble, but I would like to know why you came here. I was under the impression you'd set up home with Lord Harlyn in the umbral forest."

"I… " She searched for a plausible lie, and failed to find one. Screw it, why not try the truth? "Etyan and I had a row. I needed some time alone."

Govand looked thoughtful, then nodded. "Fair enough." Dej relaxed a little. Then he asked. "Did you meet any other skykin on your way here?"

"Uh, no." If he started asking questions about "her people" things could get awkward. "I came straight from Shen."

"I see." He sounded like he was trying to understand her choice. So was she, but it was none of his business. "I only ask because we had a sighting."

"A sighting of what? Who?"

"We're not sure. We put out occasional patrols along the edge of the valley and about a month back one of them spotted a lone skykin. Looked half-starved and when they hailed him he ran off. We're a long way from any caravan route so presumably these were more rogue skykin, like those who originally attacked Lord Harlyn and his sister."

"I wouldn't know anything about them." Any more, she added mentally, to make the denial less like a lie.

"Never mind. I thought I'd ask. My only concern would be if they were considering offensive action."

"I doubt it." Because most of them are dead. And the clanless were cowards anyway. Which she may as well say. "Those types would never take on the duke's soldiers."

The way he raised his eyebrow made her wonder if he knew she'd been one of "those types" once, but he just said, "That's good to know. I'll let you rest now."

She thought resting would be easier said than done in a cave full of strange men but she'd apparently done it for a week already, and it wasn't like she had much choice; in this state if she went to sleep outside and something nasty found her, she'd hardly be able to defend herself. She dozed as the Sun came up, then slept through until evening.

For the next few days she took Gerthen's advice, resting, and eating and drinking everything put in front of her. The men who shared the cave were polite if distant, like they'd been when she was with Etyan – presumably because she still was, in their minds.

Thinking of Etyan hurt, like the mental equivalent of touching the tender wound on her side. And she couldn't shake the image of him giving up on her and returning to the city to be married off by his sister, like she always knew he would.

As soon as she was strong enough she tried standing, leaning against the cave wall. As her strength returned she took to sitting at the edge of the awning, out of the way. The workmen were wary of her; she must look pretty odd to them; slender, hairless and covered in gold-and-brown scales. Not to mention half naked.

There were about three dozen men in total, mostly craftsmen. They worked by night to "refine the iron" which looked like a tricky business. Rocks and charcoal from great piles were shovelled into the two "furnaces". The bellows made sure the fires inside burned hard. After some time, hot squishy stuff was pulled out and hit with the hammer, then rolled into heavy clay pots. The pots were shoved back into the furnaces and heated until the contents turned to bright stuff the colour of the Sun in Shen. This liquid might look like fiery honey but it was dangerous: one man who got a splash on his hand was burnt to the bone. No wonder they needed Gerthen here. The runny iron was poured into the clay moulds. Some moulds made odd shapes, strips and spikes and flattish lumps, but most produced weapons: spearheads – the leaf-shaped objects – and knives. Apparently, much as they'd like to make swords to replace the diamond-toothed weapons carried by militia officers, the iron wasn't strong enough.

Once she no longer needed to sleep most of the time she began to keep more normal hours, mainly resting at night, taking short walks by day to build her stamina. She'd be up to leaving soon. But where to? She found herself looking for signs. If rain came, she'd head back to Shen now. If all the iron cast today came out whole, she'd go her own way for a while longer. She'd wanted to decide her fate for herself, but now it came to it, she couldn't.

On the seventh day after she woke the weather changed from the overcast that had hung over the valley all week. The wind picked up and clouds swirled away to return the land to burning skyland brightness. Dej sat at the edge of the camp looking down over the valley, watching the heat-haze make the remaining clumps of vegetation shimmer and dance.

When she first saw the dark shape weaving through the landscape she thought it was a mirage, or just some local wildlife. But it walked – staggered – upright. It was a person. She stood, and held a hand up to reduce the glare not blocked by her third eyelid. Definitely a person. And she knew who.

She broke into a run. "Etyan!"

He stopped, and swayed on his feet. Dej careened down the slope to grab his shoulders. He sagged in her arms. His face beneath its scale-patterning was drawn and thin, but smiling.

"Etyan!" She grinned back. "You came after me!"

CHAPTER 14

"The bread is not as fresh as it might be m'lady." Rhia looked up as her maidservant placed the lunch plate on the corner of the dining table-turned-reading-desk, next to the Book of Separation.

"What? Ah, the shortages are biting, are they?" Prices went up every week, and even House Harlyn's resources could not guarantee fresh food on the table any more.

"I fear so, m'lady." Nerilyn turned to go.

"Wait, you went to the palace last night, didn't you? To see your young man?"

"I did, m'lady."

"What news of the duchess?" Francin had hurried Rhia away when he was called to attend to his wife. He had sent a messenger the next day with a typically terse note: *Alharet will live.* In the week since, Rhia had heard nothing more.

Nerilyn looked away before saying, "Begging your pardon m'lady, it was unseemly talk."

"Unseemly, how?"

Nerilyn's brow furrowed, "Well, it was about... how she did it. Tried to do it."

"Go on."

"You know she's not allowed anything sharp or dangerous in her rooms?"

Ever since her incarceration for treason, Alharet had been confined to her suite, save short and heavily guarded walks in the palace gardens and attendance at the royal chapel on restdays. "Indeed not. Did she somehow get hold of a knife?" Rhia went cold at the thought of what Alharet might do with a knife. And at the thought that she might still have allies in the palace who would procure her one.

"Not a knife. One of the scullions said Her Grace hid a horn spoon, brought with one of her meals. She sharpened it, over some weeks, using the stone corner of her window alcove." The window itself had been covered by a carved ironwood shutter; the duchess's only view of the outside world was through ornate filigree bars. "Then she, ah, she plunged it into her breast."

"Oh."

"They say she wasn't ever in danger of her life. The wound was shallow. She's expected to recover fully."

"Good." Guilt nibbled at Rhia. But Alharet had caused death and suffering, and betrayed her shadowland. By rights, she should have been executed. Yet the duke had refused to publicly try her, perhaps fearing to worsen relations with her old homeland. "And how about the duke's unscheduled absence? Have you heard anything else regarding that?"

"No one knows. Some still say it's got to be down to a woman, begging m'lady's pardon."

"They would. Thank you, you may go. But please remember that no rumour is too unlikely or… unsavoury to be of interest."

"Yes, m'lady."

She should try to get more reading done while she waited for Kerne, who appeared as tardy in his habits as Etyan.

Oh, *Etyan…* She sighed. Her brother's lack of communication was exasperating. Surely he must have been to the estate and seen the letter by now! If this was some game, some protest or ploy his lover had put him up to then they were going to have harsh words when he finally deigned to turn up. And if he did not return… no, he would come home in his own time, smiling and insouciant as ever; damn him.

Their shared tardiness aside, Kerne was the opposite of Etyan: attentive, eager to please, always willing to put in the effort. Markave had apologised for his boy's lack of punctuality, as though it were his fault. Her steward seemed stressed. Was it just the ill times? Or had Alharet's foolish act brought back bad memories? His second wife had been one of Alharet's victims. Or rather she had been one of the duchess's agents who, being of the lower orders, *had* been tried and executed for her treachery. Relations had already broken down between them before that – his wife had already taken a foreign lover – but even so the recollection must hurt.

When Kerne's voice broke her reverie her head was drooping over the Book of Separation. She jumped up, eager to move on to happier pursuits.

Up in her study she got Kerne settled at the day's copying. Rather than having him just read primers on the study of the heavens, by copying them he would hopefully gain better understanding.

She was frowning over her calculations when Brynan brought the day's post: three more refusals to attend her trial, including one from Engineer of Dolm; he had been Father's closest correspondent, but all he had to say was that he wished her well.

At least Examiner of Rern said he would check over her workings; he also included a two page commendation of her mental acuity and ability to express logical thoughts in a clear manner. Unlike the other two testimonials she had received so far, it did not mention how unusual such a sharp mind was in someone of her gender, which was a bonus.

Given the negative responses she might almost think Theorist of Shen had written to her fellow enquirers advising against lending their support. But she was being unfair. Most enquirers, secure in their studies and workrooms, would baulk at the thought of the journey across the skyland to another shadowland. And to go by some of the stated reasons and incidental comments in recent enquirers' correspondence, Shen was not the only shadowland suffering at the moment. The Harbinger would have brought consternation to weaker minds across the world, and the same drought that held Shen in its grip was causing similar deprecations in Erys and Dolm, the two nearby shadowlands on this side of the mountains.

"I've finished!"

She looked up to see Kerne smiling at her from the far end of the desk. "Excellent. And have you had any further thoughts on my theory regarding the mechanics of day and night?"

"I have been thinking about it, yes, m'lady."

She was coming to recognise that tone: he acknowledged the validity of the idea, but did not grasp it. Yet. "So, what still puzzles you?"

"Begging m'lady's pardon, but even with the world and the Sun as globes, it still seems simpler that night should fall due to some obstacle coming between the world and the light of the Sun rather than all these complicated revolutions."

"I can see how you might think that." She was not sure she could. But she was working from assumptions held for years. Kerne had a week's reading. "However, it is not so. When darkness falls I will take you to my observation platform and we will observe how the stars appear to wheel overhead as the night progresses to illustrate the point."

He sounded puzzled. "I have seen that for myself, m'lady."

"Yes, but only when you thought of the sky as a tableau that moves while we remain static. You need to learn to see with new eyes, Kerne."

"I will try." He sounded embarrassed at having disappointed her.

"Good. Was there anything else you wished to ask in relation to this theory, before we test it with observation?"

To his credit, Kerne was always ready with his questions. He nodded and swallowed. "What about the shadowlands? Given we live in shade, could whatever shades us in the day not block *all* the light at night?"

"That's... " She stifled her initial response. "That's a creative approach. I believe there are structures in the sky which come between us and the Sun, and diffuse its light. But they do not block it entirely."

"And we cannot see them..."

"No, we cannot, because we see the Sun *through* them. Do you understand?"

"I think so."

"What remains unclear?" she asked gently.

"There are dozens of shadowlands, so there must be dozens of such shades."

"Indeed there must, and they must be massive and complex structures. Think of it as a... shade-swarm." Although she was not clear on the mechanics, she had come up with a useful analogy on her last visit to the Harlyn estate. "Imagine a lit window, on the upper storey of a house at night. You are on the ground and there is a tree between you and the window. When you look down, you see a pattern of light and shade being cast. Those patches of shade are the shadowlands."

"Would the shades that make these patches not... interfere with each other, as leaf shadows move in the breeze?"

"A reasonable question, but I do not believe so, given the shadowlands have remained unchanged and stable for millennia. Remember what I said? Space – the openness above and beyond the world – is vast. And most likely lacking in such winds." Not that she knew for sure, yet. "Remember, my celestial model is a simplification and is not to scale."

He nodded, eager as ever. But eagerness to understand was not the same as understanding.

CHAPTER 15

Dej half guided, half carried Etyan back to the camp and into the cave, calling out for help. Gerthen laid him on the bed, and got her to fetch water to wet his lips. The other two men who slept in the cave – Captain Govand and Master Timanth, the head metalworker – woke up, then in Govand's case, went back to sleep once he saw there was no immediate threat.

Dej paced about outside. When she couldn't bear it any more she called, "Will he be alright?"

"He will," replied Gerthen, "but he needs water, and rest."

"Let me look after him."

Gerthen considered for a moment. "If you want. Give him only a dribble of water at a time, and let me know if his breathing slows or his fever grows."

The cave was awkwardly crowded now but Dej barely noticed. Etyan had come after her, and nearly died doing so. She was going to make him better.

After a while he focused on her face and whispered, "Found you."

"I hoped you would." Because she had. No wonder she'd been unable to decide what to do; some part of her had been waiting for him, knowing he'd come. "But it's been weeks!"

"I know. Not the pathfinder you are, my love." His eyes closed,

83

but he was smiling, his breathing strong and even.

She sat with him all day, dribbling water over his lips when he was awake, just watching him when he wasn't.

When evening fell, the Captain had his men set up a makeshift pallet for Dej at the edge of the awning, but she stayed with Etyan until she found her eyes closing, at which point she lay on the floor beside him and dozed.

When daylight came and they were both awake he told her how, after she had been gone two days, he went to the estate.

"You do know that's the last place I'd go?" She tried to make a joke of it.

"Yes. But if I was going to come after you I needed supplies." He'd arrived with an empty backpack. "I stocked up and left Shen on the north road, then turned off into the mountains."

"You knew I'd come here?"

"I hoped you would, given it was where we met."

Love swelled to fill her. "I'm so glad you did. So what happened?"

"I thought I knew where I was going but got lost in the mountains. I was so scared, Dej. Some of the stuff out here, like nightwings..." He'd nearly been killed by a nightwing. "I ended up more worried about finding shelter than finding you. Sorry."

"But you did find me."

"Eventually. Ran out of food and resorted to eating the local stuff first. Remember how I hated palefruit when you first gave it to me? Tastes fine now and it kept me alive long enough to find you."

"Thank the First!" She slipped her hands under him and held him to her, though it made her damaged chest twinge. She sat back. "I'm sorry I ran off. You must have been so worried."

"I was. I mean, I knew you'd be all right – you're tough and smart and you know how to survive – but of course I had to come after you."

"I'm so glad you did." For now, said a small nagging voice. What about when they went back to Shen? Would they just fall back into fighting and fucking and not really talking. Should she try and get him to talk now? Maybe when he'd recovered a bit.

"Dej?" He was looking up at her in concern. "Are you alright?"

"Yes. I was... just thinking."

"Listen, we're out here now. Why don't we do what you always wanted? Let's explore the skyland, together."

Dej's face broke into a grin. "I'd love to!"

"Good. Because I've been thinking about why we keep fighting and a lot of it... Don't take this the wrong way, but we were bored. Once we'd got the shack built, and set up regular visits to the estate so we had supplies there wasn't much to do." He grinned. "Other than the obvious, of course. But we need to do stuff together, besides that. We could spend a while finding out about the world at large. What do you say?"

"Yes, obviously! Yes, yes, yes!" She hugged him again, pulling him as tight as she dared given his feeble state and her damaged ribs. "Just as soon as we're both fit enough."

"Have you been ill then?"

She pulled back. How would he react if she told him she'd been shot trying to steal some iron? He'd be happier not knowing. "It was nothing. I'm pretty much over it now."

"Oh. If you're sure you're alright."

"I'm fine."

"Good. We'll have to tell Ree."

Her warm heart cooled a fraction. "Tell her what?"

"What we're doing. I got to the estate before she was due. I should have left a note or at least told someone where I was going, but I just wanted to get out here and find you."

"You're right, I suppose. It's only fair to let her know we're leaving."

"And when we'll be back."

"Will we? Be back I mean?"

"I can't just disappear forever, Dej. But we could spend, I don't know, three months, maybe four, out in the skyland. It's not like there's much going on with my sister except her eternal studies."

And worrying about marrying her brother off. Both of which she could keep doing by herself for all Dej cared. "All right. Four months then, yes?"

"Yes. Four months, just us, seeing the world."

She sat with him all day, sometimes talking, sometimes just holding his hand and looking out over the skyland. She wondered if the men dozing in their beds overheard them. So what if they did? When the shadowkin got up for the night's work and left them alone she cuddled up to him on the bed. But despite her elation, she was exhausted. She needed a proper night's sleep. She considered using one of the other pallets but didn't like the idea of sleeping in a strange man's bed, even when it was empty.

"Etyan, I need to sleep, just for a while. I've got a pallet outside. You should rest too. Then tomorrow you can write a note for your sister, and I'll ask about getting some supplies. We can leave as soon as you're able. All right?"

"All right." He looked as tired as she felt. "If you think you can sleep with all the noise."

"I hardly notice it." The to and fro of the craftsmen was no more intrusive than the background fuss and mutter of the crèche dormitory. "I'll be back before dawn." She gave him a lingering kiss, and left.

Her new pallet was between a pile of boxes and one of the supply tents, out of sight of the men. She dragged it round to align with the north then fell into it. Sleep came quickly, her last amused thought being that she was sleeping within an arm's reach of enough iron to buy her old crèche.

She woke to a greying sky, and sat up. The men were winding down for the night.

"Got that end?"

Someone in the supply tent next door, their voice loud through the canvas. She thought it was the soldier who kept losing at dice.

"Wait. Yep, got it now." That was Lanen; Govand had made him apologise for shooting her but he hadn't met her eyes when he did so. "I know she hasn't got tits any more, but is she scaly down below too, d'you think?"

They were talking about her. Her breath caught.

"No idea. Not going to bother his lordship if she is, though."

Something being lifted, and some sloshing; they were manhandling a barrel. "What d'you mean?" asked Lanen.

"Don't you remember? Couple of years back a guildmaster's girl got her throat slit, body dumped in the dyer's pools."

"What was that to do with Lord Harlyn?"

"The murder was down to hired thugs. Some sort of House feud. But I heard a rumour that before she got herself killed his lordship had his way with her, and not gently either."

"Oh. Didn't know he was the type."

"Oh yes. Got a cousin does door-work on a brothel. His lordship was a regular. That sort, sometimes they don't want to pay for it, even if they've got the money. They just take it."

Dej pressed her hand against her mouth. They were lying. Or they meant someone else. She jumped up off the pallet. Then she made herself walk sedately through the camp, like nothing was wrong.

When she reached the cave she looked down at Etyan. He was half asleep but opened his eyes and smiled up at her. Oh, that smile. But who else had he used it on?

"Etyan, I need to ask you something and I need you to answer honestly."

"What is it?" He struggled to raise himself on his elbows. "What's wrong?"

"Have you ever… did you visit brothels?" It sounded so absurd, so unlikely. "Back in Shen, before you met me."

He gave up trying to sit, fell back, and exhaled. "I did a lot of stupid things before I met you."

"So that's a yes then. You went with whores."

"Why are you asking this now?"

"Never mind why I'm asking. Did you?"

"I… yes. I did. Lots of us did. Young men, with money, out to have fun. We lived life to the full. I'm not proud of it. But I wasn't the only one."

Perhaps it had been normal, then. Perhaps he really did regret it, now. But that wasn't all. "And what about the girl?"

"What girl?"

"You know what girl." She fought to keep her voice down. "The one who died."

"I didn't kill her, Dej. I wasn't even there when it happened."

"But you were there before, with her."

He said nothing.

"You were there," she continued, "and you… " She couldn't say it, and instead settled on, "…attacked her."

"I don't know where you're getting this from, Dej—"

"That doesn't matter. What matters is what happened. What did you do to her?"

"Do to her… " His voice died away.

"Answer me Etyan! Did you rape her?" There, she'd said it.

He looked at her sharply, and at that moment she knew the truth. She pulled away. He put a hand out. "Wait, wait…" She paused, out of range of his touch. "Dej, you have to understand, it wasn't like you think."

"How was it then?" Each word felt like a stone she was spitting.

"I was set up. The whole thing. My so-called friends got me wrecked, found this girl, said she was a whore. I didn't know any better."

"Yes, because if she had been a whore it would've been *just fine* to do whatever you wanted to her."

"Yes. No. I really thought she… "

"Wanted you?" *Like I've wanted you, so many times.* Dej gulped back bile.

"No. She wasn't… She didn't act like a whore. But they said that was part of the game. She was play-acting, pretending. That's what they said."

Pretending to be what he wants, because you want him to want you. "And you believed them! You didn't think about her at all. You just fucked her. Even though she was just a scared, innocent girl."

88

"I really didn't know! I barely knew what I was doing, I was so out of it—"

"That's no excuse!"

"No, it isn't. And if only she'd struggled, or cried out. Anything to make me realise what was really happening. How wrong it was. But she just lay there, just let me… She just lay there."

Looking up, at the rafters. Waiting for it to be over. Because if you struggle, it'll be even worse. Dej couldn't breathe.

"Listen, Dej, please. I did a terrible thing. If I could go back and undo it… "

"You never can."

"You think I don't know that? You think it doesn't eat away at me? But what can I do, now?"

"I don't care what you do now." She turned on her heel.

"Please!"

She paused in the mouth of the cave, not turning, speaking just loud enough for him to hear. "You will never see me again."

She stalked through the camp, blind to the craftsmen and soldiers. Once she was away from their tents she stopped, bent over, and threw up, a single violent ejection of the foulness inside. She straightened, wiped her mouth and carried on, walking faster. She was humming under her breath, the rough sound going in and out of tune but filling her head, like the act of walking filled her body.

Even so, as she strode through the dark, she couldn't help thinking of Cal. What that bastard did was part of who she was, but she'd dealt with it. She wasn't going to waste any more time worrying about a shit like him. But Etyan… how could he? She slowed and stopped when the Sun came up. Now, more than ever, she needed to think straight.

She walked back across the valley then crept up to the ironworks, using what cover she could find, every sense alert to being spotted. The Sun was high, the camp silent. When she reached the shadow of the first tent she paused and tried to sense Etyan, though even this much contact repelled her. Nothing. He'd been too weak to get up by himself. He'd probably gone back to sleep.

She swallowed hard, then got out her paring knife and slit the wall of the tent. Time to do what she should've done when she first came to this wretched place. She found a pack and filled it: a fire-kit and a soldier's travel-pot; a waterskin; a thick cloak; plenty of food; a diamond-edged shortsword strapped to the outside. The finished iron weapons were in a different tent, which was good, as that meant she wasn't tempted to take one.

She heaved her bulging pack onto her back and strode away, not looking back.

CHAPTER 16

"We won the lottery."

Sorne looked up from his bowl of sweet rice. "We what?"

"Won the regatta lottery? For seats in the stands?" Sharrey was doing that thing she did, where she made it extra-clear she was asking a question, so the stupid Shenese man would understand.

"Oh, that. I'm not really interested in going." He kept his tone neutral, indifferent.

"I know." She raised her chin. "But I am."

Ah, that little defiant gesture, made without meeting his eyes. Sorne suspected that more than one of the men who'd sat at this table before him had taken issue with her cheek, maybe made their displeasure known. "So go then. You don't need me along."

"I got four tickets." She looked over at her son, busy tucking into his breakfast across the table. "And Tamak wants to go. Don't you?"

Tamak looked up, startled, then nodded. The boy was as quiet as his mother was garrulous, but Sorne was getting to know that expression. He smiled at him. "Got the pains again, son?"

As Tamak gave a slower nod Sharrey said, "He's fine. Don't change the subject."

"We were going fishing later, but if he's not well…"

"We'll see how he is. But we need to talk about the caliarch's birthday regatta."

"Go, please. You'll enjoy it."

"So might you. It'll get you off Arec. Something has to."

"I have everything I want here." He smiled to show he meant her, rather than this dingy, cramped room, but her eyes said she didn't believe him.

"Sometimes I just don't get you. You come all this way from Shen to live in Mirror, but then you never leave the strangers' isle." He knew what was coming next; sure enough, "Not even to take me to the priory." Ever since they'd got together, coming up on a year now, she'd wanted him to take her to the restday service at the Order of the First Light. Foreigners were welcome at the service; another of the current eparch's foibles.

"Told you: I'm not that religious." He'd actually seen more of the priory than she ever would.

"It's not just about the service. It's about being seen. A matter of appearances." Sharrey was big on appearances, which was why her tiny home was crowded with knick-knacks: she felt pointless collectibles lent some "class".

"Hhhm."

"Lots of the immortal advisors go. The prince himself sometimes."

"Well you'll see the prince when you attend the regatta." *And I'd rather the prince didn't see me.*

"Yes, but that's not the point."

"Take Nishet."

"She can't leave her ma alone. Last time the silly old coot wandered off and asked a punt to take her to heaven because she was sure she was dying."

"Nishet could take her along too. Like I said, I won't need my place."

"Huh. Imagine how well that'd go, with the old lady shouting at the clouds and accusing any man in range of touching her up." Sharrey looked over at her son. "Well done: I like to see a clean bowl. Now get along to school."

"My legs hurt." Tamak hung his head.

"Then I imagine you won't be well enough for Uncle Garen to take you fishing when you finish your lessons." Everyone round here knew him by the name he'd used when he re-entered Mirror-of-the-Sky.

The boy shrugged. His mother reached over and squeezed his hand. "You've missed so much. You need to get educated so you can get a good job." Her eyes flicked up to not-quite-meet Sorne's. He kept his face impassive. He wasn't going to deny how little use he was to the woman who let him share her house and bed.

"All right." Tamak levered himself up to stand, then walked off, stiff-legged.

Sorne forced himself not to watch. "Can't Nishet get someone in to look after her ma?"

"You volunteering then?"

"Course not. But Breta might do it. She's not interested in the regatta either."

"Perhaps, if it's not beneath her."

"I'll ask Jemulf if she'd do it as a favour."

"You owe those two too many favours already."

"Perhaps. But I'm seeing Jemulf later this morning anyway."

"Why am I not surprised."

Though he'd stayed in one on the way here, Mirror-of-the-Sky itself didn't have inns. But the Zekti did meet socially, and they did drink. They just did it in public courtyards, what they called common-yards, or simply yards.

Because it was still morning, the only drink being served in Ramek's yard was tea. Because this was Arec, the strangers' isle, there were several variations of "tea" available to suit foreign tastes. But because he was broke, Sorne could only afford the local stuff, bitter and chewy as it was. He sat with his cup on the low table in front of him, shifting on the mats to get comfortable. Another thing that got him about Mirror: nothing to sit on except your arse. Avoiding furniture with spindly legs made sense when you were on an island made of packed reeds and compacted earth, but the lack of seats played havoc with his back.

Jemulf strode into the yard, saw Sorne, and waved. A raised finger to Ramek to order his usual and his friend ambled over, then half sat, half collapsed onto the matting. Being a foreigner himself, albeit from Faro rather than Shen, Jemulf shared Sorne's dislike of sitting on the ground.

"No flutes today," said Sorne by way of greeting.

"Makes a nice change."

They agreed to disagree on the ubiquitous pipe and flute musicians in public spaces here: Jemulf said it put his teeth on edge while Sorne rather liked it. He had some musical talent himself and had wondered, when he'd returned to the city, whether he might play the pipes for a living. But the standard was high and musicians were, like every other legitimate profession not relegated to slaves, either locals or outsiders with proper identity papers and references.

"How's your boy?"

Sorne both liked and disliked it when Jemulf called Tamak his. "His joints hurt pretty much all the time now, he says."

"You want to try becen-root. I told you about my aunt."

"He hasn't broken a bone, this is an ongoing thing."

"It's amazing stuff."

"But not easy to get." *Or cheap.*

"I still have contacts."

"I'm sure you do." Sorne saluted Jemulf with his tea to show he meant no offence.

The other man took a pull on his own drink; he actually liked the local brew.

Putting down his cup, Sorne said, "Sharrey won seats to watch the regatta from the stands."

"Good for her. Not making you go is she?"

"Not if I can help it. In fact, you could help there. Or rather Breta could."

Jemulf raised a pencilled eyebrow. He kept to the Faroese habit of shearing, shaving or even plucking any actual hair that had the temerity to grow on him. "How so?"

"Sharrey wants to go with her friend, the one with the loopy ma. But loopy ma needs babysitting."

"I'm sure Breta would love an afternoon mopping up piss and talking nonsense. Make her wish we'd had children after all."

"Nishet's mum isn't that far gone. But she doesn't like men. I'll teach an extra session for free." He didn't say "I'll owe you" because Sharrey was right: he already owed Jemulf and Breta too much.

"About that. We may have to move the training-rooms."

"Again?" Although it was legit to run what in Shen would have been called a gym, even though Jemulf had proper, or at least well-forged, paperwork, the additional fight-training that Breta and Sorne offered to selected clientele was borderline illegal. They'd already had to relocate once.

"Palms will be greased, the rooms will be seen to close; it'll be fine. But not much work for you for the next few weeks I'm afraid. Although…"

Sorne knew that look. "You've got something 'interesting' coming up."

"We have. And it's a real easy one this time."

"You know I don't like that sort of work." Not after he'd spent most of his life trying to put a stop to it. "A little rule-bending's fine, but nothing dodgy enough to risk getting collared."

Jemulf put a finger to his chin. "You know, I'd give a week's takings to know why you're so obsessed with staying on the right side of the law." He held to the common assumption that most foreigners on the strangers' isle were in hiding, or at least had run away from their own shadowland for good reason.

Sorne ran his finger across his lips, miming sealing them, then shook his head.

His friend smiled back. "Of course. We all have our little secrets. But this job is a peach. Obviously we'll sort your domestic problem – if not Breta then we'll find someone suitable – and

I'll waive three months' rent on your lock-up. And that's just for showing up. If the job comes off you'll get a hefty bonus. And the joy of it is, you won't even have to hit anyone!"

Sorne sighed. "All right. Tell me more." He had to at least play along.

"I heard about this house on Pahnec that's been deserted for months. Likely to remain so too. An unexpected early death led to a long-running family dispute over the inheritance."

"On Pahnec?"

"Uh-huh. So it'll be crammed with all sorts of goodies. They were parfumiers, and dealt in fine cloth too."

"And you intend to just walk in and take whatever's lying around?"

"Break in, to be precise."

"I'm not a thief, Jem. And that's not me coming over all moral. It's just not my area of expertise."

"Which is why you won't be coming in with us. We need you to act as a look-out."

"A look-out?"

"Yes, just… loiter outside with a punt."

"So actually a look-out and getaway man?"

"Strictly speaking, yes. We trust you. And it can't be Breta or me." He held up a hand; even in the relatively dim daylight under the awning, his skin was several tones darker than Sorne's. "You could pass for a local. Didn't you say you had a Zekti disguise amongst the bits and pieces you're so keen to keep out of sight of your good lady?"

"I'm not a puntsman."

"Punting's easy enough to learn."

Jemulf wasn't wrong: one of Sorne's men had picked the skill up quickly enough the last time he'd done something like this.

Jemulf continued, "It's a prime waterfront property, empty and waiting for a good going-over."

"Waterfront?" Waterfront on Pahnec; near the Eternal Isle. Now that was interesting. "It would make the getaway easier," he conceded.

"It's right on the grand channel."

"And that would make us more likely to be spotted." But location-wise… it couldn't be better.

"Which is why you need to make like a local, just hanging around, not attracting attention. When we leave we'll just be another bunch of late-night revellers out on the water."

"There'll be more activity round there coming up to the regatta."

"We're planning on going in a couple of days after; still plenty of people partying to give our local punstman the excuse for a late fare, but the militia will've relaxed a bit." Jemulf leaned across the table. "So, you in?"

He didn't want to appear too eager. "I'll think about it."

Tamak was back from school when he returned to Sharrey's; sent home early, and now confined to bed. Sorne resisted the urge to check on him. It wasn't as though the boy was his own flesh and blood. He only felt this way because Sharrey's son was eight years old, halfway between the ages of his two boys when the rain-fever took them. That had been over a decade ago. But still his foolish old heart softened for the boy, damnit.

He needed to get a grip. Because if the duke's last note was anything to go by, then one day soon those feelings were going to be a problem.

CHAPTER 17

Dej stumbled in the failing light. Her reactions saved her from a bad fall but she still came down onto her knees. The heavy backpack pulled her off-balance. She flopped onto her side to lie half curled amongst the pebbles next to the mountain beck she'd been following.

She'd walked without stopping all day; a hard, mindless march, not thinking about anything beyond where her foot would come down next.

But now her body wouldn't take her any further. And that left her mind free to acknowledge the pain. It tore through her like cold lightning. *How could he do that?* How could she be stupid enough to fall in love with someone capable of doing that?

She couldn't even name him, couldn't think directly of him. She drew a long deep breath and sobbed. Breathed again. Sobbed again, her body shaking and convulsing, the jagged throb of her injured ribs adding a physical note to her silent song of pain. She curled tighter, against the pain, but kept sobbing. Dry, quivering sobs. Skykin can't cry.

Suddenly the pain flared into anger. She put her hand to her forehead, grinding the heel of her palm into the point between her eyes where her animus had entered her. "You," she ground out, "you took all I had! I can't sing. I can't even cry!"

She'd once thought that the emptiness inside would be filled by her animus. Instead she'd just become a vessel to extend its life.

She realised she was humming. She'd stopped sobbing, at least. And she'd found something else to be angry at, besides *him*.

She hummed louder. The stronger her voice got the less musical it sounded, and she knew from bitter experience that any attempt to sing would sound like a pig being strangled, but fighting her body to make something like music gave her something to focus on. When her voice cracked and died she opened her eyes. Stars had come out overhead.

She crawled free of the backpack then pulled the cloak out the top of it. She wrapped herself up, then put her arms around her pack, pulling it close. It was all she had, and she clung to it, taking simple comfort from its heavy, neutral physicality, humming herself to sleep.

Someone was nearby. Dej opened her eyes. Still dark. A darker shape moved on the far side of the stream, between her and that glowing patch of vegetation.

She came fully awake, her skykin senses singing as her voice never could. She shrugged free of the cloak like a cat edging back before striking, paused for a moment, then jumped to her feet, snatching up her stolen sword. Diamond sparked in the moonlight as she leapt over her pack, sword whirling. An unearthly scream erupted from her throat.

The skykin who'd been sneaking up on her froze for a heartbeat, then turned and ran upstream. He had a short-stave but showed no sign of stopping to use it. Dej ran after him, splashing through the stream, screaming incoherently. He sped up. She kept running, kept screaming. Only when the intruder disappeared over the brow of the hill did she stop and look around, her chest sore and throbbing.

She was alone. She neither saw nor sensed any other threat. Shame: she was spoiling for a fight. She held herself in a combat crouch, shoulders heaving, hands twitching, while the urge to do violence drained away.

Still no one nearby. She sighed. No more sleep tonight.

She cast around until she found her pack, then shouldered it and started walking, fast and determined, down the gulley. With a low Greymoon and the skyland stars the only light, she had to keep half an eye on the terrain, but she also extended her senses farther afield, in case the attacker came back, with friends.

He had to be a clanless. She'd sensed, in the split second between waking and attacking, his gender, his race and that he was not in good health. There'd been nothing familiar about him but that was no surprise; she hadn't got to know the clanless well before inadvertently leading most of them to their doom.

The survivors would not be pleased to see her.

She upped her pace. When the gulley turned north she paused. She'd been heading northwest because that was the direction the terrain took her but the clanless settlement was north and a little west of the red valley. She needed to avoid that.

She climbed the gulley side and cut southwest. When, towards the end of the day, she came across a mountain bog she took the easier detour, due west.

As the Sun grew lower, the land opened out into a great plateau. She'd visited these uplands with the clanless, to set an ambush for the shadowkin caravan on the orders of their shadowy Zekti patron. The unguarded thought let in a surge of pain, because that was how she'd met *him*. She clamped down on the emotion.

This was nightwing country. She'd heard a nightwing once, in the distance; its unearthly cry had filled her with terror. She had no desire to get close enough to see one.

Or did she? What if she stayed out here, exposed and unprotected, and dared one of the world's most fearsome creatures to put an end to her misery? Assuming her animus let her.

She shook her head. Too easy. But if she didn't want to end up as a nightwing's dinner she needed to find shelter before darkness fell.

The vegetation on the plateau was lush but low, nothing to provide cover. Then, as the Sun touched the mountains, she saw something odd. Just off to the right a stand of plants grew high, in an unexpectedly regular shape. She hurried over.

The shape resolved itself into a roofless house, a square vegetation-covered box. No windows, but an open doorway, wider and higher than any normal door; it covered half the wall facing her. She crept closer, cautious and alert; some creatures might consider this an ideal lair. But she sensed no complex life save a faint mental warmth from one of the vines covering part of the structure: it had an animate portion that brought back dead creatures to feed the plant-part, but she was both too large and too lively to be of interest.

Up close she saw there was a roof after all, just a flat one. She stuck her head inside. The last rays of the Sun shone in slantwise, showing an open space with growths on the walls. The far wall wasn't vertical but diagonal, sloping down at a steep angle.

She entered. The plant life inside was sparser, just the carrion-vine and various moss- or mushroom-type stuff that didn't need much light. Pale grey walls showed between the multi-coloured patches of furry or scaly growth. Dej ran a hand along a section of bare wall. It was smooth, and cool. Not brick or stone or wood. Some sort of metal? She didn't think there was this much metal in the whole world.

The diagonal wall was even odder. Faint daylight shone through at the very top. It was transparent, like glass, though smothered in vegetation most of the way up.

This had to be some pre-Separation wonder, built by the Children of the First themselves. Which made it unholy, spiritually dangerous – for shadowkin. For a lone skykin, it was just somewhere to shelter from nightwings.

She examined the vegetation, locating a vine whose swollen stem-parts had a soft and succulent centre. She pulled some off the outside wall near the door, and sucked out the sweet heart of the plant. Then she settled down against the wall across from the door, wrapped in her cloak. Though this was the most alien place she'd ever been, somehow being here felt right. *It's disconnected from everything, by time. I'm disconnected from everything, by choice.*

She lulled herself to sleep constructing extravagant, limitless fancies about the god-like beings who might once have lived in this place.

CHAPTER 18

Sadakh looked down at the body. "I'm sorry, old friend," he said, as he picked up the knife.

The obsidian blade slid through Ritek's cool flesh; blood welled from the cut, thick and dark. *Blood is the source...* His ghost sounded almost gleeful. But she was right.

This was the freshest body Sadakh had ever dissected, but it brought no joy.

When Ereket, Ritek's wife, had turned up at the priory this morning Sadakh had been shocked: for her to come to him was unheard of. With the use of mime and a writing pad she explained how she had woken to find Ritek dead in bed beside her.

Pausing only long enough to summon a bodyguard, Sadakh had taken one of the priory's punts over to the islet near the edge of the city where she and her husband had their innocuous little laundry business.

Ritek had indeed died in his sleep though his face was frozen in a near-comical expression of surprised discomfort, as though he had been struck down by indigestion. Sadakh had comforted Ereket but explained that he needed to examine her husband's body before it was taken to the pyres. She had nodded, even as tears ran down her face.

Sadakh drew the blade across the soft flesh below the ribs, then downwards, and across. Ritek's skin still showed residual redness from taking the serum. He peeled back the flap of fat-crusted skin to reveal the gut. The organs within looked healthy enough, wet and shining, no obvious blemishes or swellings. So why had Ritek died?

A month ago this would have been a sad mystery. Today, it was a disaster. Ritek had been the first subject since the Shenese boy to survive taking the serum. And now he had died: suddenly, inexplicably. Despite the closeness of the room, Sadakh shivered.

He worked quickly, and did not probe as deeply as he could have. He needed to leave the body in a suitable state to be wrapped in a shroud for transport across the lake before sunset. He could hear Ereket crying in the corridor outside. Like her husband, she'd had her tongue removed as a punishment during her previous, criminal life; her empty mouth made her hollow sobs sound disturbingly childlike.

Nothing looked amiss in the body cavity, save the heart being perhaps a little bigger than expected. He took samples of blood and scrapings from various organs, placing some on his quartz examining slivers, preserving others in fluids the launderers had procured for him. Then he closed, bound and wrapped the body. His bodyguard carried Ritek's remains out to the parlour where he prayed with Ereket then left her to wait for the deathsmen.

Back in the workroom, he placed his magnifying-frame near the window. He adjusted the angle of the vertical wooden viewing-tube and tilted the specimen tray to catch the last of the daylight. He still smiled to remember the moment when he had first fitted the newly-ground lenses inside the tube and examined a drop of lake-water. He'd been amazed to find it alive with a myriad of strange creatures.

But blood had been the breakthrough. It too had structure. Comparing blood, of the living and the dead, of skykin and shadowkin, had got him thinking on its nature. Then he read a treatise from Physic of Pelk, on how the combined saliva and blood of a horse that had survived jaw-rot, when dripped into a scratch on the nose of its infected foal, had cured the young beast.

The key to creating what he now knew was called a serum, and ensuring it was accepted by the subject's body, was to combine the animus extract with the blood of the subject.

Ritek's blood looked much as he expected; similarly the samples of organ tissue. No clue as to why a substance designed to extend life might end it. This was one piece of news the caliarch would not be hearing.

He had to consider the possibility of failure, and what that meant, both for the caliarch and for himself. *Your mortality, creeping up on you...* Perhaps his ghost was right, although he felt well enough. But if his span was not near its end and the caliarch died before him then his own life would be more pleasant, and perhaps longer, if Prince Mekteph was not his enemy. And making overtures of friendship might lull Mekteph into a sense of security which Sadakh had every intention of shattering if – *when* – his work succeeded.

The prince had never made a direct threat, and was always coldly polite to his face. But there had been three attempts on Sadakh's life in the last five years, two of them within the priory walls. Every one was designed to look like an accident or unexplained death. None of them could be directly linked to Mekteph but no one else had reason or means to cause him harm. Of course, if the prince really wanted him dead then an ambush during a visit to the Eternal Isle would achieve his aims. But his death would create a power vacuum which the prince was not currently in a position to exploit; the last failed assassination had led Sadakh to re-assess the most recently appointed of his twelve poliarchs. His investigations revealed links, through a family scandal and an unfortunate debt, to Mekteph. Sadakh had demoted the priest in question and transferred him out to the provinces: where possible, he preferred to show leniency to those who wished him harm. Loyalty freely earned and rewarded was more lasting than that secured through fear and self-interest. Mekteph, proud and entitled, liked to be feared. And he liked to play games. Perhaps Sadakh needed to show some humility in these changing times, and play along.

When he got back to the priory, he penned a brief note: just the words *Would you consider a meeting, on neutral ground?* Getting it to the prince without compromising his agents on the Eternal Isle would take some care, but the eunuchs were right: it was time to open a dialogue.

A week later a note came from the launderers' house. Not from the prince; just a report from one of his skyland agents, a little earlier than scheduled. He broke the seal and read:

from your servant who watchs the red valley
i saw some odd things i think you shoud know

Sadakh grimaced to himself; the clanless, having been educated in crèches like any other skykin children, could technically read and write, but were far from erudite.

a skykin woman came here a few weeks ago from the south. i did not see her for days then saw her from a distance. she was around the shadowkin camp and the men were all right with that.

a couple of weeks later another skykin came, also from the south. i did not see him much as it was raining and i was out foraging but there was something wrong with him. he looked like he had been walking for days but there was more than that. a few days later the first skykin left the camp going north. she acted angry and upset. i followed her but she chased me off.

i went back to the camp. the next day i saw the skykin man proper for the first time. he does not look well but now i am sure that this is the one you want to know about, who is like a skykin, but not! that is why i left the valley and come straight back to give this report to your man in the umbral.

Sadakh lowered the paper, as his ghost chimed in, *Is it the Shenese boy?*

It sounded like it. Understanding the nature of his first successful test subject's change was essential to making the serum fully effective. But he had no idea who he was, save that he was a young noble who had run away from trouble in Shen, and that while his fever burned he had cried out for someone called "Ree".

He needed to get a message back, to send all the clanless – or what remained of them – to the red valley to find and capture the boy and bring him back to Zekt. If it wasn't too late...

Something else nagged at him. The spy talked about not being able to see the boy clearly because of the rain; not because it was dark, just because of the weather. And the spy's account of the boy looking "like a skykin but not" supported the clanless's seer original claim that he appeared "part skykin" now. All of which pointed to his test subject being outside, in the skyland, during the day.

The Sun! Sadakh's lips curled into a smile. Of course! His ghost voiced his realisation, the missing part of the puzzle: *The Sun is the key.*

CHAPTER 19

The next few weeks confirmed Rhia's opinion. Her apprentice wanted to learn and was no fool but trying to induct an untrained mind into her life's work in a couple of months would be a near-impossible task.

He was a useful assistant though, with neat handwriting and a good head for basic arithmetic. And his questions were just the sort that might be raised at her trial.

Kerne was also settling into the household. The youngest cat, Pathi, twined herself around his legs as soon as he walked through the door, then rolled over bonelessly, waiting to be picked up. Rhia tried not to see this as an obscure but positive omen though she did waive her "no cats in the study" rule, provided Pathi stayed on Kerne's lap or desk.

As she grew used to her apprentice's presence in the house she went back to wearing comfortable clothing; climbing up to her observation platform was much easier in men's garb. One particularly hot day she did not even bother with her mask. When she caught Kerne looking at her oddly she flushed, then made herself smile and said, "I sense a question unrelated to our work."

"I shouldn't pry."

She would rather he did not, but he was here to ask questions. "You are curious about my scars."

"I... Yes." It was his turn to flush. "I heard there was an accident with your father's chemicals."

He must have asked his own father about it. "That's right, an accident. When I was a girl." However familiar they were becoming, some matters should remain private. "If my damaged face distracts you, I will cover it."

He looked away. After that she made sure she put her mask on before he arrived, no matter how the heat made her face itch.

Though she kept up her study of it, the Book of Separation continued to appear impenetrable, paradoxical, or pointless. The gap between faith and reason was too wide. In one passage the Pillar of Fire was called "the sign and the means, given by the First, to show the sundered race they were his Children no more, but were two different peoples, forever divided" while in another it was described simply as "the First's wrath, burning down the path from heaven". That latter reference could apply to the Harbinger, perhaps in a time when its straight tail had been more prominent. Could those below have interpreted its appearance as a sign of heavenly fury? But no enquirers' papers spoke of the Harbinger being seen earlier than a few hundred years ago. And the skykin seer on the caravan to Zekt, drawing on the ancient memories of her animus, had said as much. It was disconcerting to think of such instability in the heavens.

There was instability enough in the world below. Last fourday, unrest in the lower city had become a full-scale riot. She had heard the ruckus through her study window, and had the staff close shutters and lock the doors, though the riot had petered out before reaching the upper city. Brynan later said the militia were slow to respond, and had done so only in small numbers. Perhaps Francin wished to avoid the heavy-handed tactics used during the last drought. For those who preferred piety to fury, rain-vigils had become a weekly occurrence.

Nerilyn reported no more odd jaunts from the duke. Nor, it appeared, had he further restricted his wife's movements. Rhia sometimes thought Francin still loved Alharet, in his own peculiar way. As, in some ways, did Rhia. They had been such confidantes, true friends… and when they last spoke, more than two years ago now, Alharet had thought they still could be, despite the woes she had caused Rhia.

More refusals, and a few more testimonials, came through from the enquirers. She understood why no one in the network would come to her aid, and every reason given made sense. But each refusal nibbled away at her confidence, making her feel more alone in her quest to bring this great truth to the world.

Today the post-boy brought only a note from the duke. She unfolded the letter with mixed hope and trepidation:

Cousin:

I am pleased to report that the cardinals have accepted the appointment of Lord Jertine as second judge.

Rhia relaxed a fraction. Jertine, a Viscount in House Manacar, was one of the few nobles who preferred pursuits of the intellect over politics or frivolous leisure. Granted, he mainly applied his intellect to games and wagers, but he was curious and independent-minded, and not overly pious. In short, the best they could hope for. The final judge, drawn by lot, was yet to be appointed. She read on:

However, I also have less pleasing news. Etyan and his lover were seen at the red valley where they had some sort of altercation. She stormed off. He followed on a little later. As the Sun was up my men were unable to follow, but he appears to have gone northwards, deeper into the skyland.

Rhia held the paper between her hands and took a long, slow breath. She was used to her brother's absence but considered it a temporary state. Now he was truly gone.

He wouldn't be taking a wife before her trial. And no House had expressed any interest in putting forward a husband for her. She would have one last opportunity to secure her House's future before the trial, though it was an option she dreaded. She put the note down.

Now that Etyan's self-absorption had put him beyond reach

perhaps it was safe to contact the one ally she had so far avoided calling on.

The recently appointed Meddler of Zekt also held another, more public position: he was the eparch, head of the Church in Zekt, although he did not appear to let his faith interfere with acute and objective enquiry. And what better witness than a Church grandee to support her case?

Although she had assessed the quality of his work and once heard him preach – a sermon that left her inspired, rather than exasperated – she had never met Eparch Sadakh. But Etyan had. Her brother claimed he used a false name in the Zekti priory but he could still have given away his identity while in his delirium – a delirium the eparch appeared to have induced.

Given his position, she doubted Eparch Sadakh would come to Shen in person but he might send a representative. What if that representative knew of the eparch's interest in her brother? After all, someone had employed rogue skykin to kidnap Etyan; she had assumed that had been down to politics, but it could have been the eparch trying to recover his "experiment".

The letter she wrote did not, of course, mention Etyan. It did ask whether Meddler of Zekt might consider sending "someone with weight in the Church" to speak for her in person at her trial.

She only hoped she would not have cause to regret the request.

The next two weeks brought the last few refusals to attend her trial, along with two more testimonials, bringing the total to seven. She only hoped these positive words from distant scholars would do some good.

She also received a more welcome note, from Skywatcher of Lhir. She had already worked out that the world took two years to orbit the Sun – a rain-year and a dry-year – as that was the time it took for the constellations to return to their original position in the sky. This had made sense of some mathematical conundrums, but now her fellow enquirer proposed a startling new idea. Although his main area of interest was the Moons, his reception of her new theory had been wholeheartedly positive – he had even built his own sightglass – and Rhia cursed the great distance between their two shadowlands; correspondence took months to pass between them. She had sent him her initial workings but the time lag had tried her patience – hence, foolishly, trying to enlist the mathematical skills of Theorist of Shen.

Skywatcher's latest papers proposed that the orbits of the world and the Strays – he used the general term "planets" to distinguish them from the fixed stars – might not be circular as she had been assuming but might instead be elliptical. When she read the letter she spent some time staring into space, grinning and occasionally going *ahah*, until Kerne asked if she was alright.

The next day brought another positive development. For the last three nights observations had been hampered by cloudy skies. Clouds had covered the city several times since the Harbinger had gone, sealing in the heat and promising rain that never came, but after hours of low rumblings a deafening peal of evening thunder announced a spattering of great, heavy drops. Within moments the drops thickened to a downpour. Kerne had stopped working at the sound of thunder, his mouth open slightly. Now Rhia stood, and said, "Let's have a look, shall we?"

They ran to the study window. Sense said they should close the shutters but her heart had risen as the rain fell. Rhia leaned out the window. She smiled at Kerne, who grinned back and leaned out with her. They reached upwards, catching drops in their open hands, letting the rain run into their hair and down their necks, laughing like children.

The drought had finally broken.

CHAPTER 20

This ancient shelter had a lot going for it. Water from a pool nearby. A dry place to sleep. No chance of getting eaten while you slept. Dej found herself ranging farther afield for food as the days passed, though that was fine; it gave her something to do.

But with few other distractions, unwelcome thoughts and long-buried memories started leaking in, triggered by the oddest things.

Despite the reasonable pickings she felt both nauseous and hungry, and kept dipping into her shadowkin supplies. But whenever she gave in and took a sliver of dried meat or hard biscuit from the rucksack she found herself thinking of the weekly "treats" handed out by Mar, the clanless leader, and that made her think about Kir, the only clanless who ever showed her any kindness… and whose death she'd caused. She'd had to carry her friend's severed head around until the animus inside it finally died.

The lack of distraction reminded her of the contemplation room back at the crèche, where she'd spent too many miserable days growing up. She thought of Min, her childhood friend, who had let her down at the last. Also dead now.

Etyan wasn't dead. The girl he raped was. But the person she'd loved more than Min or Kir, had loved more than life itself until she found out what he really was, he was still in the world. And despite what she now knew, he was still in her heart, damn him.

Finding a familiar stem-plant whilst foraging she remembered how he'd pulled a face when she brought some back for him, then smiled and told her it tasted of strawberry.

Watching the sky and picking out the Stepping Horse she remembered Etyan telling her it was his favourite constellation, but not to admit to his sister that he had a favourite.

One week in she tried to play the flute to entertain herself and found herself turning the instrument over in her hands, thinking about the times she'd played it for Etyan.

If anything, the pain was getting worse.

Then she saw the caravan, and realised what she had to do. As she sat in the shadow of the house's doorway one morning, two huge wagons crept into sight across the plateau, pulled by rhinobeasts. Neither the skykin driving the wagons nor the outriders mounted on smaller 'beasts gave any sign of knowing she was only a couple of hundred yards away, but being this close to the caravan with its cargo of shadowkin travellers made her uncomfortable.

She needed to move on.

The direction to head in didn't take much thought. Back at the crèche the geography tutor had called the shadowlands five bands of beads strung across the face of the world. They formed a pattern like the cells of a beehive. Each shadowland was several days' walk across, and the distance between them was that and half again.

She needed to get away from the shadowlands. That meant following her innate sense of direction, and heading north.

She set off at dawn the next day. Initially she struck northeast, because due north would take her too close to Zekt. She needed to pass between Zekt and Marn. After that, she'd be truly free.

When she came off the plateau the landscape was still mountainous but damper, with more vegetation. Occasional drizzle thickened to pounding rain as darkness approached. She stopped to put the cloak on. She was on a steep slope, and she'd been concentrating on her path through the damp scree, but now she recalled a different slope; deeper, steeper and ending in a lethal ravine. She'd led the clanless onto it without any idea of the danger, and though she'd felt the landslide a moment before it swept down on them, that had only been enough to save her and the two shadowkin captives. The others died. And it was her fault.

She started walking again, faster now. *Ignore the memory, and concentrate on the simple pleasure of sensing the land.*

Her stomach growled. *Ignore the hunger, because hunger is weakness.*

Darkness fell. *Ignore the darkness, because I can see well enough to carry on.*

The rain continued to pound down, soaking through her woollen cloak. She ignored that too, but just as the sky was lightening she tripped over the cloak's sodden hem and slammed into the mud. She lay there for a while, then shrugged off her pack and pulled herself free of the mire. She started to crawl upslope, out of the half-flooded valley. Ahead, through the rain, a rocky overhang formed a small cave. She dragged herself into the shelter, then fell onto her side, and slept.

She woke with a start in bright sunlight, her hand going to a sudden, stabbing pain in her forearm. Her fingers brushed, then crushed, the hard-bodied beastie sucking at her blood. She shrieked in pain and anger, then focused. Some sort of giant beetle-thing with a now-cracked saucer-shaped carapace of scarlet and gold. She lifted the palm-sized body, its pincers still waving. Hunger and fury took over. *You, eat me?* No, you little fucker: *I'll eat you.* Despite the warning stab of pain in her forehead, she sucked at the shattered creature's innards. The gelatinous gloop tasted like glue and boiled cabbage. When she'd sucked it dry she threw the remnants away with a triumphant *hah!*

She should've listened to her animus. The sickness came on quick and hard. She kept retching long after she was empty inside, then lay huddled amongst the rocks, the rain forming a damp curtain just beyond her nose.

Everything was gone. The past. Etyan. Hope. The contents of her stomach. She laughed, or rather croaked and called the sound a laugh. When it's gone it's gone: doesn't matter whether it's a faithless lover or a rotten meal.

The rain eased off. Clouds blew through. She watched night fall, lying on her sodden cloak, her mind as empty as her guts.

As Whitemoon rose she wondered what might find her now, lying here helpless, and eat her. Somewhat to her irritation, nothing did.

The rain returned the next day. Her stupid body demanded water. She half slithered, half pushed herself out of the cave far enough to get her head under the curtain of droplets cascading off the edge of the overhanging rock. She opened her mouth until enough liquid went in, then wriggled back inside. Night fell, and she dozed.

The next day she awoke unexpectedly clear-headed.

Picking at the thin scab that time had put over her love for Etyan hurt but she had to see things how they really were. Then she could die in peace.

He'd never loved her. That was obvious now. He'd been intrigued by her, and she provided an ideal escape from the "problems" of his rich and privileged life. And he'd wanted her. Not for herself, obviously. But he'd wanted to fuck her. She must have been quite a novelty, even with his *previous experience*.

The nausea was back, but with nothing inside to throw up it came as cramps that went on and on, blanking her mind and contorting her body.

When the cramps passed it was dark again, and her body was a wan and distant thing. She just needed to face up to the full truth and she'd be done with the world, with life.

Yes, love was illusion – or rather self-delusion. Even so, it had felt wonderful. She had enough distance to acknowledge that, to examine memories of perfect moments without being crippled by the pain: morning light on Etyan's face as he slept; laughing together at the smallest thing; just sitting, holding his hand.

Once I had that. But it wasn't real. I have nothing now. I am nothing, now. So I'm ready to let go.

The Sun was coming up.

She'd barely noticed the night-time noises, the background whirrs and buzzes of skyland life, but with the new day came a surge of sound. One whirring call grew faster, more energetic, developing a secondary drone note, a complex hypnotic rhythm. Another lilting call started up some way off, like distant breathless chanting. Nearby, something started to purr softly, gentle as a contented cat.

Now, as she was ready to leave it, the world was finally singing to her.

Sunlight touched her hand, flung out the cave. Its warmth, sustaining and comforting, felt good.

Having finally noticed, really *noticed*, the world, she felt herself expanding out into it. She'd let go yet remained conscious, and now experienced reality with an intensity she hadn't imagined possible.

She reached out a trembling finger to trace a line of white crystal embedded in the rock near her head. Her hand slipped, and her finger dipped into a tiny hollow at the base of the rock. She felt softness there, some hidden growth – her animus confirmed it was a plant, and harmless. Soft as duck down, a little warm to the touch. The faint scent of honey and summer roses. She smiled, cracking her dry lips.

The world was glorious.

Yet she'd seen so little of it! And, she realised, she wanted to. She'd been avoiding reality when she should have been embracing it. Having nothing meant having nothing to worry about. It meant just being.

But making the most of being – just surviving at all – would take some effort.

This was probably just her animus talking, trying to keep her alive so it could live. Well, they were stuck with each other. And the world would continue, with or without her. Them.

She pulled herself over the damp, rocky ground to her discarded pack, half buried in the mud. Her arms trembled as she pulled at the flap. The food was well-wrapped in wax paper, and hadn't spoiled. The first packet contained hard biscuits. She wormed an arm in deeper and found a compacted block of dried fruit. When she peeled off a strip and put it in her mouth she gagged, but she made herself suck, using what little saliva she had left. She had no idea what fruit it was, but when she mashed it against the roof of her mouth with her tongue something thick and sweet trickled down her throat. When it hit her belly it burned, and she braced herself. She would keep this down, despite the urge to retch; she needed to accept this tiny shred of nourishment. She ate another piece; it went down easier.

"I listened to you," she said, and tapped herself on the forehead with a knuckle, "all right?"

It appeared she had decided to live.

CHAPTER 21

Sorne had lost the knack of waiting. He'd had his share of keeping watch back in the militia in Shen, but two years of ducking and diving in Zekt left him out of practice. Even sitting in a punt in a darkened waterway he was restless and on edge.

Or perhaps it was just that he was waiting for his friends, or the nearest he had to friends here, to commit a crime.

The house remained dark. Two storeys, six windows. Good view from those top windows.

He'd dropped Jemulf and Breta off on the far side of Pahnec, and they'd made their way to the house's "street entrance", although with no carts or animals in the city Mirror didn't have streets as such. Then he'd come here to wait. A dark face had appeared briefly at a bottom window, so he knew they'd got in safely; now it was up to them to keep checking whether he'd raised his lantern, usually the signal that a punt was available for hire but now their agreed sign that trouble was on the way.

There was no one about, but if anyone did peg him as more than a puntsman waiting for a late-night fare, he'd be off. He liked Jemulf and Breta, and their friendship was useful, but he needed to keep his head down. He had, as the Zekti saying went, bigger fish to fry.

Last time he'd done something like this it hadn't ended well.

They'd met resistance, then one of his own men had tried to take Countess Harlyn hostage. Which wouldn't have happened had the damn woman not insisted on coming with them into the priory in the first place, but she wasn't one to be told what to do.

Tonight's jaunt wouldn't please the woman currently giving him grief. Not that Sharrey ever said anything when he stayed out late working for Jemulf. And she was happy enough to take the few extra marks he handed over. It was just that look she gave him when he did.

Her own work at the paper-pressers barely kept up the rent on their rooms and put rice on the table. Jemulf said households that took in outsiders on Arec got paid a small stipend but Sharrey had expensive habits. He liked that she wanted to send her son to school but had no idea what she saw in those painted porcelain plates she collected.

Paying the locals to take in foreigners made sense: keeping all the visitors together on one islet made it easier to keep an eye on people who'd had good reason to flee their original shadowland. Like Jemulf and Breta: Breta had been an arena-fighter; Faro was known for its women warriors. When she'd refused to throw an important match those who controlled the betting came for her. An enforcer had ended up dead. So they'd run.

He scratched under his dark wig. It was rather threadbare, having been stuffed in the bottom of his pack while he was wandering the umbral then stashed at the lock-up with everything else Sharrey didn't need to know about.

Perhaps he shouldn't worry about Sharrey. He knew the type: she didn't want to know. When he'd bought her a commemorative regatta plate to remind her of her lovely day out with her friends she'd thanked him with a kiss, and not asked where he'd got the money from.

Tonight was threeday, so not a usual late night for him – he still stayed out on the nights he'd been at the training-rooms, even though the rooms had closed – but when he said not to wait up she'd just nodded, like she expected no better, then said not to wake Tamak when he got in. The boy's aches and twinges made it hard for him to sleep through these days.

A crash from inside the house. Sorne's head shot up.

No lights, no immediate commotion. Sounded like a dropped pot.

The noise gave him the excuse for a more serious look around. A few upstairs lights still showed in some of the other houses along the waterfront. The Eternal Isle loomed close to one side, lit with lamps strung along the eaves. The only sound was the ever-present lap of water. No obvious reaction to the noise. One last glance around, then he lowered his head again.

People were such fools. Himself included, of course. Sharrey was like his own mother, and like Dulima, the mother of his boys. He'd driven Dulima off after they lost their sons, because he wanted someone to blame, and she'd been conditioned to believe that it should be her. She was right to leave him, after he hit her, after he'd broken his promise to himself that he'd never become his father. Yes, fools one and all.

But individual, foolish people made up nations. Little fools could still make something big and worthwhile. If he'd been born in Zekt perhaps he'd be comfortable with perpetual rain, ridiculous hairstyles and nothing decent to sit on, maybe even with slavery and crazy rulers. But he'd been lucky enough to be born in Shen, ruled by the smartest man he'd ever met, home to sensible clothes and proper furniture and wholesome food. What wouldn't he give for a warm cob loaf...

Movement: Breta's face at a window. He raised his head and affected a stretch, catching her eye in passing. She nodded. He lifted the pole from the bottom of the punt, stood up with care, and pushed off.

Jemulf and Breta were waiting where he'd dropped them off. They climbed into the punt without a word. Their backpacks were full; Breta's clanked; sounded like she had some metal in there. They laid their haul in the bottom of the boat then sat opposite him, still without a word. Sorne pushed off.

Round the first corner, they passed another punt. The couple in it were entwinned with each other, oblivious, but the puntsman gave Sorne an odd look, perhaps for his shaky pole technique, or for his obviously foreign passengers. Sorne made himself smile back as though nothing was amiss.

Three days passed: time enough for the Faroese pair to start selling the scented oils, fine fabric and pair of valuable bronze knives they'd stolen. Perhaps he might even expect some money today. But then Jemulf failed to turn up at Ramek's yard.

He waited through lunch, nursing the same cup of cold tea to an equally cold stare from Ramek's wife. When he couldn't stand it any longer he went for a careful stroll past familiar haunts – the rice-dealer, speaker's square, the empty rooms that had recently been the gym – to an enclosed court whose residents valued their privacy. He didn't even get as far as the entrance. When someone grabbed his arm he tensed and turned. Then he saw Breta's face peering out of the alley he was passing. She nodded, and he slid into the shadows beside her. The alley was so narrow they had to stand side-by-side to talk, but they were out of sight.

"What happened?" muttered Sorne.

"We were raided last night."

"The militia?" Sorne went cold. If the Zekti authorities got their hands on the duke's letters he was screwed.

Breta shook her head. "Locals. Woke up to a knife at my throat, damnit." She'd hate being overpowered like that.

"You all right?"

"They didn't hurt us. No point: they got what they wanted."

"The stash from the robbery?"

"That's what they came for. I told Jem that tip-off was too good!"

"So these were Zekti criminals who got you to do their dirty work, then walked in and took the goods?"

"Got it in one, my friend."

"And the lock-up?" In a city of baked brick and bundled reeds the reinforced strong room at the back of the Faroese couple's digs was a valuable resource. It'd cost Sorne a large cut of the duke's money to secure one of the ironwood-fronted lockers built into it.

"Trashed that too. That's why I stopped you. Been trying to let people know subtly. Not sure who else is watching."

Sorne's chest felt tight. "My stuff. Is it... Did they take everything?"

"You had some coin in there, yeah?"

"I did." Quite a lot. But money could be replaced. "There were some papers too..."

"The cash they took. The papers ended up all over the floor." She turned her head to look him in the eye. "Couldn't help reading some of them."

Sorne made himself breathe. "I can't blame you for that." It felt like someone else's voice speaking. "But I'd be interested to know what you thought."

"Well." She pulled her near-hairless head back a little; this was an absurd, intimate meeting. But though they might be allies, they both had secrets. And they were both killers. "Interesting to see you've got a legit identity after all."

She meant the papers he'd used when he first entered the city. Given how he'd left, as far as the authorities were concerned the Shenese baker called Sorne was still living in Mirror. "I'm really not that person any more."

She inclined her head, acknowledging the necessary expedience. "The other papers were... odd."

The duke's letters weren't written in code. That would have been suspicious in itself. But they were sparse and lacking in specifics with places or events just alluded to – "the location you were looking for" or "the events of a decade ago" – and names reduced to a single letter. The duke trusted Sorne to work out what or who he meant. "They might seem that way to you, yes." he offered.

"And one had these weird pictures on. Some sort of diagram..."

"What happened to them?"

"Your papers? I gathered them up. Got them here." She pulled a leather pouch from her tunic and handed it over. "We owe you that much for the inconvenience. But I'm afraid our arrangement is at an end."

"I see." Sorne kept his tone even.

"It's been good knowing you, for all your secrets. Good to have someone around who understands discipline, and knows the joy of the fight. But the break-in, coming on the back of the troubles with the training-room. Me and Jem are taking the hint. We're moving on, leaving Zekt."

"I'll be sorry to see you go." And he meant it, he realised. "Have you decided where to?"

"Not yet. Xuin or Marn I guess. Might even be Shen. Heard it never rains there. That right?"

"Hardly ever. You'd wouldn't need to worry too much about getting mildew on your leathers."

"Of course this doesn't have to be the end. You could come with us."

"To Shen?" He must be messed up: the thought of home made his heavy heart leap. But most of those he'd cared for in Shen were gone now, and all being well he'd be seeing his old home soon enough.

"To wherever."

He made a show of sucking at his lip. "Tempting. But I've still got unfinished business here."

Breta grinned. "I'll bet you do."

CHAPTER 22

Sadakh put down his quill with a sigh. He had promised himself he would not neglect his flock. Being eparch was his destiny and if it became an eternal destiny, that would be an honour he would strive to live up to. But as the weeks passed his spiritual energy was being drained by other concerns. He just couldn't summon the concentration to write a new restday sermon. Last night, the animus he had used to create the serum had finally died. It was not the disaster it could have been; he was already working on ways to replicate the serum without going back to the source. Not that there was much point until he had managed to prove it worked.

The caliarch was ailing. His annual birthday regatta had gone off without a hitch, but out in the daylight Numak's frailty had been evident to all. His end was not far off.

If only the prince would respond. Even if that response was just a dismissive note, at least he would know where he stood.

If only his clanless agents would report back on, or better still, bring back the Shenese boy. Assuming they dared: they would never attack the encampment directly; whatever was going on in the red valley, the Duke of Shen valued it enough to guard it. But if the boy left the camp alone, or with a minimal escort, they could take him. Blood was the key to the serum, and that boy's blood was as valuable as pure iron.

Last but not least, if only Ereket would return. It had been nearly four weeks since he had sent her out to the umbral camp he maintained in the forests owned by the caliarch.

He looked up at a knock on the door. "The day's post, your Holiness."

"Bring it in."

He had hoped the bundle of correspondence his secretary handed over might contain something to address at least one of his concerns, but it looked like the usual letters from those seeking advice or potential initiation.

Wait, what is that?

At his ghost's urging he reached into the loose pile spread across his desk. He had nearly missed the odd letter out, because it was just that: a letter. Most correspondence from the natural enquirers came as tight-wrapped packages containing multiple pages. He turned it over in his hand: vellum not parchment, and he recognised that writing. The timing fitted with the caravan to Shen too. He opened it with care, read the single-sided sheet, then sat back in his seat.

The situation Observer of Shen found herself in was no surprise. He had only skimmed most of the papers she had sent his way before passing them on to enquirers further along the network; thanks to his other commitments, he barely had time to read and copy those treatises related to his own interests, let alone those dealing with other matters of enquiry. But he knew enough of her work to see how her theories might bring her into conflict with the Church in Shen. He had cause to be grateful to her: her writings on optics had led him to come up with his magnifier-frame. He also liked the idea of a woman in the network, given how many institutions failed to credit the female gender with proper critical faculties.

That did not did mean he would drop everything and rush to her defence, of course. But perhaps he could assist her remotely. He refolded the letter. He needed to think about this.

That evening Dalent, his female Marnese guard, came to see him. She had been staying at the launderers' house, empty now Ritek was dead and Ereket absent, dealing discretely with visitors and deliveries and guarding his hidden workroom. When she reported that Ereket had finally returned, Sadakh hurried back with her.

Ereket had changed, but not the transformation the boy had apparently undergone; she was still a shadowkin, albeit one in obvious pain from her raw, burnt skin. She kept her head down and did not meet his eyes.

Taklew, the guard who had accompanied her into the skyland, said Ereket had been happy to remain beyond the umbral all day while he watched from the shade of the forest. Sadakh asked Taklew to confirm whether Ereket had also spent time out under the open Sun, beyond the umbral clouds.

"We took the tent out into the deep skyland, being careful of the creatures and plants you warned us of, Holiness." A slight puzzlement showed in Taklew's tone; perhaps he wondered how his master knew so much about the skyland. "The burning on Ereket's skin got worse and it was unpleasant for me, even in the tent."

"You have both made me proud."

Ereket looked up at that. Sadakh gave her a fulsome smile, then pushed the note paper across the kitchen table to her. "How do you feel?" he asked gently.

She wrote one word. *Burnt.*

Sadakh nodded. "I am sorry you are in pain. I will send a salve. But is the burning just on the outside? Do you feel any change within?"

She wrote. *Just out. Not in.*

"I see." Ereket's limited writing ability had been a positive feature when she was Ritek's co-conspirator – even if interrogated, she could give away little – but her limited self-expression was a hindrance now. "Can you tell me anything else about how you feel?"

Burns + pain outside. Empty inside.

When she said she was empty he suspected that wasn't related to the serum. She had lost the only person she loved. Sadakh knew how that felt, even if his own loss had left him with a unique consolation.

"Taklew and Dalent will return to the priory with me, but Taklew will come back with some medicine, and will stay with you while the burns heal."

Ereket nodded. Of the handful of trusted guards who Sadakh had taken into his confidence, Taklew was the most cultured as well as having some basic medical knowledge. And as his tastes did not run to bedding women Ereket should be comfortable sharing her house with him.

As Dalent poled the punt back to the priory isle Sadakh considered the results of the "Sun experiment" as he had come to think of it.

He had hoped the Sun's pure light might act as a "catalyst", another concept he had got from the enquirers. If the serum only worked fully once activated by the Sun, then Ritek's untimely death was merely a personal tragedy for his wife, not a result of the serum.

But the Sun hadn't changed Ereket. There must be another factor.

Or was the First truly displeased with him, as the caliarch feared? His own view of divinity was complex and ambiguous, but he was not so arrogant as to dismiss the possibility that mysterious powers could influence human destiny; after all, he had a presence in his head which did not fit with either logic or organised religion.

He spent the rest of the journey praying.

Back at the priory his secretary, Viteph, said that a messenger had arrived from the Eternal Isle. Though this was not unprecedented – the caliarch had been known to summon him for ad-hoc advice, spiritual or mundane – he kept Dalent with him when he entered the reception room. The messenger was a stranger, neither one of the handful of lay initiates who worked at the palace nor one of the few courtiers Numak trusted to run personal errands. He wore a servant's garb and stood to give his obeisance when Sadakh entered.

Remaining near the door – and next to his guard – Sadakh said, "Do you bring a message from His Majesty?"

"I have a message from the palace." The man reached into his tunic. Sadakh felt Dalent tense beside him. The man produced a folded note.

"Kindly bring that over and give it to my guard." Some poisons did not require a wound to work, only touch.

Dalent took the note without hesitation despite being aware of such risks. Sadakh observed a slight reticence in the other man, though: he knew he was in dangerous territory.

Dalent unfolded the note and held it where Sadakh could read the two short lines:

If you are serious in your desire for a meeting, come to the southeastern jetty of the Eternal Isle at the fifth hour tomorrow morning. Take whatever precautions you feel necessary.

Sadakh drew a long, slow breath. Had the delay in answering been due to machinations in the palace he was unaware of? Was this gesture a result of some unknown change in circumstances? Or had Mekteph merely chosen to leave him stewing in uncertainty? And should he refuse this offer, made at such short notice with no assurances of safety?

Sadakh looked at the messenger. "I am guessing the prince wishes a prompt answer."

"I am instructed not to leave the priory isle until I have one." The quaver in the man's voice confirmed he was afraid. Perhaps he expected Sadakh capable of the kind of capricious and barbaric acts the prince favoured when crossed.

Sadakh walked past the quaking messenger – this was no trained assassin – and sat at the table. Chin in hand, he went through the options and implications. He kept half an eye on Dalent in case the letter had been poisoned, but she maintained her usual expression, stoic and neutral. The messenger remained standing, trying not to shift from foot to foot.

Finally Sadakh said, "Tell the prince I will meet with him."

CHAPTER 23

Over the next few days Dej ate a quarter of her remaining shadowkin supplies. Not everything stayed down, but she kept eating through the nausea. If she wanted to live, she had to eat.

While her strength returned, instead of getting lost in dark thoughts she got lost in the world around her: the track of the bright Sun across the silver sky, the complex jumbles of rocks, the myriad of small life on and under the ground.

When she woke after a solid night's sleep feeling strong enough, she picked up her pack and strode away from what she had jokingly decided to think of as the cave of self-indulgent despair.

She felt like a thing new made. She lived, she was no one's victim, and she had choices. She was done with people. She would fill the void inside her with the sights and sounds of the world. It was a lot bigger than she was.

She decided to find the world-sea. It was said to be in the north, the direction that called her, and it was something no shadowkin had ever seen.

As though to test her resolve to shed the past, her path down from the mountains crossed the valley where Kir had been killed. She didn't pause, just noted the point where the chakaka hunt had been staged, and recalled how it had gone wrong, with a clinical detachment. Like thoughts of Min, of Kir, of Cal, of Etyan

135

himself, she could now examine this memory without pain.

The following morning she crested a small rise to come out onto a shallow slope covered in a low tangle of bluish fronds. Ahead, a herd of pichons raised all their heads at once, then kicked their feet and fled. She would have liked to catch and eat some of the rabbit-like beasties, but with their linked senses and fast moves, hunting them alone she stood no chance.

The low hills soon flattened out into a plain, stretching to the horizon. Dej watched the clouds boil up and disperse for a while, taking in the massive skies. The ground-cover here was tangled and mossy, like so many skyland plants. When she trod on the ankle-height pinkish-mauve growth it smelled like old linen. Tracks ran through it; something small had eaten the moss-grass down to the bare earth in meandering trails. Presumably such little nibblers fed at night, away from predators.

Though there were no nightwings here, the possibility of becoming something's prey herself was always present, especially out in the open. Dej had found a relative of the pus-bush before she left the mountains and smeared its sap over her cloak; so far it had seen off everything small and bitey.

As for bigger beasties, she had seen lone distant flyers, broad-winged and circling lazily but showing no interest in her. One day she spotted a herd of large cat-like things in the middle distance; when the wind changed to bring them her scent, she braced herself to run, but though the two largest animals at the front raised their heads and then, disconcertingly, jumped onto their hind legs, they dropped back down at once, and the herd carried on its way.

That night a shower of blowballs tumbled through, fist-sized gaseous balls of furry blue that stuck to the skin and burst with the smell of rotten wood when she brushed them off. Neither edible nor harmful, her animus informed her.

The next day she saw the glint of water to the east and went to investigate. It turned out to be a river, another geographical feature she'd only heard about. The fast-flowing water's surface rippling in the Sunlight. Unless she misremembered her lessons the river would, eventually, reach the sea. She decided to follow it.

Further downstream she came across stands of dark many-branched trunks topped with clusters of turquoise fuzz. Gnarled roots trailed down the shallow riverbank like lazily draped limbs; when one of them twitched, her animus chimed in with an unspoken warning. But the trees' fuzzy leaves were edible, so she climbed one on the landward side, away from the roots, and harvested some of the turquoise fuzz. It reminded her of over-cooked scrambled eggs.

When darkness fell, tiny golden lights rose from the river, dancing in the gloom. They moved in time to the song of the water. She fumbled in her pack, digging deep to retrieve her flute, then began to play. The lights skittered away, then flitted back a moment later. They began to dance to her tune. Dej's heart lifted. She played until her mouth was dry, then watched as the lights drifted back into the depths of the river.

The next day it occurred to her that she hadn't thought of Etyan once as she played her flute.

After a few days she left the clumps of scrambled-egg-trees behind. The river slowed and the river-lights no longer came out.

Finally the river began to broaden out, its edges becoming marshy and indistinct. The succulent reeds growing in rich clumps here were good to eat, so she gorged herself on them, sucking the pith out and chewing the stalks.

The river widened further the next day, until it lost itself in boggy purple-grey heathland. Stands of spiky reeds edged pools covered in mats of floating vegetation; no good to eat, and sharp enough to tear skin. She sensed various forms of small but nasty life in the pools themselves. Picking a safe path through the solid ground, such as it was, was slow and exhausting work, taking all her concentration.

When night fell and she was still deep in the marshlands, she began to worry: though the knife-reeds had disappeared, for the last half day she'd been dancing across barely-thick-enough-to-support-her mats of vegetation. As soon as she stopped, she started to sink. Should she turn back? But the marsh couldn't go on for much longer. She carried on. Rain started to fall, soft but pervasive.

By dawn she kept finding one leg or the other knee-deep in stagnant water. At some point it would be both legs, and she'd be lost to the marsh. Looked like she might die out here after all. The thought made her furious, but the fury had nowhere to go except into self-pity, and she was done with that. She put the emotion to one side, and carried on.

As the Sun passed noon, half-hidden in scudding clouds, she saw a paler, rough-looking patch in the flat purple marsh. It was smaller than her dorm bed, just a thick oval of knotted vegetation, but it was the nearest she'd seen to solid ground. She couldn't sense anything nearby likely to eat her so she knelt, stiff-legged, then rolled out the cloak to spread her weight and lay down, curled round her backpack. Despite the damp seeping up around the edge of the cloak, as soon as she stopped moving she fell into an exhausted sleep.

She woke just before dawn, lying in shallow water. She sat up; the submerged cloak dipped under her, but she didn't sink far. She ate a couple of hard biscuits, then extended her senses. Marsh in every direction, just like her eyes were telling her. She stood shakily and tried to pull the cloak free of the marsh, but it sucked it back.

She'd head due north; if there was no change to the terrain when she began to tire, she'd turn round and head due south to spend the night here again. It wasn't much of a plan but it beat just giving up.

Around mid-afternoon she saw taller plants ahead, the sort that wouldn't grow in a swamp. She thought she felt the change in the land too, though that might've been wishful thinking. But she upped her pace from an exhausted stumble to a purposeful stagger.

Soon, not every step sunk into brackish water. She let herself feel the exhaustion she'd been holding at bay. Shivers went through her overworked calf muscles. *Not far now, not far now.*

She was right, though the final few hundred yards took an age, and the last of her energy. As soon as she'd taken half a dozen steps without the land giving way under her feet she pitched forward. She landed in a damp springy tangle that gave a lime-scented puff and faint creak when she rolled deeper into it. Hopefully it wouldn't digest her. Actually, right now she didn't care. She sighed, closed her eyes and let herself pass out.

It was light again when she woke. Something had stung her in the night; the scales on one shoulder, exposed now she had no cloak, were sore and itchy. At least the lime-grass hadn't had a go at her.

This landscape was a bit like that near Shen, complete with stands of lemon-spikes. She ate every one she could find, sucking at the cool pith for moisture.

Her pack had dried out a little, though it, and her skin, were ingrained with marsh muck.

As she walked farther north the vegetation clumped into growths twice her height that almost counted as trees. Their long blue-green leaves shimmered in the Sunlight.

She dismissed the first presence as an illusion, her tired mind playing tricks. Nothing but a tree-bush over there. Unless the tree-bushes had minds. Perhaps they did: she projected her senses, and caught a quick flash of something being hidden. The bush-trees did have minds. She made a note not to sleep near them. *Ah, sleep.* That was a wonderful thought. Soon as she was clear of these bushes–

Movement. Something behind that tree-bush. Nothing with a proper mind... or was it? It had intent, and she was what interested it. She sped up, exhausted body responding to a threat her strung-out mind couldn't fully process. She still couldn't see the threat, but she was sure now: something was hunting her.

Her heart was racing. Her feet tried to break into a run.

Another flash of presence, ahead. She darted to the left. Her body ran off fear alone, all energy long since expended.

Running full pelt now. Movement off to the side, and behind. Presences too, lots of them, all around. Proper minds, no longer trying to hide from her.

Something whistled overhead.

Her feet stuck together, stopping her dead. She fell, boneless, seeing the ground rush up fast towards her but unable to stop the inevitable.

CHAPTER 24

"A skykin. Here?" Sadakh frowned at Taklew.

"At the house, Holiness."

Only one of his skyland agents dared come to the city in person, and only in extreme circumstances. "Was this individual... disfigured?"

"He has a missing eye."

Yes, it's him. His ghost's disdain was clear. "Did he say what he wants?"

"Just that he had important news."

"Well, he had better have." The timing was appalling. "Go back, tell him to wait for me. I'll be along as soon as I can."

The bodyguard left. Sadakh had already summoned two others of his trusted cadre. Since taking the first office of the day he had been meditating alone in his study, centring himself for the upcoming encounter, but the prospect of the unexpected visitor from the skyland had shattered his inner calm. *One crisis at a time please,* he silently beseeched the First.

Outside, the day was fine, though swirling breezes ruffled the waters of the lake. Approaching the Eternal Isle Sadakh noted that the prince was already standing halfway down the southeast jetty. He was flanked by two individuals who, like Sadakh's own guards, were not obviously armed but wore unusually voluminous robes.

He had one guard, Penek, wait with the punt. Penek was his best puntsman. Also, it would be a sign of trust to bring one fewer guard than the prince himself. The other guard, the dour and unflappable Klimen, walked half a pace behind as he strode along the wooden planking. The twisted hallways and manicured terraces of the Eternal Isle rose behind the prince, the golden stone of the walls gleaming in the morning light. As far as he could see no one was looking their way from the palace, though he had no doubt this meeting was being observed.

Sadakh stopped half a dozen steps from the prince's party. The prince did not bother with the pretence of an obeisance. For a few moments neither of them spoke.

Finally the prince raised a hand, gesturing for his guards to step back out of earshot. Then his face broke into a wolfish grin and he said, "You feel your end approaching."

A chill gripped Sadakh's heart. His ghost spoke in reassurance: *Surely he cannot know the truth.* But what if the prince did know what he truly was? With some effort, he replied evenly, "I will accept my death however and whenever it comes."

The prince inclined his head, as though making a gracious concession. "You have done well for yourself, and will go to the First knowing this."

What is he playing at? Despite his ghost's suspicious tone, Sadakh made himself smile, as though pleased by the compliment and oblivious of the veiled threat. "I have done my best for god and for my nation."

"And from such humble beginnings. Peasant to eparch. Quite a journey."

Sadakh schooled his expression not to show his relief. The prince was referring to his cover story, not the truth behind it. The only person who knew that was Zekt's other natural enquirer, and it was highly unlikely the prince had compromised Counsellor of Zekt. "I have cause to be proud, yes." He composed his face into an expression as close to supplication as he could get. "But this is not about me. This is about our shadowland."

"How so?" The prince appeared genuinely, innocently curious.

"Much as I wish it were not so, the caliarch is ailing."

"Yes he is. And as his creature, you must be concerned, perhaps even afraid." A flash of glee showed in the prince's expression. "Are you afraid, Holiness?"

"I fear for the caliarch. But as I say, I am thinking of Zekt itself, once our beloved caliarch goes to his ancestors. A regency can be a difficult time." *Especially when the regent wants the crown for himself.* "It is important to maintain a sense of continuity."

"How so?" The prince did not sound that interested.

"A change of caliarch and a change of eparch within a short period of time could be… destabilising. Your job will be easier with the people behind you."

"Yes, and you have been such a good eparch, very popular. Notwithstanding your sexual deviancies."

A cheap shot! Sadakh agreed: it was disappointing to see base mudslinging from the prince. "You refer to the fact that I sleep with some of my initiates?"

"The phrase I was thinking of was 'take advantage of'."

"They enter into the relationship freely, and leave it when they wish." *Or when we wish*, commented his ghost. "Frankly, I do not see how this aspect of my personal life is relevant." Sadakh resisted the temptation to comment on the prince's own choices in this regard. Although he had most likely been faithful to his now-dead wife, everyone at court knew who the real object of his affections had been, even if she was long gone. That relationship had definitely been deviant.

"Perhaps not." The prince shrugged, then focused. "So, you believe that you would be of use to me when I take my uncle's place."

He isn't even pretending he'll just be regent! "I believe the benefits of allowing me to continue in my role would outweigh the satisfaction of putting this humble peasant in his place." Sadakh accompanied his words with a disarming smile; a less arrogant man than Mekteph might be insulted by such sycophantic insinuations, but the prince was not renowned for either humility or irony.

"Hmm. I wonder if you would really switch allegiance so easily."

He has no replacement planned. Indeed not. If the prince still had a man amongst his poliarchs they would not be having this conversation. But he just said, "When Numak is gone, my focus will be on Zekt itself."

"And on saving your own skin. He'll be watching you of course. Watching all of us." Sadakh wondered how literally the prince believed in the spiritual guardianship of the previous caliarchs; living on the Eternal Isle it was an accepted, if intangible, fact of life. Mekteph continued, "But experience suggests he'll not do more than watch."

If ghosts really could exact vengeance... Sadakh heard the grim humour in his own ghost's voice. She appeared to have more reality to him than the dead Zekti royals did to those living in the palace; otherwise it was unlikely Mekteph would get much rest, given how many of the palace's ghosts he was responsible for making. "I would not presume to say either way."

"What are you up to with my uncle anyway?"

"I am not sure what you mean."

"You two are thick as thieves, working on some great project... I heard the oddest rumour, you know."

"We both know how little credence to give to odd rumours."

"Something about a dead skykin."

"Well, that is an odd rumour," he managed, without giving anything away in his tone or expression.

"If you really are willing to work for me then tell me what you're up to. Let me in on this secret project. As you say, my time is coming."

That the prince suspected he was up to something beneficial to the caliarch and wanted in would explain why he had finally agreed to this meeting. Sadakh already knew his answer, but made a show of mulling over the offer. Finally he said, "It is true that, as his spiritual confidante, I have considered, and even indulged, some of your uncle's more fanciful requests over the years, although," – and here he smiled – "none of them have run to anything as shocking as procuring dead skykin. But nothing has ever come of them." *And when your plans come to fruition, this bastard would be the last person you'd grant immortality to.* "So I fear there is nothing to tell."

"Hmm. I thought you might say that."

Sadakh tensed. This could be it. The prince had hoped he was desperate enough to betray Numak's secrets, but instead he had insisted there was no secret. Even without a plan for replacing him, such a snub might make Mekteph tire of this lower-class upstart of an eparch.

But the prince just grimaced and said, "Never mind. You can go back to your holy isle now." When Sadakh didn't move at once, the prince flicked his fingers. "Go on. We're done."

Sadakh made himself incline his head in respect, and turned slowly on his heel. Klimen stepped behind him, shielding his back. Klimen had heard the conversation, but that was fine; interestingly, Mekteph's own guards had not.

From behind he heard the prince laugh, once, then shout out, "Ah yes. Do watch your back."

Sadakh made himself take measured steps, as though unconcerned by the threat.

He had Penek return to the priory isle. He could not risk being followed to the launderers' house. How much did the prince already know? And how had he found it out? Did the prince have agents on the priory isle, despite Sadakh's precautions? Or had he compromised one of Sadakh's people in the palace?

He must not allow doubt to stop him. He would up his precautions, taking the prince's last piece of advice. And he would carry on with his work.

He told his secretary to assign the rest of the day's offices to his poliarchs, changed into a plain tunic and used a postern gate to leave the priory for the launderers' house.

When he arrived Ereket and Taklew withdrew to the house's small parlour, leaving the skyland visitor alone in the kitchen. Half empty dishes, presumably from an interrupted breakfast, had been piled to one side.

The skykin was indeed the clanless's seer, although such a degenerate specimen barely deserved the title. Sadakh held up a hand, "I am sorry to have kept you waiting, however I have had an appalling morning, so kindly get to the point."

"We could not capture the boy."

"Ah, and my day does not improve. Did you even try?"

"We watched the red valley camp for some days, and saw no sign of him. I also sent out searchers in case he was nearby but they found nothing."

"It took you a long time to bring me such bad news."

"I wanted to do all we could to try and find him. And the news is not entirely bad. We know who he is now."

"You do?"

"Yes. Our spy was young, and not very brave, but some of our hunters got close enough to overhear the shadowkin men talking."

"And? Who is he?"

"They referred to him as 'Lord Harlyn'."

"Good." *We know that name.* Sadakh did, but it was not at the forefront of his mind. "Anything else?"

"We know who the skykin girl was too."

"What girl?"

"The one who arrived first. From what our spies overheard, she had an argument with the boy, but before that, they were lovers."

"And where is she now?"

"Long gone."

"Well, at least we have a name for him. And you felt the need to tell me this in person."

"Yes. In case you wanted immediate action. Also…" The half-seer shifted on his stool. "With so few of us left, my people are not thriving. Working for you has saved us. But we would do more, if we can."

And be paid more, his ghost's tone was cynical. "Like what?"

The seer spread his hands. "Whatever you ask."

Something in his tone, a mixture of the craven and the resentful, put Sadakh's teeth on edge. But he needed agents in the skyland more than ever, however inadequate they may be. "I will send a payment of food with you now. As for more work... you will keep an eye out for this Lord Harlyn, and continue to watch the red valley."

"What about getting you another animus?"

"Finding the boy is your priority. I need you to bring him to me."

Sadakh left Taklew loading up a rucksack of dried food for the clanless and went to sit in his workroom to think. Where did he know the name "Harlyn" from? *The boy called for Ree...* ah yes, so he had.

Of course. Ree... Rhia. Rhia Harlyn. The boy was a close relative of Rhia Harlyn – or as he usually thought of her, Observer of Shen.

For the first time in some months, Sadakh laughed out loud.

CHAPTER 25

"Are you all right there, old lady?"

Dej focused on the face swimming in and out of focus above her. A skykin man, teeth bared in a grin, mind projecting concern. She'd only been out of it a few moments. Her legs were still tangled in the bolas; this'd happened once before, when she'd tried to run from her bonding.

She sat up, pushing the stranger away; her hands tingled at the skin-to-skin contact. She ignored the sensation. "What did you do that for?"

"Sport." His expression softened. "We meant no harm."

"You could've fooled me."

He looked pensive, perhaps even contrite. "You're right, little one, in your state one must take care. And we normally ask before we play."

"I should hope so."

The conversation felt unreal. She'd been thinking of the skyland as empty, a place to get away from people, but of course it was home to the true skykin.

"Did Nal-Urej hurt you?" Dej looked past the first skykin to a second speaker, also male. "Uh, no." He'd said "Urej" – a warrior. As though reading her mind – which he might have been – the second skykin said, "I'm Tas-Olok. Most of our party are warriors.

149

I'm their healer. We're on our way to war."

"To… war?" She thought "war" was a shadowkin concept, a bad thing they'd grown out of – and something skykin never did.

Tas-Olok laughed, and Nal-Urej's lips twitched into a smile. "We use the word war but the concept is…" He paused, and Dej felt his consciousness nibbling at hers, then sliding away. These skykin were fully bonded. She sensed only shadows, compared to them. After a brief flash of frustration at her inability to comprehend he said, "Think of it as a game, with serious but temporary consequences."

"Join us." Tas-Olok sounded like the thought had just occurred to him.

"In this war?" She was strung out between wonder and irritation.

"No," said his companion. "At our camp, for a while. Share some food. Get clean. Rest."

"It is the least we can do," added Nal-Urej, "after taking the liberty of hunting you without your permission." He offered to help her up but she shrugged his hand off. Still, food and rest sounded good.

The skykin turned, and she followed. Half a dozen others melted out from the trees to join them, greeting Dej with a nod or half-raised hand, backed up by mental touches she barely felt.

The skykin seemed friendly enough though they set a fierce pace, and it took all her remaining stamina just to keep up.

Their camp was like nothing Dej had ever seen before.

Four low domes formed a square in a clearing amongst the tree-bushes. They were the colour of pale rainbows, soft shades sliding across surfaces like oil on water. Each was twice the size of her old shack and came down to four points, with open sides. Skykin sat under or near the domes, a couple working on odd-looking white swords, the rest just sitting, at peace.

They looked up as the main party returned, and Dej sensed wordless greetings being exchanged.

"Do you want to get clean first?"

She looked over at Tas-Olok who had asked the question. "When you say 'first' that's before what exactly?"

"Before we eat. Follow me."

He led her to one of the open-sided domes. The ground underneath was strewn with multi-coloured blankets. Passing one of the skykin sharpening a sword, Dej started: the blade looked like bone.

The healer picked up a clump of pale pink fuzz from an enamelled bowl. "Run the cleansing-moss over your skin; when it turns dark, squeeze it out."

Dej did as he said. Her skin tingled as the moss passed over it, an odd but not unpleasant sensation, like the grime was being sucked from between her scales. The moss soon darkened and plumped up, like a washcloth taking on water. Dej held it at arm's length and squeezed it. The moss squirmed and reduced under her fingers, releasing a cloud of tiny dark particles that blew away on the breeze. They could have done with some of this at the crèche! It took another two squeezes to complete her cleansing, and by the time she finished she was aware that all the nearest skykin were watching her.

She looked up and stared back at them. "What?"

Nal-Urej, who was loitering nearby, laughed out loud. Others smiled. One of the other watchers held up a hand, and said, "We don't mean to be rude, old lady."

"Then stop calling me 'old lady' perhaps?" She'd worked out, on the walk here, what they meant; her animus was ancient compared to theirs, old and decrepit and by implication, inferior.

"A fair request," said a female skykin who'd been looking at her sidewise. "I'm Mai-Umae."

"A storykeeper?"

"That's right. And I'd love to hear yours."

Sharing her story would make her part of their lives, and them part of hers. Except, she was done with people, shadowkin or skykin. "Maybe later," she conceded. But even so, she was curious. "I'd like to know the story here though. This war you're going to, what is it? Nal-Urej said something about a game…"

"A contest. We love contests. Some of us anyway."

"When you say 'we', is this a skykin thing?" Though the crèche had tried to prepare her for life after bonding, the shadowkin had only the sketchiest idea of how the skykin clans lived.

"Yes, for some of us. We have many sorts of contests: martial, mental, crafting, all aspects of life. Often an individual will devote a given life to excelling in one area ze wishes to perfect, or compete in."

By "a given life" the storykeeper must mean the lifespan of one body. Dej felt a peculiar stab of disappointment; given that skykin, or rather the animus inside each skykin, lived for so long it was depressing to think they spent their time trying to get one over on each other. Which she may as well say. "Don't you have anything better to do?"

Mai-Umae put her head on one side, unoffended. "Yes and no. We will, in the lifespan of our animuses, do many things. Some will spend one or more lives in contemplation, or giving service to their clan-mates. Others live to compete, for a while." Mai-Umae's lip curled in a smile. "Perhaps you assume that, given our continuity and community, our lives have higher meaning than a shadowkin's short span of care and woe?"

"Not necessarily." Dej glanced at the temporary but luxurious camp. She doubted this lot ever went hungry. "All right: do they?"

The storykeeper dropped her voice. "The first lesson, which you learnt long ago, then forgot when you grew old, is that we make our own meaning."

Dej considered this. She'd sort-of assumed that skykin did live more significant and meaningful lives than shadowkin, that maybe they knew some big, eternal secret. Apparently not. Assuming the storyteller wasn't lying. These skykin could be messing with her. She settled for saying, "War seems like a pretty grim way of making your own meaning."

"A contest of arms, that is all. Warriors compete with each other, and on occasion, with other clans."

"So you're off to, uh, fight another clan?"

"To have fights with, not to fight. We feel no animosity, off the field. Let us call it a festival, rather than war, to make you more comfortable."

"Yeah, let's. But do you fight to the death? Don't the warriors' animuses stop them?" The compulsion to preserve the life of an animus had caused Dej enough grief.

"For some of these warriors, the current life is almost over. They seek a dramatic end and their animus allows this. Those whose given lives are just beginning compete without risk of death."

"And you're all one clan?"

"These are the warriors of East-silver-flower, with Tas-Olok to tend wounds and myself to remember."

A couple of dozen warriors plus the other two here... and there were ten roles in a given clan... "So, your clan is only a few hundred strong. I thought they were bigger."

"Some are." Then Mai-Umae said, more loudly, "Time to eat now."

The skykin were already turning towards the weird little fire in the centre of the camp; though some small logs burned in the middle of it, it was set on a round grey stone which emitted its own pale blue flames, mixed with the normal flames. Two skykin had just lifted a cook-pot off a spindly frame over the heat and now served a meal of plump grains and bright fruits. Dej wanted to dislike the food but it was delicious. She ate so fast she barely had time to catch her breath. When she'd finished shovelling the warm spicy mixture into her mouth she stifled a belch, then nodded at Mai-Umae's offer to fetch more. She took her second portion more slowly.

She sensed Mai-Umae's amusement as she ate. Which presumably Mai-Umae let her sense, given the hunters had hidden themselves from her. The thought took the edge off her pleasure at eating. Mai-Umae, in turn, looked away.

"One thing you need to know," said Mai-Umae as Dej licked her spoon clean.

"Just one?" Dej decided to play the fool they thought she was, while trying to get all she could off these kindly-but-

153

condescending skykin.

"Well," conceded the storykeeper, "more than one I'm sure. But this regards your life with the clanless."

"How do you know about that?"

"I do not know. But I guessed. Or have you survived this long, and done this well, all alone?"

"Not alone, no." Until now. Now "alone" was what she wanted to be. "And yes, I lived with a group of clanless, for a while. It was... well, it was pretty shitty."

Mai-Umae nodded sagely at the profanity. "Did they tell you that you need shadowkin food to live?"

"Yes. They did. Was that a lie?"

"It may have been. Some half-bonded are still so tied to the shadowkin body that they need their food, but most do not. However, those who lead the outcasts often use that lie to keep their folk in line."

"Great. As if I didn't hate those bastards enough already."

Mai-Umae exuded something like sympathy. "We would help you, as much as we can."

"Really?" Mainly they seemed interested in demonstrating their superiority. "Why, if you don't mind me asking?" Or even if they did.

"For the lives you've lived and forgotten."

Which was at least an honest answer. "And I'd be happy to accept your help," she said, with as much good grace as she could muster.

A murmur was going through the skykin, and the storykeeper said, more loudly, "You want a tale?"

The murmur changed tone. It appeared they did. Mai-Umae said, "How about the death of Tah-Urej?"

Smiles and nods at that, most of them directed to one of the warriors round the fire, who nodded in response and said, "Remind me what I've got to live up to, Mai!"

The story was interesting enough, if you liked poetic tales of combat and glory, but Dej couldn't get past the fact that this skykin was enjoying hearing about their own death. Assuming the warrior remembered. How much knowledge an animus passed on was another question the crèche hadn't answered. Surely skykin couldn't remember everything from all their previous lives. It would overwhelm them.

At the end of the tale the warrior Tah-Urej said, "My memory is refreshed." It sounded like a ritual response.

It was dark now; during the first story the insides of the domes had begun to glow softly, supplementing the firelight. Mai-Umae launched straight into another tale, this time the deeds of a warrior of the clan who wasn't with them, as he – or rather ze, as the skykin didn't use "he" or "she" except when talking about a specific person in their current life – was now a pathfinder. Dej had noticed the lack of pathfinders in the group. Presumably they'd come this way so often they knew the route. If not, she could always offer her services... yeah right. Like they'd let an "old lady" show them the way.

The tale was a variation on the first one, and Dej found herself more interested in her surroundings. The camp was like the fire: a mixture of the familiar – woven blankets, bowls made of ceramics or hollowed gourds, stone paring knives and wooden spoons – and the weird, like the perfectly circular low tables, the bone swords, the glowing dome-tents themselves. There was a lot of gear here but just the one rhinobeast, tethered off to one side. How did they carry all this stuff?

By the time the current tale of noble combat was done, Dej was yawning. Mai-Umae said, "Take any space you want. I will show you how to make yourself comfortable."

"Uh, here's fine."

"Of course." Mai-Umae picked up a shiny blanket and gave it a sharp shake. In the blink of an eye the blanket filled out, becoming plump as the richest eiderdown. She laid it on the ground next to Dej. "We should be warm enough in here, but just pull a woven blanket over you if you are cold." Behind her, another skykin was running his hand down the opening in the tent walls. Something sparked in the air in the wake of his hand, spreading out into a faintly glowing barrier, to plug the gap.

"What's that?" Dej nodded at the glowing wall.

"It keeps the heat in, and the beasts out."

"How about if I need to get up for a pee in the night?"

"You can pass through it freely."

"Good." The idea of being trapped with the skykin made Dej uneasy. Realising that, she asked, "So am I coming with you?"

"Travel west with us if you wish. You will not be permitted to attend the festival though."

"Yeah, what with me being too old for all that." Still an odd thought, that the animus inside her had lived more lives than these people's had. "I'll move on soon but, uh, could I maybe ask a favour?"

"You can ask."

"I lost my cloak, and I wondered if you'd have something I could use. One of these neat blanket-things maybe, if it'll pack down."

"It will reduce to the size of a kerchief."

"Really?"

"Watch." The storykeeper pulled over a blanket not currently being used by any skykin bedding down around them, and slapped it with her palm; the bright fabric made an audible snap, then shrunk away, reducing to a small square before Dej's eyes.

"Wow. Do the tents do that too?"

"They do."

Which explained why they only needed one rhinobeast. "One of those would be great."

"We can give you a made item, but not tech."

"Not what?"

"Tech is not for the half-bonded."

"Yes, but *what* is it?"

"Tech is prohibited in the shadowlands, and you are part shadowkin. It is not for you."

"I guess not." Mai-Umae hadn't exactly answered her question, though she had managed to get in another reminder of how inadequate she was. "Well, I don't want to be any trouble."

"And we want to help, as much as we can." The storykeeper gestured to Dej's "tech" bed. "Rest now. You are our guest. We would help you, you who are so near your final death."

"Thanks for reminding me of that. Actually I feel fine right now."

"Your body is fine, yes. More than fine. But your animus…" The skykin shook her head sadly.

"That's all right, me and it are only just on speaking terms." She turned away from the storykeeper before adjusting her bed to align better with the north, calling over her shoulder, "Well, good night then."

She woke in darkness, needing a pee just like she'd warned her hosts she would. For a few moments she lay in the embrace of the "tech", enjoying the feeling of being safe and warm with a full belly. But the skykin's pity irritated her. She was like some sort of pet or curiosity to them. And they weren't heading her way; they were going somewhere she couldn't go. She could follow them, see if she could get into their "festival"… but given how easily they'd stalked and hunted her, she doubted it. May as well make a clean break, on her terms.

She rolled off the bed and crawled to the edge of the tent. They'd left her pack outside; no surprise given how bad it smelled. She may as well take the ordinary blanket she'd been offered. She rolled it up, breathing shallowly, listening for anyone waking up. No one did. As she tucked the blanket under her arm her eye fell on the cleansing-moss in its bowl. She snatched it up before she could think better of it. Then, crouching low, she approached the glowing barrier. What if Mai-Umae had lied? But her outstretched hand passed through the barrier with a faint, quite pleasant, tingle. She slipped out, crouching low.

She picked up her pack and crept away into the night.

CHAPTER 26

According to Counsellor of Zekt, important matters left
unregarded could surface through the dreaming mind. And Rhia
had had her fair share of disquieting dreams these last few months.

When she dreamt of Alharet twice in three nights – the first
dream gone as soon as she awoke save the memory of laughter
from behind a fan, the second something about a captive songbird
and letters to an unseen lover – she took notice. With her trial only
six weeks away she had enough to worry about, but something
below the level of thought was building inside her.

She sent a note to Francin. She half hoped he would refuse her
request. She could then tell her dreaming mind that she had done
all she could, and it could leave her in peace.

The response came back while she was working on the
celestial model with Kerne. Her apprentice was good with his
hands and, when the promised iron cogs and rods had finally
arrived, welcomed the chance to do something practical. She had
considered rebuilding the model with elliptical orbits but there
was no time. Just getting all the parts functioning in coordination
was hard enough. Despite his enthusiasm for tinkering with
her model, she remained unconvinced that Kerne believed its
accuracy; ironically, it took a leap of faith, or perhaps imagination,
to embrace the most radical theories. He was not one to take such

leaps. And he was tired all the time; no wonder, given he still spent mornings at the horticulturists before coming here, often working through siesta with her then staying up late to observe the sky. She should ease up on him. But they were running out of time.

The duke's answer to her request to visit Alharet was short, even by his standards: *If you must.*

She cleared her throat to attract Kerne's attention. "I have to go to the palace. Take the rest of the day off."

His expression went from surprise to hurt; he thought he had displeased her. But at her smile he nodded and thanked her.

Outside, the recent drizzle had eased off, leaving the city damply steaming under low cloud. No observing tonight. But the close air and occluded sky were a small price to pay for the life-giving rain.

When she stated her errand to a footman he told her to wait for "the escort". This turned out to be a guard with a short-stave and knife on his belt who, after a shallow bow, fell in behind her.

She had been visiting the palace most weeks to meet her lawyer, who she was coming to respect if not entirely trust. Sur Lectel had his own agenda, and for as long as that fitted with hers she was in good hands. But he had no interest in her theory, or even her life: just in winning her case. She had seen Francin only a couple of times, in passing. If the rumours Nerilyn brought back were true, he had taken another clandestine trip recently.

Rhia paused outside the Countess's apartment, now barred with an expensive metal-bound lock. The guard muttered "excuse me" and came forward with an ironwood key. The mechanism was heavy, and complex, and as the guard worked at it Rhia fought the urge to turn around and stride away down the corridor.

The guard opened the door. Every other time Rhia had visited these rooms, Alharet had met her on the threshold. Only a burst of fusty air greeted her today. "Your Grace," called the guard, "You have a visitor. I will bring her to you." His voice was carefully neutral. He nodded to Rhia to go first.

Rhia knew these rooms so well. A receiving room, with a

bedchamber and dressing room to either side, then ahead, the parlour: the duchess's sanctum.

The heavily screened window left the parlour shadowy and dim. Alharet sat in her usual chair. As Rhia entered she put the book she had been reading on the table next to her, where it joined a shaded lamp and a hank of crumpled embroidery. For a brief moment the duchess's expression showed her shock. Then, with a single blink, she composed her face. "This is a surprise," she said.

Alharet looked old. Grey streaked her dark, unstyled hair. Her face was puffy and oddly stark. Of course: even for their informal tête-á-têtes she had worn cosmetics, smoothing powder into her skin, tinting her lips red and painting her eyelids with iridescent greens and blues in the Zekti style. Rhia looked away, and saw what was missing from the familiar room.

Alharet followed her gaze. "Ah yes. Anat died, so I had her cage removed. Perhaps I could have asked for a replacement songbird, but I decided not to inflict my fate on another dumb animal."

Rhia flashed back to her half-forgotten dream. "I shouldn't have come."

Alharet pursed her lips for a moment, then said, "No, you should have come. You should have come before." Passion entered her voice for the first time. "You are one of very few people the duke will allow to visit me, but I haven't seen you for *two years*."

"I know, I'm sorry but I've been busy and... " Rhia caught herself. She should not be apologising to the person who betrayed her. She settled on, "You are allowed to see your children, at least."

"Once a week, and never alone." The duchess's gaze slid past Rhia, no doubt to the guard behind her. "Never alone. Or always alone." Her voice faded for a moment, before strengthening as her regard returned to Rhia. "Why are you here now?"

"To make my peace with you."

The duchess laughed, the sound as light and infectious as ever. "Oh, if only peace were something one could just *make*."

"All right." *I will not let you get to me.* "I'll put it another way. I want you to know that I'm sorry."

"You do. Really." The half-questions came out in typical flat Zekti style. Alharet put a hand to her lips and stared at the ceiling, her face pensive. Then she dropped her hand and frowned back at Rhia. "I will give you the benefit of the doubt and assume that you want me to know this because you *are* sorry, not just because you feel you should *claim* to be. Is that right?"

"Of course it is. Please, no games, Alharet."

"No games." For a moment the duchess's face flushed in fury. Then she sighed. "You're right. Much as I am enjoying the rare chance to exercise my wits, this is you, my *friend* Rhia Harlyn. With you, I don't need a mask. Ironically." She twitched a finger to indicate Rhia's own masked face. "You have no idea how much I've missed our little chats." She sounded utterly sincere.

Rhia had seen the duchess blow hot and cold like this before; it was one of her ploys, an entertaining way to toy with courtiers and dignitaries. It was less entertaining when she was the target of the duchess's antics. And these mood shifts were shockingly sudden, almost as if Alharet was intoxicated.

"However," the duchess continued more evenly while Rhia searched for a response, "I would like to know precisely what you are 'sorry' for. Are you showing sympathy for me because my life is not what it once was?" She grimaced at her comfortable but cluttered prison. "Or are you asking for forgiveness for your part in my fate?"

Rhia made herself breathe before answering. "Both, I think."

Alharet nodded. "For the former, thank you for your sympathy. For the latter… you do know I would have done the same in your position."

"Yes. Yes, I do."

"And how is your wicked little brother?"

Rhia flinched. "Don't bring Etyan into this."

"No, because you love your brother more than anyone else in the world, despite everything. I know what that is like, of course." An odd expression flitted across Alharet's face, a deep, twisted grief.

"I should go."

"But you still haven't told me why you come to me now, after all this time. Delayed concern for my welfare perhaps."

"I'm not sure what you mean."

"Did it take this long for news of my, ahem, accident to reach you?"

"No. But I am sad that you felt the need to do such a thing." Whatever else Rhia felt for her ex-friend, she pitied Alharet.

"Every day is like the last in here, you know." She twitched a hand, as though missing her fan. "I must make my own entertainment. And at least I managed to get my husband's attention. But we were talking about you. What has happened to bring you here today, Rhia?"

Francin had not warned against confiding in the duchess. After all, who would she tell? "I am being tried for heresy."

Alharet's expression remained impassive. Did she already know? Or was this just Alharet being Alharet: unreadable unless she wanted to be read? The duchess looked down at her lap and laid her other hand on the one already resting there. "That is not good." She looked up at Rhia, her expression one of genuine concern. "Heresy, you say." She gave a wry smile. "You must be in fear for your papers."

Rhia felt something uncoil inside and blurted, "Alharet, I am in fear for my life!"

The duchess looked down again, as though scalded by Rhia's outburst. "That is shocking to hear. Could it really come to that?"

"It could! One of my theories is against the will of the First. Or so the Church claim. They are holding a grand trial."

Alharet sighed. "A grand trial. Oh dear. I tried to turn you away from matters of the intellect, did I not? My reasons were selfish, yes, but I also thought you might be happier not being so outspoken and curious."

"You're saying I wouldn't be in this trouble if I had let you marry me off?"

"Well, would you?"

Rhia wanted to be angry, but Alharet was right, damn her. "No, but I would be miserable."

The duchess's voice hardened. "In a prison not of your own devising, perhaps. We have both done regrettable things. You have yet to pay the price for them."

"Is that really what you think of me? That I deserve... punishment."

"I did not say that. And I think of you as a friend. I always have. I like you most of everyone I have met in Shen. But you are also the ultimate source of my woes, the reason I am here at all." Rhia remembered the duke's comment on his wife's disconcerting ability to separate different parts of her life. Now Alharet looked wistfully out of the small gap at the top of her shuttered window, then back at Rhia, and said, gently, "But even so, you know you can say anything to me. Still."

Which was the real reason she had come here, of course. "I do know that." She blew out a long slow breath. "But I choose not to. Not any more."

"Ah. I see. Then I think we are done." The duchess looked past Rhia. "You'll forgive me if I leave seeing you out to our friend here."

Walking back through the palace corridors Rhia found herself obsessing on the conversation, on how it might have gone differently. Nothing Alharet had said was untrue. But nothing she said could be trusted. However much the duchess protested, and however much Rhia had secretly wanted it, they could never be friends again.

And she could not shake the conviction that, underneath the arch manipulation and mercurial mirth, the duchess had gone a little mad.

A letter arrived at the townhouse a few days later, from Eparch Sadakh. He opened by saying he regretted not being able to attend her trial in person to defend her, adding intriguingly, *"unless my situation changes"*. He had considered sending one of his poliarchs, but had decided not to because, as he put it *"sadly the Church is not as united as it might be across the world, and although the cardinals of Shen might be distracted by the chance to argue the minutiae of practice with the clerics of another shadowland, doing so is unlikely to serve your cause."*

He also included a long, detailed and elegantly expressed testimonial. He argued, with logic Rhia could not fault and extensive references to the scriptures how, far from challenging the teachings of the First, her theory glorified God, while reminding His fallen children to approach His creation with humility. The First Himself was at the heart of the universe, unknowable and eternal, and could arrange it in any way He saw fit.

CHAPTER 27

The joy of getting away with it thrilled through Dej as she sneaked away from the skykin camp. One thing from her old life still held true: stealing felt good.

When her hammering heart began to slow, she started to doubt. What if they came after her? Stealing from the skykin was even dumber than stealing from the duke; the duke's men couldn't follow her through the skyland, but these skykin could hunt her down with ease.

When the night began to lighten and there was no sign of pursuit she slowed her pace.

In daylight the landscape was low and undulating, with circular clumps of waist-high orange vegetation. She continued north. The skykin were heading west. Hopefully they wouldn't make a diversion to track down one small missing item. Even so, she kept moving until late afternoon, when she found a stand of tree-things that didn't smell too dangerous and slept for the rest of the day and a full night.

The next morning she tried to use the cleansing-moss on her pack, running it over the rank, mud-caked leather. Nothing happened. Her heart sank. When Mai-Umae said tech was not for her, perhaps that meant it wouldn't even work for her. This was probably one of those prohibited items the shadowkin Church talked about. Then she ran the moss up her arm, and felt a tingle. No, it still worked, but only on her, not on her possessions. Tech was inconstant stuff.

She felt a bit odd, perhaps some hangover of the encounter with the skykin, their food or the air in their tents. But the feeling persisted into the next day, when the terrain became wetter though not, thank the First, another bog. She had an odd, tight, bloated feeling deep in her guts. Perhaps her head was messing with her body. She'd been determined to ignore people, but yet again she'd stayed with them and then run off. Better to have nothing to do with anyone in the first place, shadowkin or skykin.

She woke up late the next morning, filled with an awful certainty.

She sat up and looked down at herself. Her chest had been a bit sore for a few days now, the tiny, residual breasts from her bonding oddly tender to the touch. And her belly was a little swollen.

"No."

She put both hands on the swelling, pressing down. The flesh was firm and unyielding. "No I'm not."

But she was.

What had the skykin said? "One in your state must take care". Befuddled, she'd assumed they meant half-bonded. But they'd known the unthinkable truth she hadn't even considered.

She was carrying Etyan's child.

She raised her head and howled at the world, just as she'd done when she first discovered her bonding had gone wrong. Now, as then, the world ignored her.

Such theatrics were an indulgence. She took a deep breath and focused on the problem.

Perhaps she shouldn't be surprised; burnheart blocked conception for both shadowkin and skykin but Etyan was neither.

And now, when she'd finally started to get over him, this. She carried part of the lover she thought she was free of; the beautiful boy, the only person to make her heart sing. The rapist.

She wanted to hit herself, pummel her treacherous belly, get the thing out of her. Perhaps some plant would purge her of it. But her animus was unlikely to tell her that.

"I don't want this!" she told the sky one last time. As she expected, the sky still didn't care.

How long had it been inside her, growing unseen? Two months? Three? That assumed it came from the last time they'd fucked. How long did she have before it was born? A while presumably, if it was only just showing, though skykin babies grew faster than shadowkin.

Skykin protected their children by leaving them in shadowkin crèches, to be raised away from the burning skyland Sun, suckled by wet-nurses whose breasts still produced milk. If Etyan's brat was born out here, it would die. Which would solve the problem. But could she do that?

The way she felt at the moment, she could. And that was appalling, at least as appalling as what Etyan had done.

She should just turn around and head back to the shadowlands right now.

The fuck I will.

She got up, and looked down at herself again. The swelling hardly showed.

She faced north and started walking.

CHAPTER 28

"M'lady I'm sorry!"

Rhia started awake, and focused on the boy in her bedroom. Kerne stood a few steps away, his hands tangled in front of his chest.

She sat up, sleep still clogging her mind. Now she was no longer obliged to study the scriptures in the morning – Sur Lectel had tested her knowledge and declared her as well-briefed as she was going to get – she was letting herself catch up on some of the sleep she'd lost these last few months, although the more she rested, the more tired she felt. "Kerne? What is it?"

He grimaced. "The model…"

Her mussiness evaporated. "What about it?"

"I… " His hands did another loop around each other. "I think I broke it."

"Show me!" Rhia leapt up, tugging at her shift to make herself nominally decent, and followed her apprentice out the room and up the stairs. In her study, he stopped and pointed. At first Rhia saw nothing wrong with the celestial model. Then she noticed how the Maiden, on its spindly pole, sat at a peculiar angle. "What did you do?"

"I was fitting the new metal rods to the cogs, and I tried to crank the model, to get to the smallest cog, only it jammed, and

I… I should have left it but I thought I could wind past and–"

"What broke?"

"The cogs beneath the Maiden. They locked and then… the big ironwood one cracked. The new iron cogs were too strong for it."

Rhia leant over, and confirmed the damage. Suddenly her concern and frustration bubbled over into anger. "There is not enough grease on these! How could you be so stupid?" She straightened. Everything was falling apart. No enquirer would come to her aid. The mathematics had become all but insoluble now she was using ellipses. The third judge was not someone she wanted ruling on her fate. And now this! "It's only a week until Between. We'll never fix this before the new year!"

"I know, I'm so sorry!"

Her anger fell away. "It's all right. You're tired and stressed. We both are. You were doing your best." Last week he had turned up with a black eye; when pressed he reluctantly admitted to "having a scuffle" with a boy at the horticulturists who'd referred to her as Countess Cuckoo. She'd offered to speak to his guildmaster, but he'd said it was nothing. She forced a smile. "Just imagine how much worse it would be if we had tried to rebuild the model with ellipses."

He smiled back uncertainly.

"We need to forget the outer Strays entirely. Take what you need from them. Concentrate on the Maiden. That's the key."

Once she had got him started, she returned to her bedchamber to dress. The rain was expected to clear tonight so she may as well wear men's clothes, for ease of getting up the ladder to–

"Rhia!"

She paused, hand in her clothes' chest. That wasn't Kerne's voice. And it came from downstairs.

"Ree? Anyone?"

She straightened and ran out onto the landing. Someone stood in the hall below, just inside the open front door. The kitchen door was also open but Rhia barely registered it. "Etyan?" Could this bedraggled scrawny figure really be her brother?

He looked up, and grinned. "There you are, sis."

"Etyan!" She raced down the stairs. "Have you been in the skyland all this time?"

He looked like it, pared down to muscle and sinew, the last of his boyish fat gone. And his skin was burnt to dark bronze, bringing out its odd scale-like patterning. "Pretty much. But I'm back now."

She hugged him. He was soaking wet but she didn't care. He hugged her back, and gave that mischievous laugh she knew so well.

When they broke apart Etyan took in what she was wearing and raised an eyebrow. "I see dress standards have slipped in my absence."

"What? Oh, I was just getting dressed."

Etyan looked past her, up the great staircase. "Really?"

Rhia followed his gaze. Kerne had come out of her study and was leaning over the banister. "Go back to work please!" she called up. Looking back, she was favoured with Etyan's cocky grin, looking odd on his new face. "What?" she said, trying not to snap. She knew the kind of conclusions he might draw at her being half dressed with a strange youth in the house. Except Kerne wasn't a stranger. "That's Kerne, you remember? Markave's boy." She gestured to her steward, hovering at the kitchen doorway, flashing him a sympathetic smile.

"I remember." When Markave's sons had lived in the servants' quarters Etyan had sometimes played with them, though his greater age and status had made the games somewhat lopsided; occasionally his behaviour had verged on bullying, and Rhia had intervened. "What's he doing in your study?"

"He's my apprentice."

"Your what?"

"So much has happened while you've been... absent. We've got a lot of catching up to do."

"All right. But can I get cleaned up first?"

"Of course." Rhia turned to Markave. "Please heat water for a bath. And I expect my brother's hungry." Markave nodded and withdrew.

"Hungry? I'm ravenous. Where's Yithi?"

"Out hunting I expect. The rain has brought the rats out."

"That's my girl."

Talking of girls... "Is Dej, um, around?" She wasn't sure how to phrase it.

"Dej is gone, Ree. Long gone."

Rhia tried not to let him see how pleased she was with this news. "But you're here. I'm so glad." She resisted the urge to hug him again. "Get yourself cleaned up. We'll talk later."

They ate in the dining room. Agitation dulled her hunger but Etyan devoured everything put in front of him. He was wearing one of his old doublets; it hung off his lanky frame.

He didn't interrupt while she summarised recent events, though how much was because he was listening and how much because he was busy shovelling cassoulet into his mouth Rhia could not say. But when she got to the end of her summary and sighed he reached over and gave her hand a quick squeeze, before sitting back with a stifled belch. "So I haven't been replaced in your affections by Markave's boy then?" He grinned to make a joke of it.

"Of course not." She had considered asking Kerne to eat with them, given he was not exactly staff, and she wanted Etyan to get used to his presence, but tonight was for family; her only family. "As I said, I needed an apprentice to help me with my work and in case... the worst happens."

He looked away. He'd been visibly shocked when she spoke about her possible fate, which in turn had made it one step closer to being real, and had been enough to kill the last of her appetite.

She wanted to tell him how he could help, but she doubted he'd want to talk about matrimonial matters given his recent experiences, and she needed to know where they stood before she broached the subject.

When the silence stretched she said, evenly, "The duke's men reported that you went to the red valley." When he didn't respond she added, "And that you argued with Dej there."

"Yes. I did." He pulled another hunk off the ravaged loaf next to him and, in denial of a lifetime's table-manners, used it to wipe the last of the gravy off his plate.

"Then she ran off. And you went after her."

Etyan spoke with his mouth full. "Right again."

"I'm sorry if this is painful, but I just need to know what's what with you and Dej."

He swallowed. "There is no 'me and Dej'."

"Right."

"I imagine you're happy about that." The bitterness in his voice cut deep.

"I never said that. I hate that she hurt you."

"So why keep going on about it? All right, here's how it is: we rowed, she ran off. I went after her but I was weak from wandering around so she got a good lead on me. Then I got lost. I'm no pathfinder. And maybe I didn't want to find a path, a way back. Maybe I wanted the skyland to kill me. But it didn't. It hardened me."

"Yet you came back." She could not keep the delight and relief out of her voice.

"There's nothing for me out there now."

"Oh Etyan. I love you, little brother."

"And I love you, sis." His smile was genuine, despite the pain in his eyes.Later, alone in her room, she wondered what that last, devastating row had been about. The two of them sometimes bickered when they were at the estate, but always made up. Perhaps they had just had enough, and fallen out of love. No, Etyan still loved Dej. Had Dej found out the truth about Derry, about what Etyan had done? It seemed unpleasantly likely, but Rhia had no intention of asking. On top of everything else, she could not bear to uncover that darkness again.

CHAPTER 29

Sadakh smiled at his flock from his dais. He had been letting his subordinates take too many services. This was his life, his calling.

Seeing the congregation's joyful, receptive faces lifted his heart; knowing his words touched them raised his spirits. He made a difference to many lives, leading people to fulfil their potential. There was no greater work.

But whenever he was alone, he found himself fighting off despair. Mekteph no longer attended restday services at the priory and he sensed that the prince's low-level enmity had now sharpened to active animosity, thanks to his refusal to betray the caliarch's confidence. With every visit to the Eternal Isle a gauntlet of hostile stares, trailing guardsmen and tense-not-so-chance encounters, Sadakh had only visited the caliarch twice in the last month, giving excuses for missing two of their weekly meetings. And Numak was fast losing his grip on reality. On his last visit, earlier this week, he had insisted that Sadakh pray with him. This was not unprecedented; what was new and disturbing was his insistence that surely the eparch must be able to *hear* the voices of the dead caliarchs. When Sadakh admitted he could not, Numak had cried.

The caliarch was losing faith in him. And he had begun to lose faith in himself. He had touched many lives, but how lasting was his influence? And how long did he have left to continue his work, spiritual and temporal?

His response to Observer of Shen had been a pleasing if all-too-brief diversion. His initial elation at finding she was related to his escaped test subject soon faded. Could he really expect her to sell out her kinsman in return for Sadakh's aid at her heresy trial?

Rhia Harlyn had a sharp and incisive mind, but he knew nothing of her save what she revealed through her writings. Or perhaps he did...

The Shenese boy had been abducted from the priory's infirmary. Two separate sets of intruders had taken advantage of the caliarch's birthday regatta two years ago to sneak in to steal him away. They had ended up fighting each other. One group, whose two survivors had been extensively questioned, had almost certainly been hired by the prince. Evidence suggested that the prince's interest in the boy was political, not medical. Relations between Zekt and Shen had turned frosty after a failed dynastic marriage a decade and a half ago, back before Sadakh arrived in Mirror, resulting in Mekteph's twin sister being exiled to Shen.

The other party in the priory had apparently been Shenese. One of them had turned on his comrades, and been killed by them; the rest of the party fled, taking the boy with them. And one of the Shenese had been a woman of early middle years. Could she be the boy's older sister?

If so, then given she had travelled to Zekt and put herself at risk to get him back, it seemed unlikely she would hand him over, even in return for a testimony that might help save her work. Assuming she even knew where he was. If her possibly-brother was living in the skyland, perhaps with a skykin lover, Rhia Harlyn would have even less chance of finding him than Sadakh himself did. And if she had been one of those who snatched Lord Harlyn, what did she think – and more importantly know – about the boy's presence in the religious house run by the enquirer she later began corresponding with?

He had already been inclined to help her. And if Rhia Harlyn might – perhaps inadvertently – help him find his missing test subject, he needed her on his side. The lengthy letter he finally wrote kept his options open but could, he hoped, make a potential ally of her.

Now, with no news to either encourage or dismay him for weeks, he was taking what pleasure he could in the rituals of his Order.

The service finished. He liked to remain available to any supplicant who wished to speak to him after the morning's formalities, whether it was a priest wanting spiritual advice or a trusted initiate with useful information. When he spotted Taklew he nodded to the bodyguard, and had his secretary show him in first.

Taklew was still looking after Ereket at the launderers' house. Her burns refused to heal, and she was becoming increasingly lethargic and lacking in appetite. Although Sadakh himself felt no signs of illness or impending mortality, her failing health was one more blow, one more sign his efforts might be doomed.

He continued to work fitfully on the serum, kept fresh in its stone jar in the lakewater pool in the launderers' washroom. He had investigated ways of propagating it in blood, and last week had dosed two of his guards: stalwart Dalent and Naldak, a reformed criminal turned loyal servant. Both had become ill, then recovered, but showed no other change. He was still missing something.

He showed Taklew in and closed the study door behind him. "Is it Ereket?" he asked. "Has she worsened?"

"She is stable, Holiness. But I have news from the umbral." Sadakh wondered if the Shenese boy was finally within his grasp, but Taklew's next words dispelled his hopes. "There is a problem at the camp."

"What sort of problem?" The umbral "camp" was just a single tent in the caliarch's forests, but was a vital link in Sadakh's lines of communication.

"Abandoned, apparently. The next watcher on the rota found it deserted and disturbed when he went to take his place, and reported back to the launderers' house." Aside from specific uses, such as when Ereket and Taklew made it their base to go into the skyland, the camp was manned by a string of lone hirelings.

"What did he think happened?"

"He had no idea. Obviously he knows only what he is told, to go wait there for messages or visitors. Shall I investigate?"

"Yes, but take Klimen. Bring back a full report, but don't stay any longer than you need to."

Taklew and Klimen managed the journey to the umbral and back in under four days. Such efficient, loyal servants were worth two dozen hired men. It had occurred to Sadakh that the prince's earlier reference to skykin bodies most likely came from having interrogated, or perhaps just bribed, one of his distant hirelings. They had no idea who their ultimate employer was, but Mekteph could put things together and draw his own conclusions.

His trusted guards reported that the camp had indeed been wrecked. The tent had been slashed, the fire-pit stamped on, and everything of value taken, although given how little of value there had been, robbery was an unlikely motive. There was no blood or other proof weapons had been drawn. Klimen, who had some tracking ability, said he suspected the watcher on duty had run off, possibly at the approach of superior forces. Whose forces was unprovable, but there was only one candidate. Sadakh might be safe while he remained on the priory isle, but the prince was flexing his muscles.

He would need to give more thought to protecting his people, and his work.

The next week, just before the festival of Between, he received the news he had been dreading. His secretary brought the ill tidings, daring to disturb him while he meditated alone. Seeing Viteph's pale face and sombre expression, Sadakh said, "Is it the caliarch?"

His secretary bowed his head. "I am sorry, but yes. His Majesty joined his ancestors last night, as he slept."

"Thank you for telling me."

We knew this day would come.

In his heart, he had. But he was far from ready.

CHAPTER 30

"I'm going to the Between-eve reception."

Rhia stared at her brother. "The what? Oh, at the palace." That explained the velvet and brocade. "Are you sure?" Etyan had spent most of the last three days sleeping, eating or playing with the cats. This was the first time he had come into her study since his return.

"Yes. I need to get back into my old life."

"Right. Yes. If that's what you want to do…"

"I can't just sit around in the dark moping, can I?"

It wasn't that dark in the house, but perhaps to eyes used to skyland glare it might seem so. "It's good that you want to get out. And I appreciate you telling me where you're going."

"Don't worry, I'm not planning on getting in trouble." And he was off, with a grin that looked a little forced.

Kerne was looking at her, and she raised an eyebrow to show that he could get back to work. But as he bent over the celestial model she saw how his brow was sheened with sweat. "Are you all right?"

"I'm a little tired."

Probably something of an understatement considering how hard he was working. "You can go as soon as you've fitted that last cog. Have the rest of the day off." She estimated they were a week to ten days away from getting the model working in its reduced version; she had cannibalised the cogs from the outer Strays to concentrate on fixing the motions of the world and the Maiden.

"Thank you m'lady."

If their work allowed, she'd give the boy more time off during Between which was, as Etyan had just reminded her, almost upon them.

Growing up, Rhia had loved the "free days" of Between as much as any youngster; the changing weather, the various festivities, the sense of a new and better year coming soon. But once she grew up her affection for it diminished, for two reasons.

Firstly, the whole arrangement offended her sense of symmetry. Ten months of thirty days each made an obvious pattern, but the two floating weeks of Between at the end of each year just didn't fit; to make it worse, some years it wasn't two weeks but two weeks and a day. When she'd asked Father why he said it was "to keep the years in line", which had just prompted more questions.

Between was also the season of politics, when she could not escape the obligations of her position. The purely social receptions, balls, dinners and entertainments were avoidable but some events required her to at least show her face, to see and be seen. A lot of House business was done during Between; she quashed the thought that she would once have got an inside track on such dealings through Alharet.

And there was the Grand Council, of course. That was always trying.

But when Between ended it was the new year, and her real trial would start.

She had done what research she could on the final judge. Marin Tethorn was a lesser master in the apothecaries guild, a fussy and pious man by all accounts; he would be hard to win over spiritually, but hopefully had the intellect to grasp the truth.

If memory served, the reception Etyan was attending went on into the evening; he had promised to behave but might still stay out late, after so long without the social contact he thrived on. But as she was eating supper at her desk Markave's voice drifted up the stairwell asking if his lordship required anything; Etyan's reply was inaudible. She resisted the urge to rush out of her study and ask how his visit to the palace had gone.

The next morning she ate in the dining room, hoping he would join her for breakfast. He did, initially loading his plate and tucking in, then giving her a look that said he was waiting for her to challenge him, to tell him off. Which she would not. But she did smile over her cup, and ask, "How was the reception?"

"Awful." He put his elbows on the table, and parked his chin on his hands; his carefully neutral expression dissolved into dismay.

"Oh. I'm sorry to hear that." She'd had concerns at the time, but with so many problems of her own she had lacked the energy to worry on her brother's behalf. "In what way?"

"Everyone was so horrible. Even people I thought were my friends."

"Horrible in what way?"

"They acted like I wasn't there, shutting me out of conversations, or ignoring me when I spoke to them. Then as soon as I gave up and turned away, they giggled."

"Giggled. What a bunch of children! Not worth worrying about, I'd say."

"You weren't there!"

"Sorry: I know how it hurts to be laughed at, I really do." Or at least she could remember when it had bothered her.

"It wasn't just giggling. Whispers too."

"Whispers about what?" She had an unpleasant inkling.

"I didn't always catch them. Though Warine Escar, when I turned away from him after he looked over my head, he didn't just mutter, no, he started explaining loudly how some skykin had got into the city and stolen Etyan Harlyn's old unfashionable clothes and somehow persuaded the palace staff to let him in. And everyone laughed. I mean *everyone*."

"They were just being mean, mocking you for your difference because they're all the same. Shallow idiots, obsessed with how to wear their hair and the latest dance steps and court gossip." As Etyan himself had been before he left.

"Maybe. But they're also my friends! Or I thought they were."

"It's the first time you've been back to court. Just act as though you're not bothered what they think. They'll get bored, and then you'll find out who your real friends are."

"It's not that simple, Ree. Some of what they said behind my back… it wasn't just bitching about my stupid out-of-fashion clothes and my stupid funny-looking skin."

"Oh. Right."

"Yes, you know what I mean, don't you? Talking about what happened two years ago. Calling me… I won't repeat it."

She could guess. "I wish your return to court hadn't gone like that but I'm afraid that given how you left, and given how long you've been away, you couldn't really expect to step straight back into your old life, could you?"

"Maybe. I don't know. I had to try."

"I understand. So keep trying."

"I suppose. It's not like I've got anywhere else to go. I thought I'd made a home with her, Ree, just the two of us."

"I know. I'm sorry it didn't work out with Dej." It was never going to, she didn't add.

"Don't say her name."

"All right. As you say, she's gone now." Back to her own people presumably, or what was left of them. Wherever the young skykin rebel was, Rhia had no doubt she'd cope; she was a born survivor.

"But she's still with me, here." He sat back and thumped his chest. "She always will be."

Rhia tried not to smile at the melodramatic gesture. "I know it feels like that now, but it won't always."

"You don't know what this feels like!"

"Actually I do. I have been in love, Etyan. I've been hurt like you have."

"What? Oh, that boy when you were fifteen or so, what was his name?"

"Polain." There had been several months, half a lifetime ago, when saying his name had hurt like Etyan was hurting.

"That wasn't the same. Turned out he didn't love you."

Rhia found her brother's dismissive tone unexpectedly cutting. "No, but I thought he did. And I would have done anything for him, at the time." As she had, stupidly: she had secretly burnt her own face to avoid being sent away from her "true love" and married off to a Zekti prince, forcing the prince's sister to come to Zekt to marry the duke instead. That stupid childish gesture, made in passionate ignorance, had changed the world, and not for the better.

"More fool you." Then Etyan grimaced, lowered his head and muttered, "Sorry." Then louder, "I guess I'll get used to being alone."

"We've got each other, Etyan. That hasn't changed."

He managed a half smile. "I suppose not."

She decided to risk broaching the subject they needed to discuss. There was never going to be a good time, and at least she had his full attention. "And we won't always be alone. We can't be, if we want our House to continue."

"You're talking about marriage, aren't you?"

"I am. I have tried to find a husband but… there haven't been any takers. But you're the head of the House."

"I can't think about that now."

"We must. If things don't go well at my trial, and I… House Harlyn might end up, well, just being you."

"Don't say that."

"I have to consider it. Do you want our line to end? We must plan for the worst."

He lowered his head again. "It's all the worst, now."

"Things are bad, yes, but we'll deal with them. Together." She hoped his self-absorption was enough to stop him picking up how hollow her words of encouragement sounded.

"Can we talk about this later?"

They did not have much "later" left. But what choice did she have? "All right."

CHAPTER 31

Dej found herself analysing her body as she strode across the undulating lowlands, looking for signs she hadn't noticed before. She didn't feel any, at first.

Etyan's sister had been desperate for him to produce an heir. Perhaps she'd take his brat off her hands. But Etyan and Rhia and all those complications were half a world away. And they could stay there. She was pleased, in passing, at how little emotion thinking of Etyan stirred in her now. She had extricated herself from him.

Except for this thing he'd left inside her.

Which she would deal with in due course.

This landscape was different again here. Gentle hills rolled and flowed, covered in moss-grass, grazed by assorted herd beasties and with occasional expanses of tree-type growths, the skyland equivalent of forests, forming sometimes-impenetrable thickets. These were a pain, often forcing her to detour east or west. One particular forest turned out not to be solid; lines of delicate violet bush-trees extended out across the grassland in a lacey network, their tops draped in red-gold gossamer threads. Spotting a thread-shrouded gap she almost darted through it, only alerted by her animus at the last moment. As she veered away something chittered overhead.

While she travelled she gathered burnable stuff from the forest edges to build a nightly fire. This gave welcome warmth and was enough to discourage passing predators, though without her redolent cloak she became a snack for any small biting critters unafraid of fire and able to get through her scaly skin.

As the days passed her belly began to swell and her back and legs to ache, though overall she felt well, energised, as healthy as she ever had, if permanently hungry.

It had become second nature to extend her consciousness into her surroundings, so her first clue she'd reached her destination was the gap in her sensory picture of the landscape. The gap grew, and the sense of it went from an absence to a new type of terrain, slippery and diffuse. The air began to smell odd and the wind, which had been no more than a breeze, sharpened and chilled. By the time she heard the distant swoosh and crash, she'd worked out what this was. She hurried up the next rise.

Ahead of her the land was gone, replaced by a flat plain of blue-green not-land. She stood at the top of a cliff; the ground fell away sharply to a tumble of rocks below. Dej's eye was caught by the intersection of land and sea; the sea was not flat after all, but an undulating surface, and where the undulations hit the bottom of the cliff they broke up over the rocks in spumes of white foam. She watched, fascinated, finding the name for this effect – waves – from half-forgotten geography lessons. The waves formed and died in inexplicable, mesmerising patterns, some flopping over then draining away at once, others exploding upwards in blinding sprays of white with a hollow crack; some of the spray reached her, in attenuated form, as a sour taste on a damp wind.

She sat on her pack and watched the waves while the day grew old. They were beautiful, primal, as gloriously uncaring as the Sun or the rocks, yet shockingly dramatic. When her stomach rumbled she looked around. The moss-grass here was pale blue-grey and grew close to the rocky ground in extensive patches, speckled with clusters of cream-coloured bells. These looked surprisingly like shadowland flowers, and though they smelled like the soap used in the crèche

laundry her animus indicated she could eat them, so she did. They
didn't taste soapy: they tasted of nothing at all, and stuck to her
tongue and the roof of her mouth, but they were surprisingly filling.
Dej curled up in her blanket on the top of the cliff and went to sleep
to the sound of the waves, sated and at peace.

The next day her mood darkened. So, she had reached the edge
of the world – or at least as far as she could go. *Now what?* The
pull of the north hadn't diminished or changed. If something was
drawing her, it was out of reach beyond that great mass of water.

She'd gone to a lot of effort to get this far, so she may as well
stay by the sea, at least until the thing inside her got too big to
ignore. But she needed shelter and water. Were there caves in
the cliffs below? Perhaps, but she couldn't risk climbing down.
No pools or streams here either. From the clifftop, she could see
where land met sea – the coast – as a hazy line stretching away
to the east; more cliffs that way, at least as high as this one but
more barren and forbidding. To the west she could see only water,
so presumably the coast was lower there, and curved back. After
eating as many of the bell-flowers as she could stomach she set off
westwards.

As she'd thought, the coast swept inwards in a wide arc; on the
far side, half hidden in haze, she made out more low hills. Between
the two hilly areas the land was flat, with glints of standing water.
The marshland went down to the edge of the sea and extended
as far as she could see inland. If she wanted to carry on in this
direction her only choice was to cut back in.

She kept all her senses trained on the marshlands as she made
her way down the shallow slope. They were impassable near the
sea, a maze of deep pools and treacherous bogs, but as she followed
them inland the land began to dry out. Perhaps tomorrow she
could risk a crossing.

Around noon the next day she saw taller plants ahead, slender
bushes twice her height, with fans of rustling leaves – actual leaves
– in shades of lavender and smoky purple. The leaf-fans were the
size of two hands together and opened and closed disconcertingly,

sometimes when the wind touched them, sometimes for no obvious reason. The bushes were far enough apart to walk between and the ground underneath was firm if damp. The air smelled sweet at first, but after a while walking under the hand-trees the sweetness became cloying, like rotting peaches. Her uneasiness grew the farther she went into the forest. Should she turn back? No, it was too much effort; she'd come this far.

Lethargy settled on her. The rustling of the leaf fans beat out a complex rhythm. Quite fascinating. Mesmeric, even.

She considered sitting down under a tree, just for a while.

As she wandered over to a tree with soft-looking silver-grey moss spilling down its trunk, something twitched deep inside her, a tiny spasm. She stopped dead. The child. It just moved. It was really there, inside her.

She blinked. *What was I about to do?*

Lie down and give in. Probably never get up.

She turned away from the mossy trap and carried on, swinging her arms and humming to block out the hand-tree's song.

She half expected something to drop down from above, or spring out from behind a trunk, but the predatory forest didn't actively pursue her. It had given her the option of soft oblivion and she'd turned it down.

Light ahead. The end of the forest. She upped her pace. When she emerged she paused and looked down at her gently rounded belly.

This unexpected thing inside her *was real*. And it hadn't had a chance at life yet. It was her responsibility. Just hers. Etyan had no idea it even existed. This child, this *person*, growing in her was, save the coincidence of its conception, nothing to do with the boy she'd once loved. Still loved, perhaps, given the way thoughts of him kept intruding at odd moments.

She realised something else. She no longer felt empty.

While she was busy just surviving, something – someone – had filled the void in her.

CHAPTER 32

On the morning of the Grand Council, Kerne collapsed.

Work on the celestial model was not going well: the world rotated when the handle was turned, at the same time travelling in its grooved hoop around the lamp representing the Sun. But the Maiden kept sticking, and had to be moved by hand. Rhia doubted it would be in a usable state in time for the trial. Kerne had come back after three days of illness still looking terrible, and while bent over the model this morning, he had groaned, tipped forward, and passed out.

She had fetched Markave, whose usual calm was challenged by a crisis involving his own flesh and blood, and they put the boy in the guest bedroom. She sent Brynan for a doctor, but he was still out when she had to leave for the palace.

She had served as House Harlyn's sole representative at the Grand Council between Father's death and Etyan reaching nominal adulthood. At least Etyan was with her today. And sober. The only other time he had attended Council, the year after he reached his majority, he had still been drunk from a party the night before, and had fallen asleep. He had not been happy at coming today, but had acknowledged the necessity. And he had not touched alcohol since his return; when she had voiced her approval for this he shook his head and said, "If I start drinking

193

now I might never stop."

The heads of the noble Houses filed into the Council hall and up to the steeply raked seats around the registrar's desk. They entered in current order of precedence, something which changed from year to year. House Harlyn came near the back of the fifteen Houses major. She and Etyan took their seats on the padded bench with the Harlyn crest carved into the backrest: a stylised design of a feather, a passionflower and two heads of wheat.

They had their grandfather to thank for the status and wealth they enjoyed. A stern, quiet man who died while Rhia was still a child, he had built up the Harlyn holdings, invested the financial gains well and married Francin's great aunt. The role of Observer of Shen had been taken by his more cerebral younger brother.

Everyone stood until the hall was full, with the permitted observers – mainly younger House scions watching the process they would one day participate in – arriving last to fill the upper galleries. The pause gave Rhia a chance to look around; she made herself nod at the other counts and earls and smile above their heads at nearby viscounts and baronets of minor Houses. Few acknowledged her courtesy, but it did no harm to try. As usual, she was the only woman present.

Finally the registrar held out his arms in a gesture of welcome. "It is the time of Between, when the business that changes our world is done." He delivered the Grand Council's ritual opening with the self-importance of a cardinal imparting the will of the First. She had no idea of the young man's name: he was a carefully chosen nobody with no Church or guild affiliation, selected and trained as an impartial arbiter. Her fellow nobles sometimes called him the Duke's Bastard, referring to the fact that his loyalty, like that of the archivist who recorded their deliberations, was not to the noble Houses but to the State itself; given Francin's lifestyle, and this particular registrar's youth, it might even be literally true. At least the third pillar of Shen society, the Church, had no presence here.

"Be seated, my lords."

Everyone sat, with the rustle of robes and the odd *harrumph* or creak of old joints.

The registrar consulted with the archivist. "Item one: the import rights on Xuini spices, previously held by House Lariend, are now to be the business of House Vestine…"

The first section of the agenda was the formalisation of deals and agreements negotiated during dinners, soirees and private meetings over the past year and finalised during Between. They started with matters affecting other shadowlands; Father had said this gave the Houses a feeling of their own importance. With nothing at this stage to concern her House, Rhia and Etyan simply raised their hands to show agreement, or abstained, as appropriate. Most of House Harlyn's wealth was in its physical holdings – it was one of the top five landowners in Shen – so they had little interest in external trade.

As discussions moved on to more local concerns she wondered if Brynan had found a doctor for Kerne yet. Hopefully it was just exhaustion, although if so the fault was hers. But her apprentice could rest when the model was done. In fact, she may as well just give him indefinite leave once the trial started. The phrase "once the trial started" clouded her mind but she made herself see past it to a future when, vindicated and free of other worries, she could take time to tutor her apprentice at her leisure.

"…sale of House Callorn's umbral holdings by a sealed auction…"

Her attention snapped back to the room. The agenda listed each of the many items for discussion as a single, sometimes cryptic, sentence and this one had piqued her interest. Only major Houses could own umbral plantations, given the riches ironwood brought – though perhaps the red valley would change that – so if House Callorn gave up all their forests in the umbral they were opening themselves up to a reduction in status.

But the registrar stressed that they would retain the nominal amount of forest "all Houses major know as their right and badge". Given her previous dealings with them Rhia found herself guiltily relieved that House Callorn was not about to fall.

Two more items were ratified: a new weaving co-operative being set up by four minor Houses, and the annual distribution of shares from the coinback farms; the State owned the means to produce the coinage, but the nobles still benefitted.

Then the registrar handed his pen to the archivist, and was given a new quill; more ritual. He spoke the words that, when she attended as an observer, had heralded the more interesting part of the day but which Rhia now dreaded. "So we conclude the business that passes into history. Let the new matters to be raised now be spoken of."

House Harlyn was the first item. "We begin with the petition by, ah," he consulted his notes, "Houses Ghistan, Minvar and Krathlain, that House Harlyn no longer meets the requirements of a House major. All involved may speak freely."

Rhia stood, along with the two viscounts and one baronet who had brought the motion. The three minor Houses had no doubt been persuaded to put forward this preposterous idea by a major House. Rhia looked across at the three minor nobles, cleared her throat and said, as loudly as she could manage, "I would be interested to hear your reasoning, my lords."

Viscount Minvar, a pale man with a prominent nose, spoke up. "House Harlyn takes little or no interest in the affairs of Shen at large. The bloodline is reduced to two persons, and the management of House assets is left entirely to servants. We contend that this House does not merit the status it currently enjoys as a House major."

Rhia made herself nod to acknowledge his points, then responded. "It is true we have not been as active as we might be, for some years. But those assets of ours you refer to remain extensive, and well-managed, albeit not by members of the nobility." Surely they all knew this ploy for the farce it was: the opening move in a longer game, an initial attempt to plant doubts about House Harlyn's future, no doubt timed to coincide with her upcoming trial. "Also, despite any unrelated crises I would like to assure my fellow nobles that we will continue to discharge all of our duties and participate in courtly life as required."

"May I speak?"

Rhia's head whipped round, to where a noble at her level was standing.

"We recognise Count Escar," said the registrar.

No surprise there. He was probably behind this.

"The countess talks of 'we' and 'ours', but I hear only one voice. Has the Count lost his power of speech, as well as his looks and manners?"

"How dare—"

Fortunately Etyan's outburst was lost in the wave of titters that went round the room at Escar's observation. Rhia put a hand on her brother's shoulder, then turned to him and whispered, "Remember where we are!"

He nodded, and stood. The registrar said, "We recognise Count Harlyn."

"My sister speaks for the House, and for me." His voice shook, and probably barely reached across the room.

Count Escar raised an eyebrow. "So long as we have sorted that out." More smiles greeted his observation.

Still standing, and with her hand on Etyan's arm, Rhia said, "If no one has any substantial and logical objections to my House's continued existence, may I suggest we move onto matters of actual relevance and import."

The registrar nodded. "Agreed. The discussion is noted." Meaning, nothing would come of it. Yet.

Rhia sat down and exhaled. Beside her, she felt Etyan trembling as he sat. She swallowed against a dry throat. She should have brought a drink.

More contentious items followed: an accusation of tax fraud from one minor House, brought by another, and the announcement that a business partnership between Houses Blaven and Relnarorn would be dissolved, with negotiation of terms to follow.

And then, "Next item: House Harlyn wishes to discuss possible marriage proposals."

Which was all it said in the agenda. The majors would know about this; Francin had, sometimes through intermediaries, sounded out every one of them, but even House Callorn had not shown any interest. Hence putting forward this motion, even though such business was usually conducted in private and only announced once concluded.

She stood, knees locked, awaiting leave to speak, then when the registrar nodded to her, said, "As some of you know, I am willing to renounce my unmarried status for the right match. My House has made overtures to the major Houses, but I now open up negotiations to any noble House, major or minor, provided that–"

"I'll do it."

Rhia looked round as her brother stood. Without waiting for permission he said again, "I'll do it." Rhia stared at him. Every time she had raised the subject of marriage he had deflected it. "I'll get married to save my House. I'll consider any offer."

The hall erupted. People jumped to their feet. The registrar called for order then, when he was ignored, resorted to picking up the short wooden staff of his office and rapping it sharply on the desk in front of him. "Silence, please, my lords!"

The noise quietened, but did not cease; mutters, gasps and the odd incredulous oath still came from round the hall. A handful of nobles remained standing. A little breathlessly the registrar said, "We recognise Counts Lariend, Phisten, Athlyn and Escar. Gentlemen, please keep your heads."

Umren Escar spoke up. "What in the name of the First and Last makes you think anyone will have you, boy?"

The laughter swelled.

"We don't even know what you are. No wait–" He held up a hand as Rhia opened her mouth, though she was not sure what she was going to say, other than telling him to shut up. "Actually we do know what he is." The count stared right at Etyan. "We know exactly what you are, even if no one will say it to your face."

She heard the muttered slur then, whispers and murmurs with

no one source. A cowardly consensus coming from all around: *Rapist*.

Beside her Etyan gave a single sob, then turned and fled. She watched him go, the vile mutters filling her ears. She wanted to call him back but her voice had frozen in her throat.

He reached the door. For a moment she nearly broke and ran after him. But to leave the Grand Council now, like this... She may as well hand the case for the dissolution of her House to Count Escar.

When she turned back Earl Lariend was poised to speak. He waited for the mutters to die down then raised his eyes briefly but theatrically heavenwards as though beseeching the First to give him patience, before fixing his gaze back on his fellow lords and declaring, "My noble friends, we have endured the laughable eccentricities and thoughtless arrogance of House Harlyn for too long. We have put up with one of Shen's respected Houses being run by a half-deranged and, it turns out, godless woman in the name of a worse-than-useless boy. No one will have her, this disgrace to her gender who is unable to accept the rightful rule of a man. And no one will have him, diseased by his contact with the skyland and with common whores, and a ravisher of innocent girls."

By the time the wretched man reached the end of his tirade Rhia had got enough control to speak. "Have you quite finished?"

"I think the consensus response to this ridiculous request has been made clear."

"Perfectly. However, we have broken no statute, and if my House's continued presence offends any of you then I am afraid that is not my problem. Whatever the future holds for us is... not yet known." She should perhaps say "is in the hands of the First", but the hypocrisy would have burned. She concluded, "One thing I do know, and you should know: while I still have breath in my body, House Harlyn will endure." She half sat, half collapsed onto the bench.

The registrar, looking shaken, said, "The record will show that no House chose to take up the offer of marriage made by House Harlyn. We may now move on."

Rhia stared at the empty doorway and concentrated on breathing. *Damn corset. Damn nobles. Damn Etyan.*

The rest of the session passed in a daze. But not fast enough. As soon as the ritual closing had been spoken she began to push past the nearest nobles; technically they should leave in precedence order, but now duty had been discharged she had to get out. Beyond offended mutters at her rudeness, no one tried to stop her. Which was good, as if they had she might have hit them.

She took the fastest route out of the palace, half hoping she would run into Francin, half dreading it. But he was not around; she had hardly seen him since her visit to Alharet last month. A cluster of carriages and sedan chairs waited outside but she was interested in speed, not status. She picked up her skirts and ran down the hill, bursting into the townhouse. Brynan waited in the hall, wearing the whipped-dog expression that meant bad news. "I'm sorry m'lady. He's gone."

Her fears were realised. She leant forward, trying to catch her breath against the constraints of her formal dress.

Brynan continued, "He had me order a carriage, and as soon as he carriage arrived he left."

"Where... Did he say where he's going?"

"He said to tell you, 'I'll be at the villa. I'm so sorry. I just can't stay here.'"

He had a head start, and was in a carriage. But she could still go after him. The Church had said she wasn't to leave the city, but they could not have foreseen this. But nor would they care about it. She straightened. Yet again, her brother had run. And this time, she had to let him go.

"Thank you Brynan." She needed to get out of these stupid clothes, get into her study, carry on working... "Did you find a doctor for Kerne?"

Brynan's face fell further. "Eventually m'lady. He was very busy."

"What is it?"

"We've made the boy as comfortable as we can. His father's with him, I hope that's all right…"

"What is wrong with him? Does he need medicine? Markave knows he can spend whatever he wants."

"The doctor says there's nothing to be done."

"Why not?" But she knew the truth even before Brynan spoke.

"Because it's the rain-fever."

CHAPTER 33

"Your dodgy friend called round."

Sorne looked up from his dinner to see Sharrey wearing an expression of open disapproval; she looked like that a lot these days. "Which one?" he said evenly.

"Yes, there seems to be more every day, don't there?" She cringed once she'd spoken, just in case he lashed out.

Not that he would. But he hated the groove they'd worn themselves over the last couple of months. The way she dared him to lose his temper with her. The way he refused to, then got annoyed at being goaded, and almost did. But not quite. Never quite crossing the line. "You want me to contribute to the household, don't you?"

With both the duke's money and Jemulf and Breta long gone, he'd taken on work that appalled the militia captain in him. Door duty at an illegal gambling den. Acting as strongarm for a protection scam. Beating up a man who'd annoyed another man. The jobs came through those he'd taught, or old friends of Jemulf's, or word of mouth. Mirror might be a pretty law-abiding city but out here on the strangers' isle there was still work for a man who could inflict selective damage and stay quiet. He hated it. But he had to live. And he had to live here, with this miserable, damaged woman. Even if he could've afforded a guesthouse he'd have nowhere secure to store his stuff.

He'd spent the money from his second job on a lockable box. The first job, standing guard at a meeting between two minor criminals, had earnt just enough to buy a dried twist of what the trader assured him was becen-root. The medicine hadn't helped; for the last month Tamak'd barely left his bed. The new ironwood box didn't have the fine-carved tumbler his old locker had had, but hopefully the puzzle-lock would deter curious fingers. He'd bought it when Sharrey was out and Tamak at a rare day at school, then eased the duke's letters out from the narrow gap behind Sharrey's display-cabinet where he'd stashed them, careful not to dislodge the plates. Most of them could be safely disposed of now, having informed him of what he needed to know. But they reminded him why he was here. When he'd told Sharrey that he needed to keep the box in their room but she wasn't to touch it she'd stared at him. He'd wondered if this was it, the unreasonable demand too far. Then she'd shrugged and turned away.

And now she just nodded. She'd been more subdued than usual these last couple of weeks, like she took the caliarch's death personally. Sorne's response to Numak's passing had been rather different: he could barely hide his growing anticipation.

"So then," he said, "this dodgy man. Is he coming back?"

"Nope." Before he could take issue with her terse reply she followed up hurriedly, "He asked where he'd find you. I told him you spend a lot of time at Ramek's yard."

"So he's gone there?"

"Guess so. I gave him directions."

"Wait, he didn't know where Ramek's is?" Most of Sorne's current business came through, and was often negotiated at, the yard.

"Didn't seem to. Looked like he might be one of your people, actually." She put a slight twist of disdain on *your*.

"Mine as in?"

"Shenese."

"Don't wait up for me."

He left without waiting for a response. She'd expect nothing less. And if she thought he was off to get drunk with one of his countrymen then good, because there was nothing suspicious in that.

He recognised the courier as soon as he entered the yard. But he played it cool, because he was known here. The visitor wasn't, so half of Ramek's clientele were keeping an eye on him with varying degrees of subtlety.

Sorne made a show of looking around, spotting the newcomer, then nodding in what he hoped was a casual *you look like one of my people* way. The visitor nodded back. Janave had just made corporal when Sorne left Shen; always thin, he looked downright haggard after travelling here with the skykin caravan.

Sorne sauntered over. He had an idiotic urge to grin at the militiaman, the first familiar face he'd seen for two years. He resisted and said, "You look like you've come from Shen."

"I have."

"Avoid the tea."

"I will, in future."

Those nearest were losing interest at the mundane banter. "I can show you the sights if you like."

"I would like. I hear the streets are quite safe, if a bit narrow." Janave stood.

"Most of them." Sorne gestured at the man's large backpack. "You all right with that?"

"Should be. Though an idea of the best place to stay would be good. The guesthouse the scribe on the gate recommended was pretty pricey."

As the militiaman shouldered his pack Sorne asked, "Mam Jekrey's?"

"No, Mam Mercet."

"Oh, her. Yes, I think she's put her prices up recently." Sorne had no idea whether that was true; the conversation was largely for the benefit of the observers. Whether they bought it or not he had no idea; what mattered was that they realised they wouldn't be hearing anything of interest. But he was glad that Mam Jekrey was no longer getting recommended by the scribes who logged visitors: since his first stay in Mirror he'd grown his hair long and his tan had faded under Zekt's stormy skies, but Mam Jekrey was one of the few people on Arec who might remember him. And, he now recalled, he'd left without settling the bill. He had no doubt she'd remember that.

Once they were away from the yard he let himself smile. "It's good to see you."

"You too sir."

"I'm going to want the lowdown on everything from palace gossip to the skiv-skiv league before you go."

"I don't doubt it, sir."

"Probably best if you drop the sir."

"Ah. Of course. How paranoid should we be?"

"Just careful. I'm known at this end of the isle. Which is why we'll be taking a roundabout route to your guesthouse, and watching each other's backs."

"Got you."

They had been walking side-by-side, but now Sorne slowed a fraction; Janave let him fall back. A quick glance around and behind. No sign of a tail. Stepping back up he said, "I'm guessing you're not actually short of funds."

"His Grace provided everything I might need."

"Good. And you have something for me?"

"I do."

They crossed a square, Sorne taking point while his fellow solider stopped to watch a group of youths dancing with both skill and enthusiasm to a pair of pipers. A quick nod confirmed all was well. Two more squares and several alleys brought them to Mam Mercet's. The guesthouse owner was curious about the pair of Shenese men taking a room together, until a five-mark piece distracted her.

Once she'd shown them to the room Sorne's heart lifted further. It was finally happening. Good job he'd visited Pahnec last week to take a casual daytime stroll past the townhouse. The street door had been repaired but not obviously reinforced, and the shutters were closed. The place was still empty.

When they were alone in the room he asked Janave, "How long can you stay?"

"A few days. I need to be on the next caravan back."

Sorne nodded; the duke would want to know the delivery had reached its target. "I'll need you to hold onto the package until I can smuggle it home."

Janave smiled. "Home?"

"Figure of speech. I'll check over it now though."

"Of course, sir."

He had waited so long for this, though when Janave prised open the lid of the long wooden box it was not obvious what the object was. Fortunately he still had the duke's diagram amongst his salvaged papers. What was obvious was how much iron had been used in its manufacture: the metal strips and intricate mechanisms nestled in the packed straw alongside the ironwood components could set Sharrey and Tamak up for life.

He looked up at Janave. "This red valley must be quite an operation."

"Not seen it myself sir; just the end results."

Sorne nodded. "And it's the end results that matter."

CHAPTER 34

The sky is my solace.

Rhia smiled at the remembered phrase. Or tried to: her face no longer appeared capable of even fleeting joy. And up here on her observation platform was the only place she could feel any peace, any hope.

She leaned back on her stool and tipped her head up.

The sky was not entirely clear; wisps of cloud still hid the high heavens, but she could see a couple of constellations, the Twins and the Stepping Horse. And two Strays: the Crone, peeking out from clouds halfway between horizon and zenith and the Maiden, low as always and shining pure, virginal white to the Crone's faded red. The planet was almost round when observed through her sightglass, the once-slender Maiden's belly now swollen in a way that implied the Stray was indeed a misbehaving young woman.

Tonight even active observation was too much. Just bathing in the starlight, just being and not speaking – or thinking – was what she needed.

Yet thoughts still came.

That phrase, *the sky is my solace*: she had taken comfort from it as Father lay dying. He had told her to come up here, to take a rest from his bedside, his voice cracking and weak, and while she looked up that night, the phrase had arrived in her head. Trite and sentimental, of course. But when the rain-fever finally took him, she had found herself repeating her new mantra all the time, while the grief tore into her.

And now the rain-fever had marked another victim. She knew the odds, the "doom of ten": when the plague returned, one in ten would contract it; it would take up to take ten weeks to run its full course, during which time the sufferer would be up and down, sometimes seeming to recover, sometimes relapsing; ultimately, only one in ten who caught the rain-fever would survive. Had she felt herself capable of praying, she would have prayed that Kerne was one of those lucky ones.

Snatches of this afternoon's Grand Council meeting kept coming back to her. No doubt Etyan had thought he was doing the right thing, finally facing up to his responsibilities. But why hadn't he told her what he was planning? Assuming he had planned it, rather than the offer of marriage being a spur-of-the-moment decision. Still heartbroken, he'd appeared so against the possibility. Not that it even was a possibility, it now appeared.

The noble Houses held more power than either Church or State but their constant bickering and politicking meant they rarely acted in unity. Yet they had united today, against her House.

Of course Francin had had no luck finding her a husband. Any man coming into the Harlyn household on her terms would have to give up his old affiliations: he would be marrying into her House, rather than her marrying into his. He could use Harlyn resources and influence to help his old House, but how many noblemen would consider that a price worth paying to become, in effect, a male wife? Perhaps she should have tried the minor Houses, as they might view being a consort in a major House as a step up, although the majors would have taken great offence at that. Or perhaps she should have offered a far-greater-than-usual dowry to pay off the groom's House. But she had not thought to do either of those things. Her mind, which she prided herself on keeping open, had not been able to see the offer as her fellow nobles saw it. She had assumed, in her arrogance, that marriage into House Harlyn was attractive enough by itself. It had been once, to House Callorn at least.

But no longer. Though they would want to keep details of the charges secret, the fact that she was being put on trial by the Church was known amongst the noble Houses: many high clerics, including two of the three cardinals, came from the nobility, and though they were meant to renounce their worldly affiliations once ordained, lines of communication remained open. No one wanted to marry a heretic.

The majors had much to gain by her downfall. The minor Houses had only called for a reduction in status, but if House Harlyn was actually dissolved – as could happen if she and Etyan both died without heirs – then the Houses major would get a third share of its assets between them. A third of the Harlyn wealth was significant, even split fifteen ways. More, in fact, than any one House could expect from giving up one of their own to be a subordinate partner in a marriage. Enough, it seemed, to bring the squabbling Houses major together in what appeared to be a genuine conspiracy.

At least Viscount Manacar, the one judge at her trial she hoped would take her side, was from a minor House, like most noble magistrates. Any conspiracy would be amongst the majors, as only they would benefit from her House's dissolution. Except, three minor Houses had spoken against her today. They might not be in on the majors' scheme but they could be reacting to pressure from one or more major House. If she had to guess which, she would say the instigators were House Escar: her grandfather had built up the Harlyn fortune at a cost to them, a slight they still remembered, and they had not come off well from their part in the conspiracy to frame Etyan. It was possible House Manacar could be put under the same pressure, in which case every judge might be against her before her trial even started.

No, she must not think that way. She must not assume the worst, and lose what little hope she had left. But she must plan for it.

Etyan was still nominally head of House Harlyn. But his

dramatic and impulsive gesture had publicly undermined his fitness as Count, after the House's status had already been openly questioned. If she was not around this time next year, she had no doubt that the next Grand Council would dissolve House Harlyn.

Unless...

Perhaps, with the world against her, the solution lay close to home. After all, every sensible, reasonable option had been exhausted.

She needed to speak to her lawyer.

Movement above caught her eye. Focusing on the sky she saw the clouds had cleared. There, again: a streak of silver. A falling star. Rhia's attention snapped fully back to the sky. Another. And another. Star-falls occurred midway through most dry-years, but rarely at other times, and rarely in such numbers. They were not stars, of course; the stars remained fixed. She had no idea what caused this breathtaking phenomenon, and tonight she did not care. She watched, entranced, lost for a while in the wonder of the skies.

"Is it hopeless?" Rhia found herself wringing her hands where they sat in her lap. She untangled them and laid her palms flat on the dining table.

Sur Lectel, looking over the cup of cooling tisane in front of him, pursed his lips. "Not at all. You have prepared well, although the lack of a working celestial model may be an issue–"

"I'm close, as I said! Sorry, I shouldn't snap. I should complete the model any day now."

"So we must hope. Although in some ways, it would be easier should you fail to prove your theory..."

"What do you mean?"

"Forgive me for mentioning this m'lady, but if you are mistaken, or at least are ruled to be mistaken, then I believe you would recant?"

"If I am proved wrong, yes. If I am right, but they refuse to believe me, no. I will not cover up the truth."

"Ah. The reason I mention this is that I am obliged to point out again that your best chance of getting through this ordeal unscathed would still be to recant, at which point the Church would have no case and you would walk free."

"And if I did, hypothetically, recant now, would that be an end to it?" Recanting went against all she stood for, but as the trial neared and the proofs continued to elude her, she had to consider it.

"You would go free, yes, though bound under oath never to speak of the matter you were brought to trial for."

"My theory you mean. I would have to swear to abandon it."

"Yes. And your papers…"

"They would confiscate all the papers pertaining to the theory." She had suspected as much.

"Indeed. And they would have the right to examine *all* your papers."

She threw her hands up. "Then I have no way out!"

"If recanting at the cost of your work is not acceptable then your *only* way out is for us to win. Let us assume you do convince the judges – two out of three of them, anyway – of the validity of your theory. At that point the Church would be forced to consider how it can be reconciled with the scriptures, and their teachings."

"I have been through the scriptures! I found nothing that goes against my theory. What little is said about the sky is ambiguous at best."

"Which is good. However, as you have observed yourself the scriptures allow for… varying interpretations."

"Contradictions, you mean. If the Church can preach both that the First is timeless, impartial and eternal and that He created people then punished them and has now withdrawn from the world, then surely they can deal with a new way of explaining commonly observable physical phenomena the scriptures barely mention!"

"They may not see it that way."

She kept forgetting she was not dealing with rational people. "In which case it *is* hopeless."

"Please do not think that. Our first task is to convince the two impartial judges of your theory. Then, I believe that the variations within the scriptures will give us the room we need to make your case, to argue that this model of the heavens may be accurate without challenging the Church. We can do this, m'lady."

He appeared convinced. Or at least passionate about the case and optimistic about their chances. Which was the best she could hope for. "Thank you." But she had called him here for two reasons. "I also need to speak to you about another matter. Something rather... delicate."

Three days to the trial. Sur Lectel had said her enquiry could take "a few days" to research. She must be patient.

She was finding it hard to concentrate, which in turn caused more stress, because a lapse in concentration could lead to a mistake in her workings or worse, damage the celestial model. She all but gave up on work.

But she needed to do *something*, to take action, or seek diversion. There were still plenty of social events as Between drew to a close, but she would rather jump off her observation platform than attend those. However, while idly looking through her papers she realised there was something positive to be done at the palace. Francin still had some of the writings he had requested from her recently, and they had discussed the more general idea of him taking copies a while back. Thanks to poor Kerne's diligence, copies of much of her recent work already existed. Normally the second enquirer in a shadowland would hold the other enquirer's papers in trust in an emergency like the one she was facing, and she might yet have to send Theorist of Shen some of the less contentious contents of her ironwood chest. But her traitorous colleague would not see any more of her original theories, even if it meant disobeying the Church's letter.

She considered going to the palace herself but there were too many people she wanted to avoid. Markave was the obvious choice to send in her place.

Her steward was, understandably enough, spending as much time as possible at his son's bedside. The boy was livelier than his father when Rhia entered the room, sitting up and stroking Pathi, who had taken up residence on his bed. Markave, half collapsed in the chair next to him, was dozing; his conscience would not let him neglect his household duties even in the current crisis and he looked exhausted. But he straightened when she murmured his name, and agreed at once to the errand. His eager obedience set off an unsettling and complex warmth in Rhia's chest, which she chose to ignore. Even so, she found herself disproportionately relieved when he returned from the errand promptly, reporting that he had handed her note to the duke in person.

The duke's reply came back the same evening:

Of course you can send copies of your papers to me. But in order to avoid unwanted attention please send them in small parcels, to be left with one of the following individuals only:

There followed a list of six names, four minor ministers and two militia captains.

Rhia worried at Francin's paranoia. But then, as events at the Grand Council had proved, sometimes she was not paranoid enough.

CHAPTER 35

Dej shadowed the hand-tree forest, heading back towards the sea. Rain fell intermittently from a heavy grey sky.

The coast here was flat and the skyland growth petered out before it reached the sea. This gap – the "shoreline" the geography tutor had called it – was covered in smooth, rounded pebbles. Something else the tutor said about the world-sea came back to her, but she hoped he was wrong. She walked down the pebbly shoreline, taking care on the uneven footing, to where the waves lapped and frothed. She filled her empty waterskin from the sea, then tipped it up to her lips–

And spat and sputtered, even as her animus sent its belated warning like a rap on the forehead. The geography tutor was right; the sea was poisonous. But she wouldn't give up; she'd find an alternative water source.

Half a day later, a stream tumbled down through a cleft in the hills that had been rising behind her as she walked along the shoreline. The water seeped away into the pebbles before it reached the sea, but a short and easy clamber upstream brought her to a pool large enough to fill the skin.

The coast continued to sweep southeast. At some point she'd need to cut due south, back to the shadowlands. Unless she could raise the child out here. Perhaps there was some foodstuff she could feed the baby…? She had a while to find a solution.

But she also needed shelter.

The next stream she found came down to the shoreline in a stand of reeds. The huts at the clanless settlement had been roofed with reeds. She sawed at some sturdy-looking stalks then bundled them into her half-empty pack.

The next day she was walking along the shore in the shadow of low cliffs when she spotted something odd on the lower shoreline.

She'd already explored the edge of the sea, looking for food, though she didn't risk venturing into the water. But she'd noticed how the extent of the shoreline changed. The sea moved up it and receded by various amounts, two, three, sometimes four times a day, leaving occasional items behind.

She had already found, in places where the pebbles gave way to rocks, growths of crinkle-edged reddish weed which tasted like a combination of snot and mouldy bread but which were not actually poisonous. She'd also come across collapsed milky-coloured gelatinous spheres the size of her hand that her animus warned her about, shiny yellow ribbons with bladders the size of a fingertip along one edge that smelt bad enough she didn't need any warning and a stringy tangle of blood-red strands that shuddered as she approached, rolling up the shore then, when she gave a surprised squeal, flopping back into the waves.

This was much larger. It looked like a bone, but it was longer than she was tall; flattened and curved. She wondered if it belonged to a relative of whatever had been making that low booming call out to sea for the last two nights. When she pulled on it, it moved easily; it was light as bone too. It would make a good support for a shelter. As she pulled it free of the waves she spotted another one, a little farther along the beach, and a third beyond that. Something big had died out there.

This might be a sign. The cliffs here were compressed and weathered yellow stone layered through with bands of charcoal grey and ochre. She spent a while casting along the base of them, until she found a fold in the land. She dragged the bones up the beach and propped them up against the slope to make the skeleton of a lean-to shelter. Nothing fancy: although she had to make sure it was aligned properly, the structure only had to be big enough to crawl into.

Still easier said than done. The materials for the shack in the umbral had been provided by Etyan's sister and the result had still been somewhat ramshackle, and leaked in heavy rain. This was an even less impressive effort, just bundles of reeds lashed with vines and pinned down with small rocks, the result barely big enough to lie down full length in, but she still took pride in it. After a day's foraging she would sit outside her shelter, playing her flute for her unborn child, sometimes getting a kick in response. On one clear night she was treated to a spectacular display of falling stars.

But the next week billowing clouds blew in as dusk faded. Dej eyed them up as she crawled into her shelter, but there was nothing she could do. If it rained, she would find out if the shelter was watertight. If it wasn't, she would fix it.

She was dragged from sleep by a crash of thunder. She hadn't heard thunder since leaving Shen, and for a moment she was back in the umbral, wondering why the bed was so hard and where Etyan had gone.

She sat up, shocked by the memory. Her head hit the reed roof, and a trickle of chill water ran down her back. A gut-shaking roar nearby reached a sudden crescendo. She scrambled out of her shelter in alarm.

The waves had been whipped to a froth by the gale, their white tops seething in the moonlight before crashing up the pebbles. But the waterline was far enough down the beach not to be a threat, even if it sounded like the end of the world. She made herself take a calming breath. She should get back into the shelter, and take what protection it offered, even if sleep would be out of the question in this—

She knew that sensation. The land was moving!

She whirled on the spot just as the slope behind her shelter shuddered, then slumped. Orange mud and dark vegetation slid down the slope and into her shelter. The support-bones exploded outwards. Dej jumped back as the mudslide erupted out across the pebbles.

The torrent of earth slowed. She dug her nails into her palms and breathed hard and slow, oblivious of the rain running down her bare scalp. When she'd calmed down she unclenched her hands, put one on her belly, and murmured, "Well, that was close."

She sat on the pebbles, halfway between treacherous earth and furious sea, and hugged her knees, waiting out the storm, and the night, in a state of tension. When the sea came closer she edged backwards until it receded again.

The next morning, as the storm blew away on shreds of cloud, soaked, cold and exhausted, she surveyed the damage. The landslide had buried her possessions, but the mud was soft and it wasn't hard to dig out her pack and blanket. She was no worse off than she had been.

But she wasn't going to hang around at the site of her latest failure.

She used the cleansing-moss to clean herself up, shook her pack out and washed the blanket in the now-calm sea. Then she set off along the shoreline.

The babe kicked most days now, though her belly was nothing like as big as the pregnant skykin she'd seen at the crèche. If she did give up soon, and went to a shadowland before her child was due, they were obliged to take her in while she waited to give birth. It made sense to at least be nearby, just in case. But she hated the thought of leaving the child. She shouldn't: skykin knew that they had to leave their children with shadowkin for the sake of the child's survival, so they did. But she wasn't a pure skykin. And the baby was all she had.

The landscape remained rugged and hilly, which beat swamps and marshlands, but with her belly swelling and her energy flagging, the terrain was hard work. When she could she walked on the shoreline, but half the time there wasn't a shoreline to walk on, as the sea kept cutting into the hills. At night she huddled in what shelter she could find, wrapped in her blanket.

Soon she would have to turn south.

Then, as she heaved herself up a rock-strewn slope she sensed a change ahead. The land fell away in a valley, a dip in the hills. And it didn't feel like another damn swamp.

When she reached the crest of the hill her intuition was proved right.

It wasn't another damn swamp.

It was a city.

CHAPTER 36

The opening day of the trial of the Church of Shen vs Rhia Harlyn was something of an anti-climax. Sur Lectel had explained the process but somehow Rhia still expected a formal, drawn-out session with unnecessary pomp and flourishes.

She and the lawyer reported to the Council hall at the appointed hour. It was mercifully empty; the trial was in one of the lesser chambers. Not the one she had heard the original charge in, and where she had previously seen Etyan face something-like-justice, but a larger room, containing a desk facing a long table. Three men sat behind the great table, chatting casually as she entered. Two other men, in dark clerical robes, sat over papers at small desks against the walls.

Spotting her, the three judges fell silent. The one in the centre nodded an acknowledgement. Vansel was the oldest of the cardinals, his hair wispy and white, his shoulders bent with age. When he preached he uncurled, the passion of his words burning off the infirmities of age. He came from a humble background, and she found him refreshingly lacking in the arrogant pretentions of Marsan or the distracted superiority of Charain. But he was a stickler, a follower of protocol.

"Come in then, and stand before us."

As Rhia stepped up she stole looks at the other two men who

223

would be deciding her fate.

Lord Jertine, Viscount Manacar, sat on the cardinal's right. He was about her age, handsome except for his thin mouth, and dressed well but not ostentatiously. He had not been at the Grand Council – though a viscount, he was not head of his House – and though she knew him by sight they had never met, although she remembered Etyan once losing a significant sum to him in a game of cards.

Sur Tethorn, on Vansel's left, was younger than she expected, with a weak chin but a hard stare. Unlike Jertine, he would not have had any formal training in the law and was here as a representative of "the populace", or rather of the guilds.

Vansel spoke up. "Please confirm that you are Rhia Harlyn, and that you are aware of the nature of the charges being brought against you, the process by which you shall be examined, and the consequences should you be found guilty."

Sur Lectel had not said any particular ritual response was required, so Rhia lifted her chin and said simply, "I am."

"We will start with the oaths."

One of the minor clerics came forward with a copy of the Book of Separation. The other one, Rhia was pleased to note, was a scribe, poised to write down the proceedings.

The oaths were complex, being several different ways of promising to tell the truth in the sight of the First, to respect the judges, and to abide by the laws of the State. Sur Lectel, standing half a pace behind her, had to swear variations on them too. During the lengthy process Tethorn fidgeted but paid attention. Jertine looked a little bored.

Once the oaths were complete, Vansel gestured to the desk. "The defendant may sit."

She did so, her lawyer settling next to her.

The cardinal said, "For the record, let it be noted that the purpose of this court is to ascertain whether the defendant has, in her presumption to know the nature of the heavens, caused offence against the First. Specifically, whether the celestial arrangements she suggests contradict the word of the First as given in the scriptures. At the request of the defendant's representative, the process will not only examine how these claims should be viewed in the light of the word of the First, but also whether they can be said to have any objective reality." Rhia tried not to wince at the incredulity in his tone. "Will the defence be calling any witnesses?" Although there were no events or actions to be recounted, because they were using the apparatus of the State witnesses were permitted.

"Not at this time." Sur Lectel's careful answer allowed for the possibility, however remote, that Eparch Sadakh might still appear in person to defend her.

"So that is 'No' then?"

"We have yet to hear back from a potential witness, Your Holiness." If Sadakh did participate, his word might make all the difference. "Would the judges indulge us and allow this individual to speak, should they later ask to?"

"Hmm. This is somewhat irregular. Then again, this entire procedure is without clear precedent." The cardinal looked to the scribe. "Let it be noted that the defendant may wish to call a witness at a future date." Then to Rhia, "The court will assess whether to permit this when and if it happens."

"Thank you, Holiness." Sur Lectel's tone had an unctuous edge which Rhia disliked, but she saw the need for it. "And will the prosecution be calling anyone?"

Rhia held her breath. Would Theorist of Shen want to make sure she was brought down by appearing in person?

"No."

She exhaled. Apparently her fellow enquirer was happy to leave her to her fate.

Vansel continued, "The defendant has been given ample time to gather evidence for her case, and we have been informed that this evidence is… substantial. Her representative will now submit it."

Sur Lectel had arrived with a large satchel slung across his back. Having lowered it to the floor beside the desk, he now lifted it in both hands and carried it up to the judges.

Three sets of eyebrows went up. "All of this?" said Vansel.

Rhia had an inappropriate urge to smile. Sur Lectel said, "As well as the papers she has prepared herself, the defendant is submitting a number of testimonials."

"Testimonials?"

"Yes." They had discussed how to deal with the matter of the enquirers; Rhia had had no choice other than to reveal their existence to Sur Lectel. "From individuals she is in correspondence with in other shadowlands. As the honourable judges may perhaps be aware the defendant knows, through the exchange of letters, a number of like-minded thinkers."

From their expressions, the two non-Church judges had not been aware of this. Vansel, who no doubt was, said, "Indeed, and it is a matter of concern that the idea we are here to discuss may have been shared with persons unknown in other shadowlands." He looked across at her. "Has it, Countess Harlyn?"

Rhia suppressed a cough and said, "You are asking if I have shared my theory that the Sun is the centre of the universe with anyone outside Shen?" She had known there was a risk of being asked this under oath, hence the care with which she phrased her reply.

"I am, yes."

"Before my work came to the Church's notice, I had communicated my initial ideas to an individual in Lhir."

"Lhir? That is a long way from here."

"It is. Our correspondence is consequently... slow."

"And did it cease once you were made aware that your idea was not acceptable to your Church?"

Rhia noted the phrase "your Church". This court's jurisdiction ended at Shen's umbral, which allowed her to answer with a degree of honesty. "It did not. However, my correspondent already had papers on the theory itself, and what little has passed between us since merely refines it."

"Hmm. We may return to this once the main matter is resolved." Meaning: she could be asked to give up the real name of Skywatcher of Lhir. As far as she knew the Church did not hold excessive sway there; however, Lhir was so distant that what little information she had was rumour and hearsay. "For now, myself and the other judges have reading to do. A lot of reading." As Vansel broke her gaze to look at the papers spilling from the satchel in front of him Rhia risked a glance to either side, where the other two were also staring at the paperwork; Tethorn with a degree of curious interest and Jertine with some dismay. "Given how much written evidence we need to get through, we will need several days. Let us convene again on fiveday."

And that was it.

Sur Lectel came home with her but declined the offer of refreshments, saying he was sure the duke would offer him some later; a subtle way of letting her know Francin was following events closely, Rhia thought.

"I think that went as well as we could expect," she suggested. She hadn't exactly lied under oath, just not offered facts beyond those requested.

"At this early stage, yes. All proceeded as expected."

"And I was pleased to see the trial being recorded."

The shade of a grimace crossed the lawyer's features. "Although the mechanics of the trial will remain on record, I believe that, should you be found guilty, then due to their inherently heretical nature any details about your actual theory will be expunged from the transcript."

"Oh, First's sake!" For once she felt happy to take God's name in vain. Of course the Church would go to such lengths to suppress forbidden knowledge. The few heresy trials on record had been about prohibited items. The defendant had either come into possession of some ancient artefact made by the Children of the First which they failed to turn over to the Church or else had fashioned an object forbidden by the prescriptions against unholy devices. This was the trial of an idea. And none of those had been grand trials: most had ended with the destruction of the device and a public penance for the defendant. "Regarding the other matter… have you completed your research?"

"I have, and the news is good. There is no legal bar to this course of action. Assuming you really do wish to go ahead."

"I do."

She took the "course of action" he had referred to as soon as the lawyer left, before she lost her nerve.

Nerilyn was out: it was her afternoon off, and she was spending it with her beau; Rhia had sent the first package of papers to the palace with her.

Markave was with Kerne. She called Brynan from the kitchen and had him take over watching the boy.

Markave came to the parlour looking tired and careworn, the lines in his high forehead deeper than usual. Perhaps she should not have summoned him from his son's bedside. "How is he?" she asked.

"Sleeping peacefully."

"Good." There was no point giving him platitudes about Kerne's situation, or chances of survival. "Sit please."

"M'lady?"

"This is a discussion we both need to be sitting down for." *What am I thinking?* She should just let him go back to watching over his child, and forget the whole idea. But to send him off now would start him worrying about what she had been unable to tell him. And she had made her choice.

Markave lowered himself into a seat across from her. The concern on his face was turning to confusion, with a hint of alarm.

She had considered possible ways to approach this conversation. She had even rehearsed a short speech, talking about the problems the House currently faced and how they could work together to save it. But now he was in front of her she couldn't start spouting justifications. Instead she blurted: "I want you to marry me." She sucked her lips in, as though trying to take the words back, then exhaled in a rush and added, "For the sake of the House."

Markave's eyes went wide. He blinked, then bowed his head. When he raised it again he said, "I am not sure what m'lady means."

"I mean… no one will have me." Which sounded insulting, when she put it like that. But she'd said it now. "And I need to marry, because Etyan never will, and we need continuity."

"Continuity." Her steward's voice was a flat whisper.

"Yes. I…" She could not bring herself to talk about possible heirs, not with his dying son in the house. Instead she said, "You are one of the most important people, most important men, in my life. And you are vital to this House. If I am married, there is some hope for House Harlyn."

"M'lady's words make some sense." Again, just a whisper, but from his tone he was not entirely appalled by the idea.

"Believe it or not, I would rather marry you than any of my peers." Which was true enough. "But I will not order you to do this. Given…" she nearly said "our history" but that implied a closeness which had not existed, save briefly in her adolescent mind "…past events, I will understand if my proposal is not acceptable to you. If this offer is not something you can countenance just say, and it will be as though this conversation never happened." Except it would have. Just making the suggestion had changed things between them forever, she now realised.

"I…" He looked at his hands, then at her – or rather over her shoulder. "I need to think about this."

"Of course. Take as long as you want."

"May I go now?"

"Yes. Please. I mean… Markave, I'm sorry to have to foist this on you."

"M'lady never has to apologise or explain." He stood, bowed shallowly, and left.

CHAPTER 37

Dej had seen a city before, in Shen. Buildings of many sizes
and styles, crammed together, covering a big hill. She'd been
overwhelmed by the noise, the smells, the sheer chaos of the place.

This was different. This was a skykin city. The houses were the
same design as their tents, bright domes with open sides. Some
were connected to form bigger structures, while others stood
alone. There were gaps between the dome-houses, streets and open
squares; the squares, and some streets, had stuff growing in them,
bushes and vines, some of which had rioted free to overwhelm the
nearby domes.

Her instinct was to duck down, hide and observe, avoid being
seen. But, she quickly realised, there was no one here to see her.
No figures walked the streets, no sounds drifted up from them.
She risked extending her senses.

Nothing. Unless the people were in their houses, and the houses
somehow stopped her sensing them. But that wasn't what it felt
like. This city felt empty.

She crept down the slope to the nearest dome, ready to run if
she was detected. But the closer she got the more certain she was.
There was no one here.

The dome was open, with no sparkly curtain. A scattering of
low tables and beds and some empty shelving took up some of

the space but overall it was bare. Dust had blown in to coat the furniture nearest the openings.

She checked the next house along. Same thing: some furniture but everything portable gone.

The city was deserted; had been for some time, by the look of it.

She wandered through the empty streets and squares, sometimes brushing aside or slashing at the plants that had grown up between the houses in order to clear a path, sometimes giving up in the face of a wall of foliage.

As she neared the bottom of the valley she heard running water. Pushing through a living wall of blue-green stems she found a stone-lined channel with pure fresh water running down it. She unslung her pack and filled the waterskin; this was the best water she'd found for months! Then she paused. *Why not stay here?*

She had ready-made shelter, as much as she wanted for the taking. Water too. Food might be tricky; nothing she'd found so far appeared edible, but then she hadn't really been looking. And she could always go foraging.

Assuming she wanted to live in a dead city.

It felt fitting, in some ways: empty life, empty place. On the other hand, settling here would put an end to exploring, and there was more to see. And it meant giving up on having company, acknowledging there would never be another person in her life. Except there would be, and that growing complication had to be her priority. Could she bring up her child here? Standing in the centre of one of the empty house-shells and thinking this Dej looked down at her belly, something she did a lot these days, triggering contradictory feelings of warm comfort and suppressed panic. Yes, she had shelter and water, but no way of feeding a baby.

Still, she could stay for a while. She was spoilt for possible shelters. Perhaps one further up the slope–

Someone was here. Not here as in nearby but as she thought about going upslope some part of her awareness had flicked that way, and touched another presence. She put her head on one side and concentrated.

Definitely someone here, on the far side of the valley. A skykin presumably, though too far away to sense more than that. Should she try to hide her presence? She wasn't even sure how. And they'd probably have sensed her too by now. Perhaps she should leave, given this place wasn't deserted after all.

No, if this person told her to leave she would, but she wasn't going to flee like some frightened animal.

She set off, homing in on the presence but keeping her other, non-skykin senses sharp too. This didn't *feel* dangerous, but then neither had the cliff that collapsed and nearly buried her.

As she got closer, stalking through the empty buildings and overgrown streets, she picked up the gender of the person – male – and a sense of age; he was old, whoever he was, near the end of both his life and that of his animus.

Which hopefully meant he'd be less likely to harm her. Or patronise her.

She found him in a small dome which had been partially reclaimed from nature, the foliage pulled back from one of the wall-gaps.

She hesitated a dozen or so paces off. He knew she was here. Was he going to come out? Or should she go in?

Of course she should. But perhaps she should go in armed. She swung her pack off her back and pulled the sword free. But she kept it lowered as she walked up to the open side of the house-shell and peered in.

A figure lay on a raised bed over the far side. Even as she looked his way, he spoke. "This is unexpected." He sounded weak, but calm. Unflustered.

Dej was about to lower the sword when she remembered the skykin hunters, how they'd drawn her in, flashing then hiding their presences. They hadn't meant her serious harm but even so, once she stepped inside she'd be trapped. She hesitated on the threshold, and looked closer, waiting for her eyes to adjust to the dim interior. Definitely just one person, lying still on a bed.

"If you're going to come in, come in. And if you're going to stab me with your sword, get on with it." Amused now. And still calm.

"Why would I stab you with my sword?" she asked, the words coming out hoarse after weeks of silence.

"Why carry a sword if you don't intend to use it?"

"Caution."

"Very wise." She got the sense he was subsiding, fading out for a moment. Then he focused again. "So what are you? Besides pregnant and paranoid, I mean."

She was being patronised again. Toyed with. "I'm a traveller. And that's all you need to know. What are you?"

"Oh, I'm dying. Alone, I thought."

She found herself unexpectedly upset at the idea that this stranger was dying, though that could just be her animus, trying to preserve its own. "Can I... help?"

"If you can bring yourself to use that sword you could speed things along." Her eyes were adjusting now and she saw his grimace. "But I suspect you won't be able to, will you?"

That wasn't what she'd meant but she decided, on impulse, to test their joint suspicion. She sprang forward, raising the sword. Three steps, and it felt like she was wading through mud. After five steps she gave up. She threw the sword to the floor with a grunt.

"Thought not," the dying skykin said.

She was inside now, and able to take a proper look around. The man was a shrunken shape under a beautifully woven blanket. Beside the bed, a half-empty backpack and an empty waterskin hung on a stand. Seeing where her gaze fell he said, "I brought food and water with me. I needed to convince it I'd at least try to live while I waited for my body to give out."

"This isn't your home then?"

"Not for many centuries, no."

"You came back here to die?"

"In peace, yes."

"I'm happy to leave you to it if that's really what you want." But this didn't make sense. "Are you clanless?"

"Do you see any clan-mates here?" His voice sharpened for

a moment, an acid ironic tone that reminded her of the crèche tutors.

"No. So you're…" she didn't want to say "half-bonded" or some similarly insulting term. "Your animus is dying. Not just you."

"That's right. Just like yours."

"Except I've no plans to die just yet."

"Good for you." He gave a wheezy sigh, and subsided further into the covers. "I'd forgotten how exhausting people can be."

"Tell me about it."

His eyes, which had been fluttering closed, opened at her response. "What's your name?"

"Dej."

"You can call me Yrif, if you want."

A seer. She'd only met one seer, and she'd prefer to never meet him again. "I don't want. Anyway, if you aren't fully bonded you don't really have a right to that title."

"Arguably true." He fell silent, possibly thinking or possibly resting. "Call me Jat then."

She pointed at the waterskin. "Do you want me to get more water for you, Jat?"

"My animus does. I… I should probably send you away. I'd nearly managed to escape my lives, but perhaps the world hasn't quite finished with me yet."

"What do you mean by that?"

"Aha…" he gave a dry croak that might have been a laugh. "Ah yes, I imagine you have questions. Fetch me a drink and I might even give you some answers."

CHAPTER 38

The next day a letter arrived from Etyan. Rhia had not seen Markave since their conversation, but she needed to give him space to consider her offer. She read the letter alone in her study.

Ree,

I'm so sorry. I thought I was doing the right thing, offering myself up at the Council like that, but it probably just made things worse. Of course no one wanted me. I'm a freak and a monster.

I can't stand it in the city, it's so crowded and dark, and everything reminds me of when I had a life there. I have no life now. I may as well be miserable here at the villa as anywhere! Don't worry, I'm not going to run off again, and if you need me you can send for me. I know this is a difficult time for you, but I'd be no use to you, even if I was there. I'd just make you more stressed, worrying about me too. It's better that I'm here.

I've told Mereut to keep the wine cellar locked. Like I said, I'm done with running away, inside or outside my head. But I do need some time alone, to think.

with love – E.

She refolded the parchment. Perhaps it was for the best, at least for now, that Etyan remove himself from the city. He was still a mess but he was behaving rationally. All his life she had urged him to think, and now, having run out of other options, he was finally doing so.

That evening Markave asked if they could talk alone. She led him into the parlour, sat down, smiled, and waited for him to speak.

Still standing, he said, "M'lady, I have been giving thought to your proposition but I am not sure how it would work."

"In what way?" *So many ways,* she thought despite herself, but she kept her tone even.

"I am a commoner. I could never be the head of a noble House." He sounded scandalised at the thought.

"You would not be. I have taken advice on this. You would, in effect, be my consort, with no holdings of your own save what I grant you."

"I see." He sounded relieved. "But if that is the case, how does this help House Harlyn?"

"It would give the House an heir."

"An heir?" His voice was high, panicked.

"Yes. It may be... our child, if we have one." Hurriedly, she continued. "But if not, I have drawn up documents which make your children, by your first marriage, my legal heirs."

"How can that be? They are not of noble blood either."

"No, so once we are married I would formally adopt Tador and Kerne. There is legal precedent. It cannot be challenged in law." Not that it would stop the Council trying if, this time next year, all that remained of House Harlyn was her self-exiled brother and Markave and his sons. Or son.

"And you are sure this is the best way, for the House, m'lady?"

"I believe so."

"I ask because... I heard there was some hostility from the Houses major at the Grand Council, and I can understand your ladyship not wanting to seek a husband amongst them. But perhaps one of the minor lords...?"

"That is not going to happen. They would gain very little from it, given the terms I would impose, save the enmity of the Houses major."

"Are the majors really determined to bring about our downfall?"

Rhia felt a flush of warmth at that "our". "It appears so. But I – we – will fight them. And rather than doing so in the company of some minor lord thinking to take advantage of my House's travails, I would do it with you at my side, Markave. You are... you have always been important to me." Her face felt hot. "And I trust you utterly."

Her steward nodded once. "Thank you." After a moment he said, "I need to speak to Tador, and to my sister, about this."

"Naturally. Please do that, with my blessing."

"I will visit them tomorrow." His family had come to the house to see Kerne a couple of times since he had fallen ill; Rhia had stayed out of the way to avoid any awkwardness.

The silence stretched. Rhia realised he was waiting for her to dismiss him. How would that work if they were married? She cranked her already forced smile wider, nodded and said, "I will keep you no longer."

He returned a smile as uncomfortable as hers, and left.

She should tell Etyan what she was planning with their steward. But not yet. It may not even happen. Markave left around mid-morning, having first asked her, with that uneasy air he had developed, if she might watch his boy. Although she had finally been getting somewhere with the celestial model, she agreed at once.

Kerne was not doing well. The fever had reasserted itself, bringing a cyclic delirium. He would twitch and grasp at the covers before falling back into an uneasy sleep, eyes darting behind lids as the disease infected his mind with formless horrors. It had been this way with Father too, and watching her apprentice now was an unwanted reminder of that earlier loss. But watch him she must: in this state the sufferer might swallow their tongue or fall from the bed.

Markave's first wife had died of rain-fever too. And that period, when they were both grieving, had been when she had come to see him, privately, as more than a trusted servant. It had been an odd, awkward attraction, never returned; she was not sure if Markave had even noticed. And it was long gone, replaced with something more complex, a mix of familiarity, trust and mutual understanding that she hoped they might build on now.

His second wife had died a traitor, something which still appeared to cause embarrassment, as though he were somehow responsible for her wickedness. He had not wanted to talk about it then, and she doubted he would now.

Kerne gave a weird hiccoughing gasp, drawing Rhia back into the moment. His face showed raw horror, even as he subsided on the pillows. On impulse, Rhia took his hand, offering what small comfort she could. She had read, in the enquirers' papers, that to touch an infected person was unwise, but the rain-fever did not appear to spread like other diseases, seeming to strike almost at random.

Her touch appeared to help; Kerne sighed, his face settling into less anguished lines. She looked at his hand, calloused and hot in her grasp. When was the last time she had held someone's hand? His nails were still bitten back to the quick; she never had found time to dig out that cure Father had given her.

Markave was out all day. When Brynan offered to take a turn watching Kerne, Rhia fled to her study, tinkering with the celestial model, then when that was too much copying some papers. She was too distracted for mathematics.

That evening she and her steward met in the parlour again, though this time they both sat down without anything being said. Rhia asked gently, "Have you reached a decision?"

"I believe I have, m'lady."

"Good. I... just want to say again that whatever your choice is, I will honour it."

"Thank you." He dipped his head, then raised it and managed to meet her eyes. "I will do it, m'lady."

She felt a genuine note steal into the smile she was wearing. "Thank you."

"It is, as you say, the only sensible course." His own smile softened. "And it is not an unpleasant prospect, if m'lady will forgive me for saying so."

What was he saying? Did he have feelings for her, as she once had for him?

He must have seen her expression, as he half raised a hand. "Please, do not think I harbour any… inappropriate emotions, m'lady. It is just that I have known you all your life, seen you grow and change. I respect and admire you, even as – and I hope I may speak freely here – you sometimes perplex me; your mind is extraordinary, if you do not mind me saying so."

"I… do not. I am flattered. And I think we should practise speaking freely to each other. We need to get used to that."

"As m'lady wishes." He spoke with a shy humour, something she had not seen from him before.

"You know that you will have to learn to call me Rhia."

"That thought had occurred." He cleared his throat. "There will never be a good time to ask this, so I will say it now, before we are committed further. Would I be able to draw on a small fraction of the House's funds to help make my family more comfortable? My sister's husband has been ill for some time."

"I had no idea." Why would she? Before now Markave's personal life had been a closed book to her. "You could have asked anyway."

"That would not have been appropriate."

"I suppose not. This illness, is it… treatable?"

"It is not rain-fever but a condition he has had some time. There are herbs that alleviate it but they are unfortunately somewhat beyond my sister's means."

"Of course I will make funds available to your family. They will be my family too, after all." What a peculiar prospect. With a sudden swerve not unlike that she had felt after the Council, she saw this union from her steward's point of view, of the amazing good luck it represented for an ordinary family in the middle city. But that did not change what marrying Markave did for her, and her House.

"Thank you. I imagine there are preparations to be made."

"Preparations? Oh, for our wedding." How odd to say those words. "It will not be a sumptuous affair, Markave."

"I am glad to hear it, m'lady." Then he coloured, and corrected himself. "Rhia."

CHAPTER 39

"We come into the world with nothing. And so do we leave it."

Although Sadakh intoned the words with the expected gravitas, in this case they were somewhat inaccurate.

The four poliarchs whose duty it was to bear Numak's bier stepped forward with slow reverence, although Vemmat, the last-minute replacement, was not quite in step with his brethren. The assembled advisors, courtiers and nobles stood silent and reverent as the late caliarch's funeral procession passed them. The normally-empty Hall of Eternal Guardians felt claustrophobic with so many living souls crowded in to see the dead ruler take his place amongst his ancestors.

Although the poliarchs' burden was precious, it was not heavy. One of the many rites Sadakh had officiated over during the month of state mourning was the removal of the caliarch's inner organs. He could not help thinking that Numak's brain, at least, might have been better left where it was rather than fed to the gyraptors; both the enquirers' writings and his own experience suggested that the brain was the seat of the intellect, if not the very soul. But some traditions were not to be questioned. Numak's husk of a body had then been filled with the traditional mix of consecrated and preserved plant matter brought from all parts of Zekt, his skin dried and waxed, and finally, his finest robes arranged on his reclining form.

So now, far from going to a possible heavenly reward, the late caliarch was tied to mundanity forever, his much-reduced but still recognisable body transformed into a lovingly conserved anchor to the world.

"May the First bless his favoured son, as we set him to watch over the lands he ruled so well." Numak had not been a bad ruler, by Zekti standards. He had been a gentle soul, if somewhat naive and eccentric. A better ruler than his nephew would be, for sure. Had Numak's final end been hastened by Mekteph? Quite possibly. What was certain was that the serum had not saved him – just as it had not saved Ritek, or Ereket, whose health had continued to deteriorate until she passed away last week. Just as it would not save him.

The poliarchs had reached the niche reserved for Numak. It had already been dressed in fine fabrics and set out with representations of those persons and items that had mattered to him in life. In the former case, this was a pair of carved models of his long-dead wife and son. The latter consisted largely of objects he had made, the odd, intricate items he had crafted alone in this Hall in his long dotage.

It would be inauspicious to say the least for the poliarchs to slip up in transferring the body from bier to niche. Sadakh was glad now that he brought in an additional pair of priests to assist in sliding the caliarch's bound form into place. Once he was sure the delicate operation had been concluded with the requisite dignity he said, "Before the lamp is lit, let us each send our thoughts of Numak to the First, in prayers of thankfulness and love."

From the corner of his eye Sadakh saw Mekteph's mouth twitch where he stood close to his uncle's resting place: this part of the ceremony allowed for some improvisation by the eparch and no doubt the prince and others had expected Sadakh to lead them in a formal prayer. But heads still bowed, and hands were clasped under chins.

Sadakh closed his eyes but could not summon the inner peace to pray. With Ereket dead, he had moved Taklew permanently into the launderers' house but, unsure whether the prince knew of his hideaway, he had left a rota of trusted guards to watch over the place from outside. He had already relocated some of his work, but there were limits to what could be done within the priory walls.

Then there was poor Hekmat. Determined never to need one, Sadakh had given little thought to a successor. Once he was sure all twelve poliarchs were individuals he had both vetted and won over personally, he had been happy to let the Order run itself from day to day. But he had to acknowledge that he would not be eparch forever; he had already been living on borrowed time before he took the probably-ineffective serum. And though he trusted any of the twelve to do his will, none was an obvious successor, and one of the best candidates was even now succumbing to old age himself.

He'd had no more news of Lord Harlyn, nor of Rhia Harlyn's trial, but events in Mirror were enough to keep him occupied.

Some of those nearby were fidgeting. He peered up through half-closed eyelids to see several courtiers squinting or openly looking round, uncertain whether this unexpectedly freeform part of the ceremony was over yet. They did not look their best. No one here did. During the official mourning period everyone in the city had shown their grief in acts of communal piety and austerity; tunics went un-pleated, faces unpainted, hair unoiled. He had to admit he was looking forward to having his own hair dressed after so long; a vanity, yes, but the body needed its small indulgences. He opened his eyes fully; others followed suit with suspicious speed.

"I now call on the keeper of the lamps to step forward and kindle the light that will burn eternally for our beloved caliarch."

The eunuch in question, Fidekh, was one of Sadakh's few overt allies in the palace. His assigned duty, that of keeping the hundreds of lamps in the Hall of Eternal Guardians topped up with oil and burning bright, had kept him close to the late caliarch, who all but lived in the Hall in his final years. His slight nod as he raised the taper to light the green glass globe by Numak's niche was an acknowledgement of their shared values. But although this particular immortal advisor might not like the prospect of

Mekteph's rule, he acknowledged its likelihood. Others amongst the advisors and courtiers had come to accept its inevitability; the more traditionalist eunuchs would want to consolidate whatever royal blood remained in Mirror, in the hopes that a new generation would emerge which would serve the shadowland better. Fools and madmen with that very blood might have brought Zekt to this pass, but Zekt would endure.

When Fidekh stepped back Sadakh raised his arms in blessing – it felt odd doing so indoors amongst the state's power-brokers, rather than under the open sky before a loving congregation – and said, "Be assured that Numak now watches us. We are blessed by his guardianship, and that of all his illustrious ancestors. Knowing this, go in peace and return to your lives. Your caliarch is gone. Your caliarch lives on."

People left in order of political precedence and Sadakh was surprised to find Mekteph waiting for him on the terrace outside the Hall. His entourage had gone ahead down the steps but a few eunuchs still loitered within sight. A very scripted meeting.

Sadakh composed his face into an open smile, ignoring Mekteph's more rapacious one. The prince gestured for them to step back from those still passing, to the far end of the terrace outside the Hall; just out of earshot if they kept their voices down.

The prince even managed a convincing obeisance for the observers. "Such a fitting and moving service, if a little, ah, ad-hoc at points."

"I am glad you were moved, Highness."

"You must have a lot on your mind right now, of course."

"As always." He'd let the prince work his way to the point. He had behaved with passable decorum during the mourning period and Sadakh was reasonably certain he was not about to push him off the edge of the terrace now.

"Ah yes, your ageing poliarch. Hekmat, isn't it? I understand he'll soon be going to his own eternal rest."

Sadakh forced himself not to react. Of course the prince knew that one of his most senior poliarchs was unwell. Hekmat's health had not been good for some months now. Sadakh had diagnosed an ailment of the inner organs, perhaps the liver or spleen; he had done all he could but given the poliarch's advanced years, it was unlikely he would recover. Poison was not out of the question, but it would take more resources than the prince had on the isle to get at one of the resident poliarchs; poison being very much the prince's style, Sadakh had long-ago instituted a system for tasting all food served to himself and those closest to him. "I continue to pray for his recovery."

"How compassionate. And optimistic." The prince made a show of gazing out over the islets of the city, golden and calm in the early evening light. "When he does go to his rest, I have just the replacement."

We should have seen this coming. Now they were outside the mausoleum of dead caliarchs, his ghost was back. And correct. "I will of course consult you in your capacity as his young majesty's regent when I make my choice."

"You misunderstand me. I have chosen for you."

"Ah. A new poliarch is elected from amongst serving priests of sufficient seniority. As a respecter of tradition, I am sure you would not want to change that process."

"Oh, I have a priest in mind. From the provinces. He has the relevant experience, though."

"Would this be Sholrew by any chance?" Sadakh had to hand it to Mekteph: he was persistent. "He was sent away from Mirror after some unsavoury allegations."

The prince waved a hand. "Never proved. Possibly politically motivated. He's my choice."

You should have killed that disloyal weakling when you had the chance. He feared his ghost was right. His compassion had come back to bite him. "But not mine." He kept his tone light.

"You would be wise to heed my will, Holiness. I believe we discussed the importance of continuity, tradition, and stability. Sholrew is a great lover of such things. He will serve you well. And when the time comes, he will ensure our Church gets back its strength." Mekteph leaned in close; Sadakh resisted the urge to recoil. "I can see how this talk of personal responsibility and independent thought you've introduced into the First Light might appeal to someone with your humble background, but this is the state religion. Systems of belief are there to be rigidly followed by the masses, not 'questioned' or 'explored'."

Say nothing! Sadakh hardly needed the reminder, though he schooled his face to stay neutral. But his mind was in turmoil.

Mekteph not only meant to replace him with a puppet eparch, he meant to turn the First Light religion back into a mere tool of social control. And he wanted Sadakh to know his life's work would be undone. But the prince had to act legitimately, to keep Sadakh in power long enough to see the conventions were adhered to; to do otherwise risked losing what support he had amongst the eunuchs. And why resort to open violence when you can achieve your ends as easily with unseen manipulation? The prince was obviously learning... unfortunately. Sadakh took a deep breath, and finally managed, "On that matter, we may differ. However, I shall consider your offer."

"You do that." The prince waved a dismissive hand, then as an afterthought for any remaining witnesses, gave another obeisance, before turning away to survey the vista of the city he would soon rule in all but name.

Sadakh just had to hope that Mekteph's current fondness for diplomacy would give him enough breathing space to find some way out of this mess. If not then he would have to accept that, far from being an eternal leader shepherding questing and willing souls to enlightenment, he had been but a brief aberrance in the spiritual history of this shadowland, a misguided fool who had made the mistake of trying to make people think for themselves.

CHAPTER 40

"A what?" Cardinal Vansel's high brow furrowed.

Sur Lectel replied, "A demonstration, Your Holiness."

Rhia kept silent. They had agreed the request needed to come from her lawyer, not her.

"Of what, precisely?"

"The theory which you and the other esteemed judges have spent this week reading about."

"And which, before you made this unorthodox request, we were about to discuss with the defendant."

Rhia liked the word "discuss". It implied a reasoned exchange.

"My apologies for complicating the proceedings but we are, as I'm sure you'll agree, in unknown territory here."

"Why did you not make this request at the outset, Sur Lectel?"

"Perhaps we should have. However, in order to understand the reason for, and timing and location of, the demonstration, it was necessary for you to have a firm grasp of the nature of the defendant's theory."

That and the fact that she had only completed the celestial model late the previous night. Fortunately the judges had not wanted to reconvene particularly early.

"What do you mean by the 'timing and location of the demonstration'?"

Sur Lectel took half a step back, leaving Rhia free to explain the complexities. "I have built a model to demonstrate my theory."

"Have you now?" Cardinal Vansel's tone implied he doubted that was possible.

"Aspects of it, yes. It is a delicate and cumbersome item, so cannot be moved from my study."

"Your study is in your townhouse, yes?"

"That's right. Also, I would like to show you the night sky, so you can link what you see in the world to the model, and also back to my theory."

"I think we have all seen the night sky, Countess."

"Ah, yes. I mean, as viewed through my sightglass. You will have read about that in my notes."

"Indeed we did."

Rhia knew that tone, and pre-empted the cardinal's next question. "It is a built device but breaks no prescriptions. It does not move under its own power and has no interaction with a person's body."

"Save by changing what they see?"

"Magnifying, yes. But that… I have brought the sightglass with me, if you wish to examine it."

"That would be acceptable."

Rhia returned to the desk and fished out the short ironwood tube from her satchel. She walked back to the table and handed it to Vansel. He took it with a mixture of curiosity and caution, holding it at arm's length for examination, then turning it over in his hands.

"As you see, there are two tubes, set inside each other. Moving the smaller one up and down focuses the lenses at either end." Lenses which, she noted with dismay, his bony fingers had splayed across.

"If you say so."

"May I see?" asked Tethorn. The apothecary had a surprisingly gruff voice.

Vansel handed the sightglass over. Tethorn examined it with

more care than Vansel had, and did not touch the lenses. He half raised it then looked to Rhia. "I just look through it, do I?"

"Uh, yes. The other end though."

He turned the sightglass and tried again. "I see only blurred colours."

"It is designed to focus on objects far away."

Tethorn lowered the sightglass. "I see. I for one would be most interested in this demonstration, Holiness."

"Hmm. Lord Jertine, did you wish to examine the object?"

"Why not?"

Vansel handed it across. The viscount gave the sightglass a cursory look, and shook it – Rhia managed not to wince – then said, "It seems a simple enough piece of work. I'd be interested to see what it does too."

"Then perhaps we should agree to this demonstration?" Vansel did not sound enthusiastic.

"Ah, but it has to be after dark you say?" said Jertine.

Rhia nodded. "It does, yes."

"Then it cannot be tonight. I fear I have a prior engagement." Jertine gave the cardinal an apologetic look. "Had I know my duties would extend into the evenings, Holiness, I would have left them free, but…"

"Quite. This is not an ordinary situation by any means. Hmm. But maybe we could spare the time for this demonstration tomorrow night, if that is agreeable to my fellow judges."

Jertine nodded and Tethorn said, "It is, Holiness."

"Good." He handed the sightglass back to Rhia, who returned to stand by her lawyer. "Now, if we may get back to the matter at hand. I was summarising the evidence presented which we three have now gone through, both separately and with some conferring. However, before we move onto detailed questions I would like to discuss the matter of the submitted testimonials."

"What about them?" Rhia tried not to sound too defensive.

"All speak highly of you, and some do not even make mention of your being of the gentler sex." Rhia felt her hands tighten their grip on her sightglass, and made herself relax. "It is obvious they come from diverse sources, both from the handwriting and from the travelworn nature of some of the documents. Most, I note, use peculiar titles, though they all refer to you by name." Just as she had requested. "It does seem odd that you should know so many erudite individuals in distant lands by these strange titles, yet they know your name…"

Was he about to ask her to betray the enquirers' network wholesale? Would she, to preserve this one, vital, idea?

But then Vansel continued, "However, that is not a matter for this court." Perhaps Theorist of Shen had already reached some sort of accommodation with the Church, maybe even promising to try and root out troublemakers in return for the network as a whole being left alone. "What is a matter of interest is the one correspondent who does name himself. Are you really asking us to believe that you are in regular correspondence with, and have the respect of, Eparch Sadakh of the Order of the First Light?"

Rhia gave what she hoped was a humble smile. "I am, yes."

Vansel drew a rumbling breath. "Hmmm. I for one find this hard to believe."

When she asked Meddler of Zekt if he would be willing to put his real name to his testimonial to add weight to it, she had wondered if he might back it up with some seal or secret phrase that would prove his identity, but he had not. "I swear it is the truth." She was, after all, still under oath.

"And I would not wish to directly accuse you of lying. However this stretches my—"

"Write to him, then!"

"I beg your pardon."

Sur Lectel slipped into the conversation. "Although the defendant did not mean to interrupt, her point is valid. If you are in any doubt as to the veracity of an attributed testimonial, we can put you in contact with the individual in question."

"That would take some time. I will accept your word, for now at least." Vansel steepled his fingers. "Myself and my fellow judges would now like to query the defendant on the evidence submitted, with a view to clarifying the theory being presented. As this may take a while, the defendant is permitted to sit."

Each judge questioned her in turn, starting with Vansel. His take on her theory was that he found it inconceivable that the First should arrange the heavens in such a complicated and unexpected way. Rhia was relieved at first, because he was not drawing on the scriptures directly, but as the questions continued ("Why would our creator stick us to these globes with an unseen force when it would be simpler and more comfortable to have us live on a flat world?" "Surely the heavens exist to show us His might, not to perplex us?") her irritation grew. She forced herself to guard her tongue, to answer his questions are though they were leading to an increase in knowledge, rather than reinforcing ignorance.

Jertine questioned her next. He took a similar line to Vansel at first – that this was an awfully complex way of explaining the world – and her heart sank. But he was less concerned with proving a point than with his own ignorance, which he was happy to admit to. She soon came to see that dispelling it would be a challenge – his interest was in people and their agendas, not nature or the universe at large – but the fact that he wanted to know more gave her hope, as did his growing enthusiasm for seeing her model. He even said, at one point, "The fact that I am not able to grasp your theory yet does not mean it is invalid, merely that I find it new and extraordinary."

By the time it was Tethorn's turn, it was late afternoon. Vansel asked whether the apothecary wished to postpone his questions until the next day because, as he put it, "I believe you have the most queries." Tethorn said he would prefer to ask some initial questions now, then spend the next day reading up in preparation for the demonstration in the evening.

From the start, Rhia knew that this was the judge whose mind was most in tune with hers. Master Tethorn was curious, quick-thinking and open-minded. He accepted the possibility that the world was a sphere, or at least curved and not flat. He himself had noticed the odd path the Strays took through the heavens. But he was also religious; he mentioned, albeit only in passing, his concerns at reconciling her view of the planets as spheres moving through space with the Church's idea that they were "fallen women", Children of the First who had been placed in the heavens as a punishment and example. Rhia had worked up several arguments to try to prove that the scriptures could be effectively true without being entirely literal – the "hand of the First" might be seen in the world He created, but that did not mean He had a palm and five fingers, for example – but she made herself hold back; these would be more relevant later. For now, her job was to make her theory comprehensible, and hence believable. And Sur Tethorn both wanted to listen and was capable of understanding. He even raised the matter of the shadowlands themselves, asking how their perpetual shade was maintained, and appeared happier than Kerne had initially been with her suggestion that the mechanism was a mass of vast structures in space between the world and the Sun. Carried away with the idea, he surmised that such an arrangement might even be the First's final tweak to His creation, made when the two races were divided, before dipping his head and apologising to the cardinal for his presumption.

In response, Vansel cleared his throat, and said, "You are free to air such ideas here. It reminds us to keep the First in mind in our deliberations."

Rhia was still deciding whether this was a positive pronouncement when Sur Tethorn said, "One final thing, Countess. Something appears to be missing, or at last lacking, in your evidence. You have provided detailed observations, and some diagrams, but very little in the way of mathematical workings. A few basic equations but nothing that might be considered a proof."

Rhia drew a sharp breath. "I did not want to burden the judges with dry numbers." Her voice came out higher than she intended.

Sur Tethorn smiled. "Numbers are no burden to me."

So she had heard. She had hoped he would not ask this.

"Well, Countess?" prompted Vansel. "Is there more to see?"

"I can provide my rough workings, such as they are, yes."

"Good. Were there any further questions?"

Both men said there were not.

"Then we will adjourn until tomorrow evening. Would the eighteenth hour be a suitable time for your demonstration Countess?"

"It would. Thank you."

She told herself, as she left, that the session had gone as well as she could have expected.

That evening, Rhia married her steward.

It was a modest affair. Markave had secured the services of a cleric from the middle city on short notice; the man appeared somewhat over-awed to find himself officiating at a noble's townhouse without any of the expected fuss. Rhia considered paying an additional fee to secure the man's silence, but rumours would surface anyway. And she was not ashamed of her choice.

The other two house servants acted as witnesses. Markave's brother-in-law was too ill but his oldest son and sister attended, the latter in a somewhat flamboyant scallop-edged gown that looked barely finished.

As the priest recited the formal speech of joining Rhia stole a look at Markave's family, soon to be hers too. Aside from her questionable dress sense and slight fawning air, his sister came across as a no-nonsense matron. Tador looked much like his brother, save being a little taller and having darker hair. They had visited Kerne on his sickbed when they first arrived and still looked a little shaken at seeing how his condition had deteriorated.

Speaking the vows she had heard others exchange on previous, far grander occasions felt unreal, as though she could not really mean them here and now, in her own parlour.

The exchange of tokens was awkward. She had insisted on real metal rings, rather than carved ironwood, but when the time came to put hers on she realised she still wore the Harlyn signet ring on her ring finger – though Etyan's by birth, the time had never seemed right to give it to him – and had to hurriedly ease it off.

Afterwards there was a formal meal in the dining room. It was somewhat awkward, and Rhia was glad when Markave's sister and son left with effusive thanks and good wishes.

On any other clear evening she would get some observing in. But not tonight. Brynan and Nerilyn had also withdrawn, leaving her and her new husband sitting side-by-side at the head of the empty table.

"We should retire now," said Rhia evenly.

"As you… yes, we should."

Neither of them moved.

Rhia took a breath to calm herself. "I think that whilst you should spend tonight in my room, we should not feel obliged to, ah, that is…"

"I will follow your lead, of course. Whatever you wish."

She wished so much, but wishes were a fool's diversion, Father had always said. "Let us go up then."

He followed her without a word, out the room and up the stairs.

CHAPTER 41

As she filled Jat's waterskin Dej tried not to think of parallels with the clanless. She'd spent too much time fetching water, taking out rubbish, preparing food and cleaning whatever needed cleaning during her time with them. She was done skivvying. And Jat was a seer, or had been. But he was nothing like Cal. And she was only fetching water for him because he couldn't.

Jat was dozing when she got back, his breath rattling in his throat like a shaken seed-pod. She could just leave the water and go. This was just another skykin who thought he was superior to her. But he was also dying. If he really wanted to die alone, she'd leave. If he wanted her to stay, she'd stay. And maybe get some answers, like he'd said.

He didn't stir as she hooked the waterskin onto the stand so she decided to take a quick look in his backpack. It was smaller than hers, just basic travelling gear: knife, fire-kit, eating bowl, and a square of ordinary waxed fabric to make a shelter from. Well-made stuff, but not tech.

"See anything you like?"

She jumped, and turned to him. "Sorry, I was just... curious."

"You certainly are." His voice descended into a hoarse whisper. "I'll help you drink."

She did; he was light as a husk, the gold of his scales faded, the scales themselves pulled tight around his eyes and mouth. Her other senses registered a whiff of cold; a darkening of vision; a sour, dry aftertaste. Death approaching. "Do you want some food?" she asked when he lay back.

"No. I'm beyond all that now."

"You said you'd answer my questions."

"So I did. Good idea, not wasting any time. Not sure how long I've got. Sit, then."

Dej perched on the edge of the bed. His clouded eyes stared past her, fixed on some memory.

She said, "You talked about escaping your lives. What did you mean?"

"Start with an easy one, eh? Well, have you ever found something out you wish you hadn't, something you'd give the world to unknow?"

Dej looked away.

His gaze sharpened. "You have, haven't you?"

"I don't want to talk about it." If she'd never found out what Etyan had done, maybe she wouldn't have felt the need to run to the edge of the world to escape him. "I want to talk about you." His eyes had closed and Dej thought he was drifting off to sleep. "Jat?"

His eyes fluttered open again. "You know, I think I do want something to eat after all. Have you got any food?"

"Yes. Now don't you go anywhere." She fetched her pack, then got out some dried apricots. He hmmmed at the shadowkin food, but didn't comment, just asked her to pull them apart, as he could only manage small strips. When he nodded to show he'd had enough she gave him more water.

"I was wrong." He sounded stronger. "Thinking I was ready to go. The world surprised me one last time, and sent you."

"What do you mean, the world surprised you? You said something like that before."

"Did I? Ah. Our lives are stranger than we can know, and just when we expect things to have a simple ending, the world – reality – comes up with new complications."

"No offence Jat, but this is just the kind of cryptic shit I'd expect from a seer."

He croaked a laugh. "You have me there."

"So is there some deep meaning to everything, which you seers know, and maybe the fully bonded skykin too?" She remembered the skykin storykeeper's maybe-mocking comment about making their own meaning.

"Quite possibly. But if so, I've forgotten it."

"Of course you have." She hadn't really expected him to impart the meaning of life. If he even knew it. If she could even understand it.

"So, Dej, returning to the question I first asked you: what are you?"

She looked back at him. "Uh, a skykin." She wasn't going to apologise for being half-bonded.

"Yes, you are. But what *is* a skykin?"

"What do you want me to say?"

"What were you taught?"

"In the crèche, you mean?"

"Where else? It's not like the clanless know much of use."

"You're not wrong there. Well, in the crèche we were taught that the skykin are those Children of the First who fell and chose to make themselves as animals."

"Ah yes, the Book of Separation. The shadowkin version of history."

"So it's wrong then?"

"Not exactly wrong. But biased. And incomplete. Yes, we did alter ourselves. Why do you think we did that?"

"No idea. It was so long ago no one remembers."

"We did it to live *in* the world, as opposed to *hiding from it*."

Dej laughed bitterly. "Perhaps we should've kept hiding. It's a dangerous place."

"Which hasn't treated you well, I suspect." A feverish animation entered his voice. "I think the world sent you to me, poor lonely Dej, because it doesn't want what I know to end when I do."

"And what do you know, old man?"

"Too much." He groaned, as though the passion going through him had torn something deep inside, then swallowed. "We need to take this slowly."

"Fine. Just don't die on me. And try and keep the cryptic shit to a minimum."

He gave a wheezy laugh. "I'll do my best. Do you know what a symbiote is, Dej?"

"Nope."

The hand nearest her, lying on the cover like a dead thing, twitched once. Pointing at her, she realised. "*We* are symbiotes. A combination of two or more things."

"Person and animus."

"Exactly. Though even the shadowkin are symbiotes of a sort. All people – all humans – are. Most shadowkin would be shocked to know how their bodies teem with – in part are made up of – creatures too small to see."

"If they're too small to see, how do you know this?"

"Good question. I know because I was told by a healer. She knew because she had been told by the healer who trained her, and so on, back through time."

Dej held up a hand. "Wait, there's something that's always bothered me about you seers."

"Ask what you want, but if you distract me for too long I *will* forget what we were talking about. My mind is somewhat overfull and prone to leakage."

"I'll keep it simple. Soon as you were weaned, you got put in a cave, and all the best hunters and healers and makers and everyone else came to you as you were growing up, and told you about what they knew and what they did and where that knowledge fitted into the clan. Right?"

"Close enough."

"But you're a *seer*, you've got a closer connection to your animus than any other clan-member. How come you don't just remember all this stuff? Or rather how come your animus doesn't remember it for you?"

"For a start, a seer is given the knowledge of the clans *before* ze is bonded."

"I know that! But once you're bonded, why doesn't your animus just, I dunno, absorb what you know, and hold onto it, ready to pass on."

"You are equating knowledge with continuity."

"And what's that meant to mean?" Dej tried not to snap.

"For a fully bonded skykin, the animus gives continuity, a sense of the past lives, and sometimes allows access to specific experiences from those lives."

"My animus also tells me what's safe to eat."

"Yes it does." His tone implied she was stating the obvious. "But that's not knowledge from your clan-mates. That's knowledge about the world. From your animus. You understand the difference?"

"I think so."

He croaked a laugh. "Good, because I've already forgotten what we were talking about. Where was I?"

"You were saying you know about the shadowkin being, uh, symbiotes because a healer told you."

"Yes. Not true symbiotes though, as none of the organisms inside them have any form of sentience."

Dej considered asking what he meant by "organism" and "sentience" but decided not to distract him further. She'd work it out. "So how did the original healer know, the one who told the one who told the… however many back it is. The healer who discovered this. How did ze know?" She felt brief pleasure at talking like a skykin, using "ze" instead of "he" or "she", before tutting to herself for such pointless pride.

"Another good question." His thin lips curled into a smile. "You have a sharper mind than you give yourself credit for. The knowledge was passed forward from the time when we had the tools to find such things out."

"Tools…" A connection flared. "Tools as in 'tech'?"

"Tools as in tech, yes! But how do you, a clanless, know about tech? We never let it leave the clans."

"I met some skykin on the way here; they were going to a war. They gave me food, told me stories and generally made me feel like a stupid child." He didn't need to know the bit about her stealing some of their tech.

"Ah. That was the real cause of the Separation, you know. Tech." He wheezed, his eyes closing for a moment.

"But shadowkin don't have tech."

"Precisely. Now, they don't have tech. They're forbidden to use any sort of sophisticated machinery, or to put anything which isn't grown naturally inside their bodies and all sorts of other daft rules. Tech is the work of the Last, according to them."

"But that wasn't always how it was?"

"Indeed so. When humans first came here… " He half closed his eyes, then opened them again. Dej was having trouble seeing him clearly now; night was falling outside, and these abandoned shadowkin houses didn't light up like the tents had. "I did tell you we're not from here, didn't I?"

"Not sure you did, no. Depends what you mean be 'we' and 'here'."

"We as in humans: shadowkin and skykin. 'Here' as in this world."

"So did the First put us here, like the shadowkin say?"

"Of course not. They've forgotten so much… We came from the stars, Dej."

"Uh, how? The stars are pretty lights in the night sky. According to the shadowkin some of the brightest ones are meant to be fallen saints, though I've no idea how that works."

"No, the stars are other worlds. We came from one of them."

"Really? Which one?" Dej had a crazy urge to go outside and look at the stars to try and work it out.

"I have no idea. It was a long time ago. But what matters is that we arrived here from elsewhere. All of us. With tech."

"What exactly *is* 'tech'?"

"Like I said: machines, devices, processes used on the body or the natural world that change you or it, make things more efficient and useful. You're no idiot, but I can't think of any way to explain this in a way you would understand. Except maybe… You know those miracles the saints were meant to have performed?"

"Yeah, we got taught about some of those."

"They were probably using tech. But I'd advise not saying that in a shadowland unless you want to get buried alive."

"I'll bear that in mind next time I'm in a shadowland. But if tech's so useful, why don't the shadowkin have it any more?"

"Ah, your best question yet. The short answer – and most of the details are lost, even to us – is that those who originally came here disagreed on how to use their tech. The people who became the shadowkin somehow came to see it as the cause of their woes, not the solution. So they banned it."

"They weren't doing themselves any favours, were they?"

"No, they were making their lives more difficult. But they thought – believed – they were doing the right thing."

"Because the First told them to?"

"That appears to be what they thought, yes." He shifted his head to look to the side; every movement he made was small yet full of effort. "Is it dark in here?"

"Pretty much."

"Good. Thought it was just me."

"You're fine."

"No I'm not. I'm dying. And very tired." He sighed. "I need to rest now."

Dej didn't move.

"Hah!" His exhalation was barely audible. "Don't worry, I'll do my best not to die overnight. But I need to sleep."

Dej got off the bed.

She fetched food and water from her pack then went outside. The night was clear and she sat with her back to the house to eat, looking up at the sky. Could her people – both peoples – really have come from there? Etyan's sister would wet herself at the thought.

Assuming Jat was telling the truth. Assuming he wasn't playing some elaborate seer's game with her. Assuming he wasn't simply mad.

CHAPTER 42

Rhia expected to feel odd, not waking up alone. But when she opened her eyes she was alone, in the bed at least. Markave stood by the still-shuttered window, dressing. Not that he had entirely undressed the night before. They had, by mutual consent, stripped down to their shifts and lain next to each other. And that was all.

"I think," Rhia had said, "that though there will be a time for proper consummation, it is not now." There was no hurry: if the Church was about to condemn her she would hardly have time to conceive and birth an heir to House Harlyn before her sentence was carried out.

Markave had nodded, his eyes flitting to the room next door, where Kerne lay in delirium.

Now, he looked over at her as she watched him, and said, "Shall I open the shutters?" Spending the night in each other's company did, at least, appear to have cured him of the tendency to clip his sentences as he bit back on the urge to say "m'lady".

"Yes please."

"And then I was going to attend to my duties, if that is all right with you."

In discussing their new and unique domestic arrangements Markave had stressed his desire to continue doing his job. She could hardly refuse him. But now she said, "Tador has grown up into a fine young man. I wonder if we should encourage him to take up his role here sooner rather than later." Markave, reaching up for the shutter, looked back at her. "The plan was already that he should follow in your footsteps," she reminded him.

"It is something to consider, yes." That careful tone; she knew it from her youth, when Markave was trying to gently steer her away from what he considered an unwise choice.

"But not yet?"

"He has much to learn."

"Which you could teach him, here."

"I fear I would... I am just not sure it would work. But of course, if you order it so..."

"No. I have no intention of ordering you to do anything, Markave. We'll leave things as they are for now."

After he left – managing to walk out the room rather than to back out like a servant, she was relieved to note – she lay in her bed a while longer, thinking of the men in her life.

Etyan, of course, was a man in age now, approaching his twentieth year, even if she could not think of him as more than a boy. She must remember to tell him about the marriage; no doubt he would disapprove but that was his problem, not hers. Thoughts of him were, as ever, a tangle of love, concern and exasperation.

She loved Francin too, in a way. She thought that affection was returned, in part because she had taken the place of the sister he lost as a child, in part because she had become a useful and impartial friend as an adult. She respected Francin so much more than she respected her foolish brother. But she was not sure she trusted him.

Did she love Markave? She cared for him, respected him – there was no more loyal and competent person in her House – and trusted him more than anyone else in her life. But not love. Perhaps that would come in time.

She thought, then, of Alharet, who she had once cared for, respected and trusted; perhaps even loved, as a friend. What would she think of this situation? Once, many years ago, the duchess had secured the services of a talented and anonymous young man to remind Rhia that sex was one of life's pleasures. No doubt she would be amused to see things come to this. Hearing the duchess's high, charming laugh echo in her head, Rhia found herself unable to stay in bed any longer.

She spent the day in her study, reading and copying. No one disturbed her, not even her new husband.

Sur Lectel arrived early, on hand to season her words should she get carried away tonight. He had been his usual reassuring self after the last court session, though he had asked, regarding the revelation that the eparch of Zekt was one of her correspondents, whether there were any other relevant facts she had neglected to mention. Although his tone had annoyed her, he had a point. She assured him she did not plan any further surprises.

The judges arrived together at the appointed hour. She had Brynan show them up to her study, and offer refreshments; she did not yet feel ready to interact with her steward-turned-spouse in front of strangers. It was disconcerting enough to have outsiders in her sanctum. She'd had to clear one of the desks for them to put their drinks on.

"So this is the celestial model then?" asked Vansel, nodding at her handiwork. "How does it work?"

"It is cranked by hand, as I shall demonstrate." Making it not remotely heretical. "Did you wish to examine it before I do so?"

Jertine waved the offer away but Tethorn and Vansel both looked over the mechanisms, the latter even bending down to check the cogs underneath. "Uh, please do not touch anything down there," said Rhia, trying to hide her nerves.

When the two judges stepped back Rhia took the crank, then paused. "Is it clear to you what is what?"

"Not really," said Jertine.

"Well, the lamp in the centre is the Sun. The small globe nearest is the Maiden, and the one beyond that, the world itself."

"And these outer two?" asked Tethorn.

"The Matriarch and Crone. Unfortunately I have not yet perfected the mechanism, so they do not move. If you would all stand on the same side, where the world is please." The judges shuffled around. "Now, I will make it move…" She eased the handle round, feeling the teeth of the mechanism engage. The world shuddered and started to turn on its pole, at the same time moving around its track; a moment later, the Maiden too began to move.

Jertine wrinkled his nose. "What is that smell?"

"Tallow. I use it to lubricate the model." Rhia paused in her winding. "Observe, if you will, the current relationship between the Maiden and the world, how it is lit along one edge only." Tethorn had bent down without her asking him to, and now nodded to himself. "If the rest of you could do as Master Tethorn has done, perhaps even to take his place after he steps aside… that's it." Each judge took a turn looking across the model as instructed.

"Now, I will move things on." She started cranking again.

"Forgive me, Countess," said Jertine, "but ingenious though this model is, my poor intellect is finding it hard to relate it to the world we live in."

Rhia paused in her winding and made herself answer politely. "It is a lot to take in, but this is only the first part of my demonstration. Now, I just need to wind it a little further." She felt resistance, and paused, breath frozen in her throat. But it had stuck here before. With exquisite slowness she applied more pressure, feeling the handle judder, then shift. The model ground back into motion. She breathed again. When it reached the relevant point she released the handle. "If you would shuffle round a bit, to where the world is now, and look, as you did before, at how the Maiden appears from there."

They did so, Vansel with impatience, Jertine with bemusement and Tethorn with interest.

"As you see, the Maiden is now half lit and half in darkness."

"I have a question," said Tethorn.

"Ask away, please."

"If we grant the possibility that the world is not flat but is a sphere – itself a considerable leap of reasoning, but not impossible – why does it then follow that the world orbits the Sun, rather than vice versa?"

"An excellent question!" Rhia smiled for the first time. "Having the Sun in the centre of the universe is the only way to explain the observations I have made. And which you will now be able to make for yourselves. Now, for the second part of my demonstration we must go up to my observation platform." She pointed to the wooden ladder in the corner of the study. "Um, it's probably best not to try bringing your drink." Lord Jertine put his glass of wine back down.

Sur Lectel stayed below, but even so the observation platform was unpleasantly crowded with four people on it. Rhia, going up first, stood with one hand on the sightglass, now locked in its tripod. She tried not to wince when Vansel, staggering slightly as he got to his feet after climbing the ladder, nearly jogged it.

When they were assembled she pointed to the Maiden, lying low over the city's rooftops. "We all know that the Maiden, unlike the Matriarch and Crone, appears only at dusk and dawn, and never rises high. As you may or may not be aware, all the Strays trace erratic paths in the sky. All of these facts are explained by their going round the Sun, as our world does. My sightglass is trained upon the Maiden now, and I invite you to look for yourselves."

As she had expected Tethorn went first. His indrawn breath at seeing the half full Maiden lifted Rhia's heart. "Do you see how its real state mirrors that shown in my model?"

Without taking his eye from the sightglass Tethorn murmured, "I do."

He looked a while longer then let Jertine take a turn. "Impressive," the viscount conceded.

Finally Vansel stooped to try the view, one hand braced on

the platform rail. He straightened after little more than a glance. "Hmm. This is an interesting sight, but what is to say it is real?"

"But you can see it for yourself, through the sightglass!"

"I look into this tube and I see a half-lit sphere, yes. For all I know I just see an image you had put into the tube."

"You cannot…" Rhia made herself breathe. "I have extensive writings on optics, the branch of learning that allowed me to create this sightglass. Would you like me to provide them?" She already had a bundle of papers for Sur Tethorn, showing her mathematical workings to date.

"I think you had better." Vansel held up a finger. "Even if I concede, for now, that what I saw was real, I am most disconcerted at such imperfection."

"Imperfection?"

"That these so-called spheres in the sky should be half in darkness… I am not sure the First would permit such a thing."

Rhia had a sudden desire to push the cardinal off the roof. She blew out an explosive breath to drive off the urge. "If you mean the phases, then surely you would have the same complaint of the Moons, whose phases can be seen without the aid of any sightglass."

"I suppose so."

"Actually," said Tethorn, "I was wondering about the Moons. How do they fit into your model?"

"They orbit around the world."

"Ah," chipped in the cardinal, "so not everything goes round the Sun, then?"

"No. As I say, moons orbit the world – in fact, worlds."

"Worlds?"

From the cardinal's tone, Rhia suspected she may have gone too far. But the truth was the truth. "Yes. The Strays are globes, so they are worlds too, and the Matriarch – which, unfortunately, is not currently in our skies – has a moon of its own."

Beside her, Vansel shook his head

Jertine said, "Talking of moons, could we not settle the

argument about whether the sightglass shows a true image by looking at one of them? I believe Greymoon is up."

"It is!" Rhia tried not to sound too triumphant. "If you stand back as far as you can I will move the sightglass." Greymoon was off to one side, beyond the tripod's limited arc, so she had to call each of the judges forward to take the sightglass, then point it as she directed.

This time, Vansel went first, by dint of having ended up standing closest to her on the crowded platform. "Hmm," he said. "The image is different, yes. Somewhat... shaky."

"That is a problem, yes," Rhia conceded. "Hence the tripod. But you can see the surface of the Moon, yes?"

"I can. It appears... barren and pitted. There are no celestial settlements there."

At least it was Greymoon, not Whitemoon, that was visible. Her answer to his query would not hold for the larger Moon, said to be the heaven to which worthy shadowkin ascended to live in harmony close to the First. "As the scriptures themselves say, we are very different to the skykin. I do not believe they live in cities."

"But you don't know that, of course."

"There is much I do not know." Whether people could live in the sky at all, for example. Not that she was going to mention this. She had given them enough to fill their heads.

Vansel must have thought the same. When everyone had viewed the Moon, he said, "We have much to consider as a result of this demonstration."

The other two nodded, shadowy forms off to one side.

"Tomorrow is restday. I propose we three spend firstday discussing what we have been shown and what it may mean. We will reconvene on twoday. I will send word as to when."

CHAPTER 43

Dej slept on the floor at the foot of Jat's bed, wrapped in her blanket. The seer was already stirring when she woke. She gave him water but he refused food. "You'd only end up having to clean up after me," he croaked.

"I've changed nappies, back in the crèche. At least you're not screaming and puking."

"I might… if I had the energy." But his humour felt forced. He seemed weaker today, every breath heaved in with an effort. She doubted he'd last another night. "Sit then."

Dej did, and waited for him to gather his thoughts.

Finally he said, "We talked about tech, didn't we? And what the Separation really was."

"Sort of. But I still don't understand why the shadowkin rejected tech."

"No one does. Some great difference in worldview. A split. Long time ago. We'll never know the full truth." He drew a long wheezing breath. "Just have to deal with the consequences." He smiled. "At least we got the useful stuff. Not that most of us understand our tech, even though we use it every day."

"So where does it come from?"

"Old, old processes and skills. Our ancestors combined the original tech they brought here with the plants and animals they found, and with themselves. Much to the irritation of the shadowkin."

"If tech's so ancient, and you don't understand it, how come it's still working? Wouldn't it have broken or gone rotten or something?"

"It's grown as much as made. It won't break as such, though it does stop working sometimes, or work in odd ways. But we have some skills, still, to fix it up. You were told there were ten roles in a clan, weren't you?"

"Yes. I'm guessing there are more."

"One more: technician. A manipulator of tech."

"Do they go to crèches?"

"Of course, even seers start off in crèches."

"So what's their parting-gift?"

"The shadowkin think technicians are destined to be builders; as with builders their mother leaves them with a perfect carved cube the size of a thumb-tip. Only while the builders have cubes of stone, technicians have cubes of… to be honest I don't know the name of the stuff, but I do know the crèche-mothers would have a fit if they knew what it really was." He gave a tired but amused *hah*, then spent a few moments just breathing.

She had so many questions, but he didn't have long now. Her job was to listen.

He noticed her again, and said, "The world is changing, Dej."

She nodded. This was what he needed to tell her. "In what ways?" she prompted gently.

"Ways we can't be sure of. That's the problem. But a lot of us have felt it."

"When you say 'us'…"

"Seers. Old seers, in tune with the world. Perhaps it's not so much changing as fighting back…" He frowned, then said, "Worlds have cycles. This one does, anyway. Long slow cycles, so slow we don't notice they're happening. Even with a memory going back over a thousand years."

"But you're sure."

"As I can be. Have there been any changes in the weather in the shadowlands?"

"The weather? Well... when I left the crèche, a couple of years back, there was a drought. And again this year. Is that what you mean?"

"That could be part of it, yes."

"Is this something to do with the Harbinger?"

"The Harbinger? Oh, the wandering star, you mean." He thought for a moment. "I'm not sure. It hasn't been visiting the skies for long, no more than four centuries I'd say. So maybe, by some unseen means."

"Don't take this the wrong way, Jat, but there's a lot you don't know."

"An near-infinite amount. And yet I know too much."

"So what else is happening with these changes? I'm thinking it's nothing good."

"Oh yes. Nothing good." He slipped into silent contemplation.

"Is this place, this city, deserted because of the cycle, the bad stuff happening?"

"It is, Dej, yes." His voice was a whisper now.

"So what happened here?"

"People left."

"Why?"

"There were not enough of us." He seemed half lost in memory, barely aware he was talking to her. Slipping away fast.

"What do you mean?"

"The skykin are dying, Dej."

"Is it some disease?" Was she infected? Her hand went to her stomach. Would it harm her baby?

"Not a disease. More complicated... Our animuses. The world has finally noticed what we've done... the crime against it." He was getting breathless again. She made herself wait in silence until he got his voice back. "This is... you need to know... ah, no time. Not sure you'd understand. There is one way, but... you don't deserve any of this, but if it's what the world wants, I have to..."

"Jat!" He was leaving her, his voice a dying murmur. She covered his hand with hers. Perhaps responding to her touch, he opened his eyes.

"I've travelled so far…" He focused fully on her. "You too, to come here." His gaze dropped to where her other hand rested on her swollen belly. "But you have to go back now."

"Back where?" Not to Etyan. Never to Etyan.

"The child. Can't survive out here."

"I've got shelter, I just need to feed–"

"No!" His vehement whisper stopped her. She could feel him fighting to stay conscious. "You can't do it alone, Dej…" His hand, under hers, quivered in agitation. "Find a crèche. Please. Promise me."

"I promise. Now stay with me!" His eyes had closed again. "Jat! No!"

He sighed, an oddly contented sound.

She waited for the next breath.

It didn't come.

"Not yet, damn you! Not yet!" Grief and frustration warred in her.

But he was gone.

With a certainty she hadn't felt in weeks, she knew what she had to do now. And she needed to hurry.

She fetched her knife.

CHAPTER 44

Rhia offered to watch Kerne while the servants went to the restday service. He was sleeping a lot at the moment, and drowsy and confused whenever he awoke.

On their return Markave entered the room where she sat with the boy. "I have a favour to ask." He sounded uncertain.

"Ask away, please." Every conversation changed things between them, as he became more used to treating her as a sort-of equal, and she came round to thinking of him as more than a faithful servant. But it would take time.

"Will you pray with me, for Kerne's recovery?"

"Pray?" She prayed in public when required, and that was what this was, in effect. "Of course, if you wish me to."

So they knelt, and clasped their hands, and Markave asked the First to show mercy and save his boy. Rhia joined in when he spoke the ritual lines to open and close the prayer, and tried to compose her mind and face accordingly. This was, she reminded herself, for Markave as much as for his son.

When they straightened Markave said, "I would like to ask you something personal, Rhia." He still said her name like it startled him. "If you don't mind."

"You are my husband. You can ask me anything." Just as the word "husband' startled her.

"Yes. Of course. It's just… Do you really not believe in the First?"

"Ah, an easy question." She considered how best to put it. "I believe in the possibility of God, but am unsure of such a being's reality. And as the First is worshipped, and with some of the acts done in His name, I cannot give Him my allegiance."

"Forgive me, but that sounds like arrogance."

"Perhaps it is. Or perhaps, if those who claim to serve the First were not intent on destroying me, I would be better inclined to respect their rules."

"I should not have asked." He got up.

"Where are you going?"

"Although it is restday I still have duties to attend to. I will return to watch Kerne when I am done. Unless you wish otherwise?"

"No. Of course. Do what you need to do."

Markave left without another word.

Firstday was agony. For months she had been trying to complete her celestial model and now, with the demonstration done, she could not bear to look at it. She copied some more papers, and sent them off with Brynan to the palace, then whiled away the day reading random writings from the enquirers, not really taking anything in. When darkness fell and the sky remained cloudy she got a rare early night, alone again, as after she and Markave had been seen to spend their wedding night together, he had suggested he rest in his room when he was not watching Kerne. She had agreed without argument.

"We have reached a decision."

Rhia made herself breathe, deep and even, deep and even. With the rains gone, the weather was hot and close; she had been summoned back after a late lunch and the small courtroom felt uncomfortably stuffy.

Cardinal Vansel continued, "Each judge will speak their piece, so you may understand what has been decided and why, starting with myself. As a representative of the Church it will not surprise you that I am not able to accept this complex and preposterous theory."

"You saw the evidence for yourself, Holiness!"

Beside her, Sur Lectel suppressed a groan at her outburst.

"Kindly do not interrupt. What I saw is irrelevant. The First can make the world appear any way He wills it. If He wishes us to see half-lit spheres in the sky, we will. If He wishes to hide the celestial settlements on the Moons from our gaze, He will. However such deception is more suited to the wiles of the Last. I suspect that the Great Deceiver has acted upon your mind, which, whilst surprisingly sharp, is still that of the lesser sex. You have been taken in. Your theory has no merit. And I believe that to pursue it further may imperil your very soul."

Rhia seethed but stayed silent. She had expected something like this.

Lord Jertine spoke up next. "Whilst I respect his Holiness's judgement, I am not obliged to agree with it, and indeed I do not. I cannot claim to comprehend the intricacies and implications of the idea that we live on a globe that orbits with others in a vast nothingness, but your demonstration impressed me, and everything you showed us supported your theory. I was particularly taken with your sightglass; should you be in a position to make another, I would be most interested in owning it. But as for the theory, I am willing to accept its validity, even if its detail escapes me."

Rhia found a smile stealing onto her face.

Vansel looked to his other side. Tethorn steepled his fingers and said, "I too see the merits of your theory." Rhia stifled the urge to laugh aloud. *They believe me!* "However, there are many unknowns, such as where the Harbinger fits in—"

"I would happily—"

Rhia bit her tongue at Vansel's raised finger.

Tethorn continued. "I also share some of His Holiness's concerns regarding how complex such a universe would be, and how impersonal; like some great mechanism running on by itself. I cannot see why the First would create such an untidy and hard-to-grasp arrangement. Last but not least, I have looked at your detailed workings and, frankly, they do not work. You also seem to have changed your mind, and started trying to make your mathematics fit orbits which are not circular – even though the model shows them as being so."

"But it represented the–"

"Silence, if you please!"

Rhia recoiled. Her heart had been sinking at Tethorn's words, and she felt Vansel's reprimand like a blow.

Tethorn concluded, "Whilst this theory is intriguing, I cannot give it my belief or support."

Rhia just stared at him.

The cardinal said. "Two out of three of us must agree for a decision to be reached, and such is the case. Your theory is ruled a dangerous delusion, with no basis in the reality we live in or in the all-encompassing mind of the First."

"May I speak?" Her voice was shaking.

"Briefly, if you require clarification."

"I do. You are, I believe, telling me that I am deluded, possibly that I have been tempted to my delusion by the Last, and that my ideas have nothing to do with the world as you see it."

"That is one way of putting it."

"Then can I go now?"

"I'm sorry?"

"If I am harmlessly crazy, or at least inclined to credulity, then is there any reason I cannot return to my foolish diversions? If I feel the touch of the Last in my thoughts I will of course seek spiritual guidance." Her voice sounded shrill in her ears.

"No, you may not go. We have not delivered our judgement."

"But surely there is nothing to judge! I am just a foolish woman who does not know her place, and therefore not a threat to the natural order the Church seeks to maintain!"

"That your ideas are delusions does not make them acceptable."

"What? Either my theory is true, and I must prove it does not offend the Church or it is false, and therefore inoffensive by definition. You cannot have it both ways!"

"That you would spread such lies is not acceptable. Doubts would be raised, questions asked. This cold, mechanical universe is not one we wish to live in. All writings and other items pertaining to your theory will be destroyed under Church supervision–"

"No!"

"–and you will swear on the Book of Separation that you will never undertake to recreate them. Furthermore, representatives of the Church will search your property and confiscate any other papers deemed to stand against our teachings."

"You cannot do this!"

"We most certainly can. And if we wished we could impose further punishments, including a fine and public penance. Do not tempt me to do so."

"A public penance. Hah!" She felt light-headed, infused with a cold, surreal fury. "If I have to crawl between every church in the city in my underwear with ash in my hair, aren't you worried that people might start *asking questions* about what I did wrong?"

"Countess, do not push me! You will come away from this with your life and, hopefully, your soul. Be thankful for that."

"But *this* is my life! You are taking everything that matters from me."

"Sur Lectel, please remove the Countess from the courtroom and explain that due process has been followed and judgement given. Either that or I shall send a clerk for the guards."

"I'm going!" She shook her head. "You've won!"

Outside, Sur Lectel strode in her wake. When it became obvious he was not going to leave her alone she turned on him, uncaring that they were in a public corridor. "How can they just take everything like that!" But even as she spoke she knew she had lost; had, perhaps, been bound to lose from the day Cardinal

Marsan had read the charges.

"You will not want to hear this, countess, but perhaps this is the best outcome we could have hoped for."

"Really? Because that's not how it feels."

"I understand your anger, but think of the price you could have paid."

"I would have died for the truth!"

"Which the Church would then have suppressed anyway."

"Maybe. I... Can I appeal?"

"You know you cannot. Not after a grand trial."

And even if she could, the process would be slow; it would be too late to save her papers. "This was what they planned all along, wasn't it?" Some of the fury was draining away.

"Perhaps." Sur Lectel glanced around; the corridor was empty. Even so he dropped his voice. "The Church wanted to prove their point, but they might have baulked at putting a high noble to death."

Rhia answered in a venomous whisper. "Certain individuals in other Houses would have been quite happy for that to happen."

"Which is one reason it did not, if I may be blunt. The Church would not want to be seen to do the dirty work of the Houses major."

"Politics again! Does no one care for the truth?"

Sur Lectel said nothing.

"All right. You did what you could. I am going home now."

But home no longer felt like a haven.

What the trial had really been about, what had really offended the Church, was how her theory challenged the shadowkin's exulted status. Vansel had said it himself: *this cold, mechanical universe is not one we wish to live in.* She had questioned the idea that the world – the universe – existed to serve, test and please the tiny, brief creatures who lived in it.

She had feared she was facing faith, which could not be reasoned with, but she was also facing arrogance, the innate sense of superiority in those who would not brook being mere observers of a cosmic miracle. She had been doubly damned to fail.

She could not face her study. Until today, surrounding herself with accumulated learning had been her comfort. Now much of that learning was going to be ripped from her, destroyed and lost forever... seeing what she was about to lose would be salt in an open wound.

Instead she asked Markave to distract her with a game. He fetched the board and pieces for set-squares, which had been her favourite as a girl.

They played in silence a while, though Rhia's mind was only half on the moves she was making.

"What is it?" asked Markave gently. He had been about to win, which never happened.

"The judges ruled against me today."

"No!" His face fell into lines of horrified dismay. "Will they...?"

"Oh. No. I'll live. Survive, anyway. But they'll take my papers. My work, Markave. It'll all be lost."

Finally the tears came. She had been strong before, held herself together for her people, her House and her work. But the world didn't care for her people, her House or her work. It had trampled over it all. A few leaky sniffs, then the damn broke, and she was sobbing and wailing like a hurt child.

She felt arms go around her, and flinched, then relaxed. Markave held her, not tight but enough for her to know he was there for her, while she cried her heart out.

CHAPTER 45

A note sealed with the Church's Pillar of Light arrived the next morning. Markave had spent the night in her room, having helped her up to bed, and continued to hold her until she finally slept. He was there when she awoke, and she managed a smile for him. She had lost a lot, but not everything. Not everyone.

Her hands shook as she opened the note, and what little peace she had salvaged overnight left her as she read:

In accordance with the judgement given on the 9th day of the 1st month of the year of Separation 5362, the writings of Rhia Harlyn on the nature of the universe are deemed to be inaccurate and fanciful fabrications, an affront to the civilised state of man. As such, they are to be disposed of discreetly, along with any related devices or other writings on similar matters deemed to likewise cause offence.

Offence to whom? Vansel had said the Church could, and would, take whatever they wanted of her work but seeing it written down was a knife to her heart.

The process will begin this afternoon, when Church representatives will call to collect all writings on the misguided celestial theory discussed and dismissed during the recent trial. They will return the next day to go through any and all other works held at the countess's city property.

*The countess should be aware that due process will be
followed.*

Meaning: don't go running to the duke. Even he couldn't help
her now.

*Any further writings not currently at the townhouse will also be
examined and, if necessary, destroyed. If any such writings are
held at other Harlyn properties the countess must send for them.
Let it also be noted that those writings given to your lawyer, and
also those sent into the keeping of His Grace the Duke in express
defiance of the Church's admonitions, will be gathered and
destroyed.*

"No!" Had Francin betrayed her? No, he'd never do that. Even
without her papers, her mind was of use to him. And they were
family. But someone had. She raised her head and met Markave's
eyes, where he sat on the edge of the bed. "When you took my
papers to the palace who did you give them to?"

"The militia captain who His Grace named; Tador is friends
with his nephew and I knew him by sight so I thought him my
best contact."

Not Markave, thank God. "Fetch Brynan and Nerilyn please."
Suddenly her frustration had a focus.

The two house servants crept into the bedroom looking
uncertain, though Brynan briefly smirked at the sight of her and
Markave together, in their underclothes. She turned to him first.

"Brynan, when you went to the palace with my papers, who did
you give them to?"

"One of the ministers on the duke's list."

"And how did you locate him?" It seemed unlikely Brynan had
any personal contacts at the palace.

"I asked a footman. When the footman asked me why I needed
to speak to a minister I said I had a message from Countess
Harlyn, and it was House business."

"A plausible lie."

"Was that... all right? You said no one must know you were
sending your papers to the duke. I spoke to the same minister both

286

times. He was very helpful."

"You did the right thing." Rhia turned to her maidservant. "You've also taken papers twice. Who did you give them to?"

"One time the militia captain and the other time a minister."

"And how did you find the right individuals?"

"I asked Adern."

Rhia sighed. "Tell me you did not let him know what you were up to."

"He asked…" Nerilyn wouldn't meet her eyes.

"And what did you say?"

"The first time, I said it was none of his business. He was a bit funny about it, but he plays around, does Adern; sometimes I don't know whether he's annoyed at me or just having fun."

"And the second time?"

Nerilyn looked at her feet. "I didn't mean to say anything. Only he was mocking me, so I said my mistress had a great mind, and he said he'd heard she wrote crazy stuff, and I said no, it's just you wouldn't be smart enough to understand it, and he said, so would the duke then? And I, I didn't say anything, I really didn't. He worked it out. But when he asked directly if I was smuggling papers to the duke for you, I couldn't lie, not to him. I made him swear not to tell anyone."

"You foolish, foolish girl!" But Rhia was a fool too; she'd been thinking how she could use Nerilyn's lover as a source of useful information. Why had it not occurred to her that someone else might do the same in return?

"I'm so sorry! Please I never meant to, I just–"

"Get out!" The fury boiled up, cold and bitter. "You have no idea the harm you have done, girl. No idea."

"But m'lady–"

"Not a word. Not one more word. Get out and don't come back. I will not have traitors in my house! I never want to see you again, do you hear me?"

Tears starting from her eyes, Nerilyn nodded, then turned and fled.

Rhia waved an exhausted hand, "Brynan, you can get on with whatever you were doing."

Which just left Markave. He said nothing, but she sensed a new distance between them at seeing her treat Nerilyn so. "Shall I go too?" he murmured.

"Yes. Please." She did not trust herself with company.

The Church sent a canon and his clerk. They introduced themselves but Rhia instantly forgot their names. She met them in the dining room and handed over a thick bundle of papers without a word.

"Is this everything you have on the theory the Church has ruled against?"

"Everything I have in this house, yes."

The churchman looked around the well-furnished but book-free dining room. "We would like to see where the other papers and potential items of interest are please."

"If you must."

She led them up to her study. Their faces fell at the sheer volume of papers, books and instruments on every surface. "This may take a while," said the clerk.

"Good," said Rhia, then changed her mind. "Actually I would like you done and out of my house as soon as possible."

The canon said, "I will recruit an additional clerk and we will return first thing tomorrow."

"Well, I'm not going anywhere."

She did wonder, after they were gone, whether she should go away rather than stand helplessly by while her life's work was destroyed. No: she would watch the Church's minions, and fight them if they overstepped their admittedly wide remit.

But thinking about the estate jogged her memory. She needed to write to Etyan! *As soon as I can face it*, she told herself.

The churchmen returned the next morning. Rhia fluttered in and out of the study, staying for as long as she could bear while they rummaged through everything, then withdrawing to her room when the sight of their desecration became too much. At one point the canon pointed to the celestial model and said, "Tomorrow we will bring someone who can safely dismantle this."

"Oh, you're not just going to take a mallet to it then?"

"No Countess. The materials are your property. You can have them back."

"How magnanimous."

"There was one other thing though."

"What?"

"You have a device which was produced at your trial, which claimed to magnify the sky."

"What of it?"

"We need to examine it, and if necessary remove it as well."

"Oh no. You are not having my sightglass."

"I am sorry Countess, but if it breaks the Church's proscriptions–"

"It does not! And Cardinal Vansel used it safely without fear of imperilling his immortal soul. It stays."

"We have our instructions…"

"And they do not include taking items which the Church has no problem with. I have acquiesced to the Church's demands, I am cooperating fully, but if you want my sightglass you will have a fight on your hands!"

"We will deal with the other items first, then."

"You do that."

She was glad now that she had already secreted the sightglass in her bedroom.

That afternoon, as she was steeling herself to return to the depredations in her study, she ran into Markave as he was pulling the door closed on the guest room.

"How is he?" she asked.

"He woke up enough to ask for water a while back." Kerne was unconscious most of the time now; unable to eat, drinking no more than a sip once a day, he was fading away in front of them.

"I can take a turn, Markave. It might distract me."

"I won't ask you to, unless you want to."

They stood facing each other in awkward silence, then Rhia said, "Was I too hard on Nerilyn?"

"That's not for me to say."

"But it is, doubly so now. I was so angry, and she was there, and couldn't answer back."

"She is a well-meaning but foolish girl. This is not the first time she has made a mistake then covered it up." He shrugged. "But she did not betray you on purpose, and I know she will be truly sorry."

"Maybe I'll take her back in a while. Or else look for a new maid who isn't such a fool." She'd had to hunt around for clean clothes this morning. "I just don't think I can face either option right now."

"I understand." He put a tentative hand on her arm. She smiled back at him. "Just let me know what you decide and we can sort this out together."

When he was gone she paused, his touch lingering. She did not feel anything like lust for him, but his physical presence was not unpleasant. Now that she knew she would live they might consider having a child together, if they were not too old. Other women seemed fulfilled by motherhood. Perhaps she could learn to be too.

The next day, true to their word, the churchmen dismantled the celestial model. All that work she and Kerne had put in, undone in half a day.

She could not stand to watch for long, so she went and wrote the long-overdue letter to Etyan. She stated the facts baldly: *I have married Markave to save our House; it is legal and has been accepted.* Or at least not challenged. *The Church found against me in my trial.*

They did not have the courage to harm me, but my work is all undone.

Sometimes she thought of everyone on the world – shadowkin, skykin, everyone – as mere animals, living in a deep well. With such limited horizons, they never saw the full reality beyond the hole, only what fell in, or could be glimpsed passing over it. She doubted this analogy would stand up to the full force of logic, but then logic was not valued by most people anyway. The Church, despite its talk of 'the heavens', did not even seem capable of looking up out of the hole. And when she had dared to, she had been put firmly back in her place.

CHAPTER 46

Dej woke from dreams of other lives.

She was lying on the floor, in darkness.

Where? The city of Foam-cast-north, the beautiful vibrant settlement by the sea.

When? At noon, reclining while giving advice in dappled shade. At cool midnight, making love on the shore, lost together in the murmur of the waves. During the festival of lights, fading to sleep after a joyful day, the dancers receding into the dusk. The dusk... the dark...

She sat up, grabbing her head in her hands, palms pressed to forehead.

She wasn't them. That wasn't then. The city was dead now. Empty. Overgrown. Everyone long gone.

And it wasn't her city; those weren't her people. These weren't her memories.

She blew out a long slow breath, and raised her head. She was lying at the foot of the seer's bed. A sweetness, the beginning of decay, wafted down.

It took a while to get her legs under her. Her limbs were weak and she was appallingly thirsty; she'd been out of it for days. Felt like years. Lifetimes. But already the seer's past lives were fading, some gone forever, others forever deeply embedded in her.

The darkness wasn't as thick now; it would be dawn soon.
She stood, sighed, and rubbed her back. The seer's body looked
undisturbed, except for the head. Good. In time local creatures
would find it, eat it, return it to the world. But that was something
she didn't want to see. Bad enough, in the pre-dawn shadows,
to see that deeper shadow between the eyes. A knife hadn't been
enough: she'd had to use a sharp stone to smash Jat's skull, working
fast, feeling the animus's life drain away, following its host into
oblivion. When she finally uncovered it, nestled between two
squishy grey masses, it was smaller than she expected; no bigger
than a finger, bone-white and segmented. It looked like a maggot,
though rather than wriggling it had just shivered as she plucked it
out, as though shying away from the outside world.

Her gorge rose for a moment. But only a moment.

The animus had tasted of nothing and everything. The texture
had been nauseating, the way the segments rolled then burst
against the roof of her mouth, releasing an earthy, salty warmth.
Swallowing had taken all her willpower. But even while its
gelatinous texture and foul taste lingered in her mouth, its essence
had begun to fill her head.

Crèche tattle said that skykin relived past lives in their dreams.
Before now, she never had, being incompletely bonded; the only
time she'd accessed her own animus's memories had been fleetingly,
at her bonding.

She hadn't eaten the seer's animus to dream about his past lives.
And she hadn't eaten it to prolong her own life, as the clanless
elder, Mar, had done. She had consumed Jat's animus to gain the
knowledge he hadn't had time to pass on.

His final life, the one that had broken him, had contributed
few dreams to her menagerie of memory. He hadn't wanted
to remember. But while the sensual specifics of dozens of lives
drained away, the cold details of the vital, terrible work he had
done as his last duty to their people sharpened, became more real,
a part of her worldview.

It had been bad enough knowing what Etyan had done. He'd

ruined an innocent girl, and hurt those who'd cared for her. But this ongoing horror affected every skykin who'd ever lived. She sagged and tottered, half putting a hand out to the seer's deathbed for support. This knowledge had destroyed a seer. Who was she, a rootless nobody, to know the awful truth? And it would die with her, out here. Her worldview shattered, for nothing.

Her flailing hand brushed her swollen belly, felt the life within. She paused, focused.

It's not just me any more.

No, it was *her* too. The innocent child inside. A girl: yes, she knew that now. A moment of cold, personal doubt intruded on her attempts to dispel the world-shaking desolation. Back at the crèche, Min had been sure her child was a girl, sure without any skykin intuition. Maybe she'd been right. But she and the baby had both died.

"You'll survive," she told the child. "I'll make sure of it."

The world might be built on a lie, but her daughter still deserved the chance to live in it.

She turned away from the mangled body of the seer, and tottered out into the pre-dawn light.

CHAPTER 47

"Rhia! Rhia wake up!"

"What? Are they here already?" In the week or so since the Church had begun their vile work she had become increasingly lethargic, exhausted by losing her battle. She had taken to sleeping late. It was bright daylight already.

"No, not the churchmen." In the light pressing in through the shutters Markave's face was a mask of horror.

"Kerne! Oh no." She struggled to sit up. Kerne had reached the stage of the fever when his pain was constant and his skin bruised at a touch. Death was not far off, and she wanted to be with Markave when his son died.

"Not Kerne."

She looked more closely. Markave looked stricken. "What is it? What's happened?"

Markave took two halting steps to the window, then tugged one shutter open, jumping back at once as though scalded.

Light flooded the room. Not just normal daylight but a burning blue-white radiance that made Rhia throw her hand up to shield her eyes.

She knew that light.

No. It can't be.

She turned to Markave. "When did... how..."

"Everything was like this when I woke up. What's happening? What is this?"

"This," she pointed at the window, squinting against the glare, "or rather that, is the Sun. What the Sun really looks like."

"I don't understand."

"In the skyland. The Sun looks like that in the skyland."

"How can this be?"

"An excellent question." A breathless animation gripped her. How can this be indeed. "I need to go to the palace."

"Is it… safe?"

"No. But given the fact we can endure this light at all I'd surmise we have a cloudy sky."

"More than cloudy. There's a storm brewing."

"Ah yes, that would make sense. I'll need my thickest cloak. You and Brynan must wait here."

"I have no intention of going out in that."

Rhia did not want to. But she had to know how bad it was.

Markave was right about the storm. Clouds swirled and billowed overhead, while menacing rumbles of thunder sounded in the distance. As she turned the first corner, a fierce gust of wind yanked at her cloak, blowing the hood down. She pulled it back up, holding it in place with one hand. She should probably have worn gloves to protect her hands too.

The streets were empty – it was still early – but there were distant shouts from farther down the hill.

At the palace a pair of demoralised guards half made to stop her, until her glare silenced them. She took back corridors unused since childhood, when she had become Francin's regular playmate after he lost his sister and they had run riot in places they were not meant to go. The servants she passed were either making a point of going about their business as normal or muttering fearfully in corners. Rhia ignored the air of restrained panic, heading ever upwards.

She emerged on the noon tower – so named because of an old, complicated and probably untrue story about a distant ancestor of the duke who had ended up throwing himself off it at midday. It was the highest point of the palace.

Up here the wind was a gale. Rhia stayed back from the parapet, and crouched down against the constant buffeting. Overhead, the already-bright clouds flashed searing white, and a moment later a thunderous crash reverberated across the city. She flinched, then made herself untense. With one hand on the tower's flat roof for support, she looked out over what Francin called "the best view in the land".

Normally the skyland was a silver-white band along the far horizon. Now, the whole land was lit silver-white, in every direction.

It was as bad as she feared. The celestial shade that made Shen what it was hadn't just moved. It was gone.

A splat of warm rain hit her cheek. She recoiled, then scuttled back down the stairs.

A staircase and two corridors later, the courtier heading towards her stopped and said, "The duke would–"

"Where is he?"

"I'll take you to him." The man, some scion of a minor House, took her to one of the duke's meeting rooms. Francin was huddled round a table with half a dozen minsters. He looked up when she burst in, and said, "Gentlemen, please wait here. I need a quick word with my cousin."

The men muttered, horrified gazes going to her scarred and mask-less face, but Rhia ignored them. Francin opened a side door to a smaller chamber, containing just two chairs and a desk. He did not sit. He looked as agitated as she had ever seen him, and before she could speak said, "Something far above us has gone awry, hasn't it?"

"I believe so."

"You believe so. Can you be sure?"

"Yes. I am as sure as I can be." With a jolt she realised that her theory, which the Church had dismissed as delusion and which she had begun to doubt herself, may just have been unexpectedly, terrifyingly vindicated. She had an inappropriate urge to laugh.

"And whatever has gone wrong has left us exposed to the unshielded Sun."

"Yes. Thankfully there are clouds, at the moment."

"Is it just us?"

"Us? Oh you mean just Shen." The thought that this might be a worldwide phenomenon stopped the breath in her throat. She made herself inhale, and think. "I can't be sure." The shade-swarm consisted of structures whose motions and interactions were beyond her ability to model, but it must be sophisticated, dynamic and, until now, reliable. If one part of the system failed, others would compensate. "But I don't think every shadowland will be affected, at least not immediately."

"And will it... remedy itself?"

"I don't know. Probably not."

"So this is permanent." His gaze went briefly heavenward, then settled back on her. "You need to go home and pack now."

"Pack?"

"Yes. One bag, as much as you can carry. No more."

"Pack for what?"

"You're leaving, with me. With us."

"Leaving? To go where?" There was no shelter, no safe haven. No Shen.

"Just be ready to leave at dusk."

"I don't underst—"

"For once, don't try and understand. Just do it. It's your only chance of survival. And wear riding clothes."

"Riding clothes? You can't outrun this!" But he was already hustling her out. He shoved her, gently but firmly, to one side and returned to his huddle of ministers.

Bereft of other choices, Rhia left.

Outside, the storm was whipping itself into a frenzy. Flurries of hot rain smacked her, and the wind harried her all the way home. There were more people around now, most dashing between shelter. The odd shout and, once, a woman's scream, were audible above the howl of the wind.

Back at the townhouse all the shutters were closed. *Well done, Markave*. Markave. Francin had said he could save her but what about Markave? And Brynan? Assuming Francin had not just gone mad. No, she had to assume he had some plan, however unexpected. The alternative was unthinkable. She had lost so much – her work, her confidence, her hope in the future – yet she had survived, at least. But this could kill them all. She went to find her staff. Brynan was sitting at the kitchen table, looking morose. Markave was cleaning dishes; hardly steward's work, but without Nerilyn… *should I fetch her back?* No: there was enough to worry about already.

Brynan jumped up, and Markave turned and put down the bowl he'd been washing.

"We are in trouble." They knew that. She tried again. "The duke has a plan. He wants to… go somewhere, and he wants me to go with him. I'm not sure where but we need to trust him. Now, he didn't say as much but I am sure you can come with me. He has asked me to pack a bag so I suggest you both do the same."

"What about his lordship?" asked Markave.

She'd been too stunned to give any thought to Etyan! "He won't be harmed by the Sun but… I need to get a message to him."

"Brynan or I could go to the villa, tonight," said Markave. "With a carriage we could reach it before dawn."

"No, we're leaving tonight. I… Etyan has survived worse than this. I'll leave a note here for him." Not ideal, but what other choice was there? "Be ready to leave at dusk." She turned without waiting for an answer. Her own packing conundrums were already consuming her.

She fetched her satchel and travelling bag and took them up to the study. For a while she stared at its denuded state: half the books and papers either gone or stacked in random piles; nothing left of the celestial model save a sad pile of hoops, rods and cogs in one corner.

Thankfully, the most valuable writings were untouched. The churchmen had noticed her locked ironwood chest, and asked what was in it. She said, truthfully enough, that it contained more papers, which she was sure they would deal with in due course but which they could kindly let be for the moment. So, she still had the enquirers' papers. The question was, how many could she carry?

She unlocked the chest and lifted the papers out in careful bundles. She must take all of Father's writings: no one else had some of his more unformed musings, and his work was all she had left of him.

While the storm rattled the shutters she sorted her papers, trying to whittle them down to a selection that would fit into her pack. Brynan brought some food around noon; he said Markave had gone to visit his sister and other son, so he would watch Kerne now.

Kerne! She'd forgotten all about him. But she had no room for that concern now. "Did Markave cover his bare skin?"

"He took a cloak."

Cloak. Clothes. She should probably take clothes. What about food? No, clothes and food could be replaced, or found. These papers could not. She went down to her room to put on her oldest mask, and men's clothes; they'd be best for travelling. Wherever they were going. As a concession she balled up her somewhat grubby kirtle and rammed it into the bottom of the pack. Yithi came into her room as she finished dressing. *The cats!* Was there any way of taking them? Of course not. But perhaps they'd be all right, somehow. She decided to believe that. Today was all about deciding to believe, and the truth be damned. The truth was unbearable. Thinking about anything beyond immediate choices would paralyse her. She stroked the cat's head for a while, then murmured *sorry* to the poor beast and fled back to her study.

The rain outside turned to hail, barrages of ice drumming on the tiles and pummelling the shutters. Thunder rolled around overhead. And the light, the terrible light, still shone bright, waiting to kill them.

The storm began to abate as the day began to fade. She looked at her efforts. So much would have to be left behind.

Someone called her from below. She hoisted the bulging pack onto her back and cast a last look around her sanctum, then made herself walk out and close the door. Looking over the banister she saw three figures below, lit by soft lamplight. She hurried downstairs as fast as her burden would allow.

"This gentleman has come from the palace," said Markave, indicating their visitor, who wore militia uniform.

The militiaman bowed. He looked rather young. "I'm Captain Deviock. The duke has charged me with your safety, m'lady."

"Has he now?" She looked to her servants. Brynan had a bag at his feet. Markave did not.

Captain Deviock said, "With apologies, it is only your ladyship who I am to accompany."

"What? No, you must take my people as well."

"My orders are to bring your ladyship and one bag. That is all."

"Your orders! Well you can take your orders and—"

"Rhia."

She looked over at her steward; her husband. His gentle eyes were sad. "It's all right."

"Markave, he has to let you come at least!" She turned back to the militiaman. "Markave is not merely my servant. I have married him."

Captain Deviock's brows went up at that, but he said nothing, save to shake his head slowly.

"Rhia, I have to stay."

"What?" She looked back at Markave.

"I can't leave Kerne."

"But he's going to die anyway!"

Markave recoiled as though struck.

"God, I'm so sorry, I shouldn't have said that. But… if you stay you'll both die."

"Then I'll die with my family." He turned away.

"Wait!"

He paused but did not turn. His tone was soft. "Is that an order, m'lady?"

"I don't, *can't* order you any more. Please!" But she was not sure what she was asking.

"I'm afraid my mind is made up. I'm staying." He looked over his shoulder. "I will pray for you, Rhia." Then he walked away.

The captain's voice was quiet but firm. "M'lady, we have to go now."

"What? Yes. Go now." She wanted to say something, to find some comfort for these two loyal men she had relied on so much. But Brynan was sagging where he stood, defeated but obedient to his superiors' wishes to the last, and the kitchen door was already closing behind Markave.

She let the militiaman take her bag and lead her out into the storm-lashed twilight.

CHAPTER 48

The streets were crazy. Groups of young men ran past shuttered houses, shouting incoherently. A priest was leading a procession of loudly praying nobles up the duke's parade; some of the small children being dragged along were crying, not praying. Rhia smelled smoke, and looked up between the houses to see a bonfire of expensive furniture stacked up against a house wall; a shrill female voice was ordering the servants to burn it all until a man started shouting at her, telling her she had gone mad.

Captain Deviock shepherded her through the growing mayhem in silence.

The storm was easing off, reduced to odd spatters of tepid rain and squalls of half-spent wind.

They entered the palace through a gateway near the militia barracks, coming out into a large, crowded courtyard. Rhia started at finding herself in a controlled bustle of men and horses, and turned to the militiaman. "What is this?"

"This is our departure from Shen."

A militiaman came up to them, looking uncertain. Rhia thought how she must look, dressed in man's clothing. "Is this the countess, sir?" asked the man.

"Yes," said Deviock. "Please fetch our horses."

"You're staying with me?"

"To keep you safe, yes."

"But where are we going? What's happening?"

For the first time Deviock's impassive expression cracked, his lips twitching into a smile that made him look nervous rather than happy. "The duke said you'd be full of questions."

"Which I expect answered."

"He said to tell you that all will become clear, but that you have to trust him."

"Right." She wasn't going to get more out of this young man right now. Instead she looked around, a task made easier when a sturdy bay horse was brought for her. She mounted and, after watching her bag get safely lashed to a pack-horse, sat up tall on her mount's back to survey the sea of heads. This was a huge, regimented endeavour, militia everywhere; checking loads, mounting up, waiting for orders. On the far side she thought she saw Francin's chestnut curls, and near him, two cloaked figures with their backs to her. Other than them, she appeared to be the only person here who wasn't a soldier.

"We need to move."

"What?" She looked at Captain Deviock, sitting on his grey horse beside her.

"We have to wait off to one side. We'll be near the back of the column."

"What column?"

But the captain had manoeuvred his horse close enough to hers that the bay twitched and sidled. Rhia took control; she was a competent rider, but out of practice, and it took concentration to stay alongside Deviock without getting in anyone's way. He led her along the edge of the courtyard. It was pitch black overhead, though torches had been lit all around. The main bulk of the militiamen were facing forward now, out of the gate. About a quarter were mounted, with more horses, and some donkeys, laden down with supplies. The militia stables must be empty. Francin, on horseback, was a little way back. Just behind him she saw three small figures riding two-up with militiamen. Francin was taking

306

his children. Somehow the thought was simultaneously reassuring – if he was risking the young prince and two princesses he must be sure they were heading to safety – and disconcerting, because it implied this was a one-way journey. Most of the faces around her looked determined, in control, though sometimes a flash of panic showed, the same panic that she, that everyone, must be feeling deep down inside.

As the mass of men and horses began to advance, Deviock gestured at her to stay back. She obeyed, and contented herself with watching. Amongst the packs strapped to horses she saw the glint of metal: bundles of long staves with metal tips. Now she knew where all that iron from the red valley had gone! She also spotted more unusual items strapped across some officers' backs. When she realised what they were her mood darkened further. Amongst her papers were a few writings from Tinkerer of Yost; the last but one holder of that post had had a fascination with devices that bordered on the heretical. He had an interest in weapons, and one in particular, a variation on the bow, had intrigued Father, though less as a weapon than because of the ingenious winding action used to fire the ironwood bolt, which employed controlled storage and release of energy. It required metal to construct, and Tinkerer of Yost called it a handbow, though the larger versions the soldiers carried looked like they took two hands to operate. But Francin had never asked for the papers describing the handbow, so despite his protestations to the contrary he must have copied the weapon design while she was in Zekt. Which meant that whatever he had been planning probably went back that far, had in fact been in train for at least two years. But how could he have known the shade would fail? And what was his plan?

"M'lady." Deviock was indicating the approaching end of the column. They slotted into a gap, with the captain riding on her outside. When they rode out under the gateway the clatter of hooves on stone was deafening.

Full darkness had not improved conditions in the city. Shouts, chants and the odd scream echoed through the streets. The column of militia, travelling six abreast, would have to take the widest roads that wound round the hill. As they left the duke's parade, a mass of people, perhaps the group of worshippers she had seen before, intercepted the hundreds-strong column. From her position near the back Rhia heard only faint shouts, and saw distant, shadowy movements ahead, but she found herself remembering the riot last rain-year, so brutally repulsed by the militia. From the glimpse of rising batons and swinging swords, Francin was not treating these people with any more consideration. That day she had been an unwilling witness to the duke's "necessary" cruelty. Now she was standing by again, but this time she was part of what was happening – was letting herself be drawn along by it. Saved by it. She must remember that: this was the only way. Even if she was not sure what way this was.

The column started moving again. Passing the point where the disturbance had been Rhia saw a dark splash on the cobbles, and a fallen figure being tended by others off to one side.

In the middle city they passed an old man in torn and stained guild robes sitting in the gutter, sobbing inconsolably. He did not look up as they passed.

The sounds became wilder the lower they went, but the streets to the side of the main thoroughfare closed in as they became poorer, so there was little to see.

Suddenly a woman hurtled out of a side-alley, throwing herself against a foot-soldier three ranks in front of them. From her bright but minimal clothes, Rhia suspected she was a prostitute.

"Take me with you! Wherever you're going I... oof!"

Her hysterical demand was cut short when the soldier she had flung herself at shook her off. "Back with you! We can't take anyone!"

"I'll earn me keep!" She straightened, standing out of baton range, and exposed a painted breast to the passing militia.

Rhia winced, half expecting the men to mock the whore, or worse. But the column barely faltered, and the man who'd pushed her away shouted back, not unkindly, "First have mercy on your fallen soul!"

They came out onto the north road shortly afterwards, and crossed the stone bridge across the rain-swollen river. The road would eventually fork, becoming the two routes to Marn and Zekt, but to get to either shadowland they had to cross the skyland, several days impossible journey. Except everything was skyland now.

They had been walking the horses through the city but once on the road the column kicked into a trot, the motion passing down it from front to back. The unmounted men in front of her upped their pace to a loping jog. The road was well-surfaced, though mud still kicked up to spatter her legs.

The increase in speed wouldn't have allowed for much conversation even if Captain Deviock had been willing to talk. Rhia concentrated on her riding. Unused to it as she was, her thighs soon began to twinge.

After a while they slowed their pace to a walk again, much to Rhia's relief. They were onto rougher road now, though the ground was relatively firm underfoot.

They slowed further, then stopped. Rhia dismounted stiffly and accepted a drink from Deviock. The horses were led away to drink at a roadside ditch. She tried to work out where she was but beyond the ditch the land was an identical mass of dark fields. At least the rain had stopped. Looking up, faint moonlight showed through the clouds.

The stop was brief. All too soon Deviock was holding her horse for her to mount up again.

The pattern was repeated; this time when they stopped, Rhia almost fell from the saddle, her legs weak and shaking, her body heavy. She was exhausted. This stop was longer, with the horses eating from nose-bags and having saddles adjusted. Her bay hung its head, looking as tired as she felt.

Shortly after they started up again she saw lights ahead. Her addled mind took a while to identify the inn she'd stopped at on the way to Zekt to fetch her brother. It had been a lively place then. Tonight it was wild. Every window was lit and shouts and

309

shrieks drifted out on the night breeze. Someone had lit a bonfire in the courtyard.

Closer, and some of the inn's customers became visible, standing, swaying and even dancing outside. Many had drinks in their hands, and some shouted incoherently, or even jeered, though none dared approach the column of armed men. As they passed, Rhia saw, to her horror, that something was moving in the bonfire. A body, twitching in the flames. She smelt a whiff of burnt meat and her gorge rose. She looked away. Beside her Captain Deviock spoke for the first time in hours, his voice muted. "Frightened people do terrible things."

She nodded, gaze still averted, and concentrated on staying on her horse and not being sick.

The column sped up again once they were past the inn, but not for long. When they dropped back down to a walk, Rhia found herself swaying in the saddle. When she got off at the next rest-stop she locked her legs, resisting the urge to sink to the ground. If she sat down now, she'd never get up.

Staying here wasn't an option: overhead the sky had cleared enough that stars showed. When the Sun rose, there would be nowhere to hide. She made herself accept a meal of leather-tasting water and hard bread, to chew and swallow, to not fall over.

She had only been in the saddle a while when, despite the constant pain of legs and buttocks and back, she began to doze. She caught herself the first time, a moment of vertigo as she pitched forward towards the horse's neck. The second time sleep crept up on her she flinched awake at the touch of Captain Deviock's hand on her arm. The third time she nearly fell when her horse stumbled, and she was jerked from fitful half-sleep into full wakefulness, grabbing for support that wasn't there. Instantly awake but confused, it took a moment to realise the horse had stopped. She felt it shudder under her.

"She's gone lame."

Rhia focused on Deviock's voice, then worked out what he meant. "I suppose I'd better dismount." Her voice sounded creaky and cranky in her ears.

The column flowed past them. Deviock had also dismounted, and now indicated his own horse. "Please mount up quickly, Countess."

"But I…" He was right. If riding was almost beyond her, walking certainly was. She realised she was still holding onto her horse's saddle for support. She made herself let go and stagger free.

As she pulled herself onto the grey's back she saw the militia captain undo the saddle on her old horse, which stood with its head bowed, one front leg lifted. "What are…?" She didn't have the energy to finish the query.

"So she stands some chance."

Rhia just nodded. From the captain's voice he was at least as upset as she was at leaving the poor animal to die.

They carried on. Deviock walked alongside her, shoulder not quite touching her leg. Whether from the shock of losing her mount or the closeness of a strange man, Rhia found herself wide awake. Craning her aching neck she saw a sky full of stars. But in the east, the velvet darkness was tinged with grey. Dawn was coming.

She looked ahead, and in the distance saw a solid line of darkness: the umbral forest. But which part? She must have been dozing when they took the fork in the road. "Are we…" She tried again; even speaking took too much effort. "Are we going to Marn or Zekt?"

"Zekt."

Captain Deviock spoke without turning his head. He hadn't dissembled, so perhaps she should try asking more questions. Except, she didn't have the energy.

Shortly afterwards the column slowed and stopped. Rhia tensed, ready to dismount, but they weren't taking a rest; the front of the column was moving off the road, striking out across muddy fields. The exhausted men and horses slowed to a crawl to pick their way over the uneven ground in the dark. *We can't afford to slow down!* The sky to the left was silver now, the stars washed out.

A curse to one side: someone else's horse had gone lame. Rhia's kept plodding along, its hooves dragging in the cloying earth. It stank of sweat, and her trousers, against its lathered flanks, were damp. The combined lethargy and urgency turned their flight into an endless nightmare of fear and frustration.

But, slowly, the umbral forest became clearer. Rhia could see individual trees now, and for a moment that lifted her heart: they were close. But it was almost light.

The front of the column reached the trees as the first rays of the Sun raced across the land. Rhia felt it strike her cheek, and screwed up her eyes. Why hadn't she thought to bring her cloak?

But it didn't burn her in the saddle, even though she could feel the heat build by the moment. Just a few more steps... They entered the shade of the trees. They didn't stop at once, but carried on deeper. *Please just let me stop, let me rest!*

She got her wish shortly afterwards. The horses and men fanned out, and stumbled to a halt. She let Captain Deviock help her from the saddle, but her knees gave way when she touched the ground. He half caught, half supported her, then lowered her down. She stretched out gratefully. All that mattered was that she could finally, finally rest.

CHAPTER 49

The journey south was very different. Fleeing north, Dej had been empty inside, shedding her love for Etyan step by painful step. Now she was doubly full: her body of the life he had sparked in her; her head of Jat's many lives.

Damn him.

Many of the memories she had inherited gave her joy – echoes of Jat's past moments of love and wonder still warmed her, and she was delighted at the confirmation that skykin *did* have music, drums and flutes, which they danced to unselfconsciously, extravagantly – but the knowledge of what the skykin really were and what was happening to them now weighed her down.

The low hills continued inland. On the first night, she lit a fire with wood-stuff taken from the ruined city. As the sparks rose, a cloud of floating, translucent creatures drifted towards her out of the night, converging from several directions. She tensed, in case they meant her harm, but both her animus's response and her newly acquired seer's knowledge said they were no threat. There were about a dozen, each a cluster of bubbles, each bubble with a single dark, thick spot shifting across its surface; currently all the spots were directed towards her.

Dej smiled, pointed back at the creatures and said, "What do we think those are then?" Speaking to her unborn child was a habit that came easily now. At the sound of her voice the eyes, or whatever they were, slid back inside the mass of bubbles. Dej opened her arms to show she meant no harm, and stood still. The bubble-creatures came closer and began circling the fire, a slow bob and drift. After a while two approached each other and the bubble masses merged for a moment. Then they whirled apart, a motion accompanied by a sigh like distant wind. A few minutes later another pair did the same and, Dej saw as they glistened in the moonlight, one of the bubbles had transferred itself from one cluster to another. She grinned; she was pretty sure this was the skyland equivalent of wild sex.

Dej watched the float-bubbles at play until they finally drifted away again. She hoped they might return the next night, but they didn't.

After a few days the hills flattened out, with more bare earth and boulders between patches of vegetation. Soon she saw a new type of landscape ahead, massive rock formations, red and imposing. She doubted there would be any water there, and probably not much to eat either.

"Let's see what we can find here first." Her girl kicked in response. She moved a lot now, getting ready to meet the world.

She stood stock-still on the barren plain and let her awareness roam over it, drawing extra strength from the life inside her. She picked up the presence of a few interesting creatures, but they were for later.

Aha. A little way southwest, the scent of water under rock. She opened her eyes, gave her perpetually sore back a rub, and set off.

Her instinct was true: a spring in a boulder-filled dip in the land. She filled both waterskins; she'd taken Jat's too, given he had no further use for it.

Now: food. She picked her way over to the area of jumbled rocks she'd sensed earlier, careful of her footing. She couldn't afford a fall. As expected, the rockslithers heard her coming and burst from their nest, darting off in every direction. Which was fine. Dej tasted the wind, and found a place to wait where they wouldn't catch her scent. She sat back on her haunches and let thought drain away, aware only of her immediate surroundings and her gravid body. It was a battle to keep her over-full head empty, to still her thoughts, but she managed it.

Slowly, cautiously, the rockslithers ventured back. The first few didn't come near her. She shifted to relieve a cramped shin. This would be easier without the extra weight she carried. Finally a fair-sized 'slither passed within reach. She jumped up, one foot pinning it down at the same time as she drew her knife and plunged it in between the creature's first and second segments, killing it at once. She felt its life flee, and offered up something between a prayer and an apology for having taken it.

It was a big beastie – a full five segments – and once she'd got back onto even ground she prised off the fore-segment, cracked it open, and scraped it clean of meat. A full segment on a 'slither this size was a hearty meal. When she'd eaten, she curled the remaining four segments up in the bottom of her pack.

The next day she reached the maze of wind-sculpted rock. Her choice was to go round or through, and round was a long detour. At first the rock walls loomed overhead and she doubted her decision. But the gulleys soon widened out, and her unerring sense of direction allowed her to pick the best path.

No chance of firewood here, which was less of a concern given the lack of predators – this land was as empty as any she'd passed through – but she'd have liked a cooking fire. As well as tasting better cooked, the rockslither meat would keep longer that way. After eating another segment that night while camped under a rocky overhang, she considered discarding the final segments but decided they might keep for one more day.

She came out of the rocky maze the next afternoon. The land was less arid here, similar to the scrublands around Shen, but still with no standing water and nothing to eat or burn. In the evening when she opened her pack she could smell that the rockslither meat was spoiling. She tipped the pack out; hopefully any staining would just be at the bottom.

That was odd: one segment had indeed discoloured, turning from mauve to brown, and going soft in places. The other two looked fine. She examined them more closely. There was something stuck to the un-rotted segments: the cleansing-moss. She'd forgotten about her stolen tech but it looked like, as well as removing dirt, it could preserve meat. Useful stuff indeed.

That night she extended her senses as far as she could while on the verge of sleep and utterly relaxed. She estimated she was about a week away from the band of shadowlands around the world's equator – another term she'd got from Jat's knowledge – but given the large gap between each shadowland she could pass between any two, most likely Marn and Zekt, without realising it. If the terrain was favourable a shadowland might be visible from several days walk away, but if she approached in a valley, or if the clouds remained as low as they had been today, she could easily overshoot. Her child was only a couple of weeks away. She might only get one chance.

CHAPTER 50

Broiling heat dragged her into wakefulness. Rhia gasped, coughed and rolled over. Next to her a strange man in militia uniform lay stretched out on the ground, asleep. He had his hands curled loosely on his breast, and looked as unselfconscious as a sleeping child.

Captain Deviock. That was Captain Deviock. And she was in the umbral, on the way to Zekt. But how could that be? How could any of this be?

She levered herself up onto all fours, feeling sweat break out across her body at even this minimal effort, then stood. Her throat burned, and she reached for the waterskin next to the sleeping militiaman. Someone had filled it, thank the First. Her head as clear as it would get in this heat, she looked around. Men sat or lay in the close, hot shadow of the ironwood trees. There were no horses in sight.

Her papers! They'd left several horses behind on the road: what if one of those poor beasts had been carrying her possessions? Spotting a pile of baggage next to a pair of sleeping soldiers she staggered over. Yes, she recognised that backpack. She clung to this small, momentary reassurance in an impossible new world of danger and uncertainty.

At the edge of the forest the light burned bright but she recognised that worn quality from her days in the cave at the red valley: a skyland evening. She'd slept all day. It didn't feel like it.

Though heat and exhaustion made lying down again tempting, she needed answers. She walked through the dim, hot forest, past resting soldiers. Those few who were awake gave her uncertain but respectful nods. She asked one of them where the duke was. The man pointed through the trees.

She found Francin sitting on a camp stool. Asleep on his side on the ground nearby lay Lord Crethen; seeing him here, now, Rhia suspected he had known full well why the duke was absent when she had asked him what seemed like a lifetime ago. Beyond him, sitting on the ground and chewing on some rations was General Prendor, head of the militia. On his other side, by contrast, was Francin's close family – all of them. Princess Yorisa, his oldest child, sat on the ground, looking sullenly solemn as only a girl being thrust towards adulthood can; her younger sister and brother slept next to her. Beyond them lay Alharet, curled in a loose crescent, one hand half flung towards her children. Seeing the duchess free, out of doors and oblivious added yet another layer to Rhia's sense that the world had been turned upside down; then she saw the militia captain who sat beyond the family tableau, just behind Alharet, keeping watch over her.

"Cousin." Francin's voice was quiet and tired.

When Rhia turned to look at the duke she saw the dog at his feet, flopped onto its side and panting hard.

"You brought your *pet*?" Though she didn't raise her voice – it was too much effort in this heat – an odd, detached rage bubbled up in her. Francin had his whole family, even his dog. She had left everyone she cared for behind, and though no doubt Etyan would make his way somehow, her family servants, her new husband and her poor cats had all been condemned to a slow and awful end.

"I did, yes." At his bleak tone her anger abated a little. "I need to know there is one living creature who loves me unconditionally. Can you understand that, my genius confidante?"

"Perhaps." She gestured around them. "But what is all this? I thought you were up to something but this is… staggering. I had

JAINE FENN

no idea. So I'm hardly your confidante, am I?"

Francin smiled and cocked his head at her. "Cousin, even if the affairs of state were of interest to you, they are not your business."

"I know, but... this is something else. Did you plan it?"

"Not exactly."

"But you had a plan, you were already making preparations when it all went wrong. Where are we going, Francin? Zekt?"

"That's right."

"How? We can just about wait out the day here in cover, but we can hardly travel to Zekt in a single night! It took a week by caravan."

"Our route is quicker, though whether it is quick enough..." He shook his head.

"What route? How are we getting there?" Perhaps he planned to camp during the day, hiding from the Sun in wagons and under canvas as his expeditions to the red valley had. But there were no wagons, and only minimal luggage.

"Remember that glass book from a few years back?"

"What? What has that to do with this?"

"Well, it didn't come from one of those isolated treasure-rooms the Church get so worked up about."

"I'm not following you."

"Some tree-cutters in the umbral saw something odd out in the skyland a while back, a shadow in the evening light. They came back in the dark to investigate. It was a sinkhole, a pit that had opened up just beyond the umbral. It gave access to a great underground room. And, leading out of that, a tunnel."

"A *tunnel*? To Zekt?"

"That's right. Pre-Separation work. Full of incomprehensible and miraculous stuff."

She found her imagination filling with possibilities, thinking on what wonders he might have found... but she needed to stay focused. "You're sure this tunnel goes to Zekt?"

"Oh yes. I did my research. I've even travelled part way along it myself."

Which explained his odd absences. "But how can you be sure where it comes out?"

"I found a very old map, then had a trusted agent look for the far end. It took a while, as that was outside Zekt's umbral too–"

"Sorne! That was why Captain Sorne stayed in Zekt!"

"One reason, yes."

"You've been planning this for years!"

"For a couple of years, yes."

"But you had no idea about the shade failing?"

"The shade... ah, you mean waking up to find my shadowland had ceased to exist overnight." His tone showed a dark humour. "No. I had no idea that was going to happen. But I did know Shen was in trouble. Every rain-year we endured droughts while Zekt prospered. Yet it did so without stable leadership, under a dynasty of madmen. I could see a better way."

"Wait, you were planning to *invade* Zekt?"

"Not invade as such. But the eunuchs are all about stability. If they invited me, or rather my children by a Zekti royal, to take an active role in Zekt's future, then I would be happy to accept their overtures, backed up by a degree of military force of course–"

"Alharet!" Rhia looked over to the sleeping duchess. "That's why you never tried her for treason, why you kept her confined to her rooms. You wanted to use her to get access to the Zekti throne!"

"My children are half Zekti, but yes, the presence of their mother would make the proceedings smoother, when it came to it."

"And she agreed to this?"

"Discussions had been initiated."

"How close were you to carrying out this plan?"

"A matter of weeks."

"So you brought it forward when the shade fell?"

"As best I could, yes." A childish voice said something about being too hot. Francin looked over at his youngest girl, just awakening. "I know, sweet. But it'll be night soon, and you'll be cooler then." Beyond her, perhaps in response to her child's voice, Alharet was stirring. The duchess looked pale and woozy. Rhia half made to call out to her, but what would she say?

The duke murmured, "Rhia, go get some more sleep. You'll need it. We leave before dawn."

Rhia nodded, and left. She considered going to the skyland side of the umbral, to see if this tunnel entrance was visible, but lacked the energy. She'd see it soon enough.

Captain Deviock was awake when she got back, and volunteered to fetch some food. For the first time she looked directly at him. Her inital impression was correct: he was young; probably had minor noble or high guild blood to be a captain barely into his twenties. The upright way he carried himself implied good breeding, although that might have just been stress. Discipline and willpower kept the men around her functioning, but they too must have left people behind.

The ration of bread and jerky Deviock brought back was small and far from tasty, but Rhia did not complain. After they had eaten she asked her escort where the horses had gone.

"They are being rested. The strongest will be our pack animals; the others will remain here with some of the men until they recover fully from the hard ride." He grimaced. "I am afraid you will have to walk from now on, m'lady."

"Into the tunnel, you mean?"

"Ah. You know about that?"

"I spoke to the duke."

He looked relieved, perhaps at no longer having to field her questions. As though she did not have more, starting with, "Have you been into the tunnel, Captain?"

"A little way. I was mainly working with the night-crews, clearing the vents."

"The what?"

His expression closed again. "You'll see."

He obviously took his duty to give her only the information she needed. seriously Which just meant she would have to pick her questions with more care.

The darkness under the trees was deepening. As the last beams of silver light fingered their way through the forest she lay down. Despite her exhaustion, heat and worry kept sleep at bay. Now the immediate panic was over her mind kept going off into wild fancies, considering options and possibilities, none of them good. The overall picture was too terrifying so she concentrated on the next part of this bizarre not-invasion. Had the tunnel always started outside the shadowland? It had to date from before the Separation, as it was definitely "tech" – a term she had come across in her recent reading on prohibited devices and practices.

What would the priests make of all this? She hadn't seen any clerical robes amongst the duke's expedition. Back in the city, they must be praying hard. Everyone must be, for all the good it would do. At times like this she almost wished she had faith, for the comfort it brought.

No: don't think of what this disaster is doing to people. Think of the cold theory, of the mechanics of what is going on.

If the tunnel between shadowlands started outside them then, logically, the shadowlands had been larger once. Given how slowly the ironwoods grew, that must have been millennia ago. Perhaps they had been shrinking steadily, imperceptibly, ever since the Separation. It was an unpleasant thought, that her people had trapped themselves in pools of shade that would, slowly but inexorably, diminish and reduce. And it had tricky implications for her fledgling model of how the shade-swarm worked.

But her last thought, before sleep finally came, was that all this was academic. What had just happened was not part of a natural process: it was a catastrophic failure.

CHAPTER 51

"Thank you Shenvet."

"You are welcome, Holiness." Shenvet smiled and picked up her robe.

For a few short hours she had helped Sadakh escape his troubles. Shenvet was one of his occasional lovers, the handful of initiates who understood that sex with the eparch was not about power or lasting emotional attachment, but a brief, mutual solace. He had found himself resorting to such comforts more often as the coronation approached, even as he knew they were just a temporary respite.

He dressed alone, only summoning a servant to see to his hair. Last night had brought more bad news: one of the First Light initiates on the Eternal Isle, a junior mistress of the royal wardrobe, had been dismissed from her post. For stealing, apparently. It would not be hard for Mekteph to identify the initiated lay members of the Order in the palace. That he had chosen to expel only one was a warning, a subtle reminder of his power.

Poliarch Hekmat had no more than a week to live. And in three days, young Prince Shirakeph would be crowned caliarch. How quickly his father took the reins of power remained to be seen.

If you are still here then...

His ghost wanted him to leave Mirror, though she had no

suggestions as to where he should go. Perhaps he could idle
out the last of his days in some distant rural village, such as the
prince believed he hailed from, paying his way with his medical
knowledge, preaching to peasants. *Like a sulky martyr,* his ghost
offered unhelpfully.

Or perhaps he could go to Shen. Rhia Harlyn was a Shenese
noble; she might provide lodgings for him, even facilities. And if
that brought him into contact with her young kinsman, perhaps
he could find out where he had gone wrong with the serum. But
that assumed she had survived her trial unscathed, and would be
willing to take in an outcast from another shadowland and allow
him access to the boy.

Or you could go back to your real home.

It was the first time his ghost had said it, though he had
previously sensed, or thought he sensed, that this was what she
wanted. The skyland was her home too, after all. Or had been,
when she was a living seer. Maybe the Sun was the key for him;
maybe it would trigger a change that would allow him to survive
in the skyland, even if it did not grant him a longer life. Unless it
just granted him a lingering and miserable death, like Ereket's.

But no skykin clan would take him in. The clanless would,
perhaps. Then again, how welcome would he be when he had
fallen to their level? At least his skyland business was beyond the
prince's reach now, the compromised umbral camp abandoned
permanently.

How fortunate, given how little he had to look forward to, and
how much he had to worry about, that he was being kept so busy
with preparations for the coronation.

That evening brought more bad news.

His secretary interrupted a round of tedious but suitably
distracting paperwork to tell him that one of "his people" was in the
infirmary. Viteph knew his master had interests outside the priory
and the way he said "your people" implied his secretary meant one
of his bodyguards. He put down the pen and went at once.

It was Klimen. He had been badly beaten, face bruised and

bloody, but what drew Sadakh's attention was his eyes. They were gone, the empty sockets weeping blood and clear fluid down his face. He lay flat, although from the way his hands clenched and unclenched he was fully conscious. The hospitaller tending him looked up as Sadakh approached, his face pale.

Sadakh gestured at his wounded bodyguard, "What happened?"

"Something sharp, driven into the sockets—" said the hospitaller.

"No, I mean how did he get here?" Klimen had, he now recalled, been watching over the launderers' house.

"I... I believe a hired punt dropped him off. I do not know more than that."

"Do everything you can." He wanted to help, but would only be a hindrance. His medics knew their business. "Send someone for me when you have tended to him."

This is the prince's doing!

Yes, it had to be.

He went to find Naldak, and told him to get Penek to take him to the launderers' house. "Do not approach unless it is safe, and you are sure no one save Taklew is there. Remove everything you can carry from the workroom at the back." He had already brought most of his notes and the magnifying frame to the priory, but his more perishable materials were still at the house.

He returned to his office, and stared at the pile of paperwork until summoned back to the infirmary.

Klimen's head had been cleaned and bandaged. The hospitaller said he'd given him poppy-milk, but he was awake and relatively alert.

Sadakh took the stool next to the bed and called his name softly.

The bandaged head turned on the pillow. "Holiness?" Klimen's normally firm and confident voice was faint and rasping. "I am sorry, I failed you."

"You did not! Never think that. But I need to know what happened."

"I was on watch. They jumped me."

"Did you..." He paused; he'd been about to ask if he'd seen anything. He settled on, "Tell me exactly what happened."

"There were three of them. Low-lifes, locals I think. Came at me from behind. I headbutted one, managed to punch another, but they caught me unawares. Before I could draw my stave they'd battered me down. They just kept hitting me. Then I felt something in my eye..." He shuddered.

"Yes," said Sadakh gently. "I'm so sorry."

"I shouldn't have let them take me like that!" Klimen's voice broke. "Sloppy. So sloppy."

"It's not your fault. You were outnumbered and ambushed. And someone will pay for this. I promise."

"Thank you Holiness." Klimen sounded like he might cry, had that still been possible for him.

Sadakh laid a brief hand over his, then left.

Mekteph had gone too far. *But what can you do?* Very little. He knew that, despite his promise.

Naldak found him in his office shortly afterwards. "The house looked quiet, Holiness, so I went in."

"And?"

"Someone'd trashed it."

"And Taklew? Was he all right?"

"Been knocked out. He was just coming round. Sent him to the infirmary when I got back."

"And the house itself..."

"They'd ripped off the doors, broken the furniture, smashed everything breakable and smeared... muck over the walls. Reckon they'd've set fire to the place if they hadn't been worried the whole neighbourhood'd go up."

"The room at the back I told you about, was anything salvageable in there?"

"Don't think so. The table was just splinters, and all the jars were smashed. Guess they took anything small that might've been valuable."

"Did you go into every room?"

"Yes, Holiness. Same everywhere."

"And in the washroom, where they used to do the laundry."

Naldak's heavy brow furrowed. "That was odd. The place was wet, smashed containers and soap and that, but also smears of blood. Dunno where that came from."

You do. The serum, the fruits of his labour, destroyed in passing by vengeful thugs. The anger was a constant now, spinning inside him, building and flaring. He made himself take a deep breath, then exhale. He must not take out his feelings on those around him. "So just to confirm: there was nothing to bring back, is that right?"

"Nothing. I'm sorry, Holiness."

"No, you did all you could. Make sure the others don't leave the isle." By which he meant the other bodyguards. Other potential targets.

Naldak nodded and left.

Sadakh sat on the floor and made himself go through an advanced meditation exercise, closing down senses and emotions, drawing on the well of peace deep within. It was hard, but he must not let the anger take over.

Finally he managed to regain some perspective. But the outlook was grim. His contacts and schemes beyond the priory isle had been cut off, his options pared down to the choice to obey the prince, or suffer.

Now do we run?

Tempting. Don a disguise, sneak out the city. Just disappear. But he would have nothing, have achieved nothing. And he'd be dead soon enough whatever happened.

No, he would stay, and crown Shirakeph, because it took an eparch to crown a caliarch, and Zekt needed a caliarch, even one who was only the puppet for a monster. It would take all his willpower to get through the coronation with that monster looking on, gloating, but he would do it. It was his duty.

The next day was restday. Sadakh tried his best to deliver a sermon that would make the world a better place but in his head his ghost kept saying *What is the point?*

Afterwards, he was tempted to avoid the post-service

encounters, until he saw Philekh, one of the initiates who worked at the palace. The young man's expression was strained, and Sadakh invited him to his study.

Once they were alone Philekh handed over a sealed note without a word, then found his voice. "I was just leaving the Isle when a courtier came up and gave this to me. He said, 'Give this to your master'."

Sadakh took the note. As he was breaking the seal the young man blurted, "Should I be worried. I mean, I heard about Emshet losing her job, and everyone is so tense at the palace…"

"I pray that matters will soon resolve themselves favourably." Prayer was about all he had left now. "But if you choose to worship alone rather than attend the service here until they do, I will understand." He hated cutting off any sources of information, but it was unfair to draw his initiates into this deadly game.

"Thank you, Holiness. I think I may do that."

When Philekh left Sadakh unfolded the note. It was unsigned, but written in the prince's extravagant hand:

Take your guard's fate as a reminder that not all eyes belong to you.

Know as well that your woman in the kitchens is dead – how typical to use the weaker sex for your most dangerous agent!

The longer you hold out against my will, the more counters will be taken.

Sadakh crumpled the paper, and stared at his clenched fist.

Mekteph had won.

When Hekmat died he would tell the prince that Sholrew was replacing him, because all that further opposition would achieve would be more vengeance on undeserving people who had been loyal to him.

Perhaps, when he bowed down to formalise his capitulation, he should ask about the reference to "your woman in the kitchens". He hadn't the faintest idea who that had been.

CHAPTER 52

"M'lady, wake up."

"What?" Rhia twitched and stirred. Her back twinged, the movement setting off other aches and pains. She was lying in hot, heavy darkness.

"We're leaving soon."

"Right." She got up on the third attempt. Her legs and backside felt like tenderised meat. Good job she wouldn't be riding. After hurried preparations – a mouthful of tepid water and an undignified squat behind a tree – they set off. Captain Deviock led her through the dark forest to join the slowly reforming column. Against the lighter patch marking the end of the trees she made out only a few dozen figures; they were nearer the front now.

When the column broke free of the forest Rhia strained to spot their destination. She saw only the heads of marching men and the odd packhorse in the pre-dawn gloom, but they slowed almost at once, so abruptly that she nearly tripped. The soldiers stood, facing forward in silence, waiting. Disconcerting as it was to be surrounded by military types, Rhia could not imagine a group of nobles, or even guildsmen, taking this absurd and awful situation so completely in their stride.

They started up again and Rhia glimpsed a faint, white light ahead. A little later the ground began to slope downwards. They were walking on recently dug but well-trodden earth; on either side banks of soil rose up. A ramp, dug into the ground – and ahead, darkness. No, another glint of white light.

Then they were underground, in an echoey space. The column slowed and stopped again. Another light appeared, nearer, and she had a sudden sense of dizzying perspective. This room was bigger than the Council hall, but perfectly square and lacking any visible supports. There were massive doors on the side walls, larger than the palace gates. The walls looked smooth and plain and dark; not brick or wood or plaster.

"M'lady, did you want to carry this?"

"Carry what?" Sudden light flared.

Captain Deviock was holding a loose net containing a glass globe the size of a grapefruit. It glowed with the same white light touching off all around the great underground room. He gave it a shake: the light brightened.

"What is *that*?" Rhia breathed, reaching for the globe.

Captain Deviock handed it over. "We call them glow-globes. I am not sure what they actually are."

The globe was heavier than she expected. It was like a tiny, captive moon. Holding the net in one hand she reached through to poke it. Just glass, cool and smooth. She looked across at Deviock. "Are these pre-Separation artefacts?" No wonder Francin had left the clergy behind; any priest would be apoplectic at such forbidden miracles.

"Actually, no. His Grace had them made. I think the glow comes from some sort of creature, in water."

"Made? Oh." She vaguely remembered how a treatise on bad air from Seeker of Thir – which Francin had borrowed, now she thought of it – spoke of underground spaces becoming more dangerous when naked flames burned, and how other sources of light might be employed. She sniffed, in case "bad air" had a smell, but smelt only unwashed bodies.

They started to shuffle forward. Rhia held the globe high. With only a few globes dotted about, most of the room remained in shadow. The column closed up; she held the globe to her chest. It did not emit any warmth. The far end of the great room was visible now. Ahead she saw a wide semi-circle of darkness; some sort of exit. It lightened briefly, as someone carrying a glow-globe went through. After a pause, they followed on. Before they went in, Rhia turned for a moment to look back. The rear wall, above the gap where they had entered, was decorated with an intricate pattern of interlocking hexagons that reminded her of the cross-section of a beehive, with side columns of what looked like writing.

Then she was swept forward with the others, into the tunnel. It was a perfect tube, as wide as a house. However, due to its curve, they could only walk four abreast. She had let Deviock march on the outside so far but now insisted on changing places, the better to see this marvellous place. The tunnel was made of the same smooth and featureless material as the room. Closer, and with light, she could see the substance was mid-grey and mildly reflective; less so than metal – this much metal would be a dizzying impossibility – but enough to amplify the glow-globes and fill the tunnel with a cold twilight.

The men upped the pace. Rhia made sure she stayed with them.

After a while they passed another, smaller, door, set flush with the tunnel wall, with markings on it, a short string of not-quite-familiar symbols. The writings of the ancients.

A little after that she looked up at a sudden breeze. She was passing under a circular hole in the roof; this must be one of the vents Deviock had mentioned, presumably going up to the surface, allowing fresh air into the tunnel while blocking the skyland's killing light. How ingenious!

By the time they stopped, some time later, she was more concerned at how tired she was than with exploring the tunnel. The soldiers had set a fierce pace and her arms ached from carrying the globe, though she had not wanted to relinquish it.

Men sat or crouched against the tunnel's slope and passed round waterskins and rations. Rhia examined the glow-globe more closely, turning it over in her hands. It was indeed a featureless globe of thick-blown glass. The glow was even throughout, although agitating the globe made it shine brighter.

"Best not do that too much, m'lady."

"Why not?" Were the creatures within dangerous, liable to some explosive action if shaken?

"The glow is not permanent; after a while it fades. Making it brighter by shaking the globe means this happens sooner."

"Ah. And we will need this for a few days yet, I imagine."

"We will."

"How many days, Captain?"

He hesitated, then said, "Three or four."

"You cannot be sure?"

"I can only tell you what I have been told." Slight irritation showed in his tone, but his next words were polite. "Shall I carry the glow-globe for a while, m'lady?"

"Yes, please do." She had examined it as thoroughly as she could under the circumstances.

By the time they reached the next stop Rhia's feet were dragging. She hoped they might be stopping to sleep – ideas of day and night mattered little down here, but she was ready to rest – but they carried on for one more stint before the final stop, men bedding down at all angles along the tunnel floor and sides. Rhia wanted to speak to Francin, but more than that, she needed rest.

When she woke, stiff and still tired, the day's routine was repeated.

Rhia let Deviock carry the globe, but offered to take a turn holding it in the middle of the "day" to show she was not just a burden. Some time during the long dark trudge a lifetime of assuming others were there to serve her had come into question. He thanked her but said he was fine. She felt oddly offended, then chided herself.

To take her mind off the pain from her aching feet, and thoughts of what might await them and what was going on back in Shen, Rhia counted the tunnel's features, such as they were. The vents and closed doors with their odd markings appeared regular, and she had an idea the doors' markings were counting up, or possibly down. As the journey wore on she began to feel light-headed, as though mildly intoxicated.

When they finally stopped to sleep, she ignored the urge to lie down, and picked her way through the soldiers towards Francin. She needed to know more of the duke's plans.

Francin was easily identifiable amongst the shadowy figures up ahead because he was sitting on a camp stool. The privileges of rank had been reduced to this: the man in charge was the only one not sitting on the floor. His dog was curled up under the stool; beyond him Alharet was sitting with her children, not obviously guarded. Then again, there was nowhere to run to. She caught Rhia's eye for a moment, her expression dull and cowed. Rhia tensed but the duchess showed no recognition, and looked away.

Francin smiled up at Rhia. She wanted to sit, even if it was on the floor, but if she did she would end up sleeping here and she wasn't sure she wanted that; Francin's presence was a comfort, but Alharet's made her skin crawl. She contented herself with turning her back on the duchess, then crouching down with a half hiss, half groan at the pain of making her abused legs bend.

"You know, I expected more stars."

She turned her attention from her bodily discomforts to her cousin. "Not down here, I assume."

"No. But before we reached the umbral the clouds cleared and the stars came out. I thought that with the, ah, daytime shade gone, the night sky would also be brighter."

"That's not how it works."

"So it's not a single shade hovering above each shadowland, then?"

"I believe the shade-swarm is a great mass of structures, placed between our world and the Sun. They interact in complex ways, so the patches of shade they create remain constant even as the world turns. But when part of the world turns to face away from the Sun – when night falls – then it no longer faces the shade-swarm either."

He sat up straighter. "So the loss of one shadowland... you said it was probably just Shen but surely if all the shade comes from the same place, every single shadowland could be affected!" His whisper had an edge of hysterical self-doubt she had never thought to hear from her self-assured cousin. She felt her own fears rise in response.

"I don't know! As I said, this is an old and ingenious mechanism. It must be able to adjust, to compensate." To think otherwise was to despair.

"Well then..." He let one of his dangling hands brush the tiny dog's heaving flanks. "I will assume it could be worse, and be grateful." He did not sound grateful so much as desolate.

"What will happen when we arrive in Zekt, Francin?" Assuming it was still there.

"One step at a time. First we must reach it."

"And that will take, what, two more days?" Given the pace they were setting they must be under the mountains already.

"Aha, you've been pumping our militia captain for information." He gave a wan smile. Behind her, Alharet was gently chiding her children, telling them to lie down and get some sleep; she sounded oddly unconcerned, as though this were some pleasure trip. "Two days if we're lucky," the duke continued. "But they will not be pleasant days."

Rhia nodded. She had expected as much. None of the vents they passed in the second half of this day had emitted any breeze, which might explain the light-headedness. This sparked a new thought. "What is wrong with Alharet?" Though she faced away she kept her voice low; sound carried in odd ways in the tunnel.

"What do you mean?"

"She's acting strangely. Even more strangely. Are you drugging her food, Francin?"

The duke grimaced and spread his hands. "Desperate times, Rhia."

She hated him for this imposition. But she also saw his logic. And while they were talking about the duchess... "This plan of yours... does it relate to her brother?"

"That's an uncharacteristically vague question for you, Rhia."

"Don't mess me about, Francin. Not here, not now."

"All right: yes. The prince is a factor I have had to take into consideration."

"Then you should probably know that she retains feelings for him." Rhia shifted at a cramp in her shin.

"Feelings?"

"Francin, I think she's still in love with her brother."

"Ah yes, those feelings."

"You know she feels that way?"

"Cousin, I don't just know. I am relying on it."

Rhia straightened, in part because her legs were about to give out but also because, yet again, the duke's machinations had shocked her. "She's your wife, Francin."

"Technically, yes."

Rhia's taste for her cousin's company fled. "I think I will leave you to your brooding."

The next day she found herself getting breathless, though thinking this made the sensation worse so she wondered if she was imagining it. She thought she was getting hot too, which was odd as so far it had been pleasantly cool in the tunnel. Then one of blisters on her heel burst, and that took her mind off everything else for a while.

She kept counting the now-useless vents, and the doors, if only to distract herself from the pain and exhaustion. When she passed an open door she stopped mid-stride. Ignoring a mutter from Captain Deviock she hobbled up to the opening. Beyond, all was dark. She turned back to the militiaman and gestured for the light. He brought it over, looking less than pleased.

When he held it up she saw another great tube beyond the door, at least five times wider than theirs.

She stared at Deviock, who said, "We need to keep moving. You won't find anything of interest in there; we've looked."

She was too tired to argue. "All right, I'll carry on, but only if you tell me what you found."

They rejoined the column a fair way down. She was definitely out of breath now.

"I didn't see it myself," admitted Deviock when he'd caught his own breath, "but I understand there are two larger tunnels on either side of this one."

"Why aren't we using them? Surely we could move faster in a wider tunnel."

"The air is worse in the big tunnels; no vents. Also, there are blockages, at the end and along the way."

"What sort of blockages?"

"I don't know."

She let it lie. They were dealing with things beyond their experience. She could try asking Francin when they rested but she would have to get back past most of the column to reach him, and by the time they finally stopped all she wanted to do was sleep.

She awoke with a pounding headache. Someone was tightening an invisible band around her temples; another one encased her chest. Just breathing took willpower. Moving was a monumental effort. And everything seemed darker, the shadows sharper, though that might just be a trick of her increasingly clouded mind.

The men around her looked rough too, and it took an age to get going. But when they did, they kept up the pace. They had to, if they wanted to get out of here alive.

The march began to assume the quality of some relentless dark dream.

At the first stop she stood, swaying, because if she sat down she might never get up.

By the second rest stop she didn't care. Her legs just folded. Someone caught her arm. She looked up into the face of a solider whose name she had once known. "M'lady, this is the final stretch.

You must stay strong."

It took her some time to work out what he meant, but when she did she locked her knees and hugged herself. She would stay upright, because if she fell over she would shatter into a thousand pieces.

During the third stint, reality kept tilting. More than once she stumbled into her companion. Sometimes he stumbled into her, and murmured an apology.

The column slowed. It must be time to rest. She indulged in a daydream of not having to move any more, of taking the weight off her raw feet. But they didn't stop. She felt annoyed, cheated. Then her foot slipped. Her companion grabbed her, saving her from a fall. What had she stepped in? She bent over to look, holding his arm for support. The globe in the militiaman's other hand barely glowed now. Even so she could see a thin runnel of something sticky, viscous and dark running along the bottom of the tunnel. Her breath caught.

"Countess!"

She waved a vague hand. "That's blood." Her voice barely broke a whisper.

"Please m'lady, if we stop now we'll never make it. We're nearly there."

She let him haul her upright.

A little later they passed the source of the blood. A horse, lying on its side, its throat cut. Its eyes were open, staring up in exhausted desperation. Blood still trickled from the wound on its neck.

Nothing made sense any more. She'd known, once, why she was doing this. Now all she knew was that she had to keep walking, or she'd end up like that poor horse.

At first she thought she was hallucinating the faint breeze. Then she looked up and saw light ahead; very faint, grey on black. No wait: a sliver of silver, brighter by far than the near-spent glow-globe. Closer still and she knew that shape. Whitemoon. If she'd had the breath she would have laughed aloud.

CHAPTER 53

"I wish I could give you a parting-gift."

The polished stones skykin pathfinders left with their offspring were meant to be special; iron stuck to them. Not that Dej had ever seen one. "But then, you're at least as clanless as me, aren't you?"

She'd made good time. Yesterday she'd spotted the characteristic dark patch of a shadowland off to the west – it had to be Zekt – and adjusted her course. Now, as evening approached, the towering clouds of its umbral filled her vision. She would need to circle it until she found a road. Crèches were built near roads, a short walk in from the umbral, to make them easy for pregnant skykin to find.

She was hungry all the time now. The two preserved rockslither segments had lasted a couple of days but since then she'd just grazed. Before, the odd stem or fruit was enough to keep her going; now her girl demanded more. But her girl was also coming soon, so she couldn't afford the time for serious foraging.

Although the road would be farther south, she'd reach the shadowland's umbral tonight. Maybe she'd go all the way in, see if she could get hold of some shadowkin food. That was odd: the thought of committing theft no longer gave her the guilty flush of pleasure it once had. Must be Jat's influence.

What if she just stayed in the umbral? People didn't live there, and her daughter would be safe from the killing Sun under the trees. But that assumed she could birth her unaided, and then she'd need feeding with shadowkin milk; Dej could hardly steal from the very breast of a nursing mother, even if she could find one.

"I'll have to give you up to save you, won't I?" The thought hurt, but this must be how it felt to all skykin mothers, clanless or not: the drive to keep their child safe overcame the pain at losing the baby. It had to be that way. She knew that now.

Still, she'd camp in the umbral tonight, for the safety and shelter it offered. Assuming she reached it today. Used to the wide vistas of the open skyland she'd misjudged the distance. It was dusk already and she was still some way off.

She stopped between one step and the next, as her mind registered something unexpected.

The land was lush here, with moss-grass covered ground and bush things in abundance. But that bush looked wrong. It was… square. All shapes, sizes and colours were possible in the skyland, but like the ancient house on the plateau this was a manmade thing.

She changed course and walked up to the object. A square wooden box, high as her waist. Not ironwood, but sturdy enough to keep most skyland creatures out. As she got nearer she caught a familiar scent. She walked round it once; fine detail was lost in the growing darkness, but it reminded her of the storage bins back at the crèche. And like them, it contained food. She could smell it. She lifted the lid. Dark shapes inside resolved in the twilight. A large canvas bundle – a tent – a pair of empty backpacks, a coil of rope, some staves and a half full sack. The smell came from the sack. This close to this much food she could focus on nothing else. She leaned in to lift the sack out. She even placed the smell now, rice cakes and dried fruit–

"Ahem."

Dej straightened, dropping the sack. Her other hand still held the lid and now she slammed it down, revealing a skykin standing a few paces away on the far side of the box.

She knew him. Even in the dark that presence was familiar.

"Cal?"

"The very same."

Something was wrong with his eye. "I thought you died with the others in the mudslide." She'd hoped so.

"Apparently not. No thanks to you. Or your lover." His damaged gaze travelled down to her swollen belly.

"What are you doing here?"

"I could ask you the same." His glance went up, past her. "Although the answer's obvious really." She had a sensation of another presence, approaching fast from behind.

Even as she began to turn something dropped over her head, and a moment later a hand grabbed her wrist to stop her reaching for her sword.

Cal said, "You're stealing from us. Again."

Someone kicked her legs out from under her.

CHAPTER 54

"Water m'lady?"

"What? Yes please." She didn't remember getting to the umbral, or falling asleep. She had a vague memory of scrambling towards moonlight; the exit from the tunnel was just a hole in the ground. Of course: Captain Sorne would have had to excavate it alone. And now she was lying in the shade of Zekt's umbral, a bright skyland day off to one side. She sat up and drained the near-empty waterskin, then allowed the militiaman to help her stand. "Where's the duke?"

"He headed over to the far side of the umbral."

"Take me to him please."

Deeper in, and the skyland silver faded. They left behind the scatter of men sitting up against trees or lying on the ground, looking as exhausted as she felt. Faint light showed ahead. Golden, shadowland light. Rhia released the breath she'd been holding.

The duke was talking to Lord Prendor and General Crethen, looking out from the edge of Zekt's umbral forest into lush farmland and pointing at something. He turned at her approach and smiled. "Ah, our non-native guide."

"What?"

His companions did not look pleased to see her. Francin continued, "We were discussing how to re-provision the men."

"Re-provision?"

"Cousin, you are clearly still dazed from our recent ordeal."

He was right: some time during the endless march through the tunnel a mental shroud had dropped over her, an invisible barrier shielding body and mind from unbearable reality. But she could not afford to hide, to give up. She shook her head, trying to clear it. "You're planning to stay here then?"

"The bulk of the men will. Also the remaining horses; I fear it will be some days before they are of use again. I was actually wondering what the chances were of purchasing supplies from a local noble."

"I think things are more expensive here."

"Not a problem."

Of course not. *Think past the shroud.* "Obviously you'll have thought of this too, but once you reveal yourself to the locals, someone will send word to Mirror-of-the-Sky."

"Which is one reason we will be leaving for the city this morning."

"When you say 'we'..."

"Just myself, a few guards, the duchess and you. Lord Crethen would have accompanied us, but he fell in the tunnel and injured his ankle." Now she looked, Rhia noticed Francin's advisor leaning on a stick. "We need to move quickly and arrive as negotiators, not invaders. I was about to send someone for you. You have knowledge of Zekt and, unlike my wife, I know you will share all you know."

"Yes, how *does* Alharet feel about this?"

"She accepts the situation." His tone implied that was an end to it. "Rhia, do you have your sightglass?"

"Uh, yes." She had her satchel with her, as usual.

Francin took a closer look at the building he'd been pointing out when she interrupted him. He had thought it might be a manor, but viewed through the sightglass it turned out to be a barn. Prendor assured him they would still find a way to get fresh supplies.

Rhia interrupted. "How near are we to the caravan route?"

"I'm sorry," said Prendor, "but how is that relevant?"

"The caravans have way-stations in the umbral run by traders who, frankly, will sell anything to anyone."

"Good idea," said Francin, then frowned. "Our map obviously didn't show such later additions but I wonder if road parallels the tunnel. Worth sending men out I think."

The general nodded. "I'll organise a couple of small parties, out of uniform."

"Good. I know I can trust you to keep a low profile. Well, I'll leave the camp in your hands. Lord Crethen will assist."

From the look Crethen gave her he was less than delighted at losing his place in the diplomatic party. Francin left the two men making arrangements.

Rhia kept pace with him. "Right. So, we're going to Mirror. What happens then?" Other than considerable surprise and consternation amongst those in charge, she imagined.

"If all goes to plan then the new caliarch will have just had a fatal mishap."

"The new caliarch? What happened to the old one?" She had an idea Numak, or whatever his name was, had been aged and infirm.

"He died, just before Between. I believe the new, rather younger, one is being crowned, well, today. Sadly his reign will be cut short by an unknown assassin."

"Your assassin."

"Not traceably. And the eunuchs will have cause to suspect his father."

"Mekteph, you mean?"

"The very individual."

"Would he really kill his own son?" What she knew of Mekteph made her gladder than ever she had not been forced to marry him, but that did not mean he would murder his kin.

"Some in Zekt say he does not love his children, perhaps even that he wished they had a different mother. More importantly, he wants the throne for himself, not just as regent for his boy. Now as it happens the prince also has a daughter, and she is of age with Temlain."

"You plan to marry your son to Mekteph's daughter?" Once again, Francin had surprised her.

"Betroth, at this stage. They're still children. But yes, that was always the plan, eventually. Unfortunately things had to be brought forward due to... unforeseen circumstances."

"What about Mekteph? Will he agree to this match?"

"The return of his sister will be most persuasive."

Rhia was sure Francin wasn't telling her everything, but decided not to push him. She had enough to process.

"Now," said Francin, "anything you can tell me about Zekt would be of use. Obviously I have my sources, but you've been there in person relatively recently."

"I never got to the palace."

"Which was probably for the best."

"Yes." Mekteph had almost certainly wanted her brother as a political hostage, what seemed an age ago. Thinking of Etyan now, she realised that despite his self-absorption and bruised heart, his current situation was arguably better than hers. Better than anyone else's in Shen, like poor Markave. But remembering events at the priory reminded her of something else. "I, er, do know the eparch. You might even say we've become friends."

"Really?" She had actually managed to surprise her cousin in turn.

"Yes, really."

Francin clapped his hands. "Having the eparch's support would be immensely useful, Rhia. Would you be able to speak to him directly?"

Rhia considered Francin's request. "I see no reason why not. What was the other reason we have to hurry?"

"I'm sorry?"

"You said we need to get to Mirror quickly because of the, ah, tricky political situation there. Was there another reason?"

Francin's face fell. "Yes. What we left behind. My people are alone in the ruins of my shadowland, with no idea what is going on. They are dying. We have to negotiate a way for them to come here, to live here, as fast as possible; it's their only chance of survival."

She nodded again. She couldn't argue with that. But when the discomforts of the tunnel let her she had been thinking more deeply on what had happened – and would happen. "Francin, I think I have some idea of what we're dealing with now."

"And can the effect be reversed?" Brief hope showed in his voice.

Which she must quash. "No. The shade-swarm is way beyond our reach. And I'm afraid I have more bad news…"

After she had explained her new theory, and what it meant for all the shadowlands, Rhia saw surprise on her cousin's face for the second time that morning. But unlike her revelation about the eparch, this was not an expression of pleasant realisation, but of profound shock.

CHAPTER 55

Just the boy.

Sorne stared at the note. He should really have destroyed it, along with the others he'd burnt last night. He'd had this paper, with its three-word instruction, for months now, and he knew what it meant. But he needed the black-and-white reminder of his duty, in the duke's own hand.

He'd practised assembling the weapon a dozen times while Sharrey was out, and no longer needed the duke's diagram and instructions. He'd had to oil the iron components, which had developed a rough red coating, something the duke had warned him might happen in Mirror's damp air. Practising firing it had been trickier, and had involved some clandestine night-time trips ashore, but it turned out to be easier to use than an ordinary bow.

Looking at the handbow now, where it sat on the low table next to the note, he wondered who had come up with this near-heretical, lethal device. It was an object of dark and compelling beauty. It was a shame it would end up in the bottom of the lake when its work was done.

Outside, someone was singing; another voice joined them in the anthem praising the eternal caliarch which he'd heard Sharrey singing under her breath around the house. A quick glance out the window showed that the grand channel itself remained clear.

However, the edges of this isle and the one opposite, and most windows in sight, were full of people. More joined in the song by the moment. Everyone was looking left, towards the Eternal Isle, trying to catch a glimpse of their newly-crowned ruler. If anyone did look his way they would only see a fellow Zekti, sat a little way back from the window.

He'd been worried that the owners of this house would return to Mirror for the coronation, so yesterday evening he'd played the tourist and taken a punt past the house for one last check. The ground floor windows were still shuttered and he'd seen no lights. Later that night, after his last bridges had been burned, he'd put on his new Zekti disguise in an alley two islets down, then returned and levered off a shutter on a side window. Once inside he found evidence of the earlier break-in – fabric strewn over a workroom, drawers pulled open, and a broken pot – but no signs of recent activity. The family dispute really had put everything on hold, thank the First.

He'd still checked out every room before allowing himself a couple of hours' sleep in this upper bedroom.

The song was getting louder, and he could hear distant cheers now. He shook his head, trying to clear the sudden image of Sharrey singing that song, furtively but tunefully.

She'd caught him burning the duke's notes last night, just as he'd expected she would. The smoke had woken her and she'd rushed from the bedroom with a face full of fear. Fear turned to anger when she saw that her house wasn't on fire, just that her apparently-drunk partner was setting fire to random papers. She'd snapped at him, asked what he thought he was doing.

He'd shouted back that it was none of her business. She'd lowered her voice to say it was. He ignored her. She'd raised her voice, asked again what he was doing. And he'd finally let the beast out, become his father's son. He'd straightened, and slapped her.

They'd paused then, the two of them, while the duke's papers crackled and shrivelled on the stone hearth. Then her shoulders had dropped, and she'd turned away.

Even hitting her hadn't been enough to break their bond. So he'd strode over to her dresser, and swept the plates off first one shelf, then the next, then the next. Some broke; some didn't. He stamped on them, kept stamping, and then finally looked up and there, there was the hurt in her face, the sign he'd driven her too far.

His face twisted in disgust – at her, and at himself – he'd walked out without a word.

He hoped and prayed the poor cow would one day find a man who treated her the way she deserved rather than the way she expected. But he doubted it.

The row would have woken Tamak up. He should've gone into the boy's room to say goodbye before he burnt the papers. Tamak was ailing; he'd be dead before the year was out.

And now he had to think about a different boy. Or rather, try not to think.

The cheers were getting closer.

He picked up the short ironwood bolt from the table, careful of its glistening tip. Next to it was his paring-knife, sharp enough that a single slash would open his throat if necessary. Zekti torturers had a reputation for extracting truths from even the most stubborn prisoner.

The water below was rippling; a high bow eased into view. Sorne dropped the bolt into place and picked up the handbow.

The royal barge was decked in flowers and foliage, and an honour guard lined the side railings. They were armed, although dressed in their finest and standing still as statues. At the front, under the gold and black canopy, the newly crowned caliarch sat on his carved throne, there for all his subjects to see and adore.

Sorne raised the handbow to brace it against his shoulder. His fingers found the firing-lever on its underside.

The caliarch's crown was a towering construction of, Sharrey had once informed him, five sacred woods covered in actual gold leaf. The boy looked tiny beneath the absurd mass of carved and shining filigree.

Tiny, but an easy target. Sorne sighted along the spine of the bow. It only took a small motion, a flick of a fingertip

So tiny, and so terrified.

His finger froze.

I can't do it.

He willed his finger to move. This was why he was here. This was why he'd given up two years of his life, deserted his friends, hurt an innocent woman; lied and stolen and killed. So many shameful deeds, because the end would justify the means. He had to follow through.

But he couldn't. He hadn't saved his two sons. He couldn't save Tamak. But this boy, stranger though he was, didn't have to die at his hand.

The barge was passing.

He jerked his gaze up.

The young caliarch wasn't alone at the prow of the royal barge. His massive throne had half hidden the figure standing on the far side, one hand on his son's shoulder, his expression triumphant. Some of the rumours Sorne had heard about Prince Mekteph…

The duke had entrusted him with this mission. He had to follow orders.

But the duke wasn't here, had no way of knowing how things were now, in this land so distant from his own.

Someone in Ramek's had said that once the prince became regent, he'd have no further use for his son – who, given the way the Zekti royals were, might not be his son anyway. One day soon the boy would suffer an "accident", they said, and Prince Mekteph would finally get what he'd always wanted, and become caliarch.

Sorne raised his aim, and fired.

CHAPTER 56

It was amazing how simple pleasures could lift the spirits. Rhia sighed and lowered herself into the water, running her fingers through her hair to dislodge the muck and dried sweat and massaging her shoulder where her satchel had chafed. The first time she had visited this inn she had not had a bath because its bathhouses were communal. Now, by keeping her shift on and not making eye contact with the other women in here, she'd conquered her embarrassment at public ablutions.

She had asked Alharet if she wanted to join her. The duchess had said nothing on the long, hard walk from the umbral to the inn. None of them had, to any degree. Though Rhia had had her share of unusual experiences, it was especially surreal to be trudging on blistered feet through a foreign land towards an uncertain future with the duke and duchess of Shen.

Alharet's response to the offer had been to blink and shake her head. Rhia had thought that was it until the duchess said, in a small voice, "I doubt it would be permitted." As she spoke she had looked across at the silent guard shadowing her. They had three militiamen with them, including Captain Deviock, all in civilian clothes.

They attracted more attention than on that first visit. They had arrived this afternoon after spending most of the preceding day trying to locate the road, and the preceding night sleeping in a beanfield. They looked awful. And though they were obviously Shenese, the caravan from Shen was not due for several days. Francin muttered vaguely about trading opportunities when anyone showed an interest and didn't demur when they were offered a pair of dormitory rooms rather than private facilities.

Now, as she approached the room she was sharing with the duke and Captain Deviock, Rhia started. A stranger stood outside it, a man in Shenese clothing. Even as she realised it was not a stranger, the door opened and he entered. Rhia rushed in after him. Captain Deviock, who had been about to close the door, jumped back as she ran through.

Inside, Francin was just standing up to greet the new arrival. Before anyone could speak Rhia said, "Captain Sorne? It is you, isn't it?"

The man turned. Paler and with hair both longer and greyer, but still the militia captain she had persuaded to take her to Zekt over two years ago – and who had abandoned her at the umbral. His eyes widened at the sight of her, his surprise possibly compounded at finding her damp, wearing men's clothes and carrying her dripping shift and kirtle like some washerwoman. He regained his composure, inclined his head and said, "It is, Countess."

Francin cleared his throat. "I had wondered if we might encounter you on the road."

Sorne turned his attention from Rhia and bowed. "Yes, Your Grace. I just arrived. I planned to stay here before travelling back to Shen with the caravan, but the commons is full of talk of Shenese visitors…" His voice, if not his words, showed his puzzlement at finding the duke here, now.

"Did you complete your mission?"

"I…" Sorne dropped to one knee. "I am sorry Your Grace, I have failed you."

Francin's voice was soft. "In what way?"

"The boy… I couldn't do it."

"So, let us be clear: the new caliarch still lives?"

Sorne nodded. Then he said, "But his father does not."

Rhia had been half-mesmerised by the conversation. Now everything came together in her head, and she exclaimed, "You've killed Mekteph!"

The duke winced at her raised voice. She bit her lip.

Sorne murmured, "I did. Your Grace, I will accept whatever punishment you deem fit."

The duke's face clouded, then cleared. Finally he spoke, "Well, this certainly complicates matters."

"What would you have me do now, Your Grace?" Sorne sounded miserable.

"Go back to the commons. Do not admit to knowing who we are, obviously. Then be my eyes and ears for the rest of the evening. I need to think."

After the captain had gone, Rhia stayed where she was. The insulating shroud was back, keeping the full impact of their awful situation at bay like some mental version of the shades that had once protected her home.

Francin sighed and said, "Cousin, please find somewhere to hang those wet clothes. I believe you brought some of your papers?"

Rhia nodded; each had brought only what they could carry on a long walk – Francin had left his dog in the umbral – so she had only a small subset of the writings she had brought from Shen, chosen in haste and crammed into her satchel with her spare clothes.

"I am sure you are quite capable of losing yourself in them for a while. I recommend you stay here and do just that."

She did not disagree.

"Your Grace!"

Rhia started awake. Morning light streamed in through the window. She was lying in a bed. An actual bed. It felt wonderful.

She focused on Captain Deviock, standing at the foot of Francin's bed. The duke cleared his throat and levered himself onto his elbows. "What is it?"

"Your Grace, I'm sorry, but the duchess is gone!"

The duke pushed himself upright, half falling out of bed before staggering to his feet, his expression dark. "What? How?"

"She must have climbed out the window." Francin had instructed one of the two guards in Alharet's room to sleep across the doorway.

"And no one stopped her?" The other guard was meant to stay awake and keep watch.

"Captain Grithim was hit over the head; he is dazed but recovering."

"And Hislain?"

"Captain Hislain is dead."

"Dead? How?"

"The duchess got hold of an ironwood handbow bolt from somewhere. She must have taken him unawares. She stabbed him in the eye."

"Let me get dressed then show me." He looked over to Rhia. "Stay here!"

Rhia nodded woozily. She was happy to, though less to avoid the horror of her former best friend having committed murder – very little horrified her now – than because of the immediate physical pleasure of lying in bed. It occurred to her that Francin might have put her in this room, rather than with Alharet, in case something like this happened. Clever Francin.

The duke was not gone long. When he returned he was shaking his head as though to clear it. "Captain Deviock, kindly fetch Captain Sorne." He focused on her. "Cousin, I assume you have paper and pen. I need to write a note."

"Of course." Though she was not sure what, in this case, writing notes might achieve.

"And you need to get up."

She obeyed reluctantly while Francin scribbled a short note. He left it on his bed with some coins then said, "We have to leave. Now."

The duke's tone did not brook any argument. She rolled up her still-wet clothes and shoved them into her satchel. The third militiaman, Captain Grithim, returned with Sorne. He had a bruise blossoming on his temple. Everyone left the room in silence. It was still early, with few guests about. Those they met appeared puzzled but not inclined to get in their way. Rhia did whisper, as they came out into the courtyard, "There was talk of horses…"

"The inn only had two to spare," muttered Francin. "And now, I suspect, it only has one."

They strode out onto the road with as much confidence as their situation allowed. When the inn had receded behind them, Rhia turned to Francin. "What did your note say?"

He gave a bitter laugh. "Something like the truth. That our companion had gone mad and killed one of our number, then fled. That we were going after her. The authorities will want to talk to us, but it isn't as though we gave our real names, and leaving even a token explanation may make immediate pursuit less likely."

"So now we walk to Mirror?"

"Yes, cousin. Now we walk to Mirror."

They continued in silence for some time, Sorne going ahead and Grithim and Deviock acting as a nominal rear-guard to their depleted party. At one point Sorne said he heard horses, and they got off the road and hid in a ditch. So much for staying clean. It was just a couple of noble types, out for a ride. They got up and carried on, still without a word.

Finally Rhia's curiosity overcame the miseries of the road and she asked, "Francin, did you really believe Alharet would cooperate?"

"To an extent yes, because she had no choice. And because she was looking for a way to use me in return. Unfortunately there were a couple of factors I had failed to consider."

"Such as?"

"Firstly, I do not think she was as sedated as she appeared to be. She always was a good actor. Her food had been seasoned with a little poppy milk ever since her confinement and I increased the dose when we left Shen, but it appears the drug's effects lessen with protracted use. You probably have a treatise on that somewhere."

"Had."

"Um, yes. I'm afraid the other factor was probably down to those thin walls back at the inn. Just straw and mud, they looked like."

"I... oh." She got his meaning. "You mean she overheard me when I mentioned Mekteph."

"Loudly and by name, yes."

"So this was my fault?"

"Perhaps, in part. But we are beyond blame. Now, we are just salvaging what we can."

CHAPTER 57

Sadakh handed over the bowl of chocatl. "And just what is the mood at the palace right now?"

His visitor took the drink, acknowledging with a nod how Sadakh honoured him by preparing it himself. Rather than answer at once, Fidekh took a sip, beaming to discover the chocatl had been sweetened perfectly to his taste.

Sadakh made himself wait. For the keeper of the lamps to visit him at the priory showed how much the eunuchs needed his support. Still, direct questioning while they were observing the formalities verged on impoliteness, however desperate he was for reliable information. Sadakh picked up his own drink and took a sip. *Small pleasures*, his ghost commented, *can keep us sane when the world goes mad.*

Something had to. It had been a full day since Prince Mekteph's death and Sadakh had heard nothing from the palace.

Fidekh lowered his drinking-bowl. "The mood is... strained." The eunuch smiled to indicate what an understatement this was. "To be honest I was glad to get away." They were in Sadakh's private reception room; he found its sumptuous furnishings ostentatious but this visitor merited such hospitality.

"And I am honoured to provide you with some respite."

"I hope you will forgive me, but while I'm here I do have to ask some delicate questions."

Of course he does. His ghost sounded at once amused and disdainful. Sadakh put his drink down on the low table and spread his hands. "Ask away."

"You were on the barge directly behind the caliarch's. What precisely did you see?"

"Very little." Which was true enough. Mekteph, paranoid in a way Numak never was, had stationed guards on the ceremonial barges. "As soon as the prince fell, the militia closed ranks." The procession had taken the fastest route back to the Eternal Isle, but the barges were cumbersome and slow. By the time Sadakh had disembarked from the Order's barge and gone to tend the royal party the prince had died from a surprisingly small chest wound – something vital must have been hit, or poison involved – and the boy caliarch had been removed to safety by the eunuchs.

"And before the prince fell. Did you witness anything odd?"

Sadakh had asked himself that question too. "I did not. There were crowds everywhere, but nothing to arouse suspicions. May I ask what exactly killed the prince?"

"You may." Fidekh's voice was even but his eyes had narrowed. "A short, pointed-ended cylinder of ironwood. Presumably some sort of projectile, given the only people near enough to stab him were his son and the militia."

"Who are all above suspicion." Sadakh kept his voice equally even.

"No one is above suspicion, but unless everyone on the barge was a traitor, they could hardly expect to get away with it."

"Quite so. A projectile, you say?"

"So we surmise. I do not suppose you have ever come across a weapon capable of firing such a, hmm, bolt?"

He has no idea what you've come across. "I have not, no."

"I hope this next question does not cause offence but… did you have ill-intent towards Mekteph? I believe relations remained… imperfect."

Sadakh composed his answer with care. "I made overtures to

the prince, as advisor Eneph suggested, but found his demands unreasonable, not least his desire that I appoint one of his own people as my successor. Had I complied I would become of no further use to him and would presumably have suffered a fate not unlike his own."

"Yet you did not bring about his fate."

Sadakh made sure he met the eunuch's gaze when he spoke. "If you're asking whether I am behind the prince's death then I can assure you, on my post as eparch and with the First as my witness, that I am not."

Fidekh nodded, once. "I believe you." His expression darkened. "However, not everyone is willing to give you the benefit of the doubt, not least because you are right; the prince had plans in place to have you killed once you were no longer of use to him."

"I wish I could say I was surprised. Are you able to share details of these plans?"

"Not really. I can say that whilst one plot was thwarted, others may lie undiscovered. You may wish to remain in the priory for the foreseeable future."

Sadakh considered, briefly, whether he was being frightened into staying away from the palace; kept deliberately ignorant, powerless and distant. But the keeper of the lamps was a reformist by nature, and as close to a friend as Sadakh had amongst the immortal advisors. This was a friendly warning, not a devious ploy. "Thank you. I don't suppose you have any theories you can share regarding who might have killed the prince?"

"Theories, rumours and accusations are flying round the Eternal Isle like leaves in a gale."

"I imagine they are." *You didn't really expect a straight answer.* No, he had not. "Is there anything I can do, to diffuse tensions or help in some other way?"

"Spread calm and show strength; in short, continue your good work here. When and if there is something more we will let you know."

Which was all he could hope for. The prince's death was the answer to some of his prayers, but brought plenty of problems in itself.

As though there had not been enough death, Hekmat passed away that afternoon. Sadakh initiated the process to replace him at once, summoning the other poliarchs and making it clear that the final choice was down to them. And he needed to think which one of them might be his own replacement when the time came. He had increased their responsibilities but not their powers, arrogantly assuming that, as an eternal leader, he would need only minions, not successors. But if his quest for the serum had failed then in order for his spiritual work to survive him he needed to trust others to continue it.

One person not under consideration as a new poliarch was Sholrew. The prince's man had gone to ground, with not even a rumour to place him. If he had any sense, he would have left Mirror.

"Holiness?"

"What is it?" Sadakh sat up in the dark, grim possibilities crowding in.

"Someone's here to see you." Dalent's voice; Sadakh had posted an overnight guard on his chambers after the attack at the launderer's house. Such precautions spread apprehension amongst his flock, but even the most spiritually-minded acolyte knew these were troubled times. Light flared as Dalent lit a lamp. "I've put him in your study."

"Who is it?"

"That skykin seer with the missing eye." Dalent did not sound any happier than Sadakh was at the unexpected arrival.

Sadakh pulled on yesterday's tunic and went to find his visitor.

The clanless seer wore a voluminous cloak, though he had thrown back the hood. He held out a hand before Sadakh could speak. "I know you said not to come here but the house isn't secure."

"I know that." He had been a little busy to worry about the launderer's house. "But even so, you had better have a damn good reason for coming to my priory."

"Oh," said the broken seer, "I think I do."

CHAPTER 58

When the clanless had finally taken the sack off her head to feed her – with nothing like enough food – Dej made the mistake of saying that Cal's missing eye improved his looks. A petty insult, just the fear talking. He'd raised his hand to hit her and muttered about putting the sack back on as soon as she'd eaten.

He didn't hit her. Or touch her. Which was good. If he ever touched her again he'd be losing the other eye.

The other clanless was stolid, stupid Ryt, Mar's surviving boy. He'd treated her like some disobedient pet, dragging her along on a rope through the night and finally chivvying her, still blindfolded by the sack, into a cart. She had no idea what they'd been doing at the stash-site near the umbral, though presumably it was theirs. She tried not to get angry at herself for letting hunger overcome caution, for getting caught so easily.

When they put her on the cart Ryt mentioned "getting her to him as fast as possible" but Cal shushed him. She looked for chances for escape, but she was permanently hooded, her bonds checked regularly.

She was in a shadowland; she could tell that from the weakness of the Sun on her skin where she lay trussed up in the bottom of the cart, and the glimpse of green fields at the brief rest-stops. Two days lying in a cart, with nothing to see – or smell – but the sack, which'd had recently contained rotten apples. Then her limited worldview darkened with another night, and they stopped again.

This time they manhandled her onto a wooden surface somewhere chilly and dark. There was an odd noise in the background; it almost sounded like the sea. She reached out her senses and, sure enough, they were taking her out over water. She tensed, but they lowered her into some kind of floating cart – *boat*, her seer-given knowledge supplied.

This water felt different to the sea. And there were people nearby. Lots of people.

Out of the boat and onto ground that gave oddly underfoot. Then to a house. She knew it was a house because Cal and Ryt discussed how the "safe house" wasn't so safe any more, so one of them would have to keep watch. Though she was already bound hand and foot they lashed her, sitting up, to something wooden and solid.

Then left her, for what seemed like half the night.

She spoke to her girl to keep their spirits up, telling her everything would be all right, although she couldn't see how this could end well. She was being taken – sold – to someone the clanless worked for. And any day now, her daughter would be coming into the world.

Finally Cal and Ryt returned and got her to climb into a wooden crate; she had to lie on her side, back pressed against the wood, to fit her belly in. The crate had a lid. She tried not to whimper when they shut her in, because that wouldn't help. They put the crate, with her in it, onto a boat.

When the boat bumped land Cal spoke directly to her for the first time in two days. "If you know what's good for you, you'll stay completely still and silent in there."

She had an idiotic urge to agree then apologise for not staying silent but her tongue had stuck to the roof of her mouth. She really needed a drink.

The crate was lifted out of the boat; Cal and Ryt were carrying it, Ryt whining about how heavy she was.

They went indoors again; she sensed enclosure, though no people. The clanless carried her up a flight of stairs; she had to brace against the crate's walls to stop herself sliding around.

They carried her a bit further and then a gruff woman's voice said, "In here." The crate was set down. A pause, then someone pulled the lid off. She tensed, though she wasn't sure what she'd be able to do.

Bright lamplight, even brighter as the sack was removed. She saw a wooden ceiling overhead.

A man said, "First's sake! Let's get those ropes off!" He had an odd accent and sounded like he was used to being obeyed.

Hands reached in and a face blocked out the light. Someone cut the ropes off her legs then said, "Should we leave her hands tied?" This was another man, more rough-sounding. She was definitely outnumbered.

"No. I doubt she's a threat but maybe you had best stay for now." The man who'd untied her lifted her to sit up.

The crate was on the floor of a small room with shelf-lined walls; the shelves were crammed with boxes and bundles. There were two shadowkin men here, and no sign of either clanless. Then she smelled food, and suddenly nothing else mattered. A low table, just out of reach, was laden with bowls and plates. She half clambered, half fell out of the crate and crawled over to the table. She should be paying attention to her captors, but she didn't care.

No one stopped her so she picked up a cup of water and drained it in one. Then she dug her hands into a bowl of warm white stuff – rice – and shovelled it into her mouth. The initial frenzy abated when enough food had hit her stomach. She looked around.

One of the men stood by the door. He wore a leather jerkin but nothing on his legs and the way he looked at her – attentive and unsmiling – reminded her of the militia. Ah yes, he had a short-stave at his belt. The other man was kneeling on the floor off to one side, watching her. He was older, also bare-legged, and he wore a long white linen shirt cut in an odd, fancy-looking style. He had a short beard but long hair, black, curled and smelling like rosemary and honeysuckle. Seeing he had her attention he said, "I am sorry for the way you've been treated, Dej."

He knew who she was. Of course: Cal would've told him. She rubbed her raw wrists. "Really? Who are you anyway? And what do you want with me?"

"My name is Sadakh and I am eparch, that is head, of the Church in Zekt."

Which was what she'd suspected. Etyan had said this Sadakh was a great man. But Etyan also said he'd probably caused the change in him. And her suspicions that he'd originally hired the clanless to get Etyan back were already confirmed by what'd just happened to her. "And I'm here because…?"

"I think you may have some idea about that."

He was a shadowkin: he couldn't sense lies. But something about him said that playing games wouldn't work. "You want to know about Etyan."

"Lord Harlyn, yes."

"And if I tell you what I know, you'll let me go?"

He looked pained. "You're not my prisoner, Dej."

"You could've fooled me." She looked over at the guard by the door. "So I could just walk out and he wouldn't stop me."

"I would really rather you didn't. And in your current state, I'm not sure wandering a strange city would be wise."

He had a point. "So what do you want to know then?" It wasn't like she owed Etyan anything.

"Mainly, where he is."

"I have no idea."

"But you are lovers." Sadakh's gaze travelled to her swollen belly. "You carry his child."

"He fathered her, yes. But we're not together anymore." Which meant, she realised, that she had nothing to trade for her freedom.

The eparch considered for a few moments. "Can you tell me when and where you last saw him?"

Why not? "About four, maybe five, months ago. We were at…"

She was about to give away a Shenese state secret; she settled on "…out in the skyland, a fair way southwest of here."

"At the duke of Shen's camp."

"You know about that?"

Sadakh nodded. "You seem a little vague on when you were there."

"Keeping time is for shadowkin."

His lips kinked. There was something weird about this man. "So you have not seen Lord Harlyn, or had any news of him, since you left the duke's camp."

His accent made it hard to be sure if this was a question. "Nope."

"I would be interested to know what you've been up to, Dej."

"Me? Wandering. Thinking. Avoiding getting eaten."

"And where you've been."

She had no idea why he cared but she may as well tell him. "North mainly." And she pointed, due north.

An odd expression flitted across Sadakh's face. Perhaps she shouldn't be showing off her pathfinder skills. "So you came back to Zekt to give birth."

"I did, yes."

"I am interested in your baby, Dej."

"Interested, how?" She didn't like the sound of that.

"Given Lord Harlyn is out of my reach I would like to, shall we say, study, his offspring."

No: definitely not liking the sound of that. "Why? What's so special about Etyan anyway?"

"He is unique."

"Yes, he is. And you made him that way, didn't you?"

Sadakh spread his hands. "I did. And I need to know how that happened and what it means."

"Which you think you can work out by studying my daughter."

"I don't wish to harm her, Dej."

"So what *will* you do with her?"

"Forgive me for saying this, but until you were waylaid your plan was to leave your child at a crèche."

"Yes. Maybe."

"So you would be no better or worse off if you left her with me instead."

"I need to know she'll be safe."

"I would like to give you my word on that."

But, she noted, he hadn't. He sat back on his heels and said, "I need to rest, and think. I suggest you do the same."

"And you're just leaving me here in this…" she looked around "…storeroom."

"For the moment, yes. I will provide food and what other comforts I can."

"And when the baby comes?"

"By then I hope you and I will have reached some sort of agreement."

"But if not? She's about ready to meet the world."

"Shout if you feel the baby coming and assistance will be provided." He stood up.

Dej had her back to the door, so she didn't see him go out, but the guard followed him.

She ate another handful of rice and a couple of plums, then stood and examined her not-prison. Only one door of course. And one window, high and narrow. She might reach it by standing on something, though the shelves held mainly soft stuff, folded tunics and robes and bed-linen; the un-lidded boxes contained more of the same. And even if she managed to squeeze through the window, this wasn't the ground floor.

She stood still, hand going to her belly without thought, and extended her awareness.

Yes, another room below. Water nearby. All around in fact, though this building was big, bigger than any she'd ever been in. Big building, water all around. Not good. Even if she escaped this room she'd have to avoid being spotted, and then find a boat. As for getting out of here… "Hey!" she called.

The door opened and the guard stuck his head in. Beyond him, she saw another figure, just as she'd suspected; a woman, but she looked like a guard too. Sending one guard for the midwife and then running off wouldn't work. She smiled at the man. "Can I have some more water please? And maybe a bucket to pee in?"

He nodded, and withdrew.

Dej waited meekly on the floor for the guard's return. It was the woman guard this time. She nodded at Dej, but didn't smile.

So: guards on the door, no accessible window. Which left… the walls.

She pressed a hand to the outside wall, the only one without shelves up against it. It gave a little: just plaster over straw. But a two-storey building made of straw didn't sound like it'd stay up long. She extended her senses, getting a feel for the construction materials around her much as she might feel out the land. There was wood here, big beams, closely set.

She moved over to the side wall, pulled out a stack of blankets and put her palm on it. It felt less solid; thin wooden supports, quite far apart, just straw and mud packed between them and a covering of plaster. She smiled.

"I reckon we can work with this."

CHAPTER 59

The next morning there was more traffic on the road. That meant more curious glances at their foreign looks and lack of transport. But no one stopped them. Rhia estimated they should reach Mirror by late afternoon; exhausted, filthy and travel-worn, they made a sorry diplomatic delegation. But they dare not delay.

Francin had gone over the plan, such as it was, the previous night, but the shroud was still upon her, and in order to fully understand what might happen, she needed to know what *should* have happened. As they plodded along between rice-fields she asked how Francin had hoped matters would unfold, had the shade not fallen and Captain Sorne not killed the wrong person.

"You know most of it. After the young caliarch died, I would have waited a respectable time then suggested that my son married Shirakeph's younger sister. After all Temlain is half Zekti by blood."

"And Mekteph would have accepted this?"

"He would already be caliarch, and have what he wanted. He might well have considered such a placatory move, to keep the eunuchs happy and ensure a successor. And to be reunited with his sister."

"But once Alharet she saw her brother again, you'd lose her."

"If I ever had her." Francin sounded wistful. "Her love for Mekteph is beyond rational. She never took other lovers, you know. And it wasn't for fear of hurting me, given my own peccadillos. She always expected to be reunited with her brother one day."

"And now that he's dead?"

"I suspect she has lost what little sanity remained. If she finds succour in Mirror then I can only hope that the, hmm, contingency I had in place for Mekteph will deal with her instead."

"When you say 'contingency', you mean another assassin, don't you?"

"A food taster, actually. Her mother was Shenese, though her looks come from her late Zekti father, whose memory she curses. It took some time to get her into the trusted position she now holds, but happily the poison she has hidden is well preserved; she even has the antidote, to take herself, in advance."

"Right." Once she would have been appalled at such heartless scheming... The shroud had its uses. "Wouldn't it have been better to just kill Mekteph?"

"That would have thrown the Zektis in chaos, and caused widespread panic. Probably has, in fact. And killing Mekteph was the obvious thing a foreign power might do, so when I conveniently made my approaches to marry my son to Princess Desemet, then suspicions would no doubt have been aroused." Francin frowned. "Much better to discredit the prince with the slur about killing his own son. In a court with subtle but deep factions, each side blames the other when such mysterious deaths occur. Obviously at some later point, after the marriage was agreed, he too would die; poison would be suspected but never proved. He might have had thoughts about children with Alharet but neither of them would have lived long enough for that."

"All these deaths, Francin."

"They give me no joy. But this matter is – was, even before the shade fell – *the fate of nations*. Once both twins were dead, the eunuchs' only logical choice would be to call me in as regent; after all, my half-Zekti son would be betrothed to the only surviving royal, who is also my niece by marriage. One day they would produce offspring, and order would be restored. Temlain would remain heir to Shen. When he succeeded me as duke then Shen and Zekt, already brought closer by the regular use of the tunnel, would finally be united."

"You had everything covered."

"Insofar as I could, from Shen, yes I did." Francin gave her a tight, humourless smile. "Unfortunately I failed to allow for the end of the world."

Despite the need for haste, they took a break around noon. The soldiers could have carried on, but she and Francin were worn down. It rained as they sat and recovered on the bare ground, a sudden sharp shower that no one had the energy to care about and which left the air misty and damp. Now she was wet through in addition to being exhausted, hungry, footsore and afraid.

Deviock was just helping her up when she thought she heard someone call her name. The cry came again, "Ree!"

Sorne and Grithim were on their feet, facing the direction the call had come from. A figure emerged from the mist.

"Etyan! What are you doing here?"

The guards relaxed a fraction, though Sorne still covered the duke.

"I followed you, of course." He rushed up, ignoring the others, and gave her a fierce hug which she returned. He felt solid, hale, healthy.

"But why?"

"Because you're my sister. My only family."

The conversation was setting off odd echoes. "How did you know where I was?"

"I went to the townhouse, and Markave told me you'd–"

"How is he? How are they all?"

"Kerne died. Nerilyn wasn't there. Markave and Brynan were making the best of it, staying in with the shutters closed. They had enough food, but water was a problem."

Poor Kerne. And poor Nerilyn. She might have stood a chance, at the townhouse. But it was too late now. "Markave will do the sensible thing."

"Yes, he always does. Except... didn't you *marry* him?"

"Yes. We'll talk about that later. When were you... there?" She wanted to say "at home" but it hurt too much.

"A week or so ago. I came as fast as I could."

"Through the tunnel?"

"What tunnel? I followed the caravan route."

Of course, he didn't need a tunnel. He was fine in the skyland. "Right. How did you know I was in Zekt?"

"When Markave said you'd gone somewhere with the duke, I went to the palace to find out where. Funny story really..." For the first time his gaze went to the duke, "... maybe not that funny. Things are a bit crazy there." He nodded, "Your Grace."

Francin nodded back. "I would appreciate any updates you are able to give once you've caught your breath, Lord Harlyn."

"Of course, Your Grace." He turned back to Rhia. "Anyway, a girl I knew who knew a militiaman told me the duke had gone to Zekt." He gave her his infectious, open smile, then added, "I was sorry to hear about the trial, about losing your work." His grin faded. "Though I guess you've been proved right now."

"Yes," she said grimly, "I have, haven't I?"

Etyan's confidence was a front; she saw how tired he was, tired and scared. Just like them. His gaze flicked between her and the duke. "So what's the plan now?"

"Diplomacy," said the duke. "Backed up by force if necessary." He favoured Etyan with his own distinctive smile. "We did not come alone."

Etyan looked puzzled. "I didn't pass anyone else from Shen."

"We have militia support to call on. Just not immediately."

He nodded. "So for now it's just you. Us." He spread his hands, "What can I do to help?"

Rhia was not sure she had ever heard her brother ask that before.

CHAPTER 60

What a peculiar creature she was.

He had known Dej was clanless because Cal, their excuse for a seer, had told him. Dej and Cal had some history, which Sadakh had not pried into. He had initially viewed her as a route to his missing test subject. But when he met her, he realised there was far more to her than those pathetic creatures who did his will in the skyland. It could be the effect of the child she carried; if so, it was even more vital he got his hands on the baby, in lieu of its missing father. But there was something else, something not unlike the feeling he got from the clanless' seer, although more fascination than revulsion. Yet she was just a pathfinder; Cal had implied as much, and she had pointed unerringly north when asked.

His morning was taken up with necessary duties, mainly related to the appointment of the new poliarch. Still no news from the palace. He would probably have to wait until restday. He excused himself as soon as he plausibly could to visit the strange pregnant clanless.

Dej was sitting next to the table, staring at the half empty bowls. She looked up as he entered. He smiled at her. "The child has not come yet then."

"Well spotted." She sat with one hand on her belly, and waited.

As he lowered himself to sit across from her she frowned and said, "Don't you have chairs here?"

"Actually no. They sink into the soft ground."

"Oh. I see. So, once I've had my girl, do I just get to walk away?"

"Absolutely. But she stays." That was another thing; an ordinary clanless would not be so sure of the gender of her child. "Dej, what happened to you?"

"I fell in love with a pretty fool and now I'm having his baby."

Which wasn't what he meant, but they could come back to that. "So you have no feelings for Lord Harlyn now."

"None I'd share."

"And him for you?"

"If you mean, would he come and rescue me if he knew I was here, then I doubt it." Sadakh wasn't sure how she knew that, given how long it was since she had seen her lover. She continued, "Not that I need rescuing, because I'm not your prisoner, am I?"

"You are not. But I would be interested in hearing more about the father of your child."

"Ask away. I've nothing else to do while I wait to give birth."

"So Lord Harlyn… Etyan, how long were you with him for?"

"Nearly two years."

"And in that time, did you see any changes in him?"

"Changes? Like what?"

"Physical changes. Did he, ah, age?"

"He got a bit taller. And hairier in places, if you must know."

Not good. Indeed: it implied the serum did not arrest the ageing process. Then again, he had been a boy, barely older than a skykin at their bonding; he had not reached full maturity. Perhaps it had still worked. But he did not have the boy here. He did have this peculiar, intriguing skykin, and her unique child. He reached into his robe and produced the object he had found at the bottom of the girl's pack. "Dej, what is this?"

Her expression turned shifty.

She's about to lie to you, warned his ghost.

But then she met his eye and raised her chin. "It's tech." She grinned. "Which means, as the head of your Church, you really shouldn't be playing with it."

He turned the moss over in his hands. "I've decided to be honest with you, and I'd appreciate a little honesty in return. Where did you get cleansing-moss from?"

Her brows went up at hearing him name the heretical stuff. "From some skykin. Real skykin, up north."

"I doubt they gave it to you."

"No. I took it." Her tone was more puzzled than contrite. "How do you know so much about skykin?"

"Because of who I was. I grew up in the skyland." Only one other person knew this; as with Counsellor of Zekt, he offered up the truth as a token of trust. He found he wanted her trust.

Dej thought for a moment, then said, "You're a seer! I knew there was something odd about you. But you never bonded, did you?"

So quick-minded! He decided, on impulse, to give her the full truth, kept hidden for so long. "I was, and I didn't. I... had failings. I developed, ah..." He paused at the sudden pain in his head; someone wasn't happy at being revealed. He carried on in a rush against growing discomfort. "I developed an unsuitable attachment to the seer in charge of my tutoring. The bonding was disrupted by a nightwing and she... ahhh." He ground his palm between his eyes.

"Are you all right?"

"I... yes. *Damn you!*" His loud cry, mental as much as physical, made his ghost back off. "She was putting my animus into me when the nightwing attacked. I should have stayed down but I tried to defend her. I failed. She died. Not just her body." It had been his fault; picking up a rock to defend them, then in his confusion and pain hitting her instead, smashing her skull and accidentally killing her animus. Destroying the only person he'd ever loved.

He heard the door open behind him, then Dalent called, "Holiness, is everything all right?"

He waved a hand without looking. "Yes. Don't be alarmed." The pain was subsiding. He'd said it now. The terrible truth was spoken. When the door closed he continued, "My animus died in me, though I wasn't really aware of that. I was unconscious for some time. Everyone else was dead. But when I awoke some combination of my dead animus and the spirit of the dead seer remained, combined, in me." He managed a twisted grin. "You could say I have been haunted by her ever since."

Dej stared at him, frowned, then said, "Now that is seriously freaky."

"Isn't it just." He felt exhausted, as though he'd fought some great mental battle. His ghost, the dead seer he had loved but killed, was still there, deep inside. Sulking. Let her. He was master of his own mind.

"I was getting a weird feeling off you but I thought it was just... me. Turns out it's both of us."

"Yes. So what happened to you, Dej?"

"Happened?" The evasiveness was back. "What do you mean?"

"You're a clanless pathfinder but you... It's as though you have the echo of a seer in you too."

She looked at the table for a moment, then said, "I can see how you'd think that. I sort of have."

Sadakh said nothing. Let her come to it in her own time. Deep in his head he felt changes happening, his ghost receding now her existence was revealed, the poisonous wound of his old guilt lanced.

Dej raised her head. "I ate a seer's animus."

"Ah. With ze's permission?"

"Oh yes. He was dying in an abandoned city by the sea, and he was eager to tell me things I didn't want to hear that he didn't have time to tell. Some of it he told me, the rest I... well, I know it now."

"And what he knew is... something beyond what a seer is taught?"

"Something you don't know, you mean? I reckon so, yes."

"Something you would share, perhaps."

"I need to know you won't hurt my child."

"Dej, I don't want to hurt your child, but I won't lie to you: my work is more important than any one life."

"And what exactly *are* you working on? What were you trying to do when you did whatever you did to Etyan?"

"Animuses live for a very long time."

"I know."

"Their skykin hosts, however, live shorter lives than shadowkin. Perhaps two-thirds the span. I am not young. As a skykin, I cannot expect to live much longer. I was trying to prolong my life, at the very least to the full span a shadowkin can expect but perhaps, I hoped, for far longer."

Dej laughed.

Initial surprise gave way to irritation. "I'm not sure what is so funny. This genuinely is a matter of life and death!"

"Well I don't know whether you can make people live forever, though it seems unlikely. But I do know that you've got your facts wrong."

"What do you mean?"

"You're not a skykin."

"I assure you I was born to a skykin mother."

"No, sorry, this isn't funny. It's grim, actually. Really grim. But the thing is: there's no such thing as a skykin."

"What do you mean?"

"We're all the same people." She stroked her belly. "I've got a convincing argument for that right here."

"I know skykin and shadowkin can have children; I was taught as much. The offspring become clanless."

"That's just tradition. It doesn't have to be. We're the *same people*, Sadakh! Right up until the animus gets dropped into a hole between our eyes. So, given you didn't get bonded, you can expect to live as long as any shadowkin."

"No. That can't be." How dare this young clanless tell him how the world worked!

"It is. I guess having a bit of animus-juice inside you might make some difference, but it's not like it made any physical changes."

"But the Book of Separation! The First divided the two races."

"You believe in the First?" She grimaced. "Silly question, given your job."

"I do believe, yes, though I also think we should question His nature."

"Maybe we should. I'll leave that to you."

"Dej, this is knowledge you got from the seer."

"Yes, it is."

"But it goes against everything I was taught – you too, in the crèche."

"Yes, because the truth isn't something people could handle."

"And what is the truth?" He wasn't sure he wanted to know. But he was a seeker of truths, however uncomfortable.

"There was a division long ago. That's true enough. The humans – us – had a split, a disagreement. When they first arrived, one group wanted to change the world to suit them, while others wanted to change themselves to suit the world. The first lot – those who call themselves shadowkin now – set up areas of shade where the Sun couldn't kill them. The others looked for ways to adapt themselves to the world. But it was too brutal, too... alien. Then they came across the people who'd always lived here."

"What people?" Life was divided into people and animals; people were divided into skykin and shadowkin. Sadakh had never thought of the world in any other way. But it seemed he might be wrong on both counts.

"They're known as the pale sisters. They're all female, though that's not relevant. And they're... Do you know the word sentient?"

"It means they think. They are rational."

"Yes, they are. But very different. They live in harmony with the world. After all, it's their world."

"So where did humans come from originally?"

Dej pointed straight up.

"Oh. That's quite a thought."

"Tell me about it. And before you ask, no I don't know how that worked. I do know our ancestors were stuck here and had to make the best of it."

"Which they – we – did by disagreeing and dividing."

"Yep. Gets worse. The humans who wanted to adapt to the world – we'll call them the skykin – found the race that already did. Thanks to their animuses the pale sisters were – are – in tune with everything in the skyland in a way we outsiders can't ever be."

"These pale sisters have animuses?"

"More like, they *are* animuses. Proper, remember everything, effectively immortal, animuses. The animus lives in a series of bodies, same as for skykin, except they're bonded from birth."

Sadakh looked for arguments against this incredible proposition. "I can't see how that would work, physically speaking."

"Jat – the seer – thought they had pools that were somehow alive, where the old body breaks down and the new one forms round the animus, though he never saw one. Where do you think new animuses come from, Sadakh?"

"I was taught that they are formed slowly, in pools of the world's blood."

"Pools of the world's blood. That sounds like what the pale sisters have. But we don't. Though we've got something like it, modelled on theirs, where animuses wait between hosts."

"I know this."

"Course you do. But there're these other pools, near the pale sisters' lands in the south. That's where Jat was, with a few other seers, plus healers, hunters and technicians. All on their last life, because once they've done their duty this knowledge is meant to die with them."

"The knowledge of where our animuses truly come from, you mean." Sadakh swallowed. "And when you say their duty…" He couldn't say it, couldn't form the words. Assuming he understood what she was saying.

"They take the animuses out of the heads of pale sisters and use tech to make them work for us."

"Holy First. This kills the pale sister."

"Oh yes. There's a story says the first pale sister gave up her animus willingly and it was grown and changed and divided to create enough animuses for all the original settlers, though I'm not sure that works, given all the different roles in a clan. Even if it's true, they – we – still keep having to kill the pale sisters now, to get more animuses."

Sadakh wished his ghost would comment, would support or observe or be the voice of reason. But she didn't. She was an illusion. A lie. Everything he believed was a lie. "Just to be clear: you're saying that in order for our people to survive, we have, over the last few millennia, been slowly killing off this world's original inhabitants."

"That's about right."

"Why have these pale sisters not died out?"

"No idea. Jat thought that new pale sisters might be… spontaneously generated, the world replacing what it's lost. He wasn't sure. He did know that things are getting worse."

"Worse? In what way?"

"The animuses taken from pale sisters don't divide as easily now, and don't live as long. It'd been happening slowly, over the last thousand years or so. It might be to do with some sort of world cycle – that's what's been causing the droughts. Or it might be something…" She waved a vague hand above her head "…we can't imagine. The world fighting back, Jat called it. Whatever the reason, it means the skykin are diminishing. Dying out."

"I find this hard to believe." But he didn't, not really. He just didn't *want* to believe it.

"Uh," Dej was looking past him.

"Holiness?" He turned to looked at Naldak, standing in the open doorway.

He frowned. "Your interruption is ill-timed, to say the least."

"Holiness, you're needed in your reception room right now."

"Can it wait?"

"Sorry, Holiness. It really can't."

CHAPTER 61

Their entry into Mirror-of-the-Sky was marked with the uncomfortable absurdities Rhia had come to expect from this new, senseless world.

She changed into her kirtle before they walked out onto the causeway leading into Mirror. The still-damp cloth clung uncomfortably.

When they gave their names to the scribe in his little booth by the causeway his reaction went from disbelief to mortification to panic, culminating in an earnest promise to send word to the Eternal Isle at once. Francin said, without obvious irony, that he would do his best to beat any messenger the scribe cared to send.

They secured separate punts at the first jetty they found, and split up.

Francin headed for the palace with Sorne and Grithim. Before they climbed aboard their boat, Francin put his hands on Etyan's shoulders and said, "Try to keep your sister out of trouble." Then he took both of Rhia's hands and said, "Try to keep your brother out of trouble." He smiled. "And if it doesn't offend your lack of religious sensibilities, may the First have mercy on us all."

With some effort, she smiled back. "I'd say we need all the help we can get."

A fifty-mark piece secured their puntsman's unquestioning

service for the rest of the day. She sat at the back with Etyan; Captain Deviock sat opposite. He was in uniform and subtly armed. Rhia chose to think of him as an honour guard rather than a bodyguard.

While the inky water slid past under the punt she took in the view of Mirror in the waning light: the golden walls and carved eaves and gables, the blues and greens of the window-shutters. The home she almost had. The home she might yet have. Or the place that would put an end to her.

The shroud that had insulated her these last few days was shredding. Every time the puntsman lifted his pole her mind sharpened. The fear remained, but buried deep. She could acknowledge the possibility of dying without the thought paralysing her. Her life was nothing. Francin had talked of "the fate of nations" but this was even bigger than that. Bigger than a single land. Bigger than a single people. This was the fate of the world.

She turned to Etyan, and took his hand in hers. The skin was rough, the bronzed pattern suggestive of scales. He was unique. He was her brother. He was the future.

He squeezed her hand in return. "My memories of the priory are a bit mixed." He wasn't a fool, even if he could be unbelievably foolish. Had he any idea what she was contemplating?

"Which is why I suggest you don't come in with me." One reason, anyway. Her response to his earlier, unexpectedly thoughtful, offer to help had been somewhat vague. *Just lend what support you can.* He'd accepted that. He had no reason to suspect ulterior motives; after all, he had no idea of the eparch's other life, other interests. Nor did she, beyond his enquirer's papers and his written support for her celestial theories. She had never met him. She could be misreading this situation. It had happened before. At best she was facing a hard task and an appalling dilemma. At worst… Thinking of worst cases would not help, at this stage.

They were approaching the priory isle. "Which jetty?" asked the puntsman.

How should I know? Happily, Deviock answered for her. "The quietest and most discreet."

They pulled up to a side jetty, round the corner from the priory's main entrance. Deviock reminded the puntsman that whilst the small fortune they had already paid secured his time, there could be more to come. The Zekti nodded, his eyes curious but his lips tight.

"I'm guessing you're coming with me, Captain," said Rhia.

"My job is to guard you. Also, his lordship should be safe enough here."

"I'm not planning on going anywhere," said Etyan.

Deviock produced a short, sheathed knife from a fold of his leather doublet. "Then hopefully his lordship will not need this. However, I will leave it anyway."

The puntsman was doing a fine job of looking everywhere except at them. Etyan, for his part, stared at the weapon and looked pained.

Rhia murmured, "Just in case." She'd gone into the priory armed last time, and given the dagger back unused. Which was not to say blood had not been shed. *The fate of nations.* And the world. She stood.

Thanks to their choice of jetty they had to pick their way along the ledge surrounding the priory buildings. The ledge gave onto the wooden platform at the front. Last time she'd been here was with Captain Sorne, to fetch Etyan. And now she had brought Etyan back. She looked over her shoulder; the boat was not visible from here. Good.

She glanced up. For once, Zekt's skies were clear. The Sun was a soft yellow ball bright enough to make her squint but still bearable even if she looked directly at it, just as it had been in the shadowlands for thousands of years. She had lived her whole life assuming a normality that was an illusion, a fallible construct.

The priory's main entrance was far quieter than on her first visit, which had been on a restday, but they still got curious glances from boatmen waiting in their punts. A pair of men in ceremonial robes with obsidian-tipped spears flanked the wide entrance. Rhia did not remember seeing guards here before, but they would do as well as anyone. She strode up to the nearest and said, "I need to see the eparch on a matter of grave urgency."

The man's reaction was not unlike the scribe at the gates: to look at her rumpled and obviously-foreign clothes, her partly masked face, her dark expression, and take to step back. She sighed, and thrust her signet-ring under his nose. "I am Countess Harlyn of Shen and I have had a long, hard journey to get here. I must speak with the eparch. Now."

The man looked at her escort, most specifically at the weapons at Deviock's belt. "You cannot enter the priory armed."

Which had not been an issue last time, given they had sneaked in.

"All right." She turned to the militiaman. "Please relinquish your weapons to these gentlemen."

Deviock unhooked the short-stave from his belt then drew his sword. The man tensed as the diamond-dusting on the ironwood blade caught the sunlight, but relaxed when Deviock handed it over hilt-first.

"Now will you do as I ask?" Rhia demanded.

The guard placed the weapons at his feet and exchanged glances with his partner, then said, "I will find someone to escort you within and see if I can locate His Holiness."

"Yes, do that. Please." She felt her voice breaking; most undignified.

He was gone a few moments, then returned with a stout woman in a long tunic. She curtsied and said, "Kindly follow me, m'lady."

The servant led them through identical corridors; perhaps she should try and memorise their route in case she had to leave suddenly. Then again, if her words did not win the eparch over he would hardly let her walk out. Deviock padded along at her side, silent and alert. Even unarmed, she was glad of his presence.

The room she was shown to was airy and pleasant, with an excess of draperies and soft furnishings and a low central table, though no actual chairs of course. The servant curtsied and left. Despite the urgency Rhia would have appreciated being offered refreshments, but then her visit was as unexpected as it got so the lapse was understandable. No doubt Francin was causing a similar upset at the palace.

Deviock stationed himself near the door. Rhia paced as far as the cushion-scattered floor allowed, and tried not to fret. She was assuming their shared status as enquirers would make Sadakh sympathetic to her, but she knew so little of him. And the news she brought was so bad, and the proposition so outlandish; she had no idea how it would be received.

CHAPTER 62

There would never be a better moment.

Dej stayed stock-still when Sadakh left, in case he did something useful like call one of the guards away, but she heard him tell them both to stay put before he strode off. Despite the weight of the life inside her she felt oddly light. She'd shared Jat's burden. Let this churchman, this half-seer, deal with knowing just what a terrible world they lived in, and that they were all doomed.

"Except you and I aren't doomed just yet," she whispered, "are we girl?"

She felt more warmly towards the eparch now; they'd shared unspeakable secrets. But that didn't mean she trusted him. And it didn't mean she was happy to remain at his mercy.

She crawled over to the side wall and pulled away the blankets she'd shoved back to hide the hole. She'd started by scoring the wall with one claw-like nail in a criss-cross pattern; then she'd pressed on the weakened plaster with her palm until it cracked and broke. After that it had been a case of widening the hole and pulling out the dried mud and straw from the core of the wall. She'd trickled it into various boxes; the housekeepers would curse her.

Being discovered was a constant worry, as was finding that the wall's supports were too close together, or that there was something solid against the far side. She'd had to widen her initial hole to allow for a diagonal wooden batten that looked structural. Then, just before Sadakh's arrival, she'd reached the thin membrane of plaster on the far side, and it'd given way under her hand, revealing a dim but empty space.

Now she sat down, reached in, and began pulling at the plaster to widen the hole. She paused every now and then to listen, but didn't hear anything from the next room. She'd planned to break out late tonight, when no one was around and the guards wouldn't be paying as much attention, but that might be too late.

She wasn't sure what was important enough to make the eparch abandon their conversation, but she was sure he'd be back as soon as he was done. And now she'd changed the game, and revealed how unique her child was, he'd be more interested in her than ever.

A large hunk of plaster cracked, the sound painfully loud. Dej paused, hand in the wall. She stared at the door, willing it not to open.

It stayed closed. She breathed again, and poked at the cracked plaster. It crumbled. The hole looked big enough now. She shoved a tunic she'd filched from a box through, then shifted onto all fours. She paused. Her belly hung down, pulling at her spine, the child inside shifting. Was this wise? Perhaps not, but she wasn't going to wait meekly on Sadakh's pleasure. Worst case, if she was recaptured he'd just find somewhere else, more secure, to put her. He used people, but he wasn't a total bastard like Cal.

She put her head into the hole. Straw pattered down. But the wall was only a couple of handbreadths wide. She pushed through, then raised her head when it was out the far side.

Ouch. Her head hit something solid overhead. A table? She cursed and crouched lower, then eased forward, keeping her head down. Her shoulders clipped the gap; more plaster fell. The baby kicked again. But she kept going, pushing through. On the far side she went down onto her forearms and crawled, backside in the air and belly bumping the floorboards, until she was out from under whatever she'd banged her head on.

She rolled over onto her back and used the tunic to wipe the plaster dust out of her eyes. She'd come out from under a bed. She levered herself onto her elbows and looked around. She was in a deserted dormitory.

She pulled herself up to stand, wobbled to get her balance, then slipped the tunic over her head; she'd stand out a bit less to a casual glance now. As she smoothed the fabric over her belly she murmured, "Try and hold off a little longer, hey?"

The nearest window was full-sized, so she walked over and looked out. What she saw stunned her. It was a city, as she'd thought, but nothing like Shen or Foam-cast-north. It was built in the water, or rather on islands in the water. Every island was covered in sprawling, gold-coloured buildings of reed and straw. Most had just the one storey, and from here she had a clear view across an expanse of rooftops and gables adorned with carved and brightly-painted wood, broken up by the odd brick chimney.

She looked down, at what was immediately below the window. A couple of wooden platforms extended from the base of the building; one of them had what must be a boat up against it. She'd need a boat to get away, but this one was already occupied by a man in a tunic at the back and sitting in front of him–

No. It couldn't be.

"Etyan!" His name escaped before she could catch it. Surprise had stolen her voice; it was more a gasp than a shout.

Even so, he looked up. Yes, it was him! Her heart did a crazy double-beat.

"Dej? It's really you!"

"It is."

"But how–"

"Keep your voice down! I have to get out of here." Improbably, the other man appeared to be ignoring them. She had a sudden thought. "Etyan, can you shout at the window to my right, say that someone's climbing down."

"So… you're *not* going to climb down then."

"I can't in this…" No, that wasn't a conversation to have now, "No, I'll have to use the stairs."

"I'll come in and find you!"

"That's not a good idea."

"I can't just sit here! I never thought I'd see—"

"I need you to make a diversion for me. Please, Etyan."

"All right. Are you ready?"

"Let me get to the door."

"I missed you so much."

"Escape now, talk later." But despite her last words to him, despite what he'd done and what she'd experienced since, she was glad to see him. "Count to ten, then shout."

"All right." He turned in his seat.

She scuttled over to the door.

She heard him shout, "Hey, there's someone climbing out the window here!"

Dej listened and heard an opening door. She eased her own door open a crack and looked out. The woman guard stood with her back to her, looking into the storeroom. From inside the other guard called something about needing a boost up.

She slipped out the dorm and ran in the opposite direction. Stairs just ahead. She was about to turn down them when she heard voices, coming up. Two men saying something about a "poliarch". She dashed past.

Corner ahead. She went round it, but slowed as she did so, unsure what she'd find. Just a long, empty corridor.

More voices ahead, distant but many. A large group of boys and girls, talking loudly, rounded the corner at the far end of the corridor. Dej opened the nearest door and slid through. It was another dorm.

"What…?"

A girl about the age she'd been when she left the crèche was lying on one of the beds. She sat up at seeing Dej, eyes wide.

"Don't be alarmed," Dej held out a hand. "I'm the eparch's guest but I got lost. Where are the nearest stairs from here please?"

The girl looked puzzled and a little afraid, but pointed back the way Dej had come. Outside, the voices were getting closer.

"Uh, I'm just gonna catch my breath."

The girl stared at her. "Are you a skykin?"

"Yep." The youths would reach the door soon. They'd better not be coming in here.

"And you're pregnant."

"Right again." The voices were passing, someone laughing about someone else's voice breaking during the morning service.

"Shouldn't you be at a crèche?"

"Probably."

The youths went past, their voices receding.

Dej smiled at the bemused girl. "Probably best not mention you saw me, eh?"

"All right."

Dej opened the door a crack. The corridor was empty.

The nearest stairs weren't an option: the guards would've worked out she wasn't outside by now, and be looking for her. She had to carry on this way.

Another set of voices had her ducking into another, empty, dorm. This was why she'd planned to escape at night.

She reached the far end of the corridor, listened at the corner and, when she heard nothing, crept round. As she'd hoped, the layout was symmetrical: there were stairs here too. She listened before descending.

The ground floor layout was more complex, with a couple of side-turnings straight off. But she knew which direction she needed to go. She took the turning leading back towards where she'd seen Etyan. These shorter corridors meant less chance of being spotted from a distance but more chance of someone discovering her unawares. When she heard a pair of female voices ahead she picked another random room to hide in; some sort of assembly-room, currently unused. The two women took an age to walk past.

Back outside, this corridor ended at an intersection. She needed to go left. She checked both ways. There was a figure to the left, advancing slowly… and wearing familiar clothes. He had one hand on his jerkin, as though holding something there. She called his name as she rounded the corner.

Etyan's face went from fear to joy in a moment. Then his gaze fell on her belly. "Dej, you're–"

"Why didn't you stay with the boat?"

"When you didn't come out I had to come in for you. Dej, you're pregnant."

"Yes, very. We need to get out of here. Now."

"I can't leave. Ree's here."

Of course she was. "Yes, but I'm guessing she wanted you to stay with the boat?"

"She did, but when I saw you... That's my child isn't it? You're having my child!"

"Mine actually. But not here. Hopefully. Let's go back the way you came."

He grimaced. "I'm not sure which way I came. These corridors all look the same."

He hadn't changed. Or perhaps he had. Etyan had an air of purpose, and a sadness that even his elation at seeing her hadn't driven off. "We'll just go slowly. I'm good with direction, remember?"

"Yes. Of course. So much has happened, I don't know where to start."

"Start by getting back to the boat. Then we'll talk."

"Yes. All right."

They turned round. Etyan said he'd come up a side passage but he wasn't sure which one. Dej inclined her head at the first one they passed.

"No, the next, I think."

Dej nodded. She was half a step ahead, in order to check down the passage as soon as her eyeline was clear.

She stopped, Etyan coming up behind her. When he saw what was in the passage ahead he breathed, "Oh no."

CHAPTER 63

The man who entered the reception room had to be the eparch. Even aside from his ornate tunic and accessories, he had an air of authority that reminded Rhia of Francin.

Right now, however, he looked as flustered as she felt. He glanced over at Deviock, then inclined his head to her and said, "Countess Harlyn."

"And Observer of Shen." Just in case he somehow failed to make the connection. "I'm delighted to finally meet you, Eparch."

"Please call me Sadakh."

"Sadakh. Right. Then you should call me Rhia. I must apologise for turning up like this but the situation is… grave." To put it mildly.

"When you say 'situation'…"

"Of the world. All of us. We're in trouble." She should probably not be so direct, but she needed to get it said.

He did something odd then, standing unmoving and looking at her hard. It was an appraising look but there was something else going on too. Then, to her surprise, he sat down, sinking to the cushioned floor. He put his elbows on the table and half leaned forward, as though he would put his head in his hands, before catching himself. He looked up at her. "My apologies. I have had a trying day. Will you sit?"

She did, across the low table from him. "I'm going to tell you what happened to Shen, because that's the first thing you need to know."

"What happened to Shen."

She had no idea if that was a question or not, but answered it anyway, her voice catching in something like a bitter laugh. "It ceased to exist overnight."

"When? How?"

"When... a week ago, no just over." Shortly after she was found guilty of heresy, that life-changing event rendered almost trivial in comparison to subsequent ones. "As for how... I'll start with 'what', if it's all right with you." She went on, in a low voice that sounded like someone else's, to summarise what had happened since that awful day when she had woken up to find the shade gone from her shadowland. Somehow the act of speaking the horror made it fully true, forever part of her; but that in itself made it easier to face, made thinking of the future easier. And they had to think of the future.

Sadakh listened intently, his already pale face going even whiter.

Despite her enervated state, she took care to gloss over the duke's political ambitions. She must focus on the elements of the cataclysm that they, as enquirers, might deal with. She did not mention Etyan.

By the time she had finished her voice was hoarse and weak.

Sadakh had listened without interruption. Now he nodded, then said, "You have suffered greatly. The least I can do is offer you a drink."

"A drink? Oh yes, that would be good. And maybe something to eat?"

"Of course. If your man asks the guard outside, refreshments will be brought."

What guard outside? Perhaps she had been too distracted to notice. "Thank you. Deviock, if you would?"

She turned back to Sadakh. "So what I said made sense to you?"

"At one level, yes. I can believe such a thing is possible, though I have no idea how it might come about."

"How. Yes. The shade-swarm – the mechanism that blocks much of the Sun's energy in a fixed pattern across the world's surface to make the shadowlands – is unreachable. It is out in space. We cannot fix it."

"So Shen cannot be… saved."

"No. And I have worse news."

His lips kinked. "It has been a day for that."

"Did you see the Harbinger?"

"The Harbinger? I did, on a rare cloudless night. What has it to do with the situation?"

"It, like the shade-swarm, is in space. Out of reach."

"And what is the Harbinger?"

"A wandering celestial body. I think it somehow came into our system, and stayed, throwing everything out of balance. Now it orbits the Sun as we do, though not in such a predictable way. Did you see the shooting stars after it left our skies?"

"I… did not."

"No matter. At the time I didn't make the connection, but I now think they might be fragments which it shed. Debris, if you like. Debris in space. And this debris… somehow it interacted with the shade-swarm, and damaged it."

"That would indeed be beyond our control."

"And some of the debris may still be out there, in space. It might do more damage. Or the damage already done might cause… instabilities in the swarm. It's too early to know for sure. But I suspect that when the Harbinger returns, more debris may be shed. I believe the situation will worsen."

"By which you mean what precisely?" But Sadakh answered his own question in the next breath. "You're saying that Shen is the first shadowland to fall, but will not be the last."

"Exactly. This is, at the risk of sounding overdramatic, the beginning of the end."

"For the shadowlands, at least."

"Yes, the skyland is fine. In fact, there'll be more of it soon."

She bit back on the hysterical urge to laugh. "We can't stop this happening, so we need a way of dealing with it."

"You do not ask much do you, Rhia, Observer of Shen." His voice was low and oddly bitter.

"So you won't help?"

"I never said that." He looked at her, eyes narrowed. "Do you have a solution to this world-shaking problem?"

"No. But you do."

"I'm not sure I—"

"You changed my brother. He can live in the skyland now, like a skykin." She watched his face as she spoke. "You know that, don't you?"

He nodded slowly.

"Well that is what we'll all have to do, in the long run. You need to reproduce your experiment. Make the change for everyone! It's the only way."

Sadakh's laugh was harsh, almost mocking. "If only the effect was reproducible."

"You've tried?"

"Oh yes. It doesn't work. I refined the serum, I tested it – on myself for a start – and it does nothing."

"It needs the Sun! That's what triggers the change."

"I tried that. It didn't help."

"But... I was sure that was it. Etyan was unwell but not much changed. Then he was exposed to the Sun, and within a day he became what he is now: half shadowkin, half skykin."

"I said I tried that! The test subject didn't change. Or rather they did: their skin burned, and eventually they died."

"Oh." Had she been mistaken? No: her brother had changed, out in the skyland. "Why would it work on Etyan and no one else?"

"I don't know. Perhaps his youth. If so, then it is too late to save ourselves, though maybe the next generation can—"

"The nightwing!"

"The what?"

"Nightwing. They're a skyland pred–"

"I know what a nightwing is. What have nightwings to do with your brother's state?"

"He was stung by one. Bitten. Whatever. He was paralysed. That was why I had to, to leave him out under the Sun." She could not afford the sudden surge of emotion triggered by *that* memory. She hurried on, "Surely nightwing venom could be the missing factor."

"Yes. Yes it could."

"Good. Because you need to reproduce the experiment, and you need to do it fast. The people of Shen are dying under the naked Sun! I will volunteer myself as your first test subject."

"It's not that easy."

"None of this is easy, Sadakh."

"I realise that. But we can hardly send people out to get attacked by nightwings. Also, you are not the only one to lose your work recently."

"What do you mean?"

Before Sadakh could answer, the door was opened from outside by a rough-looking man she had not seen before but who he obviously knew. A servant entered with a tray. Deviock helped unload a pitcher of water, and bowls containing figs, strips of white flaky meat and rice-balls onto the table. Her stomach rumbled and she found herself staring at the food and drink.

Sadakh gestured. "Eat something, please."

She nodded and gulped down some water then chewed and swallowed a rice-ball as fast as she could. It was sweet and soft and wonderful. Across the table Sadakh was looking her way but his gaze was distant. As well it might be. She ate a fig. When she had catered to her stupid, weak body she said, "I'm sorry. You were saying something about losing your work."

"Things have been difficult here too. Nothing like as bad as Shen, but politically this is a very volatile time. Much of my equipment and research, and all of my samples, have been, shall we say, lost."

"Oh. I had no idea…" Damn politics.

"So whilst I may know what is needed for a serum that allows survival in the skyland, I do not have the means to make it."

"Actually…" She hesitated. She had known when she came here that this might be the only way. She could not afford to lose her nerve now. "What you need most, what you've needed all long, is not lost."

"Meaning?"

"Etyan. My brother. Your successful test subject." After all, he had sent the clanless to retrieve Etyan from the caravan. "I assume you can get new equipment and suchlike. But he is the, uh, the ultimate sample."

"Yes," said Sadakh. "He is. And I can." He looked at her hard. "And you know where he is."

So, it came to this, the impossible choice she had seen coming but hoped never to make. The food curdled in her stomach. But it was no choice at all really. She did not matter. Etyan did not matter. Not given what they faced.

Rhia looked over to the door. "Captain Deviock, please fetch my brother."

"M'lady?"

"Bring him to me, please. Tell him… tell him there is something he can do after all." She hesitated then added, "You had better get that knife back off him first. We don't want any misunderstandings."

When the door closed behind the guard she looked back at Sadakh. She could only describe the expression on his face as admiration.

Before he could speak she blurted, "Yes, I am willing to sacrifice the person I love most in the world in order to save it." She took another drink of water, as much to deflect his attention as to quench her thirst.

Sadakh inclined his head. "Which is admirable. And if I can do my work without harming the subject permanently, I will."

"His name is Etyan. But thank you for that assurance." She

wanted to take heart from the eparch's words, to assume that her brother would survive Sadakh's attentions, even though what she knew of him implied otherwise. She already hated herself for her choice. But before the guilt took hold, she had more to do here. "Sadakh. Eparch Sadakh, what we plan to do – what we *have* to do – will need the cooperation of those in charge. And at the moment, I believe that is a matter of some contention."

"I am not sure what you mean."

"The duke of Shen is, even now, on the Eternal Isle, speaking to the eunuchs." Talking politics was easier than she expected now she had done the impossible thing, and condemned herself as both brave and heartless. "He is seeking an alliance between Shen and Zekt. He calls it that anyway. In truth he is throwing our shadowland, what is left of it, on the mercy of yours." She leaned forward. "Francin understands the problem, how every shadowland will one day fall. You can be sure he will support us in finding a way to adapt to live under the Sun."

Sadakh was studying her with care, like some specimen. "Are you asking for my help in matters other than those of the intellect?"

Had she got this wrong? She knew nothing of Sadakh's political life, beyond his suspected antipathy towards Mekteph. As enquirers they might be in accord, but when it came to matters of state, they had very different experiences, and agendas. "Yes," she managed, "I am." But her confidence was faltering. Ironically, one reason Francin had suggested she visit the eparch while he went to the palace was that, should the worst happen to him, one of them at least would escape to send word back to what was left of Shen. But what if Sadakh saw Francin's presence as an affront, and her as the duke's agent?

Evenly, he said, "You wish me to openly support the duke of Shen."

"I… If you can, without compromising your own position."

"Whilst you have my unconditional backing in your enquiries, when it comes to politics, I must be careful."

"I am sure, but we both know the importance of–"

An incoherent shout from immediately outside cut her off. Sadakh began to scramble to his feet.

The door burst open.

CHAPTER 64

We've upset the apple cart, thought Sorne, *now see those rats run!*

The panic caused by the duke's arrival on the Eternal Isle had been near-comical, with servants looking round like this was some joke or test, open-mouthed astonishment from passing courtiers, and a wave of hushed whispers following them through the painted corridors and terraced walkways. When their route brought them out into the open Sorne looked up to where the gyraptors circled the Isle's summit; the sleek and featherless birds were flying low today. Perhaps the taste of Prince Mekteph disagreed with them.

The duke's party had been hurriedly shown to an audience chamber halfway up the steeply sloping island. Around the middle city, Sorne thought, if you saw this settlement on a hill as an analogy of Shen. Which it wasn't, other than in form.

The room had a table and low chairs; Sorne had almost forgotten what actual chairs looked like. Francin took the seat facing the door; Sorne stationed himself next to him; Captain Grithim stood near the window which, like far too many around here, gave onto a steep, manicured but eminently climbable slope.

Then they waited.

Sorne suspected the wait was more about panic than politics: the locals weren't letting them stew, they were just trying to decide what to do about them. Finally a eunuch entered, scribe of the shallows or some such, his excessive embroidery and braid indicating he was someone of importance. He brought two guards: if it came to it, the odds were even. They moved to the sides of the room, allowing the soldiers to eye each other up from appropriate distances.

Despite having thrown the palace into disarray, the meeting started with formalities, including a round of vile tea. The eunuch, advisor Eneph, expressed his insincere apologies that the caliarch could not receive them in person; he explained that His young Majesty was grieving for his father, so was to be spared "further shocks". And also, Sorne imagined, under heavy guard right now, just in case. He tried not to dwell on what might be going on elsewhere in the palace in response to their arrival while the duke and the advisor traded pleasantries. He just needed to be ready to respond to it.

When the eunuch asked how His Grace came to be here, the duke provided a short and selective account of their flight from Shen. No mention of Alharet of course. Hopefully his agent here had dealt with her. Advisor Eneph was predictably amazed at the disaster that had overtaken Shen and the existence of the tunnel and asked, "So you came through with a large, ahem, force?"

"And more coming. I am sorry, advisor, but we have no other choice. I must trust the mercy and compassion of our friends in Zekt to provide us with succour and shelter."

"Our resources would be stretched thin by this…"

"I fear so, yes, and I know this is a difficult time for you also."

"Our problems are minor in comparison to what you say has happened to Shen."

"But still a concern. When it comes to it, we will salvage what we can from our shadowland before we abandon it."

"So this is permanent then. The, ah, shade will not return."

"So I believe." Francin looked pained. "In fact, I have it on good authority that the same fate is likely to befall other shadowlands in due course."

"No! That cannot be!"

"Believe me, I wish it were not so at least as much as you do."

"But if what you say is true then there is no hope in the long run. For any of us."

"We will find new ways. The tunnels, for example."

"Tunnels? There are more of them?"

"We found a map of sorts. More of a diagram. It shows all the tunnels, and indicates how to locate the entrances." Sorne's own map had been a paper copy of a fraction of the great engraving in the Shen tunnel's entrance-hall.

"But they were hidden with good reason."

Francin sagged, then straightened. "Advisor Eneph, I suspect you are a pious man, perhaps alarmed that these tunnels have the taint of 'tech', but we must face facts. Firstly, they were hidden but not destroyed, something which the First, in His wisdom, could easily have done at the time of the Separation. One of our forbearers left that diagram, indelibly etched and carefully detailed, for us to find. More importantly, I do not think our ancestors could have foreseen the changes we are on the verge of."

"I... suppose not. But the tunnels will not save us. Unless you suggest we move into them."

"We may have to make use of them but no, the tunnels will not save us. There is something which might but... we cannot know yet." All Sorne knew was that the possible solution had something to do with Lord Harlyn. "We are at the beginning of great changes, Advisor Eneph. Each shadowland has survived divided, alone. But now the isolation of the shadowlands must end."

The eunuch nodded; Sorne wasn't sure he was agreeing, but he was at least acknowledging the problem. "I need to speak to my fellow advisors, and brief the young caliarch. Will you remain as our guest, Your Grace?"

"Your hospitality honours me. However, I must return to my people."

"So the men you came with are nearby."

"Not yet."

"Ah."

"But neither did I come alone." Francin spread his hands. "I was not sure how safe I would be on the Eternal Isle."

The eunuch looked surprised at such a frank admission, but quickly regained his composure. "You are the caliarch's guest, and none of my fellow advisors would consider harming the sovereign head of another shadowland."

"If only everyone in the palace was as honourable and open-minded."

The eunuch dipped his head. "Perhaps you are right. We advisors have much to discuss. How should we, ah, get in contact?"

"I will send a man back this time tomorrow."

Sorne had already volunteered for this unsavoury duty.

That had gone as well as they could have expected. The duke appeared relieved. Not that either Sorne or Grithim would let their guard down until they were off the Isle. Grithim went a step ahead, while Sorne covered the duke's back at the same distance.

They had nearly reached safety when the attack came, in a narrow, enclosed corridor leading to the outside jetties. A perfect location for an ambush, so both he and Grithim had their hands on their weapons already; in the fuss they'd caused, no one had thought to disarm them.

The first Sorne knew was when Grithim stopped and drew his sword in one motion. Sorne was going for his own weapon even before the two men burst out of a side entrance just ahead.

Grithim timed it perfectly; his initial slash caught one man in the neck. The attacker reeled backwards, clutching his throat. As the other man clashed with Grithim's backswing Sorne looked to the duke, assessing the situation in the immediate, timeless moment that preceded action. Francin was stepping back, pressing himself against the wall. Good. Sorne considered edging past to assist his fellow militiaman but decided he was better deployed here, because if this was an ambush, it would be on two fronts.

Decision made, he whirled on the spot.

A figure was careening down the corridor towards them. Some part of Sorne's mind acknowledged that this had always been a possibility but even so he started at the sight of the duchess running towards him, knife in hand. He'd seen anger before, and moments of madness due to fear or grief, but the sheer insane fury that contorted Alharet's face froze his heart.

His sword came up automatically, ready to meet her frenzied attack. But she wasn't after him. She wanted Francin.

He adjusted his stance, or tried to. The angle was wrong; she'd be inside his guard before he could get his arm round to land a blow. He stepped back and to the side, blocking the duke with his body. Alharet held her obsidian knife ineptly, pointed straight ahead like a tiny lance. It pierced his side just below the ribs. She drove him back into the duke, who grunted in surprise.

Alharet howled, clawing past Sorne's shoulder with her left hand. Sorne had caught her right hand in his as she released her grip on the knife. His sword arm was trapped, pinned across his body where she pressed close to him, trying to get to her husband. How odd, Sorne thought with the clarity of combat, that a battle affecting two nations should be played out like this: not even a duel, but a mere domestic tiff.

But he was a solider, and absurd as the situation was, he looked for ways to secure victory, despite the incoherent screeching in his ear and the heaving warmth of the duchess's body as she tried to press past. Pushing her backward would be the obvious move but her manic strength had made her his match, and he could feel a chill spreading from the blade in his side. Her blade. Yes, that was it.

He unclenched his right hand, and dropped his sword. He closed his fingers around the hilt of the knife, slippery with his own blood.

He took as deep a breath as he could – not very, it seemed – then pushed back with his left hand, where it grasped Alharet's right, simultaneously pulling the knife from his side with his other hand.

The gap he made was not great, but it was enough. He flicked his wrist round to drive Alharet's own blade into her, up under her ribs in a killing blow.

Her screech faltered and she convulsed, then fell backwards, away from him.

But he was falling too.

A terrible cold radiated from the wound in his side, racing up and down his body. It took his legs. He fell forward, onto his knees.

Everything had gone quiet. From deafening shouts to deafening silence.

The chill reached his chest. Each heartbeat fought against it. But he wasn't going to fall, and fail, not while his master was in danger.

The cold reached his neck, icy fingers stroking his face.

Behind him, a voice, oddly distant. Grithim was asking someone whether they were unharmed. Francin said something; it was too far away to hear the words but the tone was calm and measured.

Thank the First: the duke was safe. His duty was done.

He could finish falling now.

CHAPTER 65

"Who is he?" Or rather, was he. Dej felt the life leaving the man lying across the corridor. Which was no surprise, given the rapidly spreading pool of blood he lay in.

Etyan's voice was panicked. "Captain Deviock. Our guard. We have to—"

"You there!"

She looked up. An elderly man accompanied by two youths stood in the intersection they had just run across, looking understandingly confused.

"Run!" said Dej, and grabbed Etyan's free hand. His other hand was still in his jerkin. Was he hurt?

"We have to find Ree!"

"What?"

"She's in danger. We have to help."

Less of a priority than getting back to the boat. But they were deep in the great building, and the alarm had been raised. For now, she'd settle on not getting caught.

Up ahead, a woman carrying laundry saw the two strangers hurtling down the corridor and dropped the bundle of sheets she was carrying. She pressed herself back into the wall. Dej was about to run past, then skidded to a halt beside the quivering woman. "You," she said, while Etyan pulled at her sleeve. "Where's the reception room? The eparch's reception room."

The woman pointed ahead. "Go round the next corner, take the first right, it's the second door you come to."

Dej carried on.

Beside her Etyan gasped, "What are you—"

"Doing what you wanted. Helping your sister."

She rounded the corner, and took the first right turn.

Ahead, two men in local clothes were going at each other, sword against stave, beside an open door. At least one other person had just gone in through that door, greeted by a man's shout from inside.

Etyan ran past her. He had a knife in his hand.

"Etyan, no!"

The pair in combat were intent on each other. Etyan dodged past them, into the room. Seeing no other option, Dej darted in after him.

Rhia sat up straight, heart pounding. Sadakh, on his feet now, turned to face the two armed men who had just burst in. "What is this?" he shouted.

One man advanced on him, sword drawn. He showed no inclination to answer the question. Sadakh stepped back.

The other man was looking over the table at Rhia. He was smiling as though he didn't see any problem here, because an unarmed woman was not going to put up much resistance.

She grabbed the nearest large object from the table and threw it as hard as she could.

The pitcher bounced off the man's groin and he yelped, hands going to his privates. But he recovered quickly, and Rhia saw fury in his eyes.

Behind him, someone ran through the door. Etyan!

Her brother had one arm raised, knife in hand. He leapt straight onto her attacker's back, stabbing downwards with a boyish shriek.

Unarmed, gravid and out of breath, Dej's options were limited. But instinct and training had taken over. The path to one opponent was blocked: go for the other. Two steps then a savage kick to the back of the man's knee. He toppled towards the eparch, who stepped sharply aside.

But the intruder knew what he was doing. While she was still looking round for a weapon he regained his footing and turned. He had a sword, held low, ready to come up and gut her.

His surprise at seeing he was facing a skykin bought her a moment's advantage. She used it to kick his sword arm. Her balance was off, but her foot connected with his wrist. The sword went flying.

Now they were both unarmed. But he still had the advantage and he knew it: she could see that in the way he appraised her, deciding on the best approach.

Behind her, someone screamed.

Despite herself, she flinched. She knew that voice.

The man lunged.

Rhia saw her brother's fate unfold like a nightmare. Trapped behind the table, with no idea what to do, she had no choice but to watch.

His initial, clumsy attack hit home; the knife went into the intruder's shoulder. But the man didn't go down. He gave an explosive "oof!" then jabbed his elbow back into Etyan's stomach.

Etyan gave a corresponding gasp, and staggered backwards.

The knife was still in the man's back. That arm hung limp. But his sword was in his other hand, and his legs worked just fine. He advanced on Etyan.

Her brother looked around, terror in his eyes. But he didn't run. For a moment Rhia saw his gaze slide to the side, to where Dej faced her own opponent.

His attacker used the distraction.

The man brought his sword up, towards Etyan's face. Etyan's

gaze caught the blade even as he tried to step back: too slow, too slow.

The blow was a feint. The man stepped forward as the sword came round and across. It sliced into Etyan's stomach, the obsidian edging ripping through cloth and skin and innards without stopping. Etyan screamed and toppled forward, clutching at his guts.

Sudden movement behind her opponent. Before Dej's eyes the man she'd been fighting transformed from a person to a pile of saffron-coloured cloth.

What?

Someone had flung a load of drapery over his head.

"On the table!" The eparch's cry, coming from behind the swaddled man, made little sense but his voice commanded respect and her gaze flicked to the table to see the man's dark-bladed sword. She scooped it up, caught her balance against the weight of her belly, then thrust the weapon hard into the cloth-wrapped intruder. It caught bone; a rib, she suspected. The man grunted. Red blossomed across the pale fabric.

She tugged at the blade, expecting resistance, but it came out cleanly.

Out of the corner of her eye she saw her opponent fall but she was already turning.

A sudden cramp seized her.

She curled into herself, managing to turn, managing to keep hold of the sword, but not aware of much beyond the pain and the need to stay upright. *Not now, girl!*

Someone coming up from the side. She straightened as fast as her aching, heavy body would allow. And another attacker coming in, from the other side. She was still off-guard.

The dull thud of a parry.

The cramp eased. She finished straightening. Overhead, a sword had been blocked by a heavy short-stave. The stave's wielder stood next to her; a stranger, but on her side.

Dej brought the sword round and slashed at the man in front of her. The blow wasn't her best; she barely nicked his ribs. But he flinched back, attention going to her. Her new ally let his stave drop, parry coming round and in, defence becoming offence while his opponent was distracted. The stave crashed into the attacker's neck; bone crunched. The man dropped like a felled ox.

Dej looked around, dazed, ready for the next threat. But all the attackers were down.

Etyan lay off to one side, curled tight. His eyes were open but he was pale as milk, whimpering under his breath. Dej staggered over. His hands, pressed to his stomach, were red with blood.

She fell to her knees beside him. "Etyan, no. You idiot..." Words failed her. She could feel his life ebbing.

She was dimly aware of someone kneeling next to her and looked up to see his sister, her face stricken. "Oh Etyan," Rhia murmured.

He focused on them, distracted from his suffering by the presence of the two women in his life. He tried to smile but his teeth were clenched in agony.

Rhia whispered, "Don't leave us, little brother."

But he was. Dej put her hand on his sweat-sheened forehead. "You saved us, Etyan. And..." She had to say it, for so many reasons, "I love you."

Beside her, at the same time, she heard Rhia murmur, "Love you, little brother."

Etyan's gaze sharpened for a moment. "Love you..." he breathed, "...both." Then he was gone.

CHAPTER 66

It was quite a view.

Rhia wondered if any other shadowland had built a city in a lake. Crazy idea. But the Zekti had pulled it off. From the top of the Eternal Isle the crowded islets of Mirror formed a chaotic pattern of pale gold on dark water; up here it truly did look like a mirror of the cloud-speckled sky.

High overhead a pair of gyraptors traced lazy circles; the rest of the sacred birds must be feeding behind the Hall of Eternal Guardians. They had plenty to eat. The eunuchs had offered the chance to "rest above the Isle" to her brother, but that was not to be the fate of his mortal remains. She suppressed a shudder. It was just dead flesh. Not her Etyan. He was gone, having died trying to do the right thing, finally. And his legacy would long outlive him.

She had been prepared to argue that Captain Sorne had earned the "honour" of going to the gyraptors, rather than being sent to the pyres as poor Captain Deviock had been, but to her great relief it now looked like he would survive, thanks largely to Sadakh's ministrations, although the poison from Alharet's blade would leave lasting effects.

Dropping her gaze she saw Francin coming up the steps. She moved over to give him space on the stone bench.

He sat, and she turned to him. "Well? Did they reach a

decision?"

"Of course not. The eunuchs' skill in seeing the big picture is matched only by their ability to argue about small details."

"But you think they will make you regent eventually?"

"Eventually. I'll be living here anyway so I may as well make myself useful."

"And no one brought up any, ah, previous complications." Some of the eunuchs must have known the duchess was on the Eternal Isle; no doubt they had encouraged her to stay hidden, but the temptation to avenge herself on her husband had proved too much for her fractured mind.

"Expedience and pragmatism are the laws they live by." They also had their spies, and no doubt knew that the tunnel entrance was guarded by a large military force, well-drilled and armed with iron. Given the choice between pitting Zekt's minimal militia against such a force and allowing Shenese evacuees into Zekt without a fight, the eunuchs had capitulated. "Between you and me, I'd rather deal with gently squabbling but adaptable advisors who consider every contingency than strutting nobles mired in their own interests."

"So you won't reinstitute the Council?"

"At this stage, the priority is to evacuate Shen. How far we recreate it here remains to be seen. Which reminds me; I've had confirmation that your, ahem, man Markave will be coming through the tunnel in the next group."

"Thank you. Any news on Brynan?"

"No. I think you must assume the worst. Much of the city was lost." Reports from the first evacuees spoke of a great fire that started in the lower city and burned for days. It had not reached her townhouse; she still had what remained of her study. And she still had a noble House, insofar as any Shenese did now. With a husband. And an heir, perhaps.

"So," continued Francin, "when do you leave?"

"First thing tomorrow." She had unfinished business to deal with this evening.

"And you are sure you're strong enough?"

A fortnight on from their flight from Shen she had just about recovered, though Francin still looked drawn. Then again, he was too busy to rest. "We cannot afford to waste any time. We must know if the serum works." She smiled. "Besides, I'll get some rest in the cart there."

"I'm no doctor, but I am not sure being unconscious counts as rest."

"I might not be unconscious for long. We don't know."

"There is a lot we don't know, Rhia. Does it really have to be you?"

"Cousin dear, do you even have to ask?"

Sadakh sat back from his magnifier-frame with a sigh. The last of the blood was still viable after two weeks, thanks to Dej's cleansing moss. Now the most urgent work was done, he should probably look to getting the rest of the new workroom set up.

The palace staff were a little perplexed at his presence so near the waterline and kitchens, but compared to other recent events finding the eparch had been assigned this odd little cubbyhole was barely worthy of comment. He could have set up his workroom in the priory; he had mentioned his other interests to his poliarchs, and they had taken it well. But he still preferred to keep his spiritual and medical explorations separate. And having a secure base on the Eternal Isle would be useful.

He had wondered if he would set foot on the Isle again after the attack at the priory. Rhia Harlyn had shared her belief that the late prince's sister was behind the incident, although some of her reasoning had been below the standard he would have expected from Observer of Shen. Patently she had not told him everything.

Naldak's interrogation of the surviving attacker confirmed her theory. The intruders were Mekteph's regular city thugs. When they were contacted by the prince's sister they already had an internal map and knowledge of a postern gate – presumably courtesy of Sholrew – as they had been awaiting the call to assassinate the eparch when the prince died. Given one of their previous jobs had been the attack on Klimen, Sadakh had been unconcerned when Naldak's interrogation had ended in the man's death. None of the bodies would ever be found.

The one body of interest to him, that of Etyan Harlyn, had served its purpose now. His sister had said her goodbyes before Sadakh started his work. It would have been hard for her to think of the body's ultimate fate, drained of the fluid that animated it. But she acknowledged the necessity; or, as she had put it, "Do what you have to do. This is bigger than any of us." The boy's lover had not said her final goodbye, being a little busy to visit when Sadakh began his work.

Still so much work to do…

His ghost was back: yes, she was almost certainly an illusion, a product of his own mind born of guilt and trauma, but we need our illusions, especially when we are facing a stark and terrible truth. Like the end of the world.

He had been so obsessed with prolonging his own life he had been blind to other, wider possibilities. Yes, he would die soon enough. But until then he would not waste a moment when he could be working, whether to save bodies or souls.

He had yet to tell Rhia the truth about the skykin, how the world was out of balance below as well as above. He would, one day. She would be able to deal with it. And the blood-serum he was creating thanks to her dead brother might yet be the salvation of both shadowkin and skykin. After all, when it came to it, they were all one people.

"You know you have your father's smile?"

Dej's own smile felt stuck to her face. Her daughter had that effect, whenever she looked at her. It was like the Sun came out, like the world stopped being a mean and shitty place and became instantly wonderful, because it contained this glorious creature;

her little girl.

The wet nurse had said that Jin – or Jinia as she called her, using the longer, shadowkin version of her name – was too young to smile, that babies took a while to develop that particular response. Ordinary babies perhaps. But Jin was special, unique. And that wasn't just a mother's love talking.

Dej stroked the back of her daughter's hand where she'd wriggled free of the swaddling. It felt soft to her, but the wet nurse insisted that her girl's skin was nothing like as soft as a shadowkin baby's.

The last rays of the Sun were disappearing behind the roof opposite. Dej spent much of her time out here at the moment, in the priory's huge central courtyard.

"Would you like some music, little Jin?"

Jin loved the flute, though playing it reminded Dej of Etyan. So many things reminded her of Etyan, still. She could never forgive the stupid, awful thing he'd done; the only person who might've done that was long dead; they could never have been together again, not once she knew about the rape. But her last words to him hadn't been a lie. She hadn't been sure when she spoke them, had said what he needed to hear, but yes, she still loved him, despite everything. Part of her always would. That was why she'd named their daughter after his own mother, whose love he'd never known.

Dej shifted the swaddled bundle to cradle her child in her crossed legs, freeing up both hands to play the flute.

"Shall I hold her?"

Dej looked up to see Rhia Harlyn standing off to one side. Rhia smiled and added, "That is, if you would like me to."

Dej shrugged, then made herself smile back. "It's all right. But you can sit with us if you want." As Rhia joined her on the mat-covered ground Dej added, "I'm guessing you've come to talk, rather than hear me play the flute."

"I have." Rhia leant back against the wall, "I'm leaving tomorrow. Just in case… things go wrong, I'd really like to know Jinia's status."

"She's my daughter." But Dej's defensiveness was instinctive, a flash of the old Dej, too busy rebelling to wonder what she was rebelling against. "But yes, she's your niece too."

"So you'll let me make her my heir?"

"If it's allowed, yes. What with her being a girl."

"I am…" Rhia gave a bitter laugh "…not currently in contact with my lawyer, but I'm sure a way can be found, with your permission."

"Then you have it. But that doesn't mean I'm giving her to you." She'd let Sadakh take a sample of Jin's blood, watching him like a hawk as he did so. But that was as much as anyone was getting of her girl.

"No! Of course not. She's yours." Rhia leaned a little closer. "She is an amazing little creature though, isn't she? May I…?" Rhia reached out a tentative finger. Dej nodded. Jin saw the finger and grasped it, hard. Rhia gave a half gasp, half laugh. "She's so strong!"

"Tell me about it."

Rhia looked up at Dej. "You'll stay here until she's weaned I assume."

"I don't have much choice." Dim and crowded as this place was, it was more pleasant than Shen city. "Should only be a couple of months though."

"And then?"

"I haven't decided. It won't be safe for Jin in the deep skyland, so perhaps we'll stay in the umbral for a while."

"It's your choice."

"Yes." Dej stroked her daughter's cheek. "It is."

Coming back from darkness…

It hurt: Etyan had been right about that.

A burning, delirious agony had run through her body. But distant, after the initial pain, as though happening to someone else. It went on forever yet was over before she knew it.

She was back in the moment now. Back, and changed.

She drew in a long, slow breath. That didn't feel so different.

But the smells that came with it did. Richer, deeper, wafts of spice and lemon and growth and comfort. That urgent scent with no name but a hint of blue-green, here and gone. Yes, this was so much more than mere smell.

Sounds too, came with echoes of knowledge; not just the wind in the umbral trees where her guard was waiting out the day but the other half-heard, half-sensed skyland noises; a churring summons, a low hum of contentment, a tiny cry of alarm. She was immersed in a soundscape of lives being lived.

Even the feel of the ground beneath her was new, each tiny crack and stone a discrete thing, yet part of the land.

The other sensation she had been aware of in the background, the drowsy warmth on her skin, suddenly intensified, sharpening to a fizzing heat. But not burning. The Sun must have come out from behind the clouds. Pure Sunlight, shining on her bare skin. For the first time in her life she felt its true touch, unshaded and without fear.

Coming back from darkness... and waking up in the light.

Rhia opened her eyes.

ACKNOWLEDGMENTS

Thanks to everyone who helped with this one. The Tripod writers group – Mike Lewis, Jim Anderson, Marion Pitman, Andrew Bland and Mark Bilsborough – did their usual good work, along with beta-readers Sue Oke, Alys Sterling and Rosanne Rabinowitz. Thanks to ValleysPixie and Flick for expert advice on, respectively, pregnancy and horses.

My ongoing gratitude to all my patrons, but especially my 'top tier' supporters James Anderson, Chris Banks, Shirley Bell, John Dallman, Gemma Holliday, Cathy Holroyd, Sara Mulryan, Pete Randall, Martin Reed and Teddy. The relevant page is at www.patreon.com/jainefenn should anyone wish to find out what all the fuss is about.

Lastly, thanks for my marvellous new agent Sandra Sawicka, and to the new Robots, Gemma and Paul, who've pulled out all the stops to get this book to you.